'This sparkling first novel is a treat for lovers of elegant mystery and exquisite prose … a delight' *The Times*

'*The Bellini Madonna* achieves more than mischief as it explores the complexities of desire in a narrative suffused with comedy and a mounting sense of loss … Lowry has composed her novel with tremendous care, daring to set puzzles for the reader that, once solved, form a portrait of lonely people with a talent for "self-sabotage". A mystery story, a love story and a comedy of errors set in that most familiar of locations – a ruinous country house – *The Bellini Madonna* is a compelling debut that entertains and unsettles in equal measure' *Guardian*

'Fusing the techniques of the thriller writer with those of historical fiction, Lowry … invokes an authentically Bellinian sense of distantly exact perspectives to create a first novel of genuine subtlety and distinction' *Times Literary Supplement*

'A complex narrative twists and turns back in time to Baedeker's Italy, and Robert Browning's aphrodisiac asparagus. This is a first novel and Lowry has thrown a very considerable talent into it, creating a splendidly quirky art historian' *Independent*

'*The Bellini Madonna* is a quite remarkable debut novel – one which takes the reader into several worlds, each so perfectly drawn that you can smell the dusty rooms of Mawle, the fragrance of roses blooming in a secret garden and come to understand the complexities that drive the central characters towards their separate ends' *Oxford Times*

'This is an unusual book; a debut novel that doesn't feel like one. A multi-layered detective story wrapped in a sardonic confession of a not-very-likeable individual, its tone is caustic and intriguing … marks the arrival of an interesting new talent' *Irish Examiner*

The Bellini Madonna

Elizabeth Lowry

Quercus

First published in Great Britain in 2008 by Quercus
This paperback edition published in 2009 by

Quercus
21 Bloomsbury Square
London
WC1A 2NS

A CIP catalogue record for this book is available from the British Library

ISBN 978 1 84724 953 1

10 9 8 7 6 5 4 3 2 1

Printed and bound in
Great Britain by Clays Ltd, St Ives Plc

For Ralph, William and Emma

What if all's appearance?
Is not outside seeming
Real as substance inside?
Both are facts, so leave me dreaming.

Robert Browning, *Asolando*

Part One

CHAPTER ONE

I met Anna Roper last month while I was trying to rob her at her home, in the village of Mawle in Berkshire.

I write this. I write this to explain – no, that is not the beginning. Let me start again. I write this out of an overwhelming need to confess, to record, and, just possibly, to apologize. There. I have set down the first few strokes of the pattern. To apologize to whom? To Anna? To myself, for making such a hopeless hash of everything? Or to the universe? I feel that it somehow deserves my most abject assurances of regret. I know that running away to Asolo now, at the end of this terrible summer, was a mistake. The stones of the buildings are still as ripe with sun as honeycombs, fat and warm with false promise. The Italian sun itself rises each day as though nothing has happened, awful in its innocence. Only the noonday shutters avert their faces, as if in sorrow or in shame. So *this* is what has become of my life's ambition—

There was a moment, on the flight over, when it all seemed insignificant. As the plane flopped down through the crevasse of summer sky that opened sheer above Treviso, the true proportions of things were suddenly revealed: a toy cow; a child's blue hair ribbon, negligently draped in imitation of a stream; a putty church. The last three weeks were erased. They belonged elsewhere, to another time and place. Here everything was newly hatched, blameless. I took a fierce gulp of aeroplane gin and peered down through the dusty doubled glass of the window at a landscape that, miraculously, did not contain me. If I could have held things there forever, with my maudlin, drunken self permanently suspended above the unsuspecting life below, I swear I would have. But then the craft dipped and we were plummeting down towards the black lip of a reservoir, a looming farm, the unscrolling tarmac of a landing strip. I had arrived in Italy, and within a few minutes everything was life-sized again.

My confession should begin here. My name is Thomas Joseph Lynch. I am fifty years old and until last year I was an art historian. In spite of everything, the term still suggests to me something harmlessly quixotic: a savant in a skull cap, a scholar in his robe; or at the very least a distinguished old fart with elbow patches, dedicated to the complex understanding of simple beauty. Simple beauty! As if the human eye is capable of perceiving any such thing! We cook up meanings, endless interpretations of what is. We smear and smudge everything with our quest for pattern, with our insane appetite for words—

Let me introduce a lapidary pause while the camera lenses sparkle and flash in the chilly shadows of the temple of justice. My reader, I know that you will be the jury in this case. Most certainly you will be my judge.

Why did I do it? Because I couldn't help myself, of course. Because Anna stood before me so meekly, holding the front door invitingly open. Question: what do such innocents have in common? They never knew what hit them – casualties, all, of a lethal convergence of apparently random currents, of an accumulation of old wrongs and hurts, not to mention old obsessions, gathering purpose in the fetid cockles of the human heart. A weal on tender skin. The cry of a child. In Anna's case, a by now faded picture in a shilling book, many years ago.

Enough; I can't bear it. Enough.

It is a shock to be here at last, in Asolo. What do the guide books say? 'Town of a hundred horizons.' 'Renaissance gem of the Veneto.' 'Home of exiled royalty and poets.' Originally home – did I dream the whole thing? No, the diary is lying here in front of me on Professor Ludovico Puppi's writing table, torn but perfectly real – of my Madonna. It was naturally to Asolo, just a few miles north of Treviso, that I came when everything went belly-up at Mawle; can you see the connection? I had to run somewhere; I could no longer live with myself. Where better for the disappointed pilgrim-scholar to go? Home, then, yes. I admit that I was hoping for some sort of miracle; for a welcome, for redemption. Instead I merely found my own self lying in wait for me here, as the little shit always does.

So what now? This is the 1st of September. Puppi, my host and former rival, is holidaying in Switzerland and cannot be reached. It's bound to be a matter of mere days before he and Maddalena discover that I am here. They'll try to squeeze the truth out of Anna. What will she tell or not tell them? How will I explain my ungainly flight from Mawle and my lubberly presence in Puppi's palazzo a full five weeks before the start of the autumn *vacanze* for which I was invited? And worse still, how am I going to account for my sudden indifference to Bellini and all things connected with him?

I am full of shame and pain. Asleep in bed at night I am troubled by dreams of a frightening delicacy and tenderness: an open sash window, a shadowed lake, a silver sandal, still bearing the impress of a woman's foot, left out in the spluttering rain. I awoke this morning with a numbness cauterizing my left arm from shoulder to elbow, as if an invisible body had been pressing against it all night.

The other, physical and more unsettling change in me continues, occurring just as regularly as it did at Mawle. Once or twice a day, for no apparent reason, all six foot two of me, lean and red-haired, starts to shake. During these fits I imagine that the mesh of fine lines on my hands and arms begins to blur, and the contours of my limbs themselves to dissolve in an electric trembling, until I resemble an enormous insect, a large fly perhaps, the last of the summer flies, twitching its wings and rubbing its forelegs together. But then, when I peer into the mirror in Puppi's bathroom (the large oval mirror, gilt-framed but not too ostentatious; although this is a palazzo it is, in spite of its ornate stuccoes, its marble stairway, its courtyard and well, its stables and *barchessa*, subdued and shabby), I see that I am after all still the same middle-aged man I was before the shaking started, T-bone of sternum and clavicles in place, my weak heart thud-thudding in its tented ribcage that still insists on rising and falling; my offending organ asleep, finally, in its bed of coir-like hair.

The self-hatred I feel is never-ending.

Artemisia, Puppi's housekeeper, goes about with as much commotion as possible during the daytime, hauling pots and pans to the *cortile* to be scoured, and beating assorted rugs and pillowcases with a rattan whisk. The transistor radio which her son bought for her is on in the chilly mornings, through the hazy orange afternoons, into the chirruping dusk, belting out *'Buongiorno Tristezza'* (*Buongiorno . . . tristezza! Oggi ho imparato che cosa è rimpianto, l'amaro rimpianto, l'eterno rimpianto . . .*) and other hits about unattainable women by Claudio Villa. They send a battery of fiery darts straight into my heart. The boy appears at midday on his scooter, forks down a silent plate of macaroni in the kitchen, and disappears in a cloud of rattling red dust.

Then I am fed. If I could just once cook my own food, dice a potato or peel a carrot, perhaps I would feel more like myself! But Artemisia has even the vegetal life of the villa under control.

Too afraid of what I might say if I were to use the telephone, I have begun two letters to Anna, one apologetic and firmly regretful and the other apologetic and tender, but the monotonous beating of rugs, so much like the pounding of a human heart, and the crooning, and the dust, make me feel like a fool.

All together it is, as my students would say, a bum deal.

To be frank, I think the heat is getting to me. Slumped between waking and sleep in the mornings I think again of the night a week ago when I crept upstairs to my old room at Mawle and saw Anna through the chink of her door, head averted and dressing gown partly unbuttoned, trying to pull the elastic band from her hair. A small porcelain lamp burning on the dressing table threw a shadow into each tired fold of her body. She must have been reading: an open magazine lay in the indentation on the bed. She did not hear me and as I could hardly bear to look at her I stared instead at her elbows moving vaguely in their loose sleeves. The August wind, more heat than air, blew through the branches of the elms outside and lifted the curtain, exposing a moon as thick as a cheese. She got up to close the window and I left.

What can I say? She was radiant, heavy, impassable, and I waited for hours for the light under her door to go out so that I would not have to feel the weight of her wakeful presence across the corridor.

Time passes very slowly here. Getting through it is no mean feat. I either crawl about the town, my heart shuddering in the heat, or sit inertly at my north-facing bedroom window, breathing in the cool slope of the Dolomites. More often – and since my stay at Mawle this has become my real occupation, one which I try to put off but always give in to – I do some purposeful snooping.

The palazzo is full of curious junk and old bric-a-brac: behind a sparse frontier population of sheeted winter coats and flaccid trousers every cupboard seems to conceal a secret interior life rich with yellowing suitcases, chipped flowerpots, cracked picture frames, skittering mothballs and, most annoying of all, shoeboxes stuffed with tight-lipped family photographs and trite Puppi family correspondence.

> My darling Ludo, beware of the American, Lynch. That slippery fish knows everything, he knows about the existence of the Bellini and has even been sending me insinuating letters! Shall I invite him to Mawle in order to reel him in? Surely he can find the damn thing, if

anyone can? Write soon to your anxious Maddalena, my big stud [*stallone maschio mio*].

No, I lie. I made that one up. There is no such vulgar and incriminating message in Signora Roper's hand, just as there is no exact Italian equivalent for 'my big stud'.

One afternoon I thought that I had at last found what I had been looking for. My wits weighed down as if with lead sinkers by Artemisia's *gnocchi margherita* (potato dumplings, pulpy *pomodoro*, glittering green oil, a talcum spray of parmesan; you try it), prowling through the flagged rooms in search of something that would pull together the bizarre web of secrets into which I had so recently stumbled, I came across a low, dusty glass-panelled bookshelf with a tasselled key, standing all on its own in a snug alcove.

Here, surely, I would discover, among a stash of calf- and leather-bound volumes, a second diary or notebook – its thick coffee-coloured pages crisp under my prehensile fingers – that would at last give me the full account of how my Madonna had arrived at Mawle in the possession of Anna's great-grandfather, James Roper; the frank story of his tragically brief marriage – every last detail! But in it I found nothing, nothing at all, except for a pile of curling *National Geographics* ('Lucy: the real Eve? An interview with Richard Leakey'), an old flower press of the kind constructed from blotting paper pinned down between wooden boards by metal screws – releasing, at a twist, a starry head of silver-haired Edelweiss – and a first edition, with some of its furry pages still uncut, of Robert Browning's last collection of poems, *Asolando*.

★

On Sunday, three days ago, I left the house a little after midday to escape Artemisia's pitying glances and strolled for an hour in the thin shade of the Foresto Vecchio. Across the rooftops the old clock-tower of Catarina Cornaro's castle stood white as a bone in the glare, its empty colonnades crowded with sunlight. The campanile of the cathedral tolled one slow saffron note: mass was long over, the throng dispersed. Behind Santa Maria a cramped piazzetta gave way to a row of stone steps, above which the faultless cornflower-bright sky unfurled its smooth banner of heat. The whole day, caught in a globe of pure colour, seemed to proclaim its radical innocence. Even the trees on the horizon looked self-sufficient, their undersides gleaming as if stroked by a glazing brush, each tiny scalloped leaf outlined by a cloisonné shadow.

I bounded up the steps into the main piazza of the town and there was the familiar lion with its left paw hooked over a shield, stone wings splayed stiffly in the windless air. I stood stock still, sweating heavily. I recognized it at once. It was the very same lion as the one hidden in the overgrown rose garden at Mawle.

At this distance the ruddy three-storey brick front of the house seems shrunken, its ten slender pilasters, pedimented door and Ionian bosses pathetically out of place, as if stuck on the face of an apple that has shrivelled too long in the sun. There is no going back. All that is left to me now is self-imposed banishment from the one place where I have been happy. Perversely, patchily, but undeniably happy. I want to confess, to confess it all; and perhaps, if there is time – if I can bring myself to do it, if I have the courage – to say goodbye.

CHAPTER TWO

Up till now I have managed to live quietly – discreetly, modestly, even. Until last autumn, when the strange sequence of events which I am about to relate was set in motion, I was content – yes, even admitting the odd lapse, mostly content, whatever spiteful rumours to the contrary may recently have been doing the rounds in the faculty – to deliver my quota of lectures, grade my hillock of paper, attend conferences, devise budgets, sit on committees, show goodwill by fraternizing with unimpressionable young minds in the cafeteria, and generally conduct myself as any senior, but unstuffy, representative of our venerable academic tradition might be expected to do. Quite apart from the problem with my heart (a slight arrhythmia; the odd angina-like twinge), this is as it should be. But you may read the board transcripts detailing the circumstances of my dismissal for yourself.

My erstwhile career? Must we? Very well; there's not much to tell. I was, as I say, once an art historian, or more precisely, Professor of Fine Art at one of those little New England colleges where the residential halls are hidden in drifts of russet leaves and the smell of spun sugar lies thick in the frosty air as gaggles of frisky students go tobogganing home. On a certain shelf in our college library in the backwoods of Vermont you will on most days be able to find my book, *Painting and Daily Life in Fifteenth-Century*

Italy: A Primer in the Social History of the Northern Italian Pictorial Tradition (1980), a volume that, with its florid colour-plates, inept enthusiasms and sudden flushes of rhetorical heat, no doubt affords the chance browser a garish contrast to the composed north-American landscape beyond the window pane.

In our little world the seasons used to come and go with a decent swiftness. The winter sky dutifully discharged its daily ration of snowflakes: many-armed, relentless, a conquering army settling into efficient possession of a country which the natives, tucked away in dorms, had abandoned. Spring I imagined as a long-haired sophomore grown pallid from hours of study in the college's leathery library (clutching a paperback edition of Whitman, perhaps), stumbling out into the sunbathed courtyard as she blinked the dusty motes from her blonde lashes. When summer reappeared, like a rosy-limbed games mistress summoning her charges to the field, her occupation was equally brisk. Out came the tennis racquets, and soon the *pok-pok* of rubber balls could be heard in every green shade, a cosy aestival Olympics lit up here and there by the swinging purple tassels of the redbud.

Then on the 23rd of September sharp Vermont revolved on its axis with an audible *tchk!* and the shadow of the autumn equinox descended. The black earth began to round out its plump pumpkins in good time for November and Mrs Platt, my next door neighbour, strained and decanted her first twenty bottles of elderberry wine ('Delicious with any savoury dish.' Dear Mrs Platt! Your last Thanksgiving offering probably still casts its lonely stoppered gules in the darkness of what was once my little pantry.) But all the eating up of shoo-fly pie, and the cooking up of gauzy cumuli of pink candy, and the toffeeing of crab apples, couldn't hide the fact that we were winter-bound. The reek of autumnal smoke filled the thin air. By early December the first crystal flakes would begin to make their determined descent (see above).

Where are they now, the velvety campus nights full of drawling voices, the sappy afternoons in the shade of the maples?

October had just come again last year. I had collected my bottle of plonk from Mrs Platt and a favourite student from the cafeteria, and set out with a protective hand on each for the college park, which at that season was a haven of crispy hollows and amber dells.

But the excursion did not go as I might have wished. No sooner had we reached the shady nook I had in mind than my disciple and I quarrelled bitterly. My young friend took one look at the wine and had a sudden change of heart. He pleaded a broken zipper, a torn fingernail. Although from my pockets I hopefully produced analgesics of various strengths, I was nevertheless sent packing, rotgut still in hand, to take solace in my solitary study.

After rebuffing me in the park my student had collected his dignity along with his trousers and lodged an official complaint. In the little broom cupboard off the main lecture theatre that served as my office I was told, one dirty grey afternoon towards the end of that week, by a special delegation of the Faculty Disciplinary Board, led by Professor Heidi Klug-Birkenstock, the faculty chairperson, that my time was up, finished.

'Is this the sum total of all your research, Thomas Joseph?' she shrilled, holding up a pair of stained Y-fronts, the spoils of an illicit raid on my desk. 'How in God's name are these briefs part of your brief? There have been rumours, of course, and now at last here's proof! So far I've tolerated your overblown ego and your flagrant lack of productivity; even your drinking, but sleeping with students – this really is the bottom line!'

I laughed encouragingly, but she was not, alas, intending to let me off with a mere *double entendre* or two.

On my sullen way home I met Mrs Platt, innocent accessory to all this trouble, coming up our shared driveway with a basket of her poisonous wine over one arm. When she saw her handsome neighbour slouching along, withdrawn and moody, her withered cheeks glowed bright red. I had barely got halfway through my accusation before she seized my tweed elbow in her eager fist and promised to make reparations of a most intimate kind, which simply confirmed me in my decision to flee – that driveway, the college, Vermont, New England, America; the whole crock of shit.

To be perfectly truthful, I was relieved to be shot of the place. I'm sure the place was equally relieved to be shot of me. How ridiculous I must have seemed, with my degraded good looks, my carefully distressed corduroys, my talent for complicating things – my air of pique. Back then I prided myself on not merely being a fiddler crab with an overdeveloped right claw, as so many of my colleagues were, and Heidi was starting to get on my nerves. Although I had long focused on the Italian Renaissance – particularly Bellini and his contemporaries – I preferred to think that I was a specialist not only in the iconography of the Renaissance Madonna, but in representations of the female figure in

Western art *per se*. In spite of this I hadn't published much for some years, though, and what I did squeeze out had latterly been received with wounding indifference.

Take my article comparing Titian's *Venus of Urbino* with his *Annunciation* in the Duomo in Treviso, which appeared in the faculty journal *Insight* to some acclaim, and more controversy. A week before the incident in the park I had received a letter from Heidi, conceding that my analysis of the contrast between the fabric and the geometry of the floor tiles in the *Venus* was nicely stated. She was also grudgingly impressed by my remark that the two paintings, in spite of their radically different subject matter – the courtesan and the Madonna – nevertheless have in common the fact that 'each is less a narrative of choice than a poignant awareness of the impossibility of any choice – the divinely elected Virgin being perhaps ultimately as powerless in the disbursement of her sexuality as the whore.' I was feeling pretty pleased, but then of course the megalomaniac harpy had to go and spoil it all.

> Can one really argue though, as you do, that the Madonna of the *Annunciation* is an object of *desire*? And was it really necessary for you to go into quite so much detail about the possible parallels between Titian's own (entirely speculative!) lust for his fleshly female subject (we do not even know who the model was!) and what you call 'the Creator's yearning to possess his creation'?

'I am sad to report, Thomas Joseph,' she concluded, swooping in for the kill, 'that this rather tasteless element in your paper was the occasion of a meeting last Tuesday between myself and the President of the College's Episcopalian prayer group, and his subsequent, rather stiff letter to the Governing Body.' Blah, blah. (But still, the pain this caused me: genuine, sterling pain!) 'I must,' yodelled Heidi, 'urge you most strongly, in your own interests and in the interests of the faculty in this year of the funding audit, to withdraw this essay from circulation. Art is art, but we must be sensitive to the public mood, if possible even sensitive and pragmatic at the same time.' And then, with a clank, she pulled the lavatory chain.

> Incidentally, Thomas Joseph, it would be nice – bearing the aforementioned audit in mind – to see something slightly more solid by you in another journal soon. A little bird tells me that you spend almost all of your time in the library stacks, pursuing your own private research into Giovanni Bellini's friendship with Albrecht Dürer. Are we ever to see the fruits of your labour? I think I'm right in saying that you haven't published anything substantial in quite a while? You can't rest forever on the glory of the Kraus Codex, you know. That was a whole decade ago now.
>
> I look forward to discussing this matter further with you if necessary. As always, the Renaissance remains such fun.
>
> With kind regards,
> Professor Heidi Klug-Birkenstock

Hi, clever-clogs Heidi on your mountain top! Heidi on Parnassus, *heil*! OK, OK. I admit that the high-flown tone of your letter galled me at the time, but I am ready to let bygones be bygones. I won't bleat. Except for the occasional moment of weakness, you see, I have always tried to let myself be guided in times of trial, and indeed in the most ordinary aspects of my daily life, by the serene example of the great Giambellino himself.

If I haven't published a great deal lately it is because for the last ten years, on the evidence of a paragraph or two in an old letter, I have been searching for one of Bellini's lost Madonnas. I mean of course not Jacopo or Gentile but Giovanni Bellini, the great Master of the Venetian Renaissance; the celebrated painter, in tempera and oils, of over eighty unparalleled studies of the Virgin and Child, and many more of the Venetian landscape.

Have you ever seen a Bellini? An idiotic question! The experience is unforgettable. One might almost say that Bellini invented the Venetian terra ferma or mainland with its winding roads, its biscuity towers and cypressed slopes, for Italian art. It is the backdrop to almost every one of his late pictures, and it is always there in the Madonnas, grounded in impeccably observed fact, but ineffably transmuted by the imagination. Colour and light are the means used to express mood; a mood not of detachment, but of a worldly serenity. Bellini's landscapes and his figures are always poised and still, for his is an art of contemplation rather than action. It is made up of a harmony of elements, a fusion of opposites, a dissolution of parts in a whole. It means nothing in particular; it means everything. It does not explain. It does not want to speak. It is, in fact, the very opposite of a pattern. It is embodied mystery, purely.

I had never seen a Bellini before when, as an aimlessly unhappy schoolboy of sixteen, I came across a bad print of his *Madonna of the Meadow* in a book. It was the surface effect of the thing that drew me back then: the trembling colour, the spent fall of a fold of drapery, the bruised light . . . It is only recently that I have been able to trace the deeper contusion, the mortal ache beneath the perfection. But I knew in that moment that I had come into my real inheritance. I thought that the rest of my life would be spent in pursuit of some sort of truth – or at the very least in pleasant pootling. After leaving my boarding school I took my degree, duly completed a doctorate on Bellini's altarpieces, and landed the post in Vermont. News of my discerning eye was soon bruited about by those in the know. And so, in the 1980s and 90s, I came to sport a tinsel wreath of fame in the international art world when I was commissioned to update the copious catalogues of the Samuel E. Kraus Collection in New York, a superlative stash of Old Masters raked together by the founder of a famous chain of five and ten cent stores; which task had last been undertaken in 1968 by a Professor Albert Ehrlich and his assistant, Mrs Nancy Fromm. In rising to this Herculean challenge I was of course fortunate to have the help of trained graduate students as numerous as they were devoted – but even so. Cataloguing can be an energetic and highly stimulating scholarly activity, yet clearly neither pious Nancy nor honest Albert had construed their work as anything more than a passive undertaking. The result was a miserable hodge-podge of fearful speculation and feeble feints at connoisseurship, in revising which I was pleased to point out several errors of attribution.

The Kraus Collection, you see, though the trustees of the foundation did not know it, contained two Bellinis. There was no way that one could have mistaken them; except that the Ehrlich-Fromm catalogue did, hilariously attributing one, a sublimely compact altarpiece showing Christ engaged in some *al fresco* washing of the feet of his apostles, to Bernardino Butinone; and the other, a self-conscious teenage Madonna with a deliciously gauche underbite, to Francesco Botticine. Butinone and Botticine – a Lombard and a Florentine! Not only did certain landscape details in the upper part of the altarpiece – a stream, diapered with wavelets, making a loop around a hill town to one side of the picture, crossed by a small arched bridge and with a bare aspen on its bank – clearly suggest an origin around Venice, but the execution and formal treatment, the most original way in which the problem of perspective in the background was tackled through moth-like gradations of light, the easy breadth of movement in the arrangement of the figures and the fine pathos of their expressions – so delicate as to suggest the hand, almost, of a miniaturist – all pointed to only one possible source. And so too with the little Virgin. It was outrageous to suggest a connection between this quiet picture of a dishevelled, brave child – her wimple had unpinned itself and was falling down – and the declamatory style of Botticine. The poor little soul's bump was trimmed (oh, telling, tender domestic detail) with a flicker of lace. I corrected the description of its colour from 'clair-de-lune' to 'pale sage green' and went off to apprise my patrons of my suspicions.

I flatter myself that Lynch's Kraus Codex, as it came to be known, remains a touchstone of scholarly chutzpah and finesse. The trustees were extravagantly grateful: I was given a fat cheque and carte blanche to mine the Kraus hoard for my own research in perpetuity. On my triumphant return to Vermont I took some of my prettier acolytes out for a champagne celebration that lasted till dawn and is still referred to in the Faculty of Arts as the Homecoming of Solomon.

And then, without fanfare or forewarning, when I was forty, *enfin*, and hard at work on thus furthering my career, I discovered it – the letter that would fix my destiny.

A decade ago, for reasons which I will shortly relate, I realized I had found conclusive proof that Bellini had painted a last Madonna, unique in its ambivalent treatment of its subject, shortly before his death. I was at the peak of my powers, with years of frantic tramping, had I only known, ahead of me. This quarry was potentially far greater, and more elusive, than anything I had ever pitted my wits against before. At times the chances that I would find it and repeat my earlier success seemed nil. But then, only a year before this story begins, I at last succeeded against all my expectations in tracing the painting to a house in England. And so I managed, without meaning it, to launch an engine of misery and destruction that has demolished every hope I have ever had. No doubt I should have looked more closely at what I was pursuing, at the sinister machinery that had delivered it up to me, and run away in fear while there was still time. Too late now! And so here I sit.

I was in Nürnberg ten years ago on a research jaunt connected with the Codex, working on a problem of provenance for some German religious lithographs that were possibly by Albrecht Dürer but showed an unmistakable Italian influence. It was while I was holed up in the archive of the Stadtbibliothek, transcribing the letters that Dürer had written about his encounters with Bellini in Venice in 1506, that I stumbled onto the most tantalizing lure.

When he was nearly eighty, Bellini was visited in Venice by the then thirty-five-year-old Dürer, who found the old Master, as he wrote in a letter to his friend the humanist Willibald Pirkheimer in Germany, 'still the best painter of them all', but also 'most equable and content, enjoying an existence of the utmost simplicity and untroubled delight, in spite of his fame and the many temptations to vexation that beset him.' I like to think of Bellini as he was in the last decade of his life: weary, reluctant to take on any more public commissions; but always gracious, always humble, always *serenissimo*; tender to his pupils, frank with his creditors, and charming in his commercial negotiations with the poet Pietro Bembo, who was then living in nearby Asolo as secretary to the exiled Cypriot queen, Catarina Cornaro.

Bellini was old, he was coming to the end. His reputation was assured; his workshop was in the hands of his sons. He had nothing left to prove, either to himself or others. Late one afternoon that autumn, in the September of 1506, Dürer nevertheless found him at work, in a small studio at the back of his *bottega*, on a picture that was quite unlike anything the Master had ever attempted before. It was a Madonna, but what a Madonna! It appeared to be an uncommissioned or occasional piece – Bellini mentioned in passing that the painting would eventually go to one of the queen's courtiers at Asolo, old Buccari, in payment of a debt – but Dürer was so struck by the picture that he took the trouble to describe it in some detail to Pirkheimer.

Moments before, Bellini had looked over Dürer's sketchbook and some small watercolours of the countryside which the younger man had executed after arriving in the Veneto. 'Of a barren hilltop scene which I was at pains to pick out in white lake and sienna, and to crown, by way of a pious allegory, with the figure of Christ crucified, Giambellin remarked that it resembled paint trying to turn itself into line, saying, "You forget Signore, that while ideas and words themselves may be abstract, painting is not."' Stung, Dürer asked Bellini what he meant. Bellini replied, 'Signore, your art has too much *rhetoric* about it. It is mass, the heavy solidity of things, that we recognize about the world, not so? Paint has the power to recreate mass with mass, for paint too is a physical thing. And like all material things it reflects light, and so can share in the very qualities of what it represents.' Dürer was sceptical as to whether such a transformation were possible, at which Bellini asserted that it was indeed, and that he would prove it.

Bellini led Dürer into his work-room, which was as usual cluttered with mixing pots, stacked canvases and drying boards, old apparel, clay casts, and all the other paraphernalia of their trade, and, pushing a way through these, lifted the corner of a heavy tapestry which the German had previously admired, upon which the latter saw that there was a low door set into the wall behind it. To Dürer's surprise this proved to be the entrance to a second room or large closet, surmounted by a high window and differing from the first in being completely bare, except for an easel supporting something shrouded with a linen cloth. 'Now,' said Bellini, removing this covering, 'you may see what I have not yet shown the world.'

There stood a rectangular board of some five or six
palms in length, on which was painted a Madonna in a

style such as I have never seen before. She was seated in a pebbled field, her hands laid slackly on her knees. This landscape was executed with the lightest of strokes on a plain ground, the strokes smudged a little here and there, as if with the fingertips, so that it seemed at once both weighty and transparent, as if the pigments had been mixed with light instead of oil.

There was no underdrawing at all. The whole was framed by a pearling autumn sky, such a sky as we see here every afternoon in the Veneto when the day is nearing its close and it is about to rain. In the distance I noticed a walled city, surrounded by waving aspens and crested by a pale square *turris*, and to the right of all these a well with a winch. The arm of the winch was snapped into two pieces.

The painting was indeed wonderful, but there was something more than technique, something perversely vital about it that seemed to resist explanation. The winch was the first thing to strike me, fool, as peculiar, for I looked with a painter's eye, and not as an ordinary man would look.

'Why do you paint the winch in this way?' I asked. 'Has the well run dry?'

'It has,' the Master replied. 'Look closely.'

Then I realized that the lady herself was no longer young, but well past the age of childbearing, and that her narrow brown face had the finely quilted texture that you see on the faces of ageing women in hot countries. Her robe was a leaden black and the dress beneath was neither blue nor red, but a souring white.

Yet it was not this that had troubled me. No, my discomfort stemmed from the hard, hollow gaze which met mine. It had the anguished persistence of a suffering thing, as if the paint, mask-like, concealed a breathing body.

And at that Dürer grasped the most glaring detail of the composition, which had so far escaped him: the Madonna's lap was empty. There was no Christ figure at all: no infant Jesus or deposed body, not even an empty cross. The painting was of the Madonna only. That was its point. 'In the past,' Bellini murmured, 'I have painted the Virgin in the prescribed way. Now that I am old myself I can only see her as she was when her son had at last left her, the great work of her life, the work of her imagination, behind her, but with the weary days of her earthly life still to be lived. *Sunt lacrimae rerum et mentem mortalia tangunt.* There are tears at the heart of all mortal things.'

Though it bears some similarities (the looming Madonna, the ochre landscape in the distance) to two other traditional *Madonne de' prati* or meadow scenes which Bellini produced around this time, the *Madonna of the Meadow* in London's National Gallery, and a Pietà in the Accademia in Venice, the picture in Dürer's account has never been identified. The conclusion was inescapable: towards the end of his life, at the height of his powers, Bellini had painted not two but three *Madonne de' prati*, the first two for public consumption, but the third – ah, the third! Into this he had distilled all his bold sympathy, his shrewd tenderness for his human subject, preferring to draw the Virgin not as a divinely favoured mother, or even as a brooding young girl, but as a bereft middle-aged woman, emptied out by her terrible sacrifice. His last Madonna is disappointed. She is profoundly alone. Perhaps she is even bitter! The centre, the whole focus, of the picture was not the executed man-god, but the cost of his life and death to the woman who bore him. If located, this painting would create a sensation. It would be nothing less than the first humanist portrait of a religious figure.

Imagine my delirium when I read this description in the original, instead of in the lopped standard translations of Dürer's correspondence, and realized that I was the first to have spotted its significance! Yet outside Dürer's letter there has been no other trace of this Madonna; no record in any catalogue, sale or collection. For nearly ten years I ransacked every archive, rifled every inventory, insinuated my way into every known stash and bolthole in Europe and America, but I finally had to admit that the picture was lost, irretrievably lost.

Then, last October, shortly before my ignominious dismissal, I made an astonishing discovery.

Where does the would-be snoop in search of art that has been overlooked go? Why, to the catalogues. The amateur catalogues are the most promising, assembled as they are by obsessive-compulsives with too much time on their hands. It was in one of these, buried in a welter of dross, that I finally found the glinting clue that would set me on the right track.

The minor Victorian collector James Roper (the sixth James Roper, that is, 1866–1940) is mentioned at some length by Henry Sanderson in the few remaining copies of his *Private Picture Galleries* (London, 1972). I have often used my copy as a doorstop or a teapot stand. Occasionally I have pressed a sentimental maple leaf or two, the souvenir of a happy afternoon with a favoured student, between its generous pages.

The Ropers, Sanderson noted, were a modest landed Berkshire family, Catholics all, who rose from humble trade origins in Liverpool about three hundred years ago. Their home was a square, red-brick seventeenth-century manor house with Victorian accretions in the village of Mawle, not far from Abingdon. The Roper heirs did to the house as heirs to large houses have always done, digging and soldering, papering and plastering, adding a kitchen here, a stable there, walling the garden and planting shrubberies. When James Roper inherited Mawle House shortly after his twenty-first birthday in 1887 there was very little left to improve. He'd just come down from Christ Church, Oxford; he was bored and, not being inclined to play with bricks and mortar, made the Grand Tour and set about covering the interior of his property with paintings instead.

It was that very afternoon of the kerfuffle in the college park. I had hoped, as usual, to commemorate the interlude with my acolyte by pressing a leaf from our bower as a tender memento to Eros, and I had optimistically selected a particularly delicate example – all sticky surfaces and tender veins – to pop into Sanderson. Now all that had gone bust. What the hell. I cracked open the book and tossed it in. Perhaps the afternoon's little tussle in the park had cleared my brain; in any case, I found myself, all at once, reading Sanderson's convoluted paragraphs for the first time in years. The answer to the question which had puzzled me for so long shivered in my hands, laid bare for anyone to see.

James Roper (wrote Sanderson) had an Italian wife, a Contessa Giulia Buccari. Apart from this girl, by the late nineteenth century only a cousin and a couple of others were still living at the Palazzo Buccari in the little hillside town of Asolo near Venice. The rest had simply drained away into the purple Venetian plain, were picked off regularly by the summer fever that rose from the Musone, or dabbled fatally in one war or another; so that the old house, with its quiet corners, its shadowed canvases and threadbare tapestries, stood almost empty. By great good luck the Contessina, Catholic, an heiress, and in every other way suitable, was married off to Roper, whom she had met – though Sanderson did not say how – while he was touring the countryside around Venice in 1889, and just managed to bear him a son before following her parents to the grave. Sanderson notes that all her effects, including the paintings which the Buccari had ignored for centuries, were carried off to Mawle. Among them, he writes, tossing out this titbit exactly like the garrulous master of ceremonies at some vulgar wedding, 'according to a long tradition repeated in the bride's family', was a previously uncatalogued Madonna *del prato* attributed to the workshop of Bellini, which had 'regrettably still to be located in the collection'.

Buccari! This was the name of the courtier to whom Bellini had promised his marvellous Madonna in payment of a debt. How sublimely and simply the pattern revealed itself! *The workshop of Bellini. Still to be located* . . . Fingers of brindled sunshine scampered from behind the shutters of my study and came to rest on the page. The room was bathed in a strange effulgence. Somewhere outside on the pavement a bicycle wheel creaked. A girl's laugh peaked and dwindled in the syrupy air. There was a peculiar ticking sound in my left ear. I was hardly aware, even, of the beating of my heart: its breathless knocking seemed to come from somewhere outside me, as if someone were rapping at the door. I almost leaped to my feet to answer it. I felt winded, light-headed. Light-hearted!

I did eventually get up, and poured myself a liberal slug of grappa, my usual tipple, to steady my nerves. The dry and drear months ahead were suddenly, unexpectedly shot through with an unearthly splendour. Did I guess even then that my life would soon be changed, that I would imminently come to live and breathe in this state of chattering expectation? Did I hear Anna tick-ticking away in my future? I did not. I was filled with a blind longing, a dumb craving for possession, and so I'm afraid I did not, at all.

CHAPTER THREE

The Bellini described by Dürer was the one at Mawle House, I was sure of it. What made my pulse race and my heart leap like a fish that had been speared was the suspicion that I was not the only one who knew this.

I had long been following the encroachments on my field of research of a spitefully productive Italian dwarf attached to Padua University called Ludovico Puppi, author, among five or six sumptuous books on the Venetian school, of *'Le residenze di Pietro Bembo in Asolo'*, published in *L'Arte*, and *'Le metafore della terra: la geografia umana'*, which first appeared in *Imago Mundi* and subsequently in translation in the Genevan journal *Géorythmes*.

The little bastard (for he was little, about five foot three) was everywhere, but he was particularly drawn to England. It was raining hard when I arrived in London that autumn, newly unemployed, another exile among the many exiles already adrift in Trafalgar Square. Puppi was ensconced in the impeccably stuffy Russell Hotel for a week, scurrying over to London University's Senate House almost daily – ostensibly to attend seminars on Titian, although a tame hotel flunkey told me that the professor had rented a car to make sorties into the beautiful English countryside.

How I wished that a landslip along one of his subterranean

or overland routes could have put paid to the activities of that energetic kobold!

At Guy Fawkes he was back again, with no more pressing call on his time, apparently, than drifting in and out of the National Gallery while scoffing cheap snacks.

I remember, I remember the 5th of November, a dark afternoon laden with fog and the stink of exhaust fumes. London at the close of the year must be one of the dullest cities in the world, a vast cage of dirty water and dirtier stone enlivened only, here and there, by a glistening yellow waterproof darting through the scrim, inhuman fluorescent smudges traversing the haze of saturnine street lamps and forked taillights. Torsoless legs brushed past me as I stooped to untangle the laces of my left brogue on the Gallery parapet.

'Professor Lynch, *come sta*?' The shoes speaking were midget tan morocco, now blackly speckled with the first drops of a November shower.

'Ah, Signor Puppi! *Molto bene, grazie.* What a pleasant surprise. I think we met in Milan not so long ago?' A vigorous pumping of hands.

'Professore, esteemed colleague. I, all my department at Padova, would wish to express our deepest disgust at your recent treatment. *Questi Americani puritani, che assurdità!* In Italy, the country of Michelangelo, you would not suffer such behaviour. And you, as we all know, a renowned expert on the incomparable Bellini! It is not to be believed. Tell me, are you still working on him?'

'Dear friend, you are too kind! I am indeed. Let us get out of the rain,' I cast a petitioning look up at the undecided London sky, 'and catch up on old times. Let us share the highlights of our research. Let us *grab a coffee*.'

As we crossed the square and raced down Cockspur Street, Puppi's doll-like skips just keeping pace with my giant strides, a gaudy Catherine Wheel unfurled above Nelson's Column, followed by a shower of squibs. The fireworks had begun.

I was still uncertain as to how much, if anything, Puppi knew about the missing Bellini, but I felt with a throb of exhilaration that I was now closing in on my quarry. While in London I did a little research of my own in the British Library on the Ropers. Tormentingly, I couldn't find any reference at all to this marriage of James Roper's, of which Sanderson made so much, to Giulia Buccari; a particular inconvenience as it happened to be the armature propping up my theory. What was more, Roper's male descendants turned out to be either constitutionally weak or short-lived. His son Edward, a sickly man, contracted a war-time marriage at the age of fifty – and died 'not long after', as I found out from the *Berkshire Herald*, leaving 'a son of tender years who, having failed to recoup the family fortunes, sadly expired while still in his prime'. For that, read middle age. This grandson, called John, had got hitched to an Italian girl whom he had met during a brief sojourn as an art history student in Padua (this was the 1960s; it made the society pages). His widow, the present Mrs Roper, apparently had some claims to noble blood and certainly featured often enough in the Italian gossip rags. I gathered that she was a great beauty, famous, in a nation of dark-tressed women, for her naturally blonde hair. Maddalena Roper spent half the year at Mawle and the other half in Venice, but beyond that, I could find out nothing about her.

★

Just two weeks after Christmas Ludovico was in England once more, this time staying in Oxford for a symposium on the Ashmolean Museum's Italian drawings to which I succeeded in wangling an invitation. Our surnames nudged each other – Louring Lynch and Prevaricating Puppi – on the programme of guests; during tea breaks our elbows nudged each other on the sticky counters of the museum's café. It seemed that Puppi had no family, no wife or bambini, who might ever miss him. His usual home when not in Padua, I had discovered, was in the fashionable hill town of Asolo – Asolo again! – in the Veneto, although he also had the lease of an apartment in a decrepit palazzo in the Dorsoduro in Venice.

By the middle of Lent I had followed Puppi to Italy. Did I imagine a slow blush of surprise on his chubby cheeks when I appeared, as if by accident, on a vaporetto weaving its way towards the lagoon from the Piazzale Roma?

'Why, my dear sir. This really is a happy day for an old Irish dog! I think we met in Oxford not so long ago?' We pumped hands vigorously.

'Professor Lynch! What a pleasing surprise.' I glanced down at his feet. He was wearing trim rubber overshoes, with the shrimp-like bump of a tassel beneath. Threateningly, I scuffed my brine-capped size eleven walking boots against the deck.

'Dear colleague! Let us get out of the cold,' I cast a complacent glance up at the bright, bare Venetian sky, 'and catch up on old times. Let us talk art. Let us *sip an espresso.*'

By late afternoon Puppi had invited me to an informal gathering of his friends, to be held at Ca' Granèllo on Saturday the following week. I wondered if I would see Maddalena there.

*

Those were salty, empty, aimless days of waiting for a party on the outcome of which all my hopes now harrowingly depended. The Accademia was temporarily shut due to a freak flood. I loitered instead in the great churches, San Sebastiano, San Salvatore, Santa Maria della Visitazione, San Giorgio Maggiore, San Zanipolo, San Zaccaria, the Frari; the goal, all, of devout pilgrimages in my art-student years, only to find that their fat candles, their sweating marbles and bursts of glassy efflorescence, now reminded me crushingly of my surpliced childhood as an altar boy.

I have a further confession to make, you see: in the beginning I was not American at all, but Irish, as I'd told Puppi. We Lynches were worse than poor. We were lower middle class – and we were from Limerick, that watery, stony city in the south of Ireland which is threaded through at its four dark bridges by the grey Shannon. Once a great outpost for Viking traders, under the English the recipient of a slim paring or two of red brick crescent, it has since been subsumed by the triumphant khaki and green of Dunnes Stores, Eason's and gaseous billboards advertising Bulmers Apple Cider. When I was a child in the '50s and early '60s the city was just emerging from the long squalor of the Depression. It was hour-glass shaped then, split into two halves: bottom-heavy with rows of drab houses and shops sprawling out to east and west at Irish Town under the neck of the Shannon; trimmer on top around English Town and the King's Island, where a mesh of crooked passages crisscrossed past the Norman castle squatting on the river with its two massive drum towers and thick curtain walls. If you walked from the castle along these gritty streets and smoggy lanes, bearing right, you would eventually come to the quay where it curved down towards the docks, a bristle of tall masts and chimney pots ending in the low thud-thudding of the brick-built corn and maize mill. Facing towards the river you could smell the sea and when you turned inwards again to face the city this salty smell was overlaid with a deeper one, the sultry smell of turf fires. On autumn days sheets of rain drove up from the south west, whipping up cats' paws along the water and painting the stone-cut houses of the city black.

But there were also the churches, our Italianate churches, that had sprung up in the last four hundred years in spite of famine, poverty and crueller diseases of the spirit. Did I mention them? St John's Cathedral, with its high-necked spire; the Franciscans, shallow-roofed and faced with pale Corinthian columns; Gothic St Saviour's, quarried from the dark local limestone; St Augustine's, standing flush with the shops and pubs of O'Connell Street, the brow of its heavy pediment twinkling in the evening haze; St Michael's, all honey and glass – a glittering bracelet carelessly looped around the black streets, a string of magic lanterns, with kaleidoscopic windows like immense, flattened Tiffany lamps, fantastically scattered in the salty drabness. They were my first taste of enchantment, of art – and of Italy.

Now, though, even the treasure heap of Venice failed to distract me: a gust of camphored breath exhaled by a tall old man in a snowy blazer who stepped over my buckled legs as I knelt in San Giobbe, busy at my sham devotions, almost arrested my pulse. I thought for an awful moment that I had glimpsed my father: his white apron, his vulpine look; that I'd smelled his medicinal smell. My Da. He was already well into middle age when I was born, and toiled in the laboratory of a large US-funded pharmaceuticals company. (I later discovered that it specialized in the synthesizing of norethynodrel, a hormone prescribed for menstrual disorders: in the belly of Catholic Ireland, my Da was a pertinacious pioneer of the Pill.) In his hunger for advancement he was quite unlike other children's fathers, who clerked meekly at the Post Office, or did the selling for Nolan's Ladies' Outfitters, a draughty linoleum-floored vault on a windswept corner of O'Connell Street which peddled a cocktail of elasticated briefs, shiny slips and pudding-basin brassieres. My Da strode out every day, girt in his apron, to do battle with the female reproductive system. He never sang in pubs. Oh, he had plans for me to be sure, and they did not include the onanistic contemplation of art (I translate, naturally; his actual words were 'friggin' over *smeadráils* of paint'.) Like me he was tall and flame-haired, with heavy slabs of white and red in his cheeks that pointed to a rogue Viking gene somewhere; we had the same long femur and the same supercilious look, but in every other detail we might have been entirely unrelated.

I left San Giobbe that afternoon feeling somehow assaulted, no, momentarily *infiltrated* by unwelcome memories, and stepped out glumly into the shrieking winter sunlight. As a diversion, the twisting Venetian *calli* were no better: there was simply no one of any interest about. While glowering disconsolately into the Canal Grande, watching its brown back twitched this way and that by the tide, I was startled by a pair of demonic seagulls shrilling down to the water on razor-bright wings. A swoop, a plunge, and they had coasted into the sky. I was so deaf with tears that I could hardly tell their fading cries from the shouts of the bored *gondolieri* who rowed aimlessly past towards the Bacino, cutting a lazy swathe through the sulphurous air.

But my patience paid off. Three afternoons later I was sitting at Florian's in the Piazza San Marco, drinking my glass of grappa and flipping idly through the pages of *Chiacchiere*, when I found the proof I had been looking for. Squeezed into the bottom right-hand corner of the page was a blurred snapshot of a man and a woman on the steps of the Abelàrdo, a brash new feeding trough on the Lido. The man, short, hairless and snugly buttoned into a dinner jacket, was Ludovico Puppi, photographed in the act of escorting his towering companion through the fake leather doors of the restaurant; plump left hand at the base of her spine, beringed right hand just grazing one of the blood-coloured panels. The woman had her back to the camera, a long, pendulously weighted white back like a teardrop, criss-crossed by black laces. Her platinum hair was gathered in a chignon, but what might have been the curve of her cheek peeping out beneath it was dissolved in the bright lights of the entrance. '*Il Professor Ludovico Puppi e la Signora Maddalena Roper all' inaugurazione del nuovo ristorante "L'Abelàrdo", sotto la luce dei riflettori*' the caption said.

For a moment the whole square seemed to go dark and slip away in a hush, until the noise of a tootling flute carried over on the chill wind from the canal brought me back to my senses.

How would I confront them? What should I do? Hell, I would make love to Signora Roper myself in order to gain access to Mawle House and oust Puppi, if necessary! I had just four days to devise a strategy, but by this time, I regret to say, I had followed the path on which my appetite for booze had set me to its inevitable conclusion. I was steeped in a bottle of grappa a day. My desperate heart bobbed about in my chest like a pickled fist.

When Saturday evening came I gave way to a sudden drunken inspiration. I wouldn't wait for the appointed hour; I would storm the citadel and launch a surprise attack. Leaving my hotel early, its string of neon lights twinkling merrily in the quiet dusk, I made my way swiftly past San Sebastiano, along the Calle Lunga San Barnabà and Calle del Tragheto to the slippery Fondamento del Tragheto, where Ca' Granèllo nestled in the shadows of the Palazzo Rezzonico. The corner of that building, a block of algae-forked plaster and crumbling stone balustrade, rose to meet me like a dark prow from the darker water as I turned the corner, but I was encouraged to see the *piano nobile* of little Granèllo lit up in a halo of electricity. The night was drawing in. The smell of burnt pitch still lingered in the air, wafted over from the dead bonfire of a distant *squero.* Behind their open wooden shutters, the windows of Granèllo's balcony rooms were occasionally crossed by a stumpy human shadow: Puppi was still dressing.

In the dim *sala* there was no one to be seen, other than a sleepy *domestica* who nodded me upstairs. At the front door of Puppi's apartment I hesitated only briefly, arrested by a stray impulse of restraint, before I noticed that the catch was drawn back. A flick of the wrist exposed a narrow chequered hallway leading off into inscrutable rooms, fringed here by the edge of a carpet and there by the twitching tail of a curtain, from which no sound came. In a trice I had closed the door firmly behind me and walked into a small sitting area, decked out in cosy oak and buff tile, and then into another, smaller passageway which led, through a series of hair-raising kinks, to the gaping entrance of Puppi's bedroom.

Snap went a wet towel, followed by a soaring tenor and a cataract of invisible taps.

> *'Maridìte maridìte, donzèlla,*
> *Che dona maridada è sempre bella:*
> *Maridìte finche la foglia è verde,*
> *Perchè la zoventù presto se perde.'*

A long gargling on A sharp, a slapping of flesh and an encroaching front of rank aftershave emboldened me to take a step forward. The room was empty, but it was tumbled from bed to closet as if a small heraldic beast with expensive taste had torn through it, ripping out entrails of cotton sheet, silk shirt and cashmere trouser before disappearing into the adjoining bathroom for a wallow.

I immediately positioned myself in a window seat and prepared to surprise my host. The sounds of pummelled fat had by now given way to a *tink* and slide of metal, the sighing billow of linen and the squeak of leather. A few minutes later Puppi bounded in, looking sleek in fawn-coloured casuals.

'*Aspetti un momento, Professore!*' His smooth jaws snapped to in astonishment. If he did not quite paw the ground, those plump hands nevertheless began rapidly to agitate the air. Frowning into the shallows of the room, he forced his mouth open again, as if to speak or shout.

In two strides I had reached the smooth slope of his convex shirt front and hooked my arm firmly around his neck. I was amused, as well as obscurely encouraged, to notice that he had a skew nose.

'Don't look so disapproving, my friend. God's in his heaven, all's right with the world! I'm a little early, I know. I found the door open. You really should be more careful. May I have a private word before we join the party?' Here I faltered. 'I believe there might be a lady present tonight whom I would particularly like to meet.'

Puppi peered intently at me from behind the chinks of his fat eyelids. In that moment I realized a dismaying thing: that he was a man to whom anger was in essence an abstract emotion. Behind his look of fury the wheels of a cool calculation had continued, all the while, to perform their orderly revolutions. Under all that flesh you could almost hear the whir and click of a hidden motor, like the secretive steely innards of a mechanical manikin.

'Ah, Browning,' he muttered. 'Such a civilized English poet. I beg your forgiveness, esteemed colleague,' detaching himself, he gave an unashamed sniff at my breath, 'but it is time for me to go through.' He pulled two cigars from his breast pocket, selected one, and offered the other to me.

'Da Vinci?'

'No, thank you,' I replied firmly. 'Not one of my vices.'

'As you prefer. Finest Nicaraguan. I like to have a steady supply myself.' With a doubtful smile, he added, 'You are, of course, very welcome to meet all my ladies.'

Through we went, along a corridor extending from a rear door that I had not noticed before, into the tiled sitting room, now mysteriously filled with people. On passing me a bellini (that foul mixture, revolting to the northern palate, of sickly white peach juice and biting Prosecco) from an airborne tray, Puppi's hot flabby hand rested momentarily in my cool thin one. I gave his fingers an affectionate pinch.

'Regrettably,' I said, 'I am not English.'

Although someone had given instructions that I should be passed efficiently from guest to guest, I did not come across Puppi again until the end of the evening. He strutted to and fro under the stone lintel framing the wooden doors of the palazzetto, cigar in hand, bidding us all goodnight, looking more than ever like a clockwork toy; a toy with a broad polished pate in which the lights from the windows shone reflected. My plan had failed dismally: his self-possession was inviolate.

There had been no sign of Maddalena Roper.

After the disappointment of Easter I began to write to her. My first letter was a brief one, asking simply to see the highlights of her English house. I received no reply, none. The second attack was more direct, backed up with a few Kraus crusts: photocopies of two of my articles on the Bellinis in that collection, posted in May. This, too, was met by silence.

By early July I had found myself rooms in a pleasant Oxford college which harboured no scruples about booting out its vacationing undergraduates to make room for real, paying scholars with money like myself. I was about to lay siege to Mrs Roper a third time when I received a few words from Puppi, forwarded from Vermont, inviting me to visit him at his home in Asolo. He would be taking a sabbatical break in Geneva until the 10th of October, but I would be more than welcome to 'poke my head through the door and make as if in my own house' on the weekend before he returned.

So – he *was* afraid of me and of what I might do. How eager he was to fob me off with a pretence of friendship! Had he already arranged to look for the Bellini at Mawle? I would have to hurry! The high summer sun had scarcely stretched a finger across my bartered desk before I wrote again to *la donna immobile*, declaring that I was now in England but that I did not have much time at my disposal since I would shortly be visiting an old friend of mine, whom I mentioned by name.

Within days I received a letter, carelessly dribbled in brown ink on onionskin paper, from La Roper herself.

This recklessness in the canny witch's penmanship was deceptive.

Eminent Professor Lynch!

I was in a transportation of delight to receive your article on the emotional value of landscape in the late altarpieces of the Venetian school, not forgetting of course your noble paper on harmony, humanity and linearity in the portable works of Bellini. My husband's family has a long 'connection', I think is the expression, with the Veneto, and has for some generations cherished a picture or two which might strum the chord of a precious sympathy in you, as indeed they have in the breast of your learned colleague, Professor Ludovico Puppi. I implore you to forgive me for my tardiness! I am but a widow living all alone in the countryside with my daughter, and have only the knowledge of the amateur about these things. I would be honoured to accommodate you for a weekend at your convenience, in order that you might gaze on the treasures of our poor house.

Please receive my most sincere assurances of esteem, respect, admiration, etc.

Maddalena T. Roper

Modestly but fulsomely, I demurred, saying that my own high standards of scholarship required that I should not rush such notes as I would want to make. Was the tease – what else could that middle initial of hers stand for? – really unaware of the nature of the thing she possessed? Or was she trying to keep the existence of the picture under wraps for some reason of her own? If so, it appeared that she was just, perhaps, beginning to perceive the advantages of allowing a degree of access to Thomas Lynch, author of Lynch's Kraus Codex and unchallenged expert on the great Giambellin. Whatever Maddalena's plans, it had surely dawned on her that it would be entirely to her advantage to let me in on them, and I drank a substantial toast to the realization that I was at last gaining on Puppi. Still, a weekend would not give me nearly enough time to conduct a proper search. There followed a short silence in which I left Mrs Roper to stew about the implications of not allowing me to have a good hard look for the Bellini – assuming that she really was hiding it, there was naturally always the danger that I would rush off and publish what I already suspected. Within a week my strategy bore fruit. A second sheet of onionskin appeared in my pigeonhole, begging to extend the invitation to five days. I accepted with alacrity.

By the 8th of August, a fittingly sunny Sunday, I had

locked up my suppurating room, rented a car, and entered the cool wedge of air trapped in front of the Chilterns.

Have you ever seen these pretty Berkshire villages in the summer? Glinting pylons stretch across acres of yellow rapeseed traversed by slender winding streams trimmed with hedges. Black crows swoop from the banked-up white cumulus, flying low against stubbled fields dotted with pollarded elms, limbless since autumn and now studded with wispy nodes. Where Saxon settlements of wood, wattle and thatch once stood, and before them, ancient temples and mossy trackways, creamy church spires rise out of every hollow. Bells ring through the buttered air, the tar on the road glistens, and all at once you are swerving past brown-and-white heritage signs into a bubble of peace. My car guttered to a stop and I was in Mawle.

The house was easy enough to find. A wizened turnip holding court in The Queen of the May pointed me down a muddy track, overarched by thick foliage, which began some two hundred yards behind the huddled buildings of the last street. I steered the protesting chassis gingerly down this rutted lane, straining my eyes through the dappled shadows of the long green tunnel that stretched for what seemed like an eternity. When I had given up all hope of emerging with my vertebrae still aligned, a final jolt delivered me onto a wide gravel sweep. The first thing I noticed was the glint of water in the middle distance; then the careful stripes of a rolling lawn, and immediately after that, the front of a faded red brick building, on which the unsparing late afternoon sunlight picked out every stain and crack.

Mawle House was just as Sanderson had described it, a

gracious pile of moderate size with two sweeping Georgian side elevations, capped by a rosy, sloping roof, and graced with views of a serpentine lake and rolling lawns. There was the broad front door, a solid structure of planed oak, painted white, with a curved transom window of dirty glass behind which the day seemed to have fled in darkness. As I put my finger on the bell my diseased heart gave a jolt of fear, of anticipation; which? The very leaves on the trees peeping over the raddled roof, shaken by a passing gust of wind, warned me off. A plaintive current brushed my face with a little moan. But I did not listen.

CHAPTER FOUR

The door of the house was opened by a young woman with apprehensive eyebrows and brilliant brown hair caught up in a silkily looped ponytail. She was dressed in a checked lumberjack shirt and tight blue leggings that made her tender legs look like knotted rope. Behind her stood the most enchanting child I had ever seen, a girl of perhaps seven or eight with an immense sleek forehead from which a bell of black hair depended to the level of her neat jaw, her miniature cinquecento head framed by the collar of a dingy gingham smock.

For a moment I was dumbfounded as I tried to reconcile my image of the writer of those letters with the sallow, unselfpossessed figure (how old was she? Nineteen? Possibly twenty? No, she was definitely a teenager!) before me.

'Mrs Roper?'

'Oh, no,' she smiled and her brown cheeks flushed a schoolgirl red. 'My mother asked me to apologize to you – she had to go away.'

So this was the daughter! Who, then, was the child – a sister? A cousin? I stared down at the sallow young woman's waxy parting. She was a good ten inches shorter than I. The scarlet lobes of her ears, exposed under the coppery loops of turned-back hair, began to emit an aching, burning smell. (Of course they did not really do so, but everything about

Anna now returns to me in this visceral way, as if I had swallowed her whole.) She rallied bravely.

'I mean, you must be Dr Lynch. From America. I'm Anna. Please come in. Mamma,' the sleek ermine of her English accent was ruffled by her determination to pronounce the word like an Italian, shortening the 'a', 'asked me to make you feel at home; she should be back tomorrow. Vicky, say hello.'

Vicky stuck out her tongue at me. I stuck out mine in return, and we went into the house. The first room, not unusually for these quasi neoclassical buildings, was a hall, with a watery coolness that stank of old exercise books. It contained a rough-looking oak settle drawn up in front of an even rougher fireplace of red pine, with pasty Dutch and Flemish oils of oranges, cheeses and half-plucked birds dotted around the walls.

'Is this charming little girl a relative of yours?'

We turned left into the drawing room. Miss Roper smiled distractedly. 'A relative? Oh, yes. Why, she's my – Jesus! Sorry, so sorry, I've forgotten – you know.' Her hands sketched a vague rectangle in the air. 'I've forgotten to take your towels out of the dryer.' She ran off.

I looked about me. After Miss Roper had been gone for a minute or two I opened the pamphlet which she had pressed on me with tremulous fingers shortly before disappearing in search of my laundry.

> The drawing room is perhaps the most charming room in the house. It has the only original carved ceiling, consisting of oak and bay leaves. Round the room is Georgian panelling of the egg and dart design. The

> figurines on the mantelpiece are Meissen and on the pretty Queen Anne chest the cups and saucers are Chinese Export and New Hall. Family portraits dating from the eighteenth century hang to either side of the fireplace. They are lit by wall sconces. The piano is a Steck, the bonbonnière on it is Sèvres. Above is a plaster relief of the Last Supper especially made for the Great Exhibition of 1851. Can you spot Judas in the picture?

Yes, yes, it was all exactly as described, except that the blurb could not possibly convey the sadness of the ribbed taupe wall-to-wall carpet with its scattering of dirty Wilton rugs, the yellowing pallor of the ceiling where each oak and bay leaf sat like a carefully placed lump of porridge, the enormous badly-matched metal brackets from which those heavy-chinned ancestors dangled on solid chains, in their scratched gilt frames, or the anthracitic glitter of the artificial coal in the cast-iron grate. My eyes darted around the walls. There was nary a Bellini among them. I reminded myself that this would have been a humiliatingly simple conclusion to my decade's quest, and I flexed my fingers in anticipation of the search.

As there was still no sign of my timid hostess after ten minutes, I reopened the guide, trying to choose between the dining room ('the silk panelling is Georgian, and the pale blue colour is the original. The main features of the room are the alcoves, which are perfectly proportioned. The furniture is generally Sheraton') and the library, advertised as Strawberry Gothic ('there are many things to see, including a painting of James Roper and his family by Josiah Lamb, c. 1896, and several books of interest'), certain that I would soon be led to the Great Staircase, the Chinese Suite, the Primrose Parlour, and the Rose Room.

'Actually, it's not really a piano. It's a pianola.'

The little girl had entered the room and now regarded me sternly, furrowing her dazzling forehead, on which the artificial light (did I mention that those sconces had electric bulbs?) played like a *son et lumière*. The effect was as if the smooth bowl of an ivory spoon had suddenly opened its lips and begun to speak.

'Oh all right, I'll show you.'

The child must have taken my amazement for surliness, for she suddenly perched herself with a didactic grimace on the edge of a nasty moss-coloured velvet piano stool.

'It won't go unless you push the pedals.'

And so I found myself furiously churning out 'Für Elise' in this frowsy drawing room with its dank, shabby furniture, where the air itself seemed to have the substance of a shadow, even though the August sun hung like a blazing eye outside. All at once I was struck by the futility of what I had undertaken. What did I really know about Maddalena Roper, or about James Roper's collection of a century before, or even the Bellini itself? I had only an aside in a five-hundred-year-old letter and Sanderson's vague intimations to go by, and what did they amount to? A stray phrase, a wishful hint, a bit of family gossip. And it all hinged on a nineteenth-century marriage of which I'd managed to find no public record. I was already regretting the journey I'd undertaken and wondering how best to make my excuses and leave, when I looked up and saw Anna, right hand resting on the door handle and her left clutching a grey towel-bale, smiling at us in her ugly clothes, her round, childish face suffused with that listening calm which I was later to shatter.

On the way upstairs to my room that afternoon I took care to get my bearings. I established that a straight trajectory northwards from the kitchen would have taken me through the dining room, past the settle in the hall, and out onto the front lawn. My own little pad (once the bolthole of some poor stunted skivvy, judging by a row of bells tacked to the wall above the abbreviated counterpane) hung suspended three floors up in a converted attic.

Over a pre-prandial sherry in the drawing room, served in glasses gritty with dust, Miss Roper ('No, really – just Anna') and I tried for half an hour to nurse an idiot conversation which died by degrees, comically crushed between her unbudgeable timidity and my rapacious desire to impress. As we squirmed on our sofa the shadowy air around us grew even staler with despair.

Was it then that I first noticed the quizzical frown, the roped nerve that skipped between Anna's eyes whenever she was afraid? If I did, I probably thought it part of her plainness. That first day she seemed to me to be crudely drawn, her body a confused web of badly balanced arcs and insufficient supporting stresses. The man's shirt she wore, the large sneakers on her feet, only added to my impression of her as clown-like, a coarse actor brought on to warm me up for the subtler main attraction. Yet even then I could not help but notice the way in which the dull drawing room sun brightened in a corolla around her bound hair. The dust motes lingering there seemed charged with a superfine electricity, as if stirred to life by her kinetic heat alone. I had her in my sights that first evening, but I am ashamed to say that I was glad – yes, actually glad! – to see her get up from her corner of our love seat and go into the kitchen to put supper in the oven. What a Tomfool I was. Moments later Vicky had re-entered the room and we were soon noisily engaged in decoding the entrails of the pianola once again.

That evening at 8 p.m. Miss Roper served up 'a typical American supper' of meatloaf in the large stone kitchen overlooking the back garden. The sun was just beginning its long descent; mackerel clouds, rose and silver, lay behind the hipped gables of the house. Beyond the kitchen window a patch of ruddy brick, shrouded in ivy, gleamed its warning like a hidden traffic light. I waited expectantly as my trembling young hostess set before me a chipped earthenware plate dotted about with archipelagos of crumbling meat, at the shores of which a quartered tomato had run aground.

'Well, alrighty!' exclaimed her sly guest, ramming his napkin into a casually unbuttoned collar. All my earlier hesitation had vanished. Leaning over to capture the mustard, I managed to tear the cuff of my jacket from Vicky's grasp. The child had taken an alarming liking to me and on sitting down had attached five of her pink suckers to my arm. She was pressed up as close to me as she could get, her faultless profile cupped in her free hand, regarding her plate with regal boredom.

Miss Roper threw me a cautious glance.

'You must be fond of children.' She fiddled with her fork. 'Vicky, eat your supper.'

'Indeed I am, ma'am. I find the children of your country especially delightful. So old-fashioned and sweet.'

Vicky kicked her legs briskly under the table.

'Hmmph. Stop it! We don't get many visitors, I'm afraid.'

'Really – in this lovely neck of the woods?'

'Oh dear, it's true.' Her mouth corners turned gamely down: a dying fall. 'Nothing ever happens here. We just go on from day to day – we rarely pause to think.'

'But how won-der-ful! Don't you feel that a quiet life is the best?' I drawled, taking a fresh stab at my meatloaf. 'So-ocrates—'

'Oh, yes?' The dim girl stopped trying to please and looked suddenly panic-stricken.

'Socrates,' I continued sadistically, closing my lips over a large mouthful of carrion while throwing her a knowing smile, 'used to say that the examined life is not worth living.'

'Ah – the examined life.'

A globe of fat cracked under my molar. Miss Roper revived.

'Would you like seconds?'

'How delicious that would be! Thank you kindly. I am sure my little friend will be persuaded to take a mouthful now. When I was a boy and had already been packed off to my boarding school by my loving father—'

But my reminiscences were cut brutally short. 'Anna, I'm tired as HELL!' announced that imperious child, sliding to her feet with an impatient moue. 'Shouldn't I be in bed by now?'

Miss Roper smirked an apology. As she shifted gracelessly from the table I noticed for the first time that she still wore a plastic apron strapped over her lumpy clothes.

'I was going to make us some tea first,' she said.

'Please,' I begged with operatic earnestness. 'By all means

make the tea and let it brew. Then tuck her in. I'll do the washing up in the meanwhile. Kiss, kiss.'

There followed a brief scuffle over the teapot and the dirty plates during which I managed, by sheer force of charm and persistence, to wrest control of the dishcloth from Miss Roper, and the child and her red-faced guardian retreated up the broad staircase. I was alone at last.

This risible introduction to Mawle was not at all what I had expected, but it had its points. The absence of the Mamma, who would have required a subtlety of mind and an outlay of manners exhausting in the extreme, was a decided plus. In spite of her terrible cooking, I felt almost grateful towards her absurd, uncomprehending daughter. The mysterious little girl, too, although an unexpected *tertium quid*, promised to be a prop to my performance, rather than a hindrance. In no time at all—

But no, no, this is hopeless! Try as I might, I am unable to recapture or recreate the exact pitch of my old, languid self-confidence. Tenderness keeps breaking through, and a queasy longing which goes straight to the valves of my heart, like a neat injection of sugar and adrenalin.

Let me bring down the sunset on that first evening, and begin again.

CHAPTER FIVE

When I was a boy and had already been packed off to boarding school by my Da, as I was about to say before that impossible child interrupted me, I would gladly have eaten excrement for the privilege of eating it at our kitchen table. My mother was there, and where she was, was Eden. Oh, the hands of the clock go whirring back, one of those good old-fashioned mahogany grandfather clocks with fading numerals and the name of the clockmaker written across the dial in copperplate. The brass pendulum swings to left and right, triggering the metallic gong: going, going, gone.

It is three o'clock in the time before my banishment. I am four years old, a strawberry blond cherub slurping a soft-boiled egg for my tea. The clock is in the hall opposite the kitchen. My mother has been feeding me this egg in succulent white and yellow mouthfuls, but she has put down the spoon for a moment and has gone out of the kitchen door to call to the woman who does for us, Mrs Morrissey, now crawling about on her hands and knees, soaping the narrow brick floor of the entryway.

'Mrs Morrissey, did my husband remember his front door key this morning or is it hanging on the hook?'

'Yes ma'am,' (puff, puff), 'he took it.' A trembling green bubble floats up under the door frame.

'Ah, then! I was almost after fetching someone to bring it to him, or running over myself.'

Where is she, where is she? When she returns her face is flushed and her lovely, pliant upper lip is damp. I do not want to finish my egg. This querulous, pathetic sense of loss is my earliest conscious memory.

My father was my Da, but since language first sank its fangs into me my mother was always my Darling. She was an altogether different type to his, small and tawny-faced, with a dark widow's peak splicing her firm young brows. Her black hair smelled of the rose-scented shampoo with which she washed it twice a week. Her eyes, like mine, were sea green. What else do I remember about her? She never shouted, and always seemed a little ashamed of herself. She had a habit of modesty, avoiding her reflection in mirrors. She was a country girl with the scrappily genteel, useless education of the self-taught, acquired in the bosom of a 'good family' that had been 'brought low', and her ankles were thicker than was considered beautiful at the time (perhaps they still would be). She could quote only a single line of poetry, by someone she referred to simply as 'Brownin'' – *God's in his heaven, all's right with the world* – but she certainly quoted it often enough to make up for this deficiency. She went to mass every day without fail, said a decade of her rosary every night, and, though constitutionally meek, could be stubborn on my behalf. And I? I was her pious, prim, most precious son, and already bore, from a very early age, the signs of an embarrassing physical beauty. Hardened police constables, hot in their pursuit of Fenian scum, would wheel about to chuck me under the chin. Old ladies I passed on their way to early mass would offer up spontaneous novenas for me. Ordinarily cut-throat grocers had to be prevented forcibly from thrusting lollipops into my rosebud mouth (you get the picture). Imagine me in St John's, an altar boy of eight with an aureole of rusty curls, skirted and surpliced in red and white like a tiny strawberry, skimming with my paten from tongue to eager tongue during communion as the organ flourishes its uplifting major chords and, the crumbs all eaten up, a satisfied hush descends on my captive audience. A rhombus of blue, then of purple light shimmers on the stones at my feet; a transfiguring shaft of pure sunshine darts through the apse and tickles my fingertips with fire. I take the ciborium with its folded pall, execute a neat bow and return the precious vessel to its niche, and only then do I look up, across the bowed heads, the sea of creaking pews and collapsed shopping bags, and find the face of my mother, with its lips opening and closing silently, far off and in shadow.

When I was twelve my father sent me to a Jesuit boarding school on the edge of the county. My mother was tearful, but saw the wisdom of the move. I was destined for university in Dublin, and grander things than our squeezed home could offer.

My boarding school, once an apostolic college that still reserved a cage or two for captive seminarians, was a wide, sheer building of grey limestone guarded by two rampant stone lions. Inside, the floors and panelling were all of unrifted oak, waxed to such a dizzying brightness that I remember my shock, when we later drew and labelled the genus *Quercus*, tree and shrub, at realizing that this noble plant was identical with the gallfly-ridden monster that grew at the back of our house. And yet it was not. Oh, it was not! We were an ersatz model, near-perfect in its careful repro detail, of an English Catholic boarding school, with a mission to turn out Irish Catholic gentlemen. The heady, arcane smell of beeswax that hung in the corridors, the opulent squeak of my little brogues as I trotted along to Latin and algebra, were enough to make me dizzy with a deep sensuous joy. Reading *Tom Brown's Schooldays* in the library, Tom Lynch dreamed of the day when he might have a study of his own and *sport his oak*. For the moment there hung above each classroom door an oaken plaque on which was painted the name, in gold letters, of a division through which I would have to travel: Elements, Rudiments, Grammar, Syntax, Poetry, Rhetoric. I was clever and poised; I was the captain of my soul; everything was shipshape. Enclosed by the wooden panels of this world, sailing swiftly from Elements through Rudiments to Grammar, sculling briefly at Syntax (thanks to a bout of pneumonia which kept me in the school infirmary for a month), coasting triumphantly into Poetry and Rhetoric, I was soon on my way to becoming a perfect little aesthete and egotist.

So much time has passed since then. I now conceive of my mother as a waft of Attar of Roses, or the shiver-inducing whisper of wool; as the rhythmical click, like the insistent piston of a far-away train, of wooden bead tumbling on wooden bead; as the slow downwards descent of a skeletal leaf, like a revelation of love, of doom, from the wet Irish sky, falling down, down, carelessly down behind the window as we kneel, aching, on the parquet floor of the parlour in interminable prayer—

Down, memory.

★

I was still dreaming of roses when I awoke the next morning at Mawle to loud bangs and clangs from the forecourt. From the dark pit of half-sleep the cacophony sounded like the roll of nightmare percussion, although a tentative tongue of sunlight flicking across my eyelids promised another glorious summer's day.

On getting out of bed I was struck with the peculiar sensation of having just missed catching the house in the act of reassembling itself after the night. The walls of my room seemed somehow flimsier than they had the previous evening, the strip of carpet on the bare boards even more provisional, while the service bells with their drooping clappers appeared still to vibrate faintly with recent motion.

The landing outside my door (the modern-day family and guest rooms were all on the same third or attic floor, the main rooms being airlessly preserved for show) was empty, however, and beyond it the Great Staircase dropped down like a plumb line into a well of quiet. A faint smell of bacon, of quickened fat and recently tossed skillets, came snaking up from its depths.

There was an evil tang in my mouth. What was the time? For a giddy minute or two I couldn't find my watch, although I was certain that I had placed it on the limping locker beside my bed before going to sleep. A frantic search at last revealed it, wedged down the back of the mattress. The hands stood at nine o'clock. I had overslept by two hours. Incredible, especially with that noise going on! The banging had now given way to a low throttle and purr. Through the grubby pane of my bedroom window I caught the orange rump of a mowing car disappearing into the back garden: Mawle had begun its daily business without me.

I noticed with distaste that the water from the cold tap in the corner sink was tepid, with a rusty tinge like blood, and while dressing I found that my clothes were mysteriously tighter, as if I had swollen obscenely in my sleep. I chose a natty and, I fancied, youthful cravat from my bag and tied it with puffy, alien fingers. A shoal of liverish flecks flitted across each knuckle. When exactly did they appear? I was unnerved. I have always depended on the disabling impact made on my victims by my looks. The looking-glass on the wall reflected a lump of khaki soap, my panicked chest and grainy eyes, the cracks in the ceiling, in that order.

Downstairs, all was silent. The kitchen, disappointingly, was deserted. The back door leading onto the lower terrace and lawn stood wide open, but there was no sign of life beyond it. The cold stove supported a pan of congealed grease. Two mugs, one with a rigid spoon sticking out of it, nestled on the peeling counter, orbited by a galaxy of sparkling sugar crystals. On the beechwood table where we had eaten the night before a pile of crumb-strewn plates – two large, one small – threatened to topple over, the residue of some juggler's trick.

I examined the pan on the stove for a clue. In the very centre lay a single trapped flap of bacon, spread out like an anatomical diagram.

All the while I was aware of my breath coming and going, of the enchanted stillness around, and of a chilling sense of being out of my depth, as if that staircase had been a slide to the bottom of the ocean. Hunger caressed my gut with an iron hook. I wondered whether I'd slept for twenty-four hours without waking; whether I'd passed a day and a night – a hundred years! – unconscious, and why no one had thought of missing me. I sprang on the pan and snaffled up the cold bacon with my fingers.

At that moment Miss Roper came through the garden door dressed in denim dungarees, her shimmering hair tucked under a broad-brimmed hat. She regarded my fatty chin affably. Oh, she was perfect! Her sunny manner suggested that I had lived there forever. I was already part of the family. She even went so far as to swirl the stale juices in the pan about with her little finger, which she licked, pulling a face. After she'd done some whisking and pounding I was presented with a grey hillock of scrambled eggs, bearded with parsley. Spinning around on the ball of her supple foot, my little hostess held up a curlicued cup which she had produced from a low sideboard. The door of this closet, left tactfully open, revealed a dusty bottle.

'My father always enjoyed a drop of grappa with his coffee, at any time of the day. He said that it reminded him of his student years in Italy. May I pour you some?'

This mercurial girl had guessed my habit.

By day Miss Roper was a very different creature from the clumsy frump who had presided over the night-time kitchen. It was as if she, too, turned suddenly fluid, had somehow been subtly rearranged while I slept my charmed sleep. After an hour we moved with the bottle to a grassy knoll in the garden, where we grew quite merry under a large old horse chestnut tree. I had a wild hope, in the light of her unexpected sensitivity to my wants, that we would soon be good friends.

The girl's thin brown fingers were touchingly unformed, but in the full blare of the morning sun I could see that she wasn't quite as young as I'd assumed. Was it the fault of the light, or did she have a wanton, hungry look? Tipsily I forced myself to revise my estimation of her age. She couldn't be nineteen but she wasn't, surely, more than twenty-two, much too old to be Vicky's sister, and certainly too young to be her mother. Moments before, the child had spotted us from an upstairs window and, having descended on me with a wail of jealousy, now leant on my knee, taking dainty sips from my glass. Miss Roper had said that she was a relative. Was she a niece? A second cousin? Some sort of ward? I tried to make out a resemblance between those two fresh faces, but could find none.

'Miss Roper. When I asked you earlier, about this lovely child – I couldn't quite catch – that is, I don't think you finished—'

But the mowing machine, driven by a fair-haired yokel in overalls, was starting to make its thundering assault on our green citadel, and I could hardly hear myself speak. Forget it. It was almost noon and there was still no sign of the widow Roper. I decided to press home my advantage.

'Look, are we expecting your dear Mamma anytime soon?'

Miss Roper clapped her hand over her mouth. 'Oh shit! I forgot to say. Mummy rang this morning before you were awake. She can't get here till the end of the week, but you're very welcome to use the library and see anything you like. Anything, just ask.' Her delicate tissues stained crimson. 'I'm to help you.'

'You shouldn't say *shit*, Anna,' decreed my thimble-sized empress, nuzzling closer and inserting her elfin hand into my shirt.

Miss Roper rolled her eyes heavenwards and began to

scoop up the debris of our little party. It was getting very difficult to hear anything above the shriek of the advancing engine.

'Have you ever been in love?' she shouted.

'What?' I hollered.

'I said: would you like to begin above? Most of Mummy's favourites are on the first floor.'

The thug on the mower waved cheerily at her and she actually waved back.

With that casual gesture it was as if she had suddenly shone a powerful torch in my eyes. So this was why we had been sitting outdoors, why she had been so pliant, so free. All morning I had intercepted the invisible waves of a transmission not meant for me.

'No thank you,' I announced spitefully, leaping to my feet and dusting my creased behind, 'I think I'll start in the library, if I may.'

There is something uniquely dispiriting about the slant of midday sunlight on old books. In a full glare, even gold-tooled morocco is obviously just a compression of dust, from which stray particles keep escaping. At the slightest pressure of a finger, entropy hangs in the air.

Cruelly exposed by the great blocks of summer sun falling across its shelves through tall Gothic windows, the library at Mawle was a woeful sight.

Generations ago someone had tried to improve its simple face with casquets and false panelling, carved partitions and ceiling vaults, so that the wide, honest doors now swung open onto a furtive thing of crooked corners and perverse angles. Upside down minarets and crenellations descended at intervals from every perpendicular surface, casting random shadows on the discoloured walls. These had once been white, thickly coated in the palest lead paint in imitation of the airy style at Strawberry Hill. A vast dead fireplace, encrusted with a plaster frieze, yawned from the far wall, holding a shrunken arrangement of dried lilacs in its jaws.

And the furniture! Delicate to start with, it was by now infirm. A lone desk and pursy chair perched uncertainly in the middle of the floor on slender ankles. Skittish side tables hovered beside the frazzled chintz skirts of two dissolute old sofas, as if unsure whether to go or stay. Where the sun settled, it illuminated a furtive-looking scattering of gimcracks: a twisted inkwell in the shape of a snail shell, the gleaming shank of a frivolous lacquered box. The only other seat in the room was a louche chaise longue which lay under the great window like an aged bather, baring its faded striped chest to the blue sky.

The books, bulky, trimly-stacked, dark-jacketed, were the one obviously high Victorian thing in the place. I could imagine James Roper, on inheriting this anaemic relic of a previous age, resolving to feed it up by stuffing it with the most modern line in paper and print that money could buy. There was a shelf of Loeb classics, which proved to be well-thumbed, and an ample set of Gibbon, less so. A fat copy of Debrett's was squeezed between the pneumatic spines of *Vanity Fair* and fibrous copies of *The Times*. I noted the twenty-eight gold-and-black volumes of Murray's *Oxford English Dictionary* with an inward yawn. A random stab with my thumb in the letter A turned up 'ampere: an intensity of constant current in two parallel straight conductors placed one metre apart in a vacuum; ampere-hour: the quantity of electricity equal to a current of one ampere flowing for one hour, abbrev. Ah.'

And of course there were fossils and photographs. A waxed oak cabinet straddling the bookcase held tidy rows of incisor-shaped orthoceras, serrated trilobites and cartwheeling ammonites. All were mounted like elfin tombstones on balsam tripods and bore spidery valedictions in blue ink. The photos, latter-day fossils without the labels, dated from the early days of the Box Brownie right up to the Polaroid. Here on the desk was a thin, dark-faced boy in his teens, his legs lost in 'artistic' navy knickerbockers, self-consciously gripping a palette and brush: the family aesthete. This must be sickly Edward Roper, the son born in Asolo in the last decade of the nineteenth century. On a side table there was one of those monochrome shots taken by a 1930s pavement photographer of a handsome, brash girl with a cinched waist and dark lipstick, tailored herringbone skirt and leather heels, and beside it the same girl, now a bride, posing in an austere wartime studio portrait with her wobbly-nosed groom, who was recognizably the sickly boy in late middle age, all forehead and thinning hair. There was another snap of a young man in a suede jacket and flares standing next to a girl with a blonde beehive; a taut flash of water in the background, tiled red roofs and *campanili*. And lastly, one of a pink-frocked baby with bracelets of fat and a fist in its mouth, squinting like a short-sighted cabbage.

Having shown me in and seen me browsing through the dictionary, Miss Roper (a fine help she was proving to be!) went off to continue her gardening, leaving me in full possession of the room. As soon as the doors were firmly shut I walked straight over to the desk and jacked open its ladylike drawers with a penknife. In them I found a shopping list for tampons, jam and eggs; a crumbling elastic band, and a red plastic fish. Absolutely no good.

Next I went to the fireplace, where Lamb's portrait of James Roper and his family depended from a rusty chain.

Sanderson's catalogue had described the picture as a family pastoral, but something about it, I couldn't quite say what, was out of key. Three figures were arranged on an ironed lawn, in prim English sunshine. A lightly ivied garden wall with a rustic wooden door ran whimsically behind them. In the foreground sat a fair-haired man, frock-coated and elegantly strangled by the severe pinned stock that was fashionable in the 1890s. His crossed knees, shiny as compasses, jabbed at the child next to him: a stunted boy of about six, spindly, skew-nosed, trussed up in a miniature gondolier's smock – a younger incarnation of the teenaged runt and war-time groom in the photographs. Two limp cap ribbons dangled on either side of the boy's sharp little chin. To the right of him perched a respectable spinster of perhaps fifty, a magpie with her gaunt torso embedded in a puff of striped black-and-white satin. Her watchful, birdlike face was tilted upwards towards the master of the house, as if he were about to say something very wise. Their three heads were framed by a mass of striated cloud and a familiar hump of grass, graced with the new shoot of a chestnut sapling.

What was it that Sanderson had written? James Roper's wife Giulia had an American mother, a Miss van der Veen, one of those rapt worshippers at the shrine of Italian culture, those venerators of everything with a whiff of old oil paint about it, which the English-speaking world seemed to export in shiploads in the late nineteenth century.

According to Sanderson, Miss van der Veen had met and wed her Count Buccari while making a visit to the Veneto accompanied by a female cousin called Miss Spragg. After the wedding Miss Spragg became part of the Buccari household; indeed, she stayed on to look after Giulia long after her cousin had died. Roper had supposedly married the girl some time in 1889, but the young Contessa did not long survive the birth of their child the following year. Wasn't this woman in the picture none other than faithful Miss Spragg, transported to Mawle? My heart gave a bibulous leap. I checked my pamphlet guide again. By 1896, when this picture was painted, Giulia Buccari would already have been in her grave for five or six years. Moved by familial pity, Roper had invited his wife's kinswoman, the loyal companion of her girlhood, to make her home with him and his boy. What could have been more natural? The child would have grown up motherless, otherwise.

And yet, in spite of the unimpeachable respectability of the portrait, I could not shake off the feeling that there was something – well, not entirely right about it. The man, who had to be James Roper, sat at an angle to the woman and the boy. He had the air of someone apart, or of a listener straining to catch a note that was just outside range – and like the eyes of a listener his were veiled, as if turned inwards towards some hidden thing.

The child, though, looked straight out of the picture. James Roper was fair, but his son was black-haired, and his eyes were black too. There was something provokingly familiar about him, as if we had only recently met somewhere. The child's dilated, tear-filled gaze fixed me as compellingly as if one of Bellini's boy angels had alighted in that ghastly

Gothic library and, seizing me by the hand, pressed its weeping face up to mine.

Well. It was all speculation.

'Cooeeee! Hey! Can't you hear me? It's time to come in now!'

From distant spaces, sweeping through the silence, a woman's voice called across the green garden beyond the window, squeezing my heart hard. I turned, gasping.

'Dr Lynch!' Vicky stood on the threshold, panting, her tousled bob askew. 'It's lunchtime! Anna says—'

But what Anna had said I was never to know, for she hovered just outside the door, her shining head now hatless and becomingly crowned with grass and pollen, beckoning me inward.

CHAPTER SIX

I had known Anna Roper for less than twenty-four hours, but her irregular brown features – I will admit to a slightly crooked nose, and heavy eyes, sometimes too dropsical, too pink, as if some mischievous sprite had pumped them full of rosewater – already seemed to me handsome, if not yet beautiful.

I was again seated at the grubby kitchen table, and from my pinched chair I had a fresh appreciation of her tiny waist and a child-like belly, just discernible under its coarse denim sheath, swelling above a pair of barely rounded haunches.

'Well, it has been a while since breakfast!' announced Anna from the stove, misinterpreting my slavering glance. 'Bloody hell, are you never going to give it a rest?'

This to the back door, behind which the *shirr-shirr* of secateurs savaged the air.

'Come on, I said lunch!' Then, grinning, pink-faced, 'Blokes! I'm sure *you* were properly brought up, though, Dr Lynch. Have a sausage.'

I had already performed two vicious circumcisions on the fat red tubers before me (chili bangers, according to Miss Roper) when the Genius of the garden appeared. He was a colossus of at least six and a half foot, his belted, glittering torso stripped bare and tanned a deep burgundy by the sun. Vertical streams of sweat ran past a set of surprisingly dainty blond eyebrows, down his riven cheeks. He pranced about on the threshold, shamefaced.

'For God's sake, you big poof,' cooed Miss Roper, 'I can't wait all bloody day for you. Eat up.' She forked at least ten sausages onto his plate. 'Harry, this is Dr Lynch from America. Dr Lynch, Harry.'

We regarded each other warily, Tom and Harry, Tweedledum and Tweedledee. Then this Atlas put out his flinty fingers and I felt the massive tendons closing over my hand with unexpected gentleness. Anna gazed at him adoringly. I was suddenly, brutally cleft by an ache of possessiveness.

'Aw, come on,' said Harry. 'Y'aren't really from America, are you? The Texas Rangers? Rusty Greer? Chad Curtis?' The raw smog of chili prickled between us. 'Fuck off, you little pest,' he rumbled at clingy Vicky, whose face crumpled. 'Get off of my arm.'

The addition to the tableau of this virile gardener – or whatever he was, with his clotted Thomas Hardy vowels – was yet another unforeseen complication. What was I to do? I made up my mind on the spot to assert my supremacy. 'Get off *her* arm before I break yours,' I muttered.

A crooked silence fell on our huddled group. Harry looked at me cautiously from under his pert brows.

'Anna, these burny sausages hurt my mouth!' wailed the little girl.

'You don't have to eat them then, pet,' Miss Roper replied, smoothing the hair on that small head. 'Harry, do you have to be so uncivilized?'

She threw me a grateful look. I clasped the crying child to my side.

'You don't have to eat anything you don't like,' I added, ramming the point home.

'Aw, Jesus!' groaned Harry, slinging out of his chair. 'You're all barking. Barking bloody toffs. Bloody rich bitch.' By a miracle, his plate was empty. 'I'll be out yonder if I'm needed.'

The back door banged. Within minutes, the sound of ferocious pruning had started again.

'Oh God,' Miss Roper whispered, cradling her forehead in her hands, 'Oh God.'

We ate the rest of our lunch in silence – or rather, Miss Roper and I finished ours without speaking; it seemed that Vicky never ingested anything. The atmosphere was strained and effortful. I could see that underneath her wobbly composure Anna was labouring with cumbersome emotions, like someone trying to shift oversized furniture around a too-small room. Unhappy girl. I touched on the weather, the rising pollen count, even put my fingertips once, lightly, on the back of her wrist, but she started and smiled such a stiffly ingratiating smile that I whipped my hand away.

Now that I think about it, she always had this faintly whorish quality, this geisha-like instinct to accommodate any fool who made a claim on her attention, her affections, her body. She was torn between the agony of trying to stay and be polite to me, and the equal agony of wanting to be under some bush, making reparations to the gardener. Her conscience was over-developed. I swallowed the tail of my last sausage and let her go.

Back in the library that afternoon I began to make an inventory of the pictures. Apart from the valueless portrait by Lamb there was a pedestrian early view of the Grand Canal by Guardi, a dim scene of two hounds coursing a fox, and the obligatory Gaspard Dughet, showing a picnic in a campagna. When identifying these I let my nose linger near the surface of each canvas for many minutes, an indispensable ritual in this sort of reconnaissance work. I merely glanced at the Dughet and went on looking; I was trying, always, to find something Italian. Contrary to popular belief, oil paints aren't all the same: as a formula medium the Italians used a transparent paste combining black oil with beeswax, and the smell of an Italian picture is quite distinct from, say, the turpsy bouquet of a Flemish or a French or even a German one.

There was another, more particular reason why such details had come to interest me: I knew that the peculiar fragrance of a picture could tell me not only where and even when it was painted, but – as was the case with Bellini and Dürer – something more interesting about the development of the artist's skill. While there is some evidence that Bellini himself was experimenting with oils as early as 1460, Dürer did not begin to paint in Italian formula medium as a matter of course until his Italian tour of 1506. Thanks to Bellini Dürer came nearer than at any other moment in his life to penetrating the mysteries of Italian technique, and the effect on the course of his art was revolutionary.

In November 1506, three months after Bellini had shown him his astounding Madonna *del prato*, Dürer completed a Madonna of his own for the German merchants based in the Fondaco dei Tedeschi on the Rialto, who had commissioned this panel for the altar of their church of San Bartolomeo. In Dürer's painting cardinals and bishops, priests and monks, knights and merchants, artists and craftsmen, led by the pope (possibly Julius II) and the emperor Maximilian I jostle together as the Virgin, crowned by putti, the Christ Child and St Dominic hand out rose garlands to the crowd. Here for the first time Dürer has used oil paint instead of tempera, and the rose golds and eggshell blues, the velvet greens and scumbled whites, the spreading brocade pluvial worn by the pope, the grave folds of the Madonna's gown and the faint smooth slopes of the Alps in the background are built up in vitreous layers that shimmer liquidly, as if the paint has never dried. There are no defining lines; there is only an ineffable transition from illumination to shadow. Somehow, against all the laws of nature, solid objects have been conjured out of pure colour, out of pure light. The picture is superior to anything that Dürer himself had ever painted before. Gone are the heavy contours, the insistent brushstrokes, the *rhetoric* that had so displeased Bellini in the work Dürer had shown him.

In the background of the San Bartolomeo altar piece, Dürer has posed himself in a fine fur-trimmed cloak boasting banded arms of peach and black silk. His long blond beard frames a cautious smile. Dürer's neighbour, a middle-aged man with a boxer's nose and a cap worn flat on a clump of brown curls, regards him with easy affection. This person is dressed much less finely in a black jacket and red tunic. It is not Bellini, who was elderly and by then entirely bald. Is he an imperial adviser? A broker? A fellow artist? I only discovered the answer last year. What is important is that Dürer knew how much the picture mattered. By stepping into the canvas with that quiet smile on his face he has made very sure that posterity will sit up and take note of what he has done. Something in his art has changed forever thanks to his encounter with Bellini's Madonna, and he knows it. He knows.

The sound of raised voices from the garden brought me back to myself. A pair of stained curtains flapped suggestively at the library window. On coming in I had propped it open a crack and could now hear the faint Amazonian cries of an argument echoing from the far end of the lawn. I was unobserved – to work!

I eased the door shut behind me and stepped into the hall. Where was that snivelling child? I expected her to appear around a corner at any moment, a tearful infanta demanding frolics from her giant.

So far, all was still. A titanic chandelier swung above my head, throwing crystal rainbows into the battered corners of the walls. The runner on the slatted floor exhaled a tired mortal smell, as if someone had rested there before giving up the ghost. From its central plinths at the end of the passage the main staircase extended upwards in ninety sheer feet of polished oak. Its carved banister was cool under my fevered palms as I climbed, listening for signs of life. But there was no sound, no childish footfall, no crackle of denim.

On the first floor I paused, catching my breath in the slow air. This, I sensed, was tourist territory. To the left of me lay a shabbily carpeted corridor, which I had bypassed on my way down to breakfast.

On stepping into it I knew that I had parted an invisible curtain separating the daily life of Mawle from an ideal if faded projection. Was Anna Roper the architect of this illusion? I doubted it. That girl would not have been able to resist a fistful of nylon roses on a windowsill, a chenille throw dripping from a chair. Whoever had originally fixed up this part of the house – some of the furnishings were hundreds of years old – had a high pure conception of the importance of Chinese wallpaper, of Dutch marquetry and Burmese parrots stitched in gold and silver thread. As I lurched from room to room I felt like a lonely Sherpa, arriving starved of oxygen before the foot of a temple where no human foot had trod for centuries.

A few of the paintings, concealed among thickets of oval-framed family silhouettes and watercolours of the family pets, were surprisingly good, but I bypassed them all with a silent salute (Toby, faithful mastiff, R.I.P.!), in search of larger game. I spied a Flight Into Egypt which, under its milky flush, might have been a Biscaino; a white-limbed, black-eyed Umbrian Apollo in the style of Balducci, seated next to the stark naked Muse of lyric poetry; a Rococo parlour piece of a child bride in a high-hipped gown, caressing her inflated infant that reminded me of something similar by Longhi in the Rezzonico. A Panini-like Capriccio of a tall marble column shimmered in a doorway and was gone. On the glowing wall of a very pink bedroom, finally, was an unmistakable, shinily varnished Murillo: a peachy Madonna with two trembling chins and a gleaming tear spilling from the corner of her disconsolate left eye.

After a few minutes my wanderings between the first and second floors had taken me over what seemed like a hundred thresholds, twisting this way and that through glossy out-croppings of yew and mahogany, to a dead end. I was somewhere in the east of the building, but whether in the main part or the wing, I couldn't say. I had long since left the larger apartments and crossed into a narrow corridor with a splintered floor. Here there were no pictures. At the very end was a modest, L-shaped white-and-blue chamber that had once perhaps been a bedroom but was now full of antique lumber. Its width was spanned by a vast carved Venetian tester heaped with old mattresses. The shutter on the single high window, in the toe of the L, was sealed fast. An intoxicating mould-scented darkness enveloped me. Leaving the room through the far exit I found myself in a sort of broom cupboard, a long back closet sheltering a single mop, its frozen head shock-haired with dust. Annoyed, I went back and looked around. I appeared to have exhausted all the options of egress, except one. There, next to the bed, half folded into a corner, was a frayed screen embroidered with a faded peacock – an alarmingly lifelike brute, with feathers bristling out of its great rump in wild arcs – and just visible behind it, if you stood at a certain angle, was a second door.

The door was stubborn but unlocked, and opened, after I had given it three or four good kicks, onto a small dressing room shaded by a lowered blind. A layer of settled white powder lay on the floorboards and over an iron truckle bed, covered with a short brown candlewick bedspread, which stood in the corner. The bedspread was resinous and grainy with age. As I sat down on it I felt the springs beneath sag under my coccyx, as if gratefully receiving a familiar weight. Opposite was a metal washstand carrying a pitcher and a porcelain shaving bowl, and a stub of filthy candle fused to its holder; and next to that, a squat leather chest or trunk of the kind once used by gentlemen travellers, with hard corner caps and a tarnished brass catch. The same dry powder coated everything.

My heart had begun to jolt erratically, and I got up quickly to call it back to heel. I tried to release the blind over the window, but the ancient pulley wouldn't budge. Lifting a corner of the faded green material (the fabric was brittle to the touch – silk, or dirt?) I found myself looking out, through a grimy window pane, onto a courtyard overgrown with nettles and unnaturally large roses.

Which part of the house had I come to? I searched for the top of the chestnut under which we had sat that morning, but couldn't see it. Had I walked all the way to the end of the east wing, and was I now peering over a part of the garden which had been hidden from view, around a corner, while I downed grappa with Miss Roper on the back lawn?

The courtyard was fenced in on two sides by a high wall of roughly-hewn yellow stone, completely out of keeping with the rest of the building. The corner of ground screened off by it was tiny, bounded on the left by a right angle where what I assumed was the main wall of the house joined another, which jutted out by not more than five feet. The sheer front of red brick to my left was broken at the near edge by two slim, brightly-coloured panels. A stained glass window? From my slant position it was hard to tell. Below me, coral and white blooms the size of saucers threatened every margin, rising from a thicket of thorny stalks, their blown heads tossed open, drooping, in the strong sunlight. The tall nettles bristled between them in sappy clusters, spikily furred. I thought I could make out the shadowy plinth of a sundial planted in the middle of a rectangular flag, but the angular weeds and tangled branches sprawling across the choked space glinted and shone so brightly that I couldn't be certain.

I realized why I hadn't noticed the outer wall of the courtyard from my seat in the garden. It was smothered in a dense clump of vegetation which pushed up against the stone from the far side and spilled or waved over the top: trailing boas of ivy, a thuggish clump of cow parsley and white willowherb, and, rising above the mess, the bulleted arms of a hoary old crab apple. Anyone looking towards the eastern wall of Mawle would see a thickening in the green border skirting the building, and nothing else.

Under my gaze the apple tree eased off one of its mean, puckered fruits and shed it, plop, into the frilly undergrowth. *Malus furioso*. Quite inedible.

The trunk, the fateful trunk, wasn't even locked.

I saw it again as I turned away from the window. My freckled claws tried the catch almost idly. The brass tongue stood to attention immediately, exhaling a listless puff of rust. The interior of the trunk was entirely empty, its smooth pale bottom unmarked.

And then, as I leaned over it, my tainted breath seemed to make the floor of the box ruffle and squirm. I blew harder and saw that it was not empty at all, but compounded of a settled layer of dust, from which a tough brown triangle of old cardboard protruded like a buoy.

You will conclude from my excitement that I am about to tell you that I had located my Madonna.

In fact, I pulled this object out and found that I held a notebook, blotched and fragile, in my hand. The front cover was missing. The first page, covered in a tangled black script, was torn across:

... of my time here already has been wasted drinking fetid cups of tea, and engaging in bland chit-chat with the

Bronsons, that I could die of frustration and boredom. Mrs B – a plump widow of middle years with the bulging blue eyes of a hydrocephalic baby – is not, I suspect, really an expatriate Rhode Island matron at all, but a lady meteorologist.

Mrs Bronson? Who was Mrs Bronson? I'd never heard the name before. How old was the book? The script was curled and clinging, extremely difficult to decipher, each letter grappling the next as though with wrought iron hooks. The pages smelled thickly of mould, of nevermore. No one had self-consciously ornate handwriting like that now. And where, come to think of it, had the anonymous writer been when writing this?

Her tedious comparisons between the quality of the summers in the Veneto and those in Newport and the respective opportunities afforded by them for boating, bathing and befriending hapless strangers like myself, her minute knowledge of warm currents, cold currents, disease-carrying midday troughs and bracing southerly breezes, have convinced me of this. Predicting an imminent barometric drop in the air pressure, she has arranged to whisk us – her calf-like daughter Edith, and me – off to the countryside tomorrow afternoon for a picnic. And yet her skills as a cicerone and general social facilitator come with such fulsome recommendations from the William Wetmore Storys in Venice that I daren't snub her. I may have to sing for my supper.

Asolo is certainly very picturesque, just as the Storys said it would be, and may be as good a place as any other in which to while away the last month or so of my journey. I have seen enough, and collected enough, and a veritable drapery of skirts has been paraded in front of me; now I want to stay put – although I fear that coming here now, at the end of summer, was a mistake.

Whoever made these notes had done so in the Veneto – in Asolo! My heart struck up a gallop again. 'Her calf-like daughter.' 'I may have to sing for my supper.' 'A veritable drapery of skirts.' The tone was dismissive, independent, cocksure; in a word, masculine. Who, in God's name, had been the author of this journal or whatever it was? I tested the age of the paper with an unsteady finger. It was expensive, fine in the grain, with a crisp watermark. It might well be a hundred years old, or even more. Could it be – ? Could it – ? No, absurd. Surely, surely not!

This is already the 1st of September, but the late summer heat is still murderous. The vegetation all around is scorched into paleness; the air itself swoons in the sun. Even my position high up near the city wall, in the shuttered room I have rented from Signora Tabacchi a few paces from Mrs B's own villa, La Mura, affords me little relief. The very stones of the buildings seem to glow with hidden fire. Perched on the shoulder of Monte Ricco, the ancient Euganean Rocca resembles nothing so much as a heap of coals about to topple over onto the town.

Above me totters the old dwelling of Queen Catarina Cornaro, who was forced by the Venetian Republic in 1489, on the death of her husband, to exchange her kingdom of Cyprus for this pretty but petty dominion (the phrase is Mrs

B's) where she kept state in a mimic court with Bembo, afterwards Cardinal, for her secretary. All of this and I know not what else is commemorated in Bembo's *Gli Asolani* or book of love verses inspired by the place, or so Mrs B tells me. I've never heard of the volume, which was not on any reading list of mine at Christ Church.

Christ Church. That settled it. My left hand had started to shake uncontrollably. I could hardly breathe; was it the dust?

This ridiculous trip had not, perhaps, been a complete waste of time. In this cubby hole, this airless cell, I had found James Roper's living voice – in a diary, of all things! Time gave a shimmy. My chest ached. My breath felt as if it were being dragged out of me, as though it were not a fragment of the past that I had just intercepted, but a mean bastard of a two-hundred-and-five-pound heavyweight with a deadly punch.

So Roper had indeed been to Asolo, that popular holiday spot for nineteenth-century English and American travellers to the Veneto, as Sanderson had claimed in his *Private Picture Galleries* – and here was the proof! This ragged notebook contained his journal for the Venetian tour he'd made in 1889. Within a few sentences, I thought in a roaring blaze of hope, the Bellini would be delivered up to me, and I flipped through the pages with jellied fingers. Bellini. Bellini. The name did not seem to appear anywhere, however, or at least not in an obvious way. The chevroned handwriting was far too dense for easy reading. Never mind, never mind! I would decipher the whole thing from the beginning, detach each hasped word painstakingly from the next.

It was time to return to the library before I was missed. I

slid the book into the breast pocket of my jacket, and, shuffling across the dusty floor so as to obliterate my tracks, closed the door tightly behind me. Then I began to trace my way back, through the lumber room, down the splintering corridor, and so, I hoped, to the wing where I had begun and thus to the giant staircase; but this was not at all straightforward. Some of the rooms had sprouted several doors where there had previously only been one. I was getting more and more out of breath, and after two further attempts at escape I found myself back in front of the Murillo. The sultry tints of that room, coming around yet again, made me feel faint. I'd suffered too much excitement for one afternoon.

The library was just as I had left it: as pallid, as dusty, and – thank Christ – unoccupied. Its cool white walls were a relief. The window still stood open, but I could no longer hear Anna's voice coming from the garden. I drew back the overstuffed chair from behind James Roper's desk, sat down, and went on reading.

The whole of the early section of the diary or journal, which took me a good few hours to untangle, concerned Roper's arrival in Asolo that September of 1889 and his first impressions of the place. There was something about the irreverent pup – I did some hurried subtractions and worked out that he would have been around twenty-three at the time – which I liked. What a pity for him that the Asolan jaunt had started off in such a dull way! I gave a violent snort of amusement. *Gli Asolani* indeed! I had read Bembo's book – a Renaissance celebration of courtly love on a grand scale, set in the castle gardens of the exiled Catarina Cornaro in Asolo – years ago, in the course of my research. It was full of the importance of refining crass earthly love into a higher love that would elevate the human spirit, of courtiers and ladies-in-waiting and people who played madrigals but never fucked. All that nonsense. How shabby it was, how seedy, to think of worldly James Roper encamped in this very spot. I felt an obscurely dirty thrill: the seedier the better.

'Is your work – is your work fun, then?' Miss Roper had come back and was hesitating at the edge of the room. The curve of her cheek was scabby with what looked like dried tears: that argument with Mr Horny Horticulture hadn't ended well, then.

I laughed wickedly. 'Oh, most pleasurable. Tremendous fun. The pursuit of great art always is, don't you find?'

At that the girl seemed to unravel before my eyes. You're unequally matched, I reminded myself: don't intimidate the poor child too much. I was on fire, ecstatic, oddly shaky. 'Do you know, I think I'm a little overwrought. It's – it's the joy of being here! This is going to be the most marvellous week.' My heart was pounding like a rainforest of pygmies. 'You've been so kind already, so welcoming. I think – my dear Miss Roper, I think I'm going to have to have a little lie down in my room.'

Miss Roper seemed to experience a spurt of confidence. 'Shall I bring you up a cup of tea?' she suggested. 'Then you can work again later this afternoon, can't you? Once you've had a good rest.'

'That sounds delightful,' I panted, strangely short of breath. 'Tea it is.'

I remember prowling the corridors of Mawle that Monday evening and the next day in a sort of exhilarated fog. I seemed to be carrying the burden of consciousness in both arms, and to be reeling wildly under the weight. Bright canvases shone at me from far walls, their lights dissolving the shadowy spaces in between with a crackle. For the sake of appearances I had started to make a list of the pictures in the house, as befitted a serious art historian, but nothing cohered properly: I was too charged, too vivid to myself. My blood felt electric. Attentive Anna, always on hand, brought me grappa and tea. I had not come across the Madonna *del prato*, but I would, oh I would! I thought of Dürer, so opinionated, so dogmatic, in spite of his youth – he was young enough, at thirty-five, to think that he was very old – arriving in the Veneto with his inks, his engraver's tools, his fixed ideas about his craft, and stepping into that cramped room of Bellini's with its single luminous board to find that his certainties had all, within the space of a minute or two, seeped away.

And then there was James Roper, more jejune still, arriving in the same place nearly four hundred years later, embarked on the course that would bring him face to face with this very Madonna, and the Madonna herself to Mawle . . . It was magnificent; it was overwhelming; it was almost too much to hold in balance. At intervals, overcome by a strange fidgety weariness that pulsed in slow waves from my heart, I retreated to my room and tried to decipher Roper's diary. For hours afterwards fragments of his webbed script sizzled on my retina as I gazed stupidly at his collection. He owned a Zuccarelli Pastorale – he had a Bernini cartoon. He had an assortment of smallish Canova marbles. He did not, as far as I could see, have anything resembling my Bellini. I closed my eyes and tried to breathe calmly. How funny. The empty teacup by my bed had grown a green penumbra: there were two teacups.

> Mrs Bronson's most solemn utterances are almost always punctuated by the snorting and yapping of a posse of pugs. There are eight of these miniature Chinese spaniels, named, in an ascending scale of absurdity, Contenta, Moretto, Tubby, Zizi, Thisbe, Trolley, Tou Fou and Yahabibi. These creatures all have an abundance of fur sprouting about the eyes, and suffer terribly in the heat . . . And, oh God, the daughter. 'Miss Edie' is a solid girl with a loaf-shaped face and a yellow crust of hair parted straight down the middle, as if carved by a particularly sharp knife. As she is very short she stands all the time, when she is not sitting over her embroidery, on tiptoes. She prides herself on having a smattering of learning and a very strong will. She seldom stirs before nine, and always drinks her first cup of morning coffee behind closed doors. I believe that she is a secret sufferer of the—

I tried to get up. 'She always drinks . . . always drinks . . .' The words rolled around in my mouth like gravel on a dry riverbed. My desiccated throat cried out for water. Heaving my carcase over to the sink and cranking open the tap, I bent down to put my lips to it and was astonished when a sudden swirl of acid in my stomach knocked me sideways. My chest was drum-tight, its contents tickly and ominously compressed. Leaning against the wall, I tried to duck the assaults of a malevolent light bulb that swooped and swung straight towards me. Whirlpools of nausea eddied under my ribs, chasing the first fumes of an oily and corrosive vomit into my gullet.

I staggered out onto the landing and began to make my way downstairs, calling for Miss Roper. Somewhere between the second and first floors I remember sinking at last against the banister, its posts turning to scorching lead in my paralysed hands, as the sticky burden of my heart burst into flames.

Lying on the stairs, a goner, I could hear swift footsteps approaching, the heavy grating of doors, a capable swish of female thighs. I was on the point of swooning away when I felt a pair of thin arms clasping my shoulders. I smelled the scent of a woman's breath, the stench of lilies, hot and past their first freshness, and was felled by the soft contact of a woman's cheek, damp and hairless, against my own.

CHAPTER SEVEN

Wednesday the 11th saw me reclining in a deckchair on the south lawn, under the fraying shadow of the chestnut tree. I wore a calf-length maroon paisley dressing gown with a corded waist and starched black cuffs like mourning envelopes, which Anna had found in a cupboard in her father's bedroom. The early afternoon sunlight drew tickly warm moustaches on my upper lip. With my pyjama'd knees and meditatively interlaced fingers I looked like a bonze stretched out on his palanquin. Since my angina attack the previous day Anna had declared me an invalid and decreed that I should rest as much as possible, a decision in which I'd had no say.

Above me the papery sky was brushed by the tall rear elevation of Mawle, rough but rosy in its green petticoat. It overlooked the long runner of velvet grass that stretched from the raised terrace with its curved flight of descending steps, past parallel beds of foxgloves, lips sleepily incensing the warm air, down to a high beech hedge screening a decayed tennis court. The hypnotic hum of insects rubbing their glassy wings together rose from a nearby azalea bush. The upholstered afternoon rounded out its silences, each hour a plump cushion of peace.

But I was not happy, not restful. Harry and Vicky were away: on an errand to the village to visit the butcher, the baker, the candlestick maker. They'd left me alone with Anna, but she was nowhere to be seen. She was hidden somewhere behind that brick façade, having been summoned indoors by the ringing telephone just minutes earlier. The deck of cards from which she was about to deal us each a new hand of Black Jack lay scattered on the grass, its cleft-chinned knaves and queens tumbled in a heap. As I lolled about waiting for her to return my oriental smile grew tight and mean. It had been ten minutes, twenty! Whom could this friendless girl possibly want to speak to for twenty minutes?

When I fainted she'd dragged me onto the bed in the Rose Room. After accomplishing this strangely tender and affecting feat she lay down beside me, listening as my breathing grew regular, my guttering heart slowed down to a regular thud, thud. How she got me onto the mattress I never knew: my weight must have been at least twice hers. Nor did she mention it afterwards, more than once or maybe three times, and then only to ask how I felt. The power to humiliate was not in Anna's nature.

When I think about those first few days at Mawle it is always in these terms: embarrassment, suspicion, contrition, abject need. The pressure of Anna's body on the febrile counterpane, the gemmed sweat on her neck, her peculiar, sweetish smell, stick in my memory like a splinter in a wound. That hauntingly maternal gesture of hers proved critical to us both. While I lay helpless under her gaze that afternoon, passing in and out of consciousness, the marble clearness of her flesh, shaken gently by the steady movement of her youthful blood, the starry wings of her hair, her earnest glance, entered into my aching heart and took their place among the co-ordinates of its world; the fixed points in a dreadful, all-engulfing landscape of nostalgia and desire. I was already lost. I was sinking volitionlessly into a state of infatuation – and with that most unlikely of creatures, a gormless girl half my age.

Many more days passed before it occurred to me to wonder why Anna hadn't immediately called an ambulance when she saw her mother's distinguished guest sprawled in agony across the banister, clutching his chest, but by then I was already beginning to grasp how mechanical and unquestioning her instinct for compliance was. Someone had warned her that I would take the first available opportunity to prowl about; that she should be on her guard against me, monitor my every move. Perhaps she had even – why not? – been told what my addictions were. I have sometimes wondered if the tipples which Anna so readily offered me contained only grappa. And what the hell was in that tea? Had she been directed to feed me some sort of stimulant and narcotic alternately? (This seems all the more likely when I consider what a little plotter and schemer she turned out to be in the end.) In coming to find me she had perhaps simply obeyed her instructions with a literalness which anyone not in the know might easily have mistaken for calm competence. They didn't know about my weak heart. I doubt that the Mamma meant to harm me, but it never occurred to Anna to temper her orders.

I was tremulous with spite by the time she reappeared half an hour later at the kitchen door, carrying cups and saucers on a tray. As she walked towards me with her swaying geisha steps she looked curiously foreshortened, as if descending from a great height. She was dressed as usual in lycra leggings and an oversized black t-shirt. I noticed for the first time that she was slightly pigeon-toed and that her knees made small kissing sounds whenever they touched. She stopped next to my chair, apparently deep in thought, and squatted on her shiny haunches in front of the tray. Her arms, busy about the sugar bowl and the milk jug, were the arms of an urchin, fleshless and frail. A blue vein darted beneath the tender skin of her inner elbow, like a sprat feeding at the surface of a pond. I inhaled her crushed lily smell ravenously.

'That was a long phone call.'

The expression on her face was abstracted, unfocused, as if I'd woken her from a deep sleep. 'Oh, that was Minnie.'

Minnie was her father's accountant, a stack-haired, bass-voiced virago (or so I imagined her) responsible for overseeing the house's finances – there seemed to be some sort of trust fund for Anna – from her London lair.

'And what does the charming Miss Minnie have to say, ha-ha?'

A pause, half hesitant, half fearful. Then Anna surrendered. 'Terrible things. If we don't do something soon we are going to be seriously strapped for cash.'

'My dear child, really?'

Anna leaned towards me confidingly, a guilty pucker on her brow. She was about to reveal a tremendous secret. 'Dr Lynch, we may look rich – this house, all that,' she waved the slender wand of her arm towards the raffish old front of Mawle. 'But we're not. The place doesn't actually belong to Mummy – it's sort of held in a special arrangement for me so that I get the interest. That's how Daddy left it. Not terribly tax efficient, Mummy says, but there you go.'

'Your father must have loved you very much, to leave you all the proceeds of his estate.'

Anna gave a deliberate shrug of resignation that made my heart trip. 'Daddy tried so hard to make this place pay, but he just couldn't do it. Anyway, what was the use? He wanted a boy, but he only had me.' She stared glassily at her flaking nails. 'In the end he said I was no bloody good to him at all, except as a housekeeper.'

'My dear, I'm sure that wasn't true.'

'Oh, well, you know, I suppose he was right.' Anna turned and glanced miserably over her shoulder. The brute building was still there, toad-like, untransformed. 'Minnie wants us to have an open day on the 15th. Run off a few extra pamphlets, show the house to the public. It's all planned, Mummy had the posters printed weeks ago.' Her tone, incongruously, was beseeching.

I braced my virile frame: ill, perhaps, but still most manly and forbearing. 'If there is anything I can do to help, my dear, anything at all, you only have to ask. I am sure it will be a great success. Whatever you touch is bound to turn to gold.'

What had I said? Anna's changeable features were suddenly lit up from within as if by a stellar light. A white-hot radiance passed across the bridge of her nose like the tail of a comet, illuminating her whole face; even the roots of her hair seemed to perk up.

'Really? Do you think so?' In her eagerness she knocked over the milk, sprinkling the grass with pearls. 'Will you stay and help? Will you really?'

'If I am not in the way, then of course! But what will your mother think?'

'Oh, Mummy will be so pleased! She always says that I'm

a simpleton.' An idea combusted inside that shapely skull, filling it with dangerous sparks. 'You can lead the donkey!'

'The donkey? Will there be a donkey?'

'Yes, for the children. 50p a ride.'

'Indeed. I am very good with donkeys. But make it a pound.' I gave an asinine bray, hee-haw, hee-haw, and we fell about, laughing.

I felt like crying, like dying, like laying my evil head in her lap and dreaming my life away. Instead I gave her beaming cheek a pat and sipped my tea, which had turned stone cold.

I beat her at Black Jack. I let her beat me at Gin Rummy. An hour passed, then another. The garden fell silent and shadows slid imperceptibly across the lawn. A distant chime struck thinly from the village church: four o'clock. Anna got to her feet, stretched, yawned, smiled a beatific smile. Time for tea; tea for two. Oh, I knew that that tea would make me deliciously, almost unnaturally sleepy. I watched the house swallow her sashaying rump. Ten minutes passed, twenty. How long did it take to boil a kettle, for God's sake? Had Harry returned? I was in agony as I willed her to reappear. The summer breeze fell silent, the trees stopped their whispering.

Ah, there she was! As she came towards me from the dark cave of the kitchen, carrying a tinkling tray, I had a sickening sensation of being stuck in a loop, of time concentrically and inevitably repeating itself.

CHAPTER EIGHT

Why did they want to keep me there? For they most certainly did. Whenever I had second thoughts in those early days at Mawle, and suggested to Anna that it might be better after all if I took myself off back to Oxford, and a hospital, she became emphatically nervous.

'Oh no, Dr Lynch, there's no need!' she chattered in the tinny tones of an automaton. 'You're very nearly well again. You look so much better! Why don't you have another squint at the pictures upstairs? You mustn't let your work suffer.' I noticed that her eyes skimmed involuntarily towards the telephone, as if it could overhear her.

I would climb the stairs dutifully and go back to my spurious inventory. When would Maddalena turn up? Anna had mentioned the end of the week: I didn't have much time. Fortified with slugs of grappa, I searched for the Madonna, tapping walls and the backs of wardrobes and sliding my penknife down the gaps along panel edges. I fancied that the old house suffered my predations nobly, permitting itself only the odd dignified gasp in the wrenching open of a drawer or a door. Its brick and plaster shell was a labyrinth of brassy Victorian and synthetic twentieth-century tat cohabiting flagrantly with the browbeaten remnants of more tasteful Ropers. For every putative Bertucci, quivering with life, there was a glazed case bursting with stuffed kingfishers and moorhens, a shag pile rug. The fading daylight created spliced shadows that suggested the elusive textures of countless substances, from shifting silk to the arrested flash of glass, from worn velvet to the specious sheen of silver plate. I hoped, every minute, to step from this opacity into the warm clear light of the cinquecento, to find myself face to face with a vision of simplicity: that pebbly field, those ethereal trees, the tower on the hill, and my Madonna. I never did. When I came downstairs again in the evenings, dust clogging my pores, Anna would offer to make me more tea.

'Miss Roper,' I pleaded on Thursday night as she saw me off to my bed with yet another cuppa, 'please stop all this – this skulduggery. I promise you solemnly that I won't run away. What on earth are you putting in this brew? My old Da was a pharmacist, you realize, and I know a few tricks myself. Come on, out with it.'

She blushed and looked down at the cloudy surface of the cup, as if she might read our future there.

'It's just a tisana,' she whispered. 'One of Mamma's traditional Venetian recipes. It will do you good.' But she poured it away down the kitchen sink, nevertheless.

How watchful they were, how careful, even when they seemed most indifferent! I had the apparent run of the house, but in fact my activities were carefully controlled. The mornings before the effects of the tea had worn off were my worst time, a compound of cantankerous nausea and leaden inertia. On Friday the 13th I prised myself from my matchbox bed by a great effort of will, long before the rest of the house had begun to stir, and crept out to the old stable block. The sun was already scaling the peeled blue sky. Two invisible blackbirds, shy piccolos, had begun a frenzied vibrato in the arms of a still sooty ash.

The stables were tucked away behind the curve of the lake, a long low building banging its saloon doors morosely in the dawn breeze. The shitlessness of the place suggested that no horse had been quartered there for years. A cobbled yard extended its mossy stones as far as the threshold of each cobwebby cell. I stuck my head inside the doors, to see what I could see. Four of the cells were derelict and empty, inhabited only by shadows. The fifth was full of junk: a Pye radio crouching on a plywood shelf, a wheelbarrow spilling yellow entrails of garden hose over the cement floor, the splayed hand of an upside down aluminium rake braced against a nest of brown plastic pots. As I kicked speculatively at these Harry strode into the building out of a sunbeam, his head a shower of gold.

'Awright, T.J.?'

'Morning, morning,' I began in my best American accent. 'Just getting some fresh air. Ah, Jesus,' I corrected myself, '*Jeez*, you're up early. Howya doin'?'

'Not too bad, not too bad, yeah.'

He cast his nervous spaniel eyes from side to side.

''Cept for the cows, the cows. I've been up with 'em most of the night. The poor darlins feel it every mizzomar. They're in heat and we're not breeding now.'

I nodded sympathetically.

'They do be calving in spring, and keening all summer long. Keening and keening after their season. But,' Harry folded his arms philosophically, 'that's Nietzsche for you. Nietzsche has 'er own way.'

In an adjacent field, a solitary Friesian let out a soulful

boom, ding dong, like the toll of a convent bell. Far off, a bull moaned in answer.

'There be a season to everything,' he continued sagaciously.

'A time to reap, a time to sow.'

'If only the ladies knew that, eh! *If only the darlins unnerstood that!* Ker-pow,' a ghostly automatic trailed my left eyeball, 'ker-pow. Bull's eye every time. Har-har.'

'How many cows do you keep here?'

'Not many now. Daisy, and Bess, and Tilda and Prue – and 'er innoors.' He risked a matey smirk.

Well, well. The impertinent yob meant Anna. Was he warning me off? I assayed my throatiest bellow.

'And only the one bull?'

'Only one bull – one bull.'

Ha, hinting Harry! 'Good luck, *larra*, and fare thee well,' I conceded. There was nothing in here. The junk-crammed cell had begun to revolve. I gave a low bow in the direction of the Pye radio, the nesting pots, the distant pasture where Tilda, or Bess, saluted the rising sun.

'Not feeling that well, eh?' Harry squinted at me slyly. 'Head a bit fuzzy? It's a wee bit soon for you to be up, entit? Wanta lie down again?'

Aha, lover boy, I thought, so you're in on it too.

My little jailer, my dearest girl, my love.

I remember the speckled length of your naked back with its shy vertebrae: tinker, tailor, soldier, sailor, rich man, poor man, beggar man – and your lightly furred coccyx, my tender maid, and the way you braced yourself at the touch of my probing finger.

But that was much later. Before we ever came to that, I had the diary to console me. And, my dear, your mother's visit to withstand – not to mention the first of those underhand assaults by the past that were to become a feature of my time at Mawle.

It was later that unlucky Friday. I was no longer strictly an invalid, but I was still lapped in purple pyjama'd bliss, discreetly infused with tea and grappa at appropriate hours, and gently encouraged to explore.

But why?

Always, always, I was animated by the rare shy ghost of Anna's company, her awkward appearances and disappearances across the browning lawn. The synthetic whisper of her thighs was like the music of the spheres to me. I longed to seize her chafed brown hands and run my tongue along each bitten nail.

I tossed about in a fever of anticipation. When I did not think of Anna I thought about the diary, and what it might reveal about the Bellini. Around midday, when I was certain of being unnoticed – the cheerful stink of singed meat from the kitchen assured me that Anna was usefully occupied, skewering our dinner joint – I went back to my bedroom to retrieve it. I had made a near-invisible slit in the base of my mattress and hollowed out a pocket in the middle where the journal now lay in wait for me, supine and broken-backed. Hooking it out, I inspected it with a churning sense of excitement. The notebook had once been bound in a fine nubbled leather, but only a fragment of the back board remained, and the binding had come off to reveal the cardboard beneath. The front cover and the earlier pages of the dairy, as I had observed on first discovering it, were missing, just as if someone had tried to rip the book in two.

I searched for the paragraph close to the abrupt beginning where I had last stopped reading. Roper had, I recalled, been describing the daughter of this Mrs Bronson whom he'd met in Asolo. The handwriting was head-splittingly difficult to make out.

> I believe that she is a secret sufferer of the migraine. Sometimes her face is savaged by a look of astonished pain, like Alberico trailed to death through raunce and bramble bush. Mrs B, meanwhile, is a slave both to her offspring's whims and to these mysterious headaches, which exert an equal tyranny over her.

My own brain had already begun to throb when, unexpectedly, a shrill yowl from outside shattered my concentration. It was a low *woo-woo-woo*, like the pining of a dog, and it drew me irresistibly to the window. Below me Anna teetered on the kitchen steps, gripping Vicky by her bare arm. The two see-sawed backwards and forwards. It was Vicky who was the source of the noise. She wore her slummy frock, and in her free hand – the other was twisted in Anna's shirt – she held a book at arm's length with rigidly pincered fingers, as if it were a turd.

'Woo-woo-woo!' yowled Vicky.

'Oh, shut up. Just shut up!' yelped Anna. 'Can't you just go and *read* for an hour on your own? Why do I always have to amuse you?'

'Well, I wish I had a real *mother*! Why must I be stuck with *you*?'

'Oh, for God's sake. Just don't start that crap again.' Anna scraped the child off with a magisterial gesture of despair. Vicky crouched on the grass, clutching her book, gazing at Anna's retreating back with vicious yearning. 'A look of astonished pain . . .' She was still crying, chewing her tears like a whelp with a bone. I turned quickly away. All at once I felt, with a sharp tweak of anguish, that I could not stand it – the virginal, sparsely furnished room, the desolation of that keening. Above all, the child's shame. No one feels shame like a child, unless it is a child who has never grown up.

I stood stock still, as if in a glare, still holding the diary. It was almost too much: the sudden influx of light, the memory. Here it was, the past – the wooden chair, my longing; the sour chalk smell of semen, the volume of poetry open on the table. The notebook slipped from my grasp and fell to the ground. I closed my eyes and hid my face in my hands for a moment. The floorboards seemed to bounce like a wave. What was that other child, wee Tommy Lynch, doing here? My heart felt bloated, full of tears and air.

Was it the effect of the sensation of time travel induced by the diary? The minutes unravelled, leaving me naked and exposed. Oh, it all began quietly, innocently enough – innocence; that word again! – as terrible things will.

Imagine a long, timbered classroom, varnished like an expensive coffin, vinegary with the boy-smell of damp grey flannel and urine. A slash of rain (for it is always raining) falls on the mullioned window panes. I have been at my new boarding school a fortnight. We are in a lesson being given by a certain Father Paine, barely released from the seminary, on something called *The Triumphs of Temper*, but just whose temper is meant to be triumphing, and over what, has passed me by as I am drowning in a swell of homesickness so perilous that it must be leaving a telltale puddle under my desk. A pair of batwing ears with fretted lobes in the very next desk fills me with disgust and fear: these belong to Gerard Byrne, who sleeps in the cubicle next to mine and who is given to loud moans and bouts of flatulence at all hours of the day and night.

This is a poetry lesson. Father Paine is so young that his jaw is still dotted with the scattered raspberry shot of acne, and he marches up and down on the dais, fingering his fluffy hair with pitiful self-consciousness.

'So, gentlemen,' he squeaks, 'so, then. The heroine's good angel is about to reward her virtue with the supreme prize of a happy marriage:

> Her airy guard prepares the softest down
> From Peace's wing to line the nuptial crown.

Who can gloss these lines for us? Can you, Byrne?'

A *peep* and a *parrp* that would not disgrace the brass section of a small orchestra, let alone the agonized adolescent male sphincter. Byrne hangs his notched lobes in shame. Nineteen sycophants (including me) titter.

'I see,' blushes Father Paine wearily. 'It is pointless to hope for any subtlety from you. You are only capable of the foulest *fortissimo*. Please report to the infirmary for a glass of salts after this lesson.' His maidenly hand creeps shyly to his upper lip. 'Can you interpret this passage for us, Lynch?'

All that these lines, coming so catastrophically out of the blue, suggest to me is the image of this guardian angel holding Peace with the firmness of an Irish housewife, and plucking her steadily in order to trim some sort of bonnet, but I can hardly say so.

'Well, Father,' I begin (though he strikes me as far too young to be called this), 'I think that they may just possibly imply the triumph of those qualities that are especially feminine – the wearing of hats, now – and the going to weddings,' this, the going to weddings, is something that my Darling is excessively fond of; almost as fond as she is of going to funerals. Is she still? I hardly know: for two weeks now she has belonged to another life, another time, and I will surely never see her again.

Father Paine pulls up short. He is not an unkind young man, but his mother chose this life for him without his say-so and he is aware that his dignity hangs, always, by a thread.

'Are you setting yourself up as a wit, boy?'

'No, Father.'

'Because I'll have no wits in my class. Get up. Quick!'

I jerk to my feet, fatuously aware of being a contraption constructed wholly of elbows and knees.

'Now, explain to us all exactly what you meant by that remark.'

I am unable to explain. All I am conscious of is that the wave of unhappiness on which I have sculled for the last two weeks has become a crested monster, and I am drowning in a tide of misery so black that it must come from the abyss. I start to stammer. Father Paine stares at me quizzically.

'My mother –' I stammer. 'My mother –'

And then I burst into tears.

There follows a solid silence that is like the dead wall of sound raised in the wake of an explosion. And then it begins:

a creeping, coruscating whisper, plopping around me in insinuating plosives.

'Ashy pet, ashy pet. Lynch is an ashy pet!'

I want lightning to strike me dead. I want the glossy floorboards to swallow me up. I notice, through a veil of snot and damp fringe, that my tormentor is still looking at me, but with a look oddly devoid of malice. His pale pimpled face seems more faded than usual, his Adam's apple intent on frantic escape. It is as if he and I are standing face to face in a strong wind. He gazes at me with naked pity, and I feel in turn as if I have been stripped bare. His look says that we are equal in suffering and are called to fortitude; that we both have to endure. Bear up, my brother! His bruised eyes look at me, in fact, with all the tenderness due to a fellow victim.

'Shut up, you evil little craturs, shut *up*! Sit down, Thomas Joseph. You are clearly the only boy in this class who has been paying any attention *at all* to what I have been saying. For your preparation,' for we always call it this, never 'homework', as if we are forever laying down the groundwork for some greater project, 'you are to paraphrase these lines *in full* in your exercise books. That is all. Now bugger off.'

But there's more. Not long after this I am invited one evening, just before bath and bedtime, to attend our Director of Studies, Father Gabriel Furey, in his study. He is a mild old Jesuit from Cork with untrimmed eyebrows like miniature Brillo pads, who is convinced that my fastidiousness and bookishness are the signs of a latent vocation to the priesthood. Well-meaning man! By now he must be dead and buried somewhere under the greening Irish sod. We used to laugh at him for his excessive pride in his native city and for his equally insane otherworldliness: his nickname was the

Angel Gabriel. I remember that he had a habit of speaking in fizzling abbreviations, as if the erratic current of his thought were perpetually being short-circuited.

'Ah, Thomas Joseph. I have asked you here this evening – not to converse with you idly, you understand. But to the point, which is. I have had a letter from your mother.'

Father Furey produces a rectangular wad of sturdy paper, lightly ruled, and proceeds to unfold it. It's a single sheet, covered in my mother's careful schoolgirl hand, with its cruciform crease thrust outwards at me.

My heart gives a hiccup, but I manage to speak. 'Yes, Father.'

'Your mother writes that you do not appear. That you do not seem. To be happy: now I ask you. Is it the point of our existence here, Thomas Joseph? Is it? When Our Lord wept and fasted in Gethsemane – he was not. When Our Lady trembled and sighed at the news brought her by the angel – she was not. Well. I do not know. Scripture does not tell us. But I assume not. Full of exultation, yes. But happy? Was she?'

'No, Father.'

'There you go, then. Whatever your unhappiness – offer it up.' He refolds my mother's letter into its painful girlish creases and thrusts it decisively under the blotter on his desk as if the matter were closed. But it does not seem to be.

'Your mother also writes that you are a most sensitive. That you have an aptitude. I would not want you to think that we are unwilling, within reasonable bounds now, to encourage—'

He coughs discreetly and twitches the skirt of his rusty soutane. The toasty jungle of hot-water pipes coiled across the ceiling above us begins to rumble in time to the evening's ablutions. Slippered feet slap the staircase in the corridor. I am already wearing my dressing gown, the belt of which is so long that it goes tightly around me twice, terminating in an umbilical knot. In spite of its protection I feel raw and strangely indecent. Father Furey gets up, goes to the window, and begins to agitate the folds of a pair of heavy velvet curtains. His arms saw like those of an accordionist, releasing a foul exudation of sardines, chalk and tobacco. There is an old brown engraving of a Venetian bridge hanging on the adjacent wall. He shuffles over, pauses in front of it, and regards it with a perplexing longing.

'Do you know where this is, Thomas Joseph? Get up and come a little closer.'

I creep forward a few paces. 'I think so, Father. Is it Venice?'

'It is. Ah, Venice – the Cork of Italy. Someday perhaps you shall see it.' He waves me closer again, until I am almost prostrate against his desk. 'Since poetry is the academic subject in which you seem to excel, Father Paine has generously and unselfishly offered. Do not think that this is an opportunity given to every boy. Most rare, and not be be sniffed at.' He sniffs. 'I have high hopes of you, Thomas Joseph. High hopes for your *immortal soul*. You are to report to Father Paine in Rhetoric after your dinner every Thursday. What is the matter, fella, are you ill?'

I am. I am more than ill: never mind my soul; my heart has been torn from my body. My jagged breath comes and goes with disembowelling force. I bend forward, doubled up with shock, and brace myself against Father Furey's oak tabletop, snuffling in the cubic foot of air above it with desperate gulps. For stealing out towards me through the miasma of the room from beneath the blotter where he has entombed it, like a plaintive revenant, is my mother's unmistakable, unforgettable, urgently longed-for fragrance.

My mother's fragrance, the jet black distillation of failed roses, seemed to hang over the days and weeks following my interview with Father Furey, as if she had given what happened next her blessing. I went to see Father Paine that very Thursday, once I had been dismissed from the refectory. He was sitting, as always, at the master's inky writing table on the dais, only this time, instead of the usual pile of skinny exercise books, there were three or four volumes the size of suitcases in front of him. Diffidently, he invited me to pull up a chair. Its legs scraped a shriek across the floorboards. We shuffled about a little in our seats without meeting each other's eyes, like two kids on a date.

'Is there a particular poet you'd like to start with, now?'

I only know the name of one poet, the one my mother is always quoting. 'Browning, Father.'

'What, Robert Browning? Or Elizabeth Barrett Browning, the poetess?'

I did not know that there were two Brownings. I take a wild guess at what my Darling's preference would be. 'Maybe the lady one, Father?'

'Very well, so. We'll begin with Mrs Browning's *Sonnets from the Portuguese*.' And he opens one of the engorged volumes and begins to wade through a lake of treacle by some wife who can't get enough of her husband. The woman had no sense of proportion. 'How do I love thee? Let me count the ways. I love thee to the depth and breadth and height my soul can reach, when feeling out of sight for the ends of Being and ideal Grace. I love thee to the level of every day's most quiet need, by sun and candle-light. I love thee freely, as men strive for Right, I love thee purely, as they turn from Praise. I love thee with a passion put to use in my old griefs, and with my childhood's faith, sit up for Jesussake, Lynch.'

'Sorry, Father.'

'Never mind. We'll try the other fellow next time, shall we? There's a good one about an Italian duke who murders his wife, the rogue, which I'll bet you'll like.'

He gives me a shy, complicit smile.

I read poetry with Paine every Thursday after that. Sweet Christ – how much of it there was! These poets never talked in their own voices; they were always pretending to be someone else. They hid behind a thousand masks. Browning was the worst offender of the lot. That Italian duke of his whom Father Paine had told me about was a real caution: a Renaissance patron of the arts who spoke with discrimination about the objects in his collection, his wife among them – I mean, a portrait of his wife. It became clear within a few lines that the duke had had the poor girl murdered, because, as Father Paine pointed out, he had found her youthful beauty and freshness far too alarming to live with until he'd tamed it as art. I was dazzled by this poem, by the way in which it so effortlessly exposed the blend of cruelty and refinement in the speaker's nature. Was I already dimly aware of an answering sterility, a ducal alter ego in myself? I do not know. I do remember that I was both enticed and dismayed by the insatiable way that language could cannibalize and digest feeling, leaving only this hard, bright simulacrum behind. I wanted tenderness, I suppose, and some shred of what I had lost in my Darling, but instead I found only words. There was nothing else on offer.

Then one afternoon as I bent over my book I realized that Father Paine had drawn his chair up close to mine and was looking in turn at me and at the yielding surface of the page. I smiled in what I hoped was a winning way, calculating that he would be reporting the excellent progress of my interest in things poetical to Father Furey. He rattled something (the sacristy keys? a rosary? Oh, my childhood's faith) deep in his trouser pocket. I was bending forward slightly from the waist, straining to trace the sinuous outline of an Italian name, when I felt a leg pressed against mine.

'Are you all right, Thomas Joseph?' A muted groan.

'Yes,' I whispered back uncertainly.

'Good so. Keep still.' A hand cupped my far buttock. It seemed to have nothing to do with me, or with my wide-eyed reflection in the classroom window opposite. Paine rocked backwards and forwards on his seat, still groaning softly. Dusk came abruptly behind the window, as it so often did in winter in that part of the world, turning the air to pitch. I cannot say how long we sat there in the dark; or rather, how long I sat there while he rocked. The experience was not unpleasant. All of a sudden he stopped and gave my arse a parting squeeze. I could see his anxious boyish reflection swooning towards me in the glass, above the now blurred words on the page. 'If you say a word to anyone,' he blubbed, 'it'll be the finish up of me. They'll crucify me.'

What, and have me lose the only raft I'd been thrown in that place? I certainly did not want this to happen. Turning to face him, I flung my arms, my crushable childish self, around his waist.

We continued to meet in Rhetoric once a week, before the term ended and I had to go back home. It was always the same: the solicitous enquiry, the rocking, the groans, the hand on my buttocks, and then the sudden arrival of night behind the window, like a curtain swishing.

'Don't waste your time on the oul' imagination, Tommy,' snorted my Da when I tried to confess my newfound, shameful passion for poetry to him. 'Fact is where it's at. Mind your books and do what the Fathers tell ye, and one day—'

He extended his arms so that the sleeves dangled down nearly into his soup (we were having our midday dinner at the time). He was wearing his white lab apron, and seemed about to take off for the lab at any moment like a fiery-headed seraph. He did not finish the sentence, but the implication was clear: one day, you will come into your proper kingdom.

'God's in his heaven,' my mother began in a plaintive voice. This was my first holiday at home since starting boarding school, and she looked wan and dilute, as if my absence had diminished her.

'Whisht, Mary, and give us more soup, can't you?' barked my father abruptly, and that was the end of that conversation.

After that I allowed these poetry sessions to suck freely, in secret, on the years of my growing up, a reechily deformed plant sprung from a single, well-worn line. I suppose all this was my fault. If I hadn't had this hunger for my old intimacy with my Darling, this lack, this voracious hole in the heart, things would never have gone as far as they did, either with Paine or with the others who came later. I don't blame Paine for a moment; he was himself still a child, stripped as I was in that sacerdotal barracks of the feminine affection that had once made life bearable. The comfort he wanted was covert, peripheral. It was my appetite for consummations, for gustation, that made a shadowy thing dark, that pushed it, with flinching sinews and shaking hocks, from the speculative to the real. Within a month, you see, following just three such meetings, and entirely at my instigation, Paine and I had become lovers.

My mother used to accuse me of no longer loving her, you know – when I returned from school for the holidays – once it had sunk in that our separation was to be permanent. Perhaps she was right. Perhaps she intuited that I had already been smeared with the stain of rut.

And I'm curious . . . Was my love affair with pimply Paine the beginning of that duality in my nature that has sometimes caused me as much irritation as it has given me delight? I have always been able, from youth upwards, to dart back and forth like a minnow in the shallows of sex. There was no channel, male or female, that was too narrow for this guppy. After my mother's death, as an art history student in Dublin, I spent nearly five years earning my bread and board by dredging the pudenda of a nearly inconsolable widow with a very nice front study bedroom, and on our campus at Vermont, well-stocked as it was with both genders, I kept my hand in (so to speak) through frequent fly-fishing. I say 'hand' because my heart was never involved: these forays were purely physiological. In fact I was already quite expert in the fishy physiology of my own kind by the time I had left boarding school.

I recall one encounter with Paine, in particular, that took place on a rainy Saturday afternoon in the old oak cupboard where we kept our mackintoshes. I had in a moment of mischievous boredom managed to tempt him away from his genuflections among the dust balls in the sacristy, where it was his weekend job to sort out the stubs of burnt-out candles from the reusable ones. His ardour, once aroused by my deft ministrations, caught me by surprise, and I found my cheek being rammed against the metal button of someone's coat for much longer than I had bargained for – I bore its round impress, like a brand, for a good hour afterwards. But there were more surprises to come. When he had finished with me my assiduous young lover turned me around and, kneeling at my feet, opened the cupboard door a crack so that the sacristy light fell on my face.

'What are you, Thomas Joseph?' he whimpered. I could see his eyes shining wetly below me as his supplicating hands roamed over my narrow chest and shoulders. 'You look like an angel. So innocent. Why are you so incapable of love?'

My innards recoiled in helpless anger. What a stupid question. Was it my fault if they threw themselves into my net? I never asked for love, much less for lasting devotion. And you could say that I've since had my comeuppance.

Oh, innocence. I was brought back to the present with a cruel jolt by the sudden banging of the window, which was still open. Bellini had saved me from all of this sordidness; from Browning, and from pimping myself to poetry, and a likely future spent pining among the test tubes in some Dublin lab, or stuck in that seminary as a second Paine – but for what? How had that flawed but feeling child become this deadhearted, rapacious buffoon? Where had it all gone so repellently, embarrassingly wrong? Didn't my genuine passion for beauty – for goodness! – in spite of the trivially awful things I had done, entitle me to something more than the tinpot martyrdom that had been conferred on me in Vermont? Where was the apotheosis, the shaft of light; where were the cheering crowds, the confetti, where was the shattering moment of transfiguration?

Mawle was silent now. How long had I been sitting there, with the present in ribbons around me? I craned my head out of the window. Vicky had disappeared from the back steps, leaving her book to wilt on the lawn.

I could have sworn that the house was waiting for something; it was as if it breathed in and out deeply in the stillness. Tropical humidity clogged the upper floor. A waft of heat made the thin curtains of my room quaver in anticipation. The thinly plastered walls seemed to be sweating, and a rancid smell of old polish curdled the sticky air. The stunted bed with its intricate folds was horribly suggestive of trivial and obscene human desire. I tucked the limp pages of the diary into my dressing gown pocket, planning to conceal myself in the library, and made my way quickly downstairs.

CHAPTER NINE

But I did not read any more that day. In the downstairs hall as I descended I found Maddalena Roper impatiently circling its cool depths. She turned towards me with a look of calculated compassion that became tinged with a most unfeigned admiration as she took in the refined features and distinguished bearing of her lodger.

La Roper, I noticed, was a carefully preserved woman of about my own age, the ruin of a great beauty, with a heavily powdered face and Anna-like hair tied back in an Anna-like chignon that differed from its counterpart only in being coarser, and a livid blonde. Her tensed body was encased in a trouser suit of a metallic blue material that flashed and winked its lights in the murk. My girl, lightly oiled with cooking fat, was pressed against the banister with her hands to her mouth. Anna's cheeks were glistening, with tears or with the grease of the roast. When she saw me she hiccupped twice and half ran, half fell, in the direction of the kitchen.

'Ah, Professore!' cried the old shark appreciatively, looking me up and down. 'How glad I am that we meet at last, but like this – no! My little Nana has just told me your sad news. If I had known of your indisposition I would have hurried back long before now. How rude you must think us, a guest in our house and so neglected!'

She urged her shiny bosom towards me, lips lightly parted,

yum yum. Her hard white fin took my palm and held it a fraction longer than necessary.

'My house, *casita mia*, is yours. I would like you to rest here until you are quite well again.'

A practised finger alternately caressed and prodded my flesh.

'Have you seen our Murillo? No? Every year I am urged to sell her, *ma, Dio mio . . .*' A shudder of exasperation shook that magnificent predator's body. 'My hands are tied. And in the meanwhile—' Her eyes flitted around the walls and came briefly to rest on the largest of the Dutch cheeses, which she regarded with anguish. 'In the meanwhile, we must make do. In America, of course, this is a foreign conception.' Her gaze strayed back to the cheese. 'You produce such large refrigerators.'

'Ma'am, we do.' I noticed with interest that the tight helix at the nape of her neck had sprung a snake of sunshiny hair. She saw that I saw and slapped it back.

'We manufacture Kittering,' I suggested seductively. 'Tricity Bendix. But not,' I elaborated, 'Neff, or Smeg.'

Signora Roper's heavy-lidded eyes became filmy. Down the corridor a dish slid and fell, cymballing to the kitchen floor. Her lids flew up.

'Forgive me. My daughter is one of these hopeless modern girls.'

Maddalena was off. I stared at the ragged hem of the chandelier, adrift. Vicky came into the hall and took my hand. We stood together so for a few moments, in the quiet dust, before venturing into the kitchen.

They were squared off on opposite sides of the Aga, the Mamma and her daughter, like Russian dolls about to spring into ugly configurations. A freckled neck of lamb dripped its bloody juices onto a plate between them. Anna was sobbing great heart-slashing sobs.

'*Donnaccia!*' Mamma Roper howled at Anna just as I came in. 'I'm gonna sack him for this! I'm gonna send that *fannullone a spasso*!'

'Mamma, don't!' Anna cried. 'Don't blame him!'

'*Be'*, don't worry, I blame you too! *Puttana!*'

I was intrigued. 'Is there a difficulty, ma'am?' I ventured. 'Would it be better if I left you two alone for a while?'

'No, no, Professore,' trilled Maddalena, remembering herself. 'My daughter,' she added in a significant undertone, 'can be a little temperamental. It is the age.' She picked up a pair of silvered ski sunglasses from a bowl on the counter, but did not put them on. 'A million pardons for abandoning you. Please do not feel any concern at our silly domestic disagreements. I only came for these.'

This time we ate in the dining room. Its watered blue silk walls with their empty alcoves grinned down at us, a pitted death's head. There were only the three of us: Vicky had run away before the last Sheraton chair shuffled into its place. My hostess had forbidden me from changing especially for the meal, and so I sat at the table still wearing her dead husband's dressing gown, which made me feel oddly insouciant and not quite corporeal.

'*Bimba*,' hissed Signora Roper, 'the Professore has too little meat.' The sunglasses had adopted the lotus position on the table top beside her, and were training their detached gaze on the pudding spoon.

Anna rattled the prongs of the serving fork against my plate and sat slackly back. The dirty straps of her dungarees rose a little above her meagre shoulders, like the supporting hooks of a marionette. Her right cheek was streaked with the yellowish sediment of a tear; a crop of goosebumps beaded her t-shirted arms. Poor child. In that long hour she had eaten a single roast potato, nothing else.

La Roper looked at me closely. Before lunch she had repaired to one of the upstairs bathrooms to apply fresh buttresses of black paint to her eyelids and the result was at once ghastly and mesmerizing. Deliberately, assessingly, her thumb strummed a gold chain at her neck.

'My husband, *buon' anima, riposi in pace*, was a man much attached to his house. He was never happy to sell a stick,' she pointed an accusing fingernail down the long marmalade back of the table, 'to make comfortable his wife or babe. And now that we finally mourn him there are legal considerations. His testament forbids the sale of any bloody thing in this bloody house. The whole thing is what you *inglese* call a trust, it does not even belong to me. Trust! What trust is there in that? *Mi ha tagliato le gambe*, completely chopped them off. I am walking legless on the acrobat's rope, a woman, alone.' She pronounced the word 'woman' with a mournful exhalation on the 'o', as though playing a flute made of human bone. I felt almost guilty.

'Not *legless*, Mamma,' chirped Anna. 'That is something quite different.'

'Well, it is what I mean,' riposted Mamma. 'I cannot sell what I have. I do not have a foot to stand on. How the hell else am I supposed to say it?'

'Excuse me, everyone,' whispered Anna, and slunk away into the kitchen.

'You must pardon her,' said La Roper. 'Today is my dear

husband's anniversary. For seventeen years we have lived like this! Seventeen! The question of his estate is naturally topmost in her mind.'

I peered solemnly into my wine glass. 'Naturally. You cannot, as you say, sell what you have. And of course you cannot sell what you do not have.'

Signora Roper's stare grew more concentrated. '*Proprio così!* And we, we are so alone here. We are so in need of someone discreet, who will be a protector, someone who understands our way of life and its peculiar restrictions.' One of her lacquered eyebrows shot up interrogatively.

At that moment Anna flung back into the room, as if responding to a powerful tug on her strings. She clutched a blackened spoon in her left fist. It came to me – randomly, irrelevantly, and utterly absorbingly – that she was left handed.

'Mummy, I nearly forgot!' cried Anna. 'I asked him if he would stay for our Open Day and he said yes. He said that he'd help us. Isn't that marvellous?' I gazed with astonishment at the girl's fiery transfigured face. She was pleased to have netted me for Mamma, to be sure, but her blush suggested a personal and genuine relief.

Strangely, in spite of her sang-froid, Maddalena seemed no less gratified. '"He", *bambina*, who is this "he"? Do you not think perhaps, Dottore, that I have raised a savage, hmmmnn? I have tried to make her an Italian, but – pah.' The savage's mother appeared to consider the possibility, a stoical smile on her glazed lips, head cocked mirthfully to one side. All of a sudden I felt, with a ripple of merriment, as if I were watching a play. 'And yet everything I do is for her.'

'Your daughter is charming, a credit to you. She is a *jeune fille* of the old school. These days one seldom meets with such naturalness, such spontaneity.'

Anna looked at me blankly. The dining room door banged open again, sending a shiver through the Sèvres. Vicky came in, her bob scraped up in a clip to reveal her perfect ears, and squatted balefully under the table.

'Ah, *la ragazza*.' La Roper became middle-aged again. 'Holy Mother, this house is full of children. Children!' She wiped her mouth on her napkin with weary disgust. The reek of stale lamb fat hung heavily in the air. A sudden surge in the electricity supply made the light overhead wobble as Anna braced herself, smiling fixedly, to deliver her concluding speech. 'Mamma, Professor. I'm very sorry, but the pudding is a fuck-up. Coffee is served in the drawing room.'

'Not coffee, Nana,' admonished Signora Roper. 'Coffee is too stimulating to the nerves. Let us have some tea.'

When Anna bolted for the kitchen, which was thick with the stench of caramelized sugar, I managed to grip her elbow tightly in the hall.

'What are you and she up to?' I snapped. 'What's your game, eh? I don't know what all that crying was about, but I know something's not right. Why are you allowing yourself to be pushed around in this way?' She did not reply, but a fierce tear spurted down her rosy cheek. In that moment she was the Madonna in the Murillo: the slightly myopic eyes, the quizzical brows, the canted nose. The virginal, wan look! 'Things aren't *that* desperate,' I whispered. 'Are they, my dear?'

In answer Anna simply wrapped her chilly arms tightly around my neck, still holding the spoon, and gave me a ferocious squeeze, smearing my left ear with something charred and granular.

*

Oh but they were. Quite how desperate, I was soon to discover.

In bed that night I was overcome with an attack of longing. The house was as still as a barque on a windless sea, but cold, as if the heat of the summer day had been displaced in a single push of the crystalline darkness. Behind the sagging wire of the tennis court, deep in the heart of the beech, an owl hooted.

On Maddalena Roper's departure it had been settled that I would stay until I felt quite well again. Satisfied on all fronts, she had scribbled the name ('in case of emergency') of an Oxford quack for me on a peeling of onionskin, and left – oh merciful saints, no, don't get up! – with a squeeze of my enfeebled knee and a promise to ring often. In fact, she would ring as soon as we had held our little Open Day. She waggled her sunglasses at me. She was about to go abroad for a skiing holiday but felt certain that we would meet again soon; a seemingly blatant piece of politesse which I ignored at the time. Now, too late, I realize how wrong I was.

Why was Maddalena so keen to keep me at Mawle? I sensed that I was being bought for a purpose that I couldn't make out, but I didn't care. The air seemed to hum with promise; the depthless dark of the night sky to flow seamlessly, in my stoked imagination, into the robe of the Madonna *del prato* herself, forming a black that was not the absence of colour but rather the quintessence of all colours so concentrated as to be invisible. And then there was Anna. I felt like a Victorian bridegroom, left legally alone for the first time with his shy bride. An air of orange blossom infected our rooms. The dank hall, the dusty drawing room, the gritty kitchen, the scene of our future private late-night suppers for many an evening after Mamma had gone, were suffused with a new hope. The grown-ups had departed. Oh, but I was shy too! How would I first approach Anna? How would I make known to her the secret desires of my cringing heart? It was not, on second thoughts, of the Murillo that she really reminded me, but that other, that *only* picture. From the start my feelings for her were contaminated by – yes, I can't deny it: indivisible from – my lust for the Bellini Madonna. Both seemed to me equally fresh, fragile, untouchable; and compelling precisely because they were, or I longed to believe they were, not ultimately unattainable. I wanted the painting, and I wanted her. Or was it already the other way around?

In this mood of longing I sank down on my bed that night and reached under it for my holdall. To my horror the bag wasn't there. Impossible! I had always stowed it in exactly the same place, making sure that it was concealed by the bedside cabinet and a heap of carefully discarded underwear. In that little room, you see, there was simply no other hiding place. I couldn't very well dangle it out of the window by a string, or prise up a floorboard, or sink it in the toilet cistern next door. I got down on my hands and knees. Nothing. My boxer shorts, too, had vanished. A ball of fluff rolled across the threshold of a dingy darkness. I stuck my long arms across it as far as they could go, and my heart vaulted with relief when my fingertips touched leather. The valise was still under the bed. But how had it got to be pushed all the way back to the wall? Even more shockingly, the lock had been forced with something sharp, and was no longer latched.

Several appalling scenes suggested themselves: Anna kneeling over the case with a hairpin as I slept, drugged, on my deckchair in the garden; Anna with a carving knife; Anna with a serving fork, one prong still slick with grease, which she was about to twist into the brass . . . Or did Maddalena Roper perform the deed herself before lunch, en route to repainting her face?

Either way, it had been a rush job. My research notes were scrambled; the translations I'd made of Dürer's Venetian letters all out of sequence. Most incriminatingly, there was an oily thumbprint on my batch of handwritten annotations to Sanderson. I read them again with an expanding sense of terror, glaringly aware of being overheard. 'The Bellini mentioned by Dürer is the one at Mawle House in Berkshire: I am sure of it. And I am convinced that Ludovico Puppi knows this too. But where can the picture be? How can the Ropers have concealed it for so long? Or don't they know what it is?'

The ransacker had held this piece of paper longer than the rest: it was darted with eager creases. I stared at it dumbly; I even held it up to my nose. The page smelled faintly of scorched fat.

Then the truth came to me, very quietly. The Ropers knew that they had the Bellini, all right. They knew perfectly well what they were dealing with. They knew what it was worth. But they did not know, any more than I did, *where* in the house the painting was. It had sat here for more than a century, concealed God knows where and for what reason by James Roper after his return from Italy, and they were desperate, as desperate as I was, to get their hands on it. They suspected I had the key to the whereabouts of the picture, some secret piece of information, some power, that they did not.

The irony of this was so perverse that I forgot my sense of violation for a moment and lay down and cackled with laughter. I must have startled the owl outside, for it gave a final, indignant hoot and fell silent. The rest of the house was still fast asleep. I put out my hand and stroked the iron curve of my bedstead, the rough old plaster of the wall: how solid it all felt, and yet how fake it was . . . It was exactly like a stage set. I understood, now, why I had been brought here – brought here, indeed, when I'd assumed that securing the invitation was all my own doing! Signora Roper knew what she was about. She'd never really been in the least bit reluctant to have me at Mawle; her feigned lack of interest had, as she'd anticipated, merely goaded me on. Had Ludovico Puppi already tried to find the painting on his own account, and failed? If so, she was maximizing her chances of success. Far from wanting to stop me from tracking the picture down, she'd planned to keep me at Mawle in doped-up dependency until she'd had a chance to soften me up, to make me feel weak and grateful and indebted.

But why not simply confide in me? She must have thought that I knew something that he didn't; she hoped that I would lead her to the Bellini before too long. Such a treasure would be worth at least seven million pounds at auction. But why such secrecy, and how, anyway, did Maddalena intend to convert this recalcitrant image into hard cash? On her own admission she was debarred by the terms of the trust her husband had set up from selling anything in the house. How would she get around *that*? I hadn't the slightest idea, but I was riled by her certainty that I could be lured like some dozy janitor into unlocking the secret of the painting's whereabouts. And to add insult to insult, she had posted her ingenuous daughter and that yokel gardener at the gate to keep guard over me until I did so. How farcical, how unmannerly of her. And yet, how strangely appetizing the situation I found myself in was, too. I had of course had no such key to the mystery when I came to Mawle, but I did – didn't I? – have it now. James Roper's diary would explain everything: it would reveal how he had come by the picture; it would lift the veil that hung over his reasons for concealing it. It would lead me, if I only had enough patience, directly to the Madonna.

Unable to sleep, I turned back to the notebook, which was still hidden in my mattress. This at least they hadn't looked for, because they did not know that it existed. And then, as I pulled the tatty thing out, the bulb in my bedside lamp, which had been burning steadily all evening, went out with a wicked crackle, leaving the room in darkness. The visible world was suddenly extinguished, and as it vanished the mood of effervescent irony drained from my body. The horns of the moon, just discernible above the window sash, stabbed the bed with their hard white light. I stood, frozen, in the moonlight, peering blindly into the shadows of the room. That gasping sound – what was it? Slowly, to my horror, as if in some indelicately close quarter, I had become aware of an intimate, stifled sobbing.

Grasping the neck of the light bulb, I gave it a screeching twist, and the iron bed frame, the unravelling rag rug on the boards, the flimsy locker, sputtered back into existence. I lowered myself onto the edge of the bed and sat there, nervously braiding the cord of my dressing gown in my hands.

Still the ghastly choking sound continued. It seemed, if anything, to be drawing even closer. My heart jigged – panic had begun to make my ribs ache. As I dived under the covers I realized, to my amazement and shame, that this sobbing was coming from my own chest.

CHAPTER TEN

I meant to plunge back into Roper's account straight away, but things were no longer that simple. My dread that night was caused in part by the slow dripping and lapping of memory somewhere behind the slippery wall of consciousness. I can't tell you how strange it was to have recalled my childhood self again here, at Mawle. My dear fellow, of all the places! After all these years! Since I'd seen Vicky crying in the garden the present had become suddenly, surreptitiously fissured. A tide of agony gathered behind it, ready to erupt: I lay in my bed and quaked. I promise you, I simply shook. I was back at school. *Woo-woo-woo.* That crack in the sink, the brown bedspread – did they belong to now, or to then? Something seemed to move in the depths of the room. I sat up, assailed by fear and yearning, and was granted a glimpse of a small boy in a belted dressing gown, weeping in a corner. Was it me, at twelve? The poppet had a clever face and a haughty, bruised look, like a superior doll that had been too roughly used. I was filled with a strange involuntary pity, as if it were another, more harmless child that I had seen.

I see that I must, after all, go on. The semblance of honesty demands it.

I have said that it was Bellini who saved me from the mess I had got myself into with Paine, the whole boring round of glassy-eyed copulations. My new life, the first twitch of my new obsession, began one hot summer afternoon when I was sixteen. My Da had decided that I would go on to study science in Dublin, but Father Furey disagreed, and did his best to supply me with the solitude needed to bring me to a proper appreciation of my future vocation. He had no idea, of course, of what a little bugger I was. Because of the lingering effects of my pneumonia (weakness, exhaustion and an aversion to the shrieks and bellows of my classmates), I was excused the weekly hurling practice to which the school's sturdier and more venal pupils were subjected every Friday afternoon between four and six. I spent this time in the school library, and that was the old man's big mistake. I can still see his eyebrows, which curled and fizzled like wire wool, fusing in concentration over some learned text by St Thomas Aquinas before he extends it, quivering with hope, to me.

'Ah, Thomas Joseph. I trust I'm not. This may possibly be. Perhaps you might just quickly, if you have a moment. Greatest of our moral thinkers. Doctor of the Church. Your namesake, too. You are quite certain? Good lad. This passage in particular, then.'

And what do I find in the book that the Angel Gabriel has pressed on me? It is big and fat and black – judging by the Roman numeral on its spine, it must, I notice despairingly, be part of some interminable series – and its title, *Summa Theologica*, is raised on the cover in crawling Gothic letters like beetles. St Thomas has much to say about Moderation, about Prudence, about Faith, Grace and Virtue, about Living Well and Living Badly, but what I really care for are his ideas about Love, more specifically that heady, sensual, engulfing love which I already feel for anything physically beautiful.

'The beautiful is a form of the good,' St Thomas explains. 'If something is agreeable we call it good, and if the perception of it is agreeable we call it beautiful. But as goodness must be known before it can become the object of love, so knowledge itself can be said to cause love.'

Oh true, true, but my problem is that the beautiful, and any goodness that it might represent, is something that I already crave ownership of more than I understand it.

The truth is that I am by now sick of school, and of Paine, and of our repellent weekly thrusting with its accompanying dry freight of words, and long for an escape from the snare of sex. Or is it the words themselves I long to escape from? Perhaps.

One afternoon not long after my sixteenth birthday I hunkered, as usual, in a nook in the library with my long legs tucked under me, trying to get on with the Angel Gabriel's offerings. The massacre on the hurling field was taking place some distance away: it would be a good hour before the wounded were carried back and the Angelus bell called us all to get cramp in chapel. Behind the library the school lawns were being mowed and the yearning smell of crushed grass stole towards me from the open window. Since I'd faked a great enthusiasm for Thomist philosophy Father Furey had plied me with another two volumes of the *Summa*, but to my relief there was a third book stowed between them, a sop from my lover, and that was what I was reading. It was called *An Anthology of the Madonna and her Angels in Poetry, by the Most Pious Authors, with Numerous Illustrations*. From this thin straw, all bad verse and smudged linotype, I did my best to spin my little hoard of spiritual gold. Most of the poems were laughably bad but one or two were passable, even good, as if the anthologizer had no palette but simply ground together whatever scraps he could find. Perish, cherish, adore, implore, do not ignore (a fecking bore) . . .

I did not expect what happened next. My fingers slid under and over another page. The drowsy sun spilled a fat sunbeam across the gaping sash, onto my folded knees. I looked down and there, cradled in my lap, was a single colour print of a painting. It was the picture of a young girl. She was sitting in a meadow, blue skirts angled around her, her heavy eyes downcast. Under her tented hands a baby lay with frogged legs, belly-up, its puffy cheeks relaxed in blissful sleep. A flush, just beading into sweat, crept over the girl's nose. Beyond a pebbled field, cows and sheep milled beneath the ramparts and tower of a walled town hemmed with feathery weightless trees. In the topmost branch of one of these perched a bloated black crow with a single, pin-like eye. To the right of the Madonna, a shrouded figure drew up water from a well. A slender green ribbon rippling beneath her other elbow turned out to be a snake, rearing its head far off at a hump-backed pelican as the bird advanced to strike.

This landscape with its mysterious figures seemed at one moment infinitely far away and at the next very close, both familiar and unfamiliar, like a reflection of something well known, but now indefinably transformed. I shut the book for a moment, but when I opened it again I found that the luminous stillness of the scene, suspended in its own bubble of watery light, was unbroken.

Bending my head towards the Madonna, lulled by the drone of the mower, I breathed my supplicating breath against the hem of her dress. Close up, I studied the secret shadows of a wrist peeping from its apricot sleeve.

So this solid, this perfect rosy solid, was human flesh! *This* was what the physical world could be! My own sparse body gave a grateful shiver of recognition. Behind that inclined head, plump cloudlets scudded across a pearly sky.

I knew then that I had stumbled into a foreign country in which the hard stone, the black lanes, and all the dreary scuffles in coat cupboards of my existence were utterly redeemed.

At that moment I came into my secret inheritance. With the tenacity which stood me in such good stead in my later career, I ripped the precious image from its tacky surroundings, hid it in my underpants (oh yes, stealing is wrong; I know, I know, but this was nothing compared to what I got up to later), and was soon free to enjoy my Madonna in private as often as I wanted to. Contact with the picture fluttered and bewildered me. I felt myself apart from it, quite apart, but – and this was the agony! – not detached, and an ache that wasn't loneliness was flowing out of my shuddering heart into the breathing air that murmured and cried as if a living thing were nudging up to me. In my better moments I knew that if I could only sustain this sense of tenderness, if I could only learn to see, always, with an innocent eye, all the purposes of my life would suddenly stand revealed.

In all these years it hadn't happened, but who was to say that it wouldn't happen now? Surely that was the real reason for my presence at Mawle? I wasn't simply hunting for a painting – I was hot on the heels of beauty. Of truth! All those fine things. I was about to uncover something rare and strange, something profoundly important, something that had no business being hidden. I was pursuing nothing less than my own salvation. And oh, I had a theory, an explanation for the importance of this lost painting I was after that would cause a commotion. If Bellini's last Madonna *del prato* was exceptional it was so precisely because of the quality of its vision. That earlier Madonna, the *Madonna of the Meadow*, may have been intensely tender in its respect for our poor humanity, but in his final treatment of his theme Bellini surpassed it in wisdom and compassion. He had painted the Virgin at the last not as a handmaid, a vessel, but as a creator in her own right, 'with the great work of her life,' as he said, 'the work of her imagination, behind her.' She may have been a simple peasant woman, but the shrewd old man could see quite plainly that the Madonna's capacity for love, the inordinate act of imaginative sympathy and courage demanded of her in becoming the mother of this particular child, was her life work, as much a great work as that of any artist – as great, in short, as any of his own.

This was the insight that I would put before the world; this was the thesis that would vindicate the life choices I had made; my passion for Bellini; all those years of seemingly wasted effort spent searching for this still unseen picture . . . And I was certain that James Roper's diary would point me to its location. So I was trembling that night, as I say, when I opened the notebook again in search of the missing clue to its hiding place. I must admit that my curiosity was also pricked by Roper's observations, not because of any merit they may have had, but because of the sense they gave me of the collector as he then was: young – as I myself had once been young! – gluttonous for such scraps of sensibility as might be thrown his way, and perhaps not quite as cynical as that earlier passage in the diary might suggest. In fact I rather suspected that, like most self-consciously cynical young men, the knowing dog was a romantic at heart.

I felt like a captive. How can I explain it? It was as if someone had put a knife to my throat, the more dangerous for being lightly, tenderly held. I felt afraid. The blade trembled on my skin, close and cool: the pressure of a word would undo me. In some cranny of my heart a new shape was gestating, putting out a shy green tendril. I had come to Mawle moved by a lifelong craving – by an irresistible quest. And this was the strange thing. The Bellini Madonna crowded my line of vision, but behind her now hovered the self-effacing figure of Anna Roper with her bitten nails and her bad clothes. Preposterous, and still it was true. I was afraid of being seduced, and at the same time I longed for it. But I reminded myself sternly that the picture was the thing, and the thing itself was, surely, hidden somewhere in these torn pages.

Following Roper's first diary entry there was a dull, circumstantial paragraph about the sedative effects of headache powders on young people (which I omit because I know, from my failed seduction attempt in the College park, how hopelessly unreliable over-the-counter painkillers can be) and then Mrs Bronson, Roper's self-appointed American cicerone, popped up again.

> Monday, 2nd of September. Underneath Mrs B's relentless good humour there is, I fear, something rather queer. While I sat at breakfast at Ca' Tabacchi this morning I received two messages in quick succession from her. First our picnic was off, as Miss Edith so delighted in the view of the Queen's

Castle from the loggia at La Mura that she was determined to take her day's refreshment entirely by walking up and down it, meditating on the poetic life of that little medieval court. A quarter of an hour later the expedition was on again, with no reason given, although the young lady's laboured breathing and flushed countenance pointed to the recurrence of one of those awkward migraine attacks which (murmured Mrs B) so frequently curtailed all exertion and made fresh air and a supine position absolutely necessary.

Ah yes, the contrary daughter. There was a surreptitious pleasure in imagining Roper and his captors setting out across the plain in Mrs Bronson's rattling red-velveted carriage, through fields and vineyards against which the white *campanili* of the villages they passed stood out like the scattered sails of ships. I had a bottle of Papa Roper's grappa tucked up in bed with me. Wrapping my lips about its neck, I took a luxurious pull. The figures seemed to come to life on the page with a cautionary lurch.

Some time after midday the carriage arrived at the hamlet of Altivole. Hoisting herself from her scarlet seat, Mrs Bronson motioned to the coachman to stop amid the pigs and chickens in the courtyard of a tumbledown farm building.

'Behold,' she droned, gesturing towards a faintly frescoed wall, 'the once-proud villa of a great lady. My dears,' she said as if in answer to our puzzled glances, 'we stand at the gates of the Barco della Regina Cornaro. This poor ruin was once the summer retreat of Queen Catherine. Here she whiled away the hot days of her exile, and here, in this modern-day farmyard, we shall have our picnic.' She added, leadenly, 'She thought this place a paradise. Ah, *tempus edax rerum*.'

As Mrs Bronson supervised the stately unloading of a fruit and cheese basket and various earthenware tureens containing macaroni, a mushroom and ham risotto, and fat golden slices of polenta, I reflected with a chortle that time was not to be the only eater up of things.

But Miss Bronson was already sitting down on a tuft of grass.

'Ye-es,' she said elastically, once she had settled herself, 'old buildings are melancholy. And yet I don't know why.' She began to peel a fig with stubby fingers.

'Your observation does you credit, my dear,' her mother replied. 'You are moved, most commendably moved, by impermanence – by the impermanence of our little life here.'

'Quite so,' said the daughter, producing some tapestry work with a contented grunt. 'The Romance of Ruins.'

'Edie finds that Italy affects her as no other place does, Mr Roper,' Mrs B went on. 'She is particularly stirred by the antiquity of her surroundings. As she has noticed, stones of this colour and consistency aren't to be found anywhere in New York.'

'One does the galleries and the buildings, you know,' Miss Bronson demurred.

'Indeed, Edie. But few derive as much comfort from a cornice as you do.'

By three o'clock Roper was nearly insensible, coshed by tedium. And then I came to it: the moment that, like a Fabergé egg, contained the shapes and spectres, the desires, triumphs and self-deceptions, of the future.

As the trio returned to Asolo that afternoon in a stupor of macaroni they saw two women about to leave a carriage in front of an imposing villa fronted by heavy arches of stone, not far from La Mura. The elder of the ladies was straight and lean, and heavily freckled in her face and arms in spite of the ruby shade thrown by a tall parasol. The younger, who had lowered her head while getting down from the carriage step, looked up at Roper and smiled uncertainly. She was little, and if she had not had her dusky hair pinned up he would, he writes, have taken her for a child. Her suggestive face with its barely sketched curves and small firm mouth was dusky too, earthy and delicate as the face of a Virgin by Lippi; not reddened by the sun like her companion's, but an even shade of brown, as if the same flames warmed her gently from within. She wore an incongruously dowdy dress of mustard and black check, a cruel chessboard suturing her meagre breasts.

Steadying herself against the carriage door with a look of growing confusion, the girl gave Roper a timid little wave, apparently unsure as to whether or not they knew each other. Momentarily jolted out of his boredom by that un-English face, he tipped his hat to her in return without thinking. A gaggle of peasant lasses trotted by, honking like geese, carrying folded sheets still damp from the wash. The elder lady turned reluctantly and inspected Roper through a lorgnette; then, on recognizing Mrs Bronson, she bowed. Mrs B nodded and let rip a gusty sigh of satisfaction.

'We are truly fortunate, Mr Roper, in our neighbours,' she crooned, tapping my knee with her knitting. 'The Buccari family is one of the oldest and most well-respected in these parts. They are also *intime* with the Contessa Adriana Marcello. And little Giulia's mother was an American, one of the New York van der Veens. Poor Giulia is not, of course, as clever or as well-grown as my Edith', giving her mother a pinch on the arm and a withering glare, that young lady shuffled from the carriage with a reproving 'Tsk!', 'but she is nevertheless as charming and refined a young woman as you could wish to meet. In these parts.'

I replied that she seemed charmingly refined, and that I should be delighted to meet her.

'Oh no, Mr Roper,' protested Mrs Bronson, 'it wasn't my intention to put you to the trouble – merely a chance encounter. There is really no necessity—'

'And yet, Mrs Bronson,' I smilingly urged, 'I should. I truly should.'

This was more like it. I had been careful to pack my copy of Sanderson's *Private Picture Galleries* before leaving Oxford, and I pulled it out of my violated holdall now. Asolo, the Musone, fatal fevers, family not strong. An American bride, an heiress, a son. A tragic early death . . . Yes, here it was! A few minutes of hasty filleting revealed what I was looking for. There sat the pulsing clue under my finger. Buccari was, as I'd remembered, the name of the Asolan family from whom Roper had acquired the picture – indirectly, of course, through marriage: Sanderson averred that according to family tradition such a painting had been part of the girl's marriage portion.

I recalled that Giulia Buccari was born not many years after Miss van der Veen's marriage to the Count, by which time the American Contessa was already in poor health. She succumbed to typhoid fever a few months later. I allowed myself a twinge of emotion – of sympathy. I could imagine it! Buccari was distraught. Would his wife's cousin stick by him? She would of course, to take care of little Giulia. Buccari himself died when his daughter was only fifteen, leaving the orphan entirely in the care of Miss Spragg. If Sanderson was right, then James Roper must have wed this very Giulia Buccari of the diary, the girl who had first waved at him in the street in the company of her guardian, during his visit to Asolo in the autumn of 1889. I was about to discover how that marriage, which was, as yet, my only real link with the Bellini, had come about.

My heart bumped and sped. I sighed, exquisitely caught between gratification and anticipation. While I was reading the room had grown very cold, and a thin arrow of air shivered under the door. Drawing the scratchy cuff of my blanket up to my chin, I settled back on my lean pillow. I told myself that I really didn't care what Signora Roper was up to. I dismissed the reappearance of little Tom Lynch and his unhappy reminders of my childhood with an equally fine indifference. I decided then and there that I would not rush this journey of discovery, but would savour it all: the house, the hot days and fresh nights, the hours of solitude, and every fleeting peep that I could get at Anna. I was going to outwit them all: I was going to play my part. I wouldn't leave until I had found the Bellini – this explosive picture, uniquely brave and fresh – and revealed it to the world.

In a rush of happiness I brought the diary blindly to my

lips and kissed it, then instantly laughed again at what I had just caressed.

The entry was followed by a sprawling ink blot, which the writer had transformed with a few deft strokes of the pen into a convincing picture of a large cock and balls.

CHAPTER ELEVEN

After her mother's visit, I am glad to say, Anna no longer pumped me full of questionable tea. She's detained me here long enough now to know that she has me, I thought. But does she know that I want *her*?

I doubted it. What a smooth, childish face she had, and how little it gave away! Except sometimes. Sometimes I caught her watching me. Her tender lips were as chewed up as her nails. In sombre moods her mild brown eyes could be as hooded as a frog's. Yes, her nose was quite crooked. Her halo of hair, when unwashed, was the colour of pond water. But oh, how beautiful she was to me, and how I wanted her! As a sensation it was quite new: she was so different from any of my conquests. She was not remotely boylike. She was raw, and girlish, and unformed, and the sheer girlishness and rawness of her made me feel uncharacteristically clumsy and ablaze in my own skin. Make no mistake: my feelings were wholly romantic and only partly sexual. I longed, I think, not to possess her, but to be enfolded by her, to yield to her. At that stage in our tragic little courtship *pas de deux* I don't think that I could even have kissed her: the act would have been too masterful.

'Anna,' I began the next morning, while we were in the kitchen. She was frying irascible eggs on the old yellow stove. *Pop! Pop!* threatened the yolks. *Psst*, *whisht*, shushed the whites. The plate of the hob smoked. 'You are lucky to have a mother who cares about you, who keeps an eye on you, who so evidently loves you.' What an unimaginative liar I was. 'I only wish mine—'

Anna whipped around to confront me, still clutching the spatula in her hand. Her face was an alarming mask of anger and disgust.

'Don't talk about her!' she whispered in a hoarse, shocked voice. 'Don't fucking talk about her, OK? I can't believe you've just said that. I can't believe it, after what you've seen, after—' She gestured with dismay at the row of glossless teacups on the kitchen shelf.

Yes, my petal? I thought. After she persuaded you to drug me so that you could have a good rummage through my things?

'My dear,' I said, 'I only meant. My own mother is no longer alive, you see.'

How simple it was! Her anger imploded, collapsing on itself, its energy expended. I felt like the finger of God. 'Oh, I'm sorry. I'm so sorry, Dr Lynch! I didn't know. I'm sure you loved her! I'm sure you were a lovely child,' Anna sighed dejectedly. 'Not like,' she flicked a gobbet of egg at Vicky, who lay asleep across two kitchen chairs with her head on my knee, 'not like this one. What a brat. Never brushes her teeth. Never brushes her hair. Never does her homework.'

'Maybe we can remedy that,' I suggested modestly. 'What do you say? Maybe we can address that, eh?'

'Oh, if you could – if you only would! She seems to have taken to you. And you know, I'm going bonkers with her. She's driving me fucking crazy. I never *chose* this. Why does it end up like this?'

I couldn't answer that, of course. I seldom thought about the tenuous connection between Anna and Vicky at all now: there seemed to be nothing of substance, hardly anything that could be called tenderness, between them. Whatever relation of the Ropers the child was – and I'd decided that she couldn't, on the evidence, be a close one – she existed almost unnoticed in that house, disturbing its current as little as a feather. Except for an erratic protectiveness sparked by Harry's sallies, Anna's lack of interest in Vicky was wholesale; as a guardian she was barely competent. When I tried to probe her about her charge, she quickly grew bored. Afraid of losing her sympathy, I drew back.

'But you,' said Anna, giving the subject a diffident nudge, 'you were only a child? When she – your mother – died?'

'No, my dear. I was already eighteen. But perhaps still a child, yes.'

Oh God yes, perhaps still a child.

At home again for the summer holiday following my discovery of that first Madonna, I took long evening walks beside the river, staring into its undulating mirror, torn this way and that way by the tide. The broad back of the water ran down under the bridge, shattering into a thousand spumed rills on the banks where tufts of white furze dipped their heads into its fast current. Rising up and up on wings of paper, high above the rheumy chimney pots, two Atlantic-bound seagulls coasted through the sweating air, each silvery up- and down-stroke a semaphore which I was pitifully unable to decipher.

One evening the next spring I announced that I couldn't study science, or enter the church, or even read poetry, for that matter, but had to *look*, steadily and intently, at the appearances of things themselves if I ever wanted to get behind them.

My father flung down his fork (we were having our tea at the time). 'What? Is it the gombeen original human X-ray ye're setting up to be, then?'

'No, Dada. I just want to be happy.'

'Happy? Through *looking*? Well, look here, you eejit. Will looking put *this* on the table?' He impaled the lamb cutlet he'd been eating and held it up for my inspection. 'Will looking tell you anything real about the world? Answer me!'

It's a question to which I actually still don't have an answer.

My news even startled the Angel Gabriel momentarily into a sub clause. 'In making this decision – I speak candidly, man to man, you understand – what I mean to ask is, there wouldn't be a girl in the picture at all now, Thomas Joseph, would there?'

'Well yes, Father, in a manner of speaking, you know, there is.'

'So, then.' The poor old fellow sparked and sighed. 'Unavoidable, really. The natural impulses that cannot. Many are called. As St Paul says, it is far better to marry. Absolutely nothing to be ashamed of. The love of the feminine perfectly normal. Healthy, even. Though in your case, perhaps, I thought,' he smiled at me doubtfully. 'Well, no matter. Wonderful are the ways. Just shows you. You never can.'

Paine took to writing me bad poetry, which I offered to show to his superiors, after which he took to Gerry Byrne.

Only my mother, in her uninformed, meekly stubborn way, supported me. Her prayers and threats must have worked, for by the start of my first year of college I was up in Dublin, living in an ugly room rented out at a reduced rate by my friendly widow on St Stephen's Green, and loping across the dewy grass of the square in the early mornings to attend lectures in Italian painting at Earlsfort Terrace.

I never saw Paine again. I heard later that he had been most cruelly chastised for his ongoing interest in boys such as me, and for attempting to inject us with an untimely knowledge of poetry: he was appointed teacher of Dogmatic Theology to the College's seminarians. Some years later he left the order and became a social worker.

Nor did I see my mother again. Just before I was due to return home for Christmas she died of heart failure.

This weakness of the heart, it turned out, ran in our family; or at least it still runs there in my valves. Not so long ago, after nearly fainting in the men's toilets of the National Gallery of Art in Washington following a particularly stirring encounter with the proto-Renaissance, I finally faced up to certain incontrovertible symptoms which had been dogging me for years and went to see a doctor. In the expensive antiseptic confines of a discreetly shuttered consultation room, I learned that I had an 'irritable heart' – a condition characterized by shortness of breath on exertion or excitement; palpitation, fatigue, acid indigestion, chest pain and dizziness (and, I add for the record, believed by some to be partly psychosomatic). My physician was a cadaverous young fellow in a frosty white shroud, with a charming southern intonation and an expansive reach of his bony phalanges.

'Please don't look so distraught, Professor. Physiologically, the term "irritable" has a wide application, and not necessarily always a negative one. For example, when an organ or tissue is capable of being excited to vital action, it is said to be irritable. So, too, a sensory nerve in its simplest form may be regarded as a strand of eminently irritable protoplasm.'

'Am I supposed to understand, then, that I am dying of an excess of vitality?'

'Look, it's up to you. You are not dying – or at least, no more quickly than the rest of us. I see from my notes that there is a history of longevity on your father's side. With proper rest, and the avoidance of strong stimulants' (here he trotted out a catalogue of foods on which I had long relied, including coffee, a certain pale, desiccated fungus freely available in most alternative health food stores, and the capsicum found in the humble chili pepper), 'there is no reason why you shouldn't live for another thirty years. Oh, and lay off the sauce.'

After my mother's funeral I went home as little as possible. Under the watchful eye of my landlady, whose appetite for my skinny body was, frankly, becoming a nuisance, I dashed off a doctorate on Bellini's altarpieces and applied for lectureships in America as soon as I had graduated. I wanted to get as far away as I could from my Da, whom I loathed now not only for his prosy certainties and his menthol-and-formaldehyde reek and his dull addiction to facts, and for having sent me into motherless exile in the first place, but for having compounded these crimes by killing my Darling with his lack of love. When the old murderer died at the age of eighty-three I was already comfortably transplanted in verdant Vermont. There I was fed, watered and tenured, a sturdy old *Quercus* among pliant saplings, until the Faculty Inquisition last October cut all of that short.

I had in fact been back to the city where I was born only

once in the last fifteen years, to arrange my father's funeral and sell my childhood home. I entered Limerick from the north. In the distance stood the old familiar castle, a pebble with bright eyelets of sunlight, above the calm river flattened by the long arm of the first morning shadow. A thin skin of cloud was already doubling across the sky. A café conservatory had sprung up in the courtyard of the castle; the quay sheltered a chrome and glass shopping mall; a shiny telephone company occupied the site where the mill used to be. In sheltered, sudden pockets, in alleys marked out for redevelopment, the old dusky city still lingered. The river, too, was still delicately frilled with furze, still mirror-bright, reflecting a pair of seagulls identical to the pair of memory. Everything else, though, had changed. What had my youthful anguish been about? I could hardly remember.

In our lane I stood for a moment in front of the iron knocker of my father's house. I was thinking not of my childhood there but of my mother's last moments on earth as she approached the door that winter of her death, back from a visit to a neighbour or the local lending library, carrying a little left-over cake entombed in foil, perhaps, or a crumbling copy of *Saints and Ourselves*. The door was black and dull. Blowsy red geraniums grew in terracotta pots to left and right of the threshold. At four o'clock the wintry light had already faded, sloping off into darkness. My mother would have noted all this in a haphazard way as she fumbled for her key, and then the serrated pain in her heart would have stopped her. What did she see before she died? A field of red? A field of light? The vulture blackness of the door, badly varnished where my father had patched it up the previous summer? Or nothing at all?

'Poor you,' Anna's brown eyes had the expectant sheen of a child's at the pantomime. 'And then – and then you had to make your own way into the great world,' she produced the word like a prize toffee from a bag, 'of scholarship.'

The beguiling wave of nostalgia and sympathy on which I had been borne aloft came crashing down. The absurd, pampered, unwittingly condescending girl. Who did she think I was – little Hansel following his trail of breadcrumbs?

In spite of my nascent feelings for Anna I was, during that first week at Mawle, still inclined to despise the Ropers for their privilege and their fiscal incompetence and their emotional inertia. And for their sheer gullibility. Anna in particular seemed to know nothing at all about the world outside her front door. I have always found it child's play to slip at will into the persona of an Irishman or an American – my default American setting was effete Bostonian, although I also offered a customized impression of a Texan ranch hand – or sometimes even both alternately, as necessity dictated. Untravelled Anna and her dumb strongman would be easy meat for my shapeshifting charm, or so I thought.

I remember, for instance, a particularly comical encounter on that very Saturday, the 14th, over a donkey – our Open Day donkey – when I was called on in the course of an hour to be not only an Irish peasant savant and a Texan cowboy, but a knight in armour leading his trusty steed. The donkey in question was a grave-looking beast on loan from the local animal sanctuary, with grey-rimmed eyes set into a scrubby brown head and a swelling under its flank.

It arrived during the gilded afternoon. After lunch I left

my usual vantage point in the library (Anna had set up a little folding table for me in the full glare of the window so that I could 'write my notes in peace' – we both merrily kept up the pretence that I was engaged in research) and set out for the territory beyond the tennis court. The Bellini was obviously not concealed in the old stables where Harry had surprised me on Friday morning, but there might be further outbuildings to the house, containing neglected canvases and other treasure, which I had not yet come across. Here, to the very rear of Mawle, there was a slight depression curving around the southern periphery of the garden, filled with buttercups, daisies and other girlish wildflowers, where Anna liked to loll unseen in the afternoons on a blanket, unclothed, browning her limbs. (Once I, the peeping Tom, had surprised her lying there, absent-mindedly scratching her crotch while poring over a dog-eared textbook with the unpromising title *Feminist Cinema of the 1940s*. She did her best to drape her nakedness with this rag while I stared at the clouds and tried to pretend an interest in cumulus. A few careful questions elicited the information that she was writing an essay, of all things, and was in point of fact a bona fide student at a university, enrolled in a correspondence degree course in Film Studies. This revelation shocked me much more than did my glimpse of her tiny dun breasts and crinkly lap.)

She was not there today, and I walked on. The sky was indecently blue, immodestly sporting a few token wisps of cotton wool. It was very hot. Behind the tennis court and the flowery ditch lay a field bounded by scraggy hedges of hawthorn and ragwort, and behind that another, and another, in a patchwork of sun and shadow. Occasionally a furtive rabbit darted out of a green hollow and chewed a dandelion. The horizon was obscured by a drift of chalk, a lazy exhalation from the limestone hills. By and by a distant figure hove into view in the midst of this stillness, labouring across the brilliant fields. It grew larger and larger, hobbling along in the heat-haze on lunatic bent legs. A cord or rope depended from one of its arms, tethered to a boneless mass that swung from side to side, head down and ears erect.

'Hi T.J., how's things?'

Oh, please. *That* halfwit again. 'Hey, Harry boy. That's quite some beast you got there. Is it a donkey or a mule? D'ya need a hand?'

'Naw. I got her sorted. She knows where she's headed. Come on, girl. Come on, you fat bitch.' The donkey staggered against its rope, its pendulous stomach brushing against the long grass.

'She sure is stubborn as a mule, boy. My daddy worked a ranch for close to fifty years. We had to break them mules, day in, day out. Son, I had to break ten of their hairy asses before breakfast.'

The donkey let out a large fart.

'Shit, you filthy bitch! OK, T.J., you take her. You break her hairy ass.'

I took the rope in my fist and gave it a twitch. The beast looked at me with its ancient suffering eyes.

'What's her name, Harry?'

'She ent got one, T.J. She's just a donkey.'

'Nope, laddie. That's where you're wrong. She's got a name all right. What's yer name, girl of my heart? What's yer name, Colleen Macree?'

The donkey brayed mournfully.

'She's my little dark rose, Harry. That's what she says. She's Roisín Dubh.'

'Yer strong on the animals in Texas, T.J. Yer strong.'

'We surely are, Harry-o. Come on, Rosie, shuffle over.'

I swung the donkey's lead and the beast gave a skip to the side, a little maid about to play jump-rope. Then she followed me quite placidly into the heart of the retreating green. Harry led the way. What madness! The distant chimneys of Mawle twinkled in the sunlight. We crossed a dry ditch fenced with higgledy-piggledy posts and trotted towards a shack marooned in a sea of rusting farm machinery. Melancholy music came from an open window at which a switch of flowered cloth hung without moving.

Rank absurdity can sometimes lead us into the heart of revelation. It was an outbuilding, to be sure, but it was not what I'd been looking for. If I remember these moments now it is because they seem always to have existed, to have lain in wait for me, like the rooms of an enchanted castle which had remained asleep for centuries and to which only I had the key. There was the thicket of brambles, parting imperceptibly as I approached, and the golden gate with its threadbare pennants stilled. There was the old moat overgrown with ivy, and the crumbling stair, and there the door of the topmost tower, awaiting my touch. And there was Anna with her hair loose, stepping over a wash-basket with a row of pegs clamped in her mouth, stooping and standing on tiptoe, pinning a row of piggy-pink boxer shorts onto a makeshift washing line. Oh, my princess. So that's what had happened to my underwear! She smiled her beatific smile and tucked a damp coil of hair behind a translucent ear. She wore tight, stretched shorts and a vest and a horrible neon hat with a visor tilted down over her eyes, so that she had to lift her chin to see me. A sloshed butterfly twitted past her nose.

'Hi, Dr Lynch! I did all yours too.' In the basket lay my stained cotton pyjamas, suckling a litter of socks. I felt my heart tearing into a thousand pieces.

'A little domestic accident, my dear? One should really wash bright colours separately.'

Lynch's handy household tips.

'Oh I know. Mummy is always telling me that. I forgot. You don't mind, do you?'

'From now on, pink will be your favour. I will wear it at my breast.'

Anna smiled again, more randomly. The donkey began to nuzzle at my crotch.

'Nar, you filthy girl.' Harry gave a tug on the rope. 'We'd better be getting you home.' His lecherous forearm coiled itself around Anna's waist. 'She was looking for you, love. She's been out by the pond this half hour.'

Anna sighed a colossal sigh. 'Oh fuck. Do I never get a break?'

'Go on, darling. I'll take Rosie.'

We all stared stupidly at the listless pants on the line. A few seconds passed. The silence grew.

'I'll go with you, my dear,' I volunteered.

'Oh, Dr Lynch,' groaned Anna submissively, taking my hand. 'I wish you lived here always.'

'Yar, he's good with children an' animals, that one,' harrumphed Harry. 'Good looking too, ent he?' His brows sank on his face like a granite cloud. For a moment he seemed to be shrinking; even his square head seemed abnormally compressed. A wicked little breeze stole across the ditch behind us and stirred the edge of the curtain at the window. Behind it stood a portable gas stove on a triangle of vomit-green carpet. One of Anna's t-shirts lay twisted in a question mark on the floor. A stale smell of frying, and maybe something else, saltier and more intimately brutal, unfurled from the interior.

How impercipient I'd been. They weren't just having a fling. They were a couple, an item. They were fucking constantly.

As we walked back to the house I stopped and drew Anna to one side, out of sight of the hut.

'Is that where Harry stays?'

She smiled ruefully. 'Yes, when he's here. He comes and goes.'

I looked sidelong at her, but she seemed innocent of any lewd joke. I put my hand on her arm. 'My dear girl, you should be careful. A young woman in your position is very vulnerable.'

What did I mean by that, I wonder? An heiress who has the run of this place? Or, a girl whose judgement of people, myself included, is so obviously up the spout? In any event, Anna laughed and chewed her lip, glancing about nervously. It was the first time I'd ever seen her looking disingenuous and I was suddenly revolted, and a little afraid.

'Oh, I'm all right. You all worry too much. Really,' shaking off my paw, 'I'm fine.'

She strode off around the corner. The afternoon was ending in a glut of purple shadows. Beyond the darkening house walls the front lawn was a restless sea of trembling grass in which the lake lay like a shattered mirror. Behind me to the left was the stable block; in the distance, beech and elm trees, peaked roofs, a spire, all blurred against the smudged sky. Vicky crouched at the edge of the water, stirring it with a stick. As Anna approached she jumped up with a sob and ran towards her.

At moments I still see them like this: two removed silhouettes, the crouching child and the advancing woman, hand on hip, holding a wash basket, nameless figures in a nameless landscape. They were none of mine. I thought I knew so much about them, but what did I really know? Half of their gestures I did not understand, and the rest I guessed at, only to discover later that I was hopelessly wrong.

CHAPTER TWELVE

That evening, the eve of our Open Day, Anna was in a festive mood. While scrabbling in the butler's pantry I had discovered a cobwebby crate of Pol Roger, shunted behind boxes of stale crackers and marrons glacés, the spoils of a long-forgotten dinner party. How old was this stuff? The colour-by-numbers packaging of the crackers had a 1940s look. The champagne had been stored upright but was still drinkable, though the cork was dry and came out of its vice with a creak and a spiral of mould. We quaffed the golden booze at the kitchen table, from old-fashioned, shallow French crystal that Anna had found in a closet in the dining room. A single glass had on her that almost magically inebriating effect produced by alcohol on very slender women.

Remembering the kitchen at Mawle now fills me with sadness. There was a crusty-lidded mustard pot that lived next to the toaster and was soldered fast to the counter by dirt. There was a lonely, stubborn sock, forever bereft of its mate, that cleaved to the radiator instead. A rogue cracked tile next to the cooker sang plangently underfoot; the beechwood table rocked like a sailor on shore leave. The table top was phosphorescent with grease. All of this, all these superfluous and magical commonplace things, I mourn, and miss. How strange the economy of the heart is, that it should attach any significance at all to them!

'These glasses were Granny Rose's,' slurred Anna. 'She and Grandpa Teddy got them as a wedding present.' She twizzled the spindly stem of a crystal bell between restless fingers and giggled; squinted down at her chest. 'D'you know, girls in those days used to measure their boobs by squishing them into these cups. If yours didn't fit the glass then they were the wrong size. I think that's disgustingly sexist, don't you?'

'Indeed, my dear,' I offered, vaguely. 'But our notions of female beauty are always changing.'

'Exactly! And now we have eating disorders and so on. If you are a normal size, like me, then you just feel fat.'

Sipping my champagne, I regarded her skinny flank.

'Yup, you're a big porker, Anna,' burped Vicky, blowing supernumerary bubbles into her thimbleful of Pol Roger through a straw.

'No, my dear,' I said. 'You are very slight. You could do with gaining a pound or two. Will you take another glass of champagne?'

As so often, my most mundane remark triggered a totally unforeseen reaction in Anna. Her relief and gratitude seemed to gather form and substance and become a separate creature that bounded over to me and stuck its furry snout trustingly under my arm.

'But, Dr Lynch, booze is so fattening!' she laughed. Her hands waved frantically over her glass. 'Oh, all right! I will! Tell you what – there's loads more drink in the cellar. Why don't you fetch us up a few bottles?'

'I will, most gladly.' Was this more than a casual suggestion, meant to give me a further opportunity to hunt for the picture? I'd looked for a cellar to the house previously while making my inventory, without any luck. 'Where *is* this cellar?'

'The door's outside, under the kitchen steps. Bottom left. The light switch is on the inside. Hang on, you'll need these.' She opened a kitchen drawer and passed me a torch and a thick iron key with a grinning shaft.

Vicky was on her feet in a flash. 'Can I come?'

Oh Christ. Well, why not? I was getting quite used to the limpet. 'I insist that you do. I don't think I'd manage without you.'

Anna smiled benignly at us. 'While you two do that I'll have a think about pudding.'

The cellar door was a wedge of sparred and bolted oak, shackled to the wall of the house with truculent hinges. In the absence of a key, dynamite would have been needed to open it. What loot did the Ropers keep in here? I applied my hip to the door, helped by the odd thrust from Vicky, and we nearly tumbled down a flight of damp stone steps. Once within, I groped for the light switch. A grilled safety lamp came on smokily above a viperous tangle of wires. Opaque dusk lay ahead for about forty feet, from which came a foul stench. It was musty to begin with, but soon other smells crept up from the ground, thickening the heavy air: the sharp smell of roots, the powdery smell of fungus, and a faint but unmistakable reek of decay, perhaps from the corpse of some creature that had crept into the cellar to die. I switched on my torch and shone it around the room. The ceiling and walls showed traces of lathing and plastering, through which the boulder-like shapes of the underlying stones had thrust themselves. The floor was bricked but mined with holes, and filthy with old paper, wisps of rotten straw, stray planks of wet wood and stagnant water. A heap of sodden sacking lay on the ground in front of me. In the distance, though, like the outline of a mighty cathedral rising from the mists, was a towering scaffold of bottles; an entire wall of venerable booze.

'Spooky,' whispered Vicky.

'Ah, but these wines must be superb,' I coughed. 'Look, here's a twenty-year-old Montrachet. And this Chianti looks just as excellent. Well, at any rate it's even older and it's really filthy.'

'Is that how you can tell if a wine is good or not? If the bottle's dirty?'

'Spot on. Listen, Miss Fidget' – she was playing hopscotch over some puddles – 'can you carry these two bottles without dropping them?'

'Per-lease! Of course I can.'

'Very well, then. Take them up to Anna and tell her I'll be along in a minute with more, there's a good girl.'

'OK. This place just creeps me out.'

Her heels flitted through the darkness along the beam of my torch, up the steps. Alone, I swivelled my light across the floor and walls. More sacking; an old mangle; thick snarls of rope; a wooden ladder; a discarded grate; some rows of shelves. I poked around on these for a while, but they held only brittle brushes, bottles of evaporated turps and tins of flaky paint; no paintings. In one corner of the cellar, mysteriously, there was a strange square enclosure made of unplaned boards, measuring about eight foot square. I leaned the ladder against its side and climbed up to investigate. A plastic cover was tied tightly across the top, held down at each corner by an enormous Gordian knot. I tried to unpick the one nearest to me, but it was as hard as cement. Taking out my pocket knife, I inflicted a clumsy zig-zagging gash on the sheet. The space beneath was acrid and dark. I plunged in my hand and closed my fingers around something cold and solid, which I extracted with a roaring in my ears.

The enclosure was a coal bin, containing, at a guess, about three tons of coal.

Ah, well. At least there was a goodly supply of grappa down here: I'd seen the distinctive long neck of the bottle stencilled repeatedly against the pallor of the wine rack in an alcoholic *mise en abyme*. I picked up four bottles in my blackened fists and was about to go back upstairs when I noticed an opening just to the left of the coal bin. It was a tunnel or passage of some sort, extending for a short way along the western foundations of the house, with a lowish ceiling, but wide enough, I saw once I was inside it, to accommodate two or three men abreast. The floor was unbricked, of raw earth, and widened after five feet into a shallow, cave-like storage chamber. It was even darker in here than in the rest of the cellar, and my torch scarcely made a dent in the thick gloom. I took a step forwards.

The air in that space was cold and unclean, like the breath of a large reptile. Through it darted that other, blighted smell. I took another six or seven steps, and all at once my knee struck rotting wood. My pulse nearly leaped from my wrist. Putting out my hands, I touched whatever it was that blocked my way with the tips of my fingers. It was most definitely something wooden, and flat, like a board; about four feet wide. Could it be a box or crate of some kind? I extended my fingers around the sides, but felt only air. Behind the mouldering board was another board, and there were more boards to the left and right too. I stroked and fumbled. What was this? I inched nearer; put my nose up to the wood. The smell of decay was so powerful that I couldn't discern another behind it, but spread across the board at the very back I thought I had detected the unmistakable, waxily ribbed patina of paint.

At this point my heart began to work so fast that I thought I might collapse. I fell to the ground on my hands and knees and flashed my torch across the surface of the wood. My God – it was not a picture, or a crate, but the remains of a crate, or rather one of several, stacked against the walls of the cave. What I'd felt wasn't paint, but a tarpaulin sheet that was nailed across the front. I prised out the nails one at a time with my pocket knife and ripped the tarpaulin away. Printed across the width of the board, in large crude letters, was the name *Eloïse*, and in smaller letters underneath it, *Portsmouth*. I now saw, with a flaring of disappointment, that these words were painted on the board in front too, and on all the others.

At that moment I heard footsteps.

'Dr Lynch, where are you?'

Thank Christ: it was Vicky, not Anna. There was no time to think about all this now.

'Just on my way!' I shouted. 'I'm just, ah, looking for more wine.'

'Hurry up, then! We've got Lo-Cal rum 'n' raisin ice cream for pud.'

'Lo-Cal rum 'n' raisin!' I cried breathlessly as my head emerged from the tunnel. 'What an inducement. I wouldn't miss it for the world.'

'Thought not,' said Vicky. 'Yuck, you're all dusty. You've got a cobweb on your nose. Actually,' she corrected herself, examining me by the light of the torch and scrunching up her diamond-cut lips, 'I think you're going to need a *bath*.'

Though my searches for the Madonna were at present coming to nothing, these silly nights with Anna and Vicky were nevertheless filled with a sense of enchantment. I was aware of how limited Anna was, but it made no difference. Being in her company raised everything to another pitch. The mere sight of her stimulated unwelcome attacks of feeling.

Oh, I remember! One of the oddest and somehow most typical things about Anna was that her footprints were warm. The patch of carpet, the corner of wooden floorboard, the square of kitchen tile on which she had recently stood would still send off a faint heat if you trod there in your bare or socked feet a few seconds later. I found myself testing this phenomenon, stepping deliberately where she had stepped before me, so that our progress around the room began to follow a rapt dance, with Anna leading. She kept on talking, opening and shutting drawers, rattling pans, refrigerating milk – in my absorbed orbit I seldom noticed what Anna did ordinarily, in the sublunary course of things.

Ah, Ah, Ah! By the light of the fluorescent kitchen filament, we spent many happy ampere hours in this way.

Another peculiar tick of Anna's delicate and well-regulated mechanism was that she could not choke, even ever so slightly, without immediately sneezing. I watched her snuffling water, coffee, sauce béarnaise (result of a brave attempt of mine to give the starved child some cooking lessons – if left to herself she would have dined exclusively on breakfast cereal and tubs of fat-free ice cream), crackers, even peas, down the wrong passageway, and each time the efficient ping-ping of her sneeze would clear the lethally blocked aperture only seconds later.

Yet she was also so ordinary, so plain, so *dull* – and in the next moment so beautiful! – so commonplace and so rare in turns. When I could see her as plain and insipid I felt relieved, momentarily in possession of my senses again. And then suddenly my perception would shift, everything would shift, and I would be plunged once more into a well of longing.

I was wrong in thinking that Anna's conscience was particularly keen. The truth was that she had no conscience, no sense of her own distinctness from others, no ability to protect the integrity of her inner life from outside attacks. She was an empty vessel, a vehicle constantly susceptible to hijacking by forces which were necessarily stronger than she, since they came from without. She was infinitely weak, defenceless, unoriginal. Physically she was just as vulnerable. Later, much later, I saw her give herself up to sex with a look of ecstatic suffering, like a saint listening to voices against which there was no appeal. Yet if she was too listless, too passive, to be good, she was still innocent in the most profound sense of the word: of all the people I have ever known she was the least able to grasp the implications of what she did, acting only from a pure, unreasoning impulse to efface herself. She should have been safe from me, and I would have been safe from her, if my heart had not played us both that terrible trick by imploding. Defeated in my search for the Bellini, I would have gone my way after five days, visited Puppi, and retired to chase *gondolieri* on the Rialto; why not?

But it was not to be. When I met her the most primitive cells of my being were already deeply stamped all over, like yards of Limerick lace, with Anna-shaped holes – a childish template of loss which her tidy young form was admirably designed to fill.

'Dr Lynch,' coaxed Anna later that night, as the kitchen filament struck up its mournful refrain. 'Tell me about your mother. Tell me about *your* Mamma. Was she anything like mine?'

'Oh no, my dear.' What could I say? Her hair was black. Her eyes were the colour of clover. She was a country girl. Her ankles were thick. She had an insensibility, an innocence, just like you. When I was a boy I assumed she was a pushover. Now I'm not so sure.

If Anna appeared vague, you see, it was not, as I then thought, because she was simply stupid. When it came to the point, much later, she was quite capable of doing what she thought necessary for her own survival. No: I perceive now that her absent-mindedness in those early days was the by-product of a steady sensual pressure, a nervous slow boil, which consumed all her resources. Would it have made a difference, to her or to me, if I had been less self-absorbed? Had I seen her more clearly, would I have behaved differently? I doubt it. In those heart-rendingly brief weeks at Mawle I was often overcome with a sense of fatality, as if I were simply performing gestures which had been prescribed for me; as if I were inhabiting another life, repeating a tale that had already played itself out, in another time, involving someone else. I would wonder, while looking at Anna's rosy shining face, or her face wet with tears, whether I had any agency in the world at all; or whether (a pulse-speeding thought, this!) the idea of agency itself wasn't just an illusion; whether every one of my actions hadn't already been determined long before, leaving me a profoundly free man – in the sense that I simply *could not* act otherwise than I did – after all.

On the morning of the 15th Anna appeared at breakfast wearing a floating blue dress instead of her usual t-shirt and leggings. She was shod in silver sandals. I noticed with delight that her toes were clean. I'd been thinking, erratically, about the rotting boards I had found in the cellar, but they didn't seem to hold any clues to the whereabouts of the Bellini. In this regard they were like so much at Mawle: underneath that surface grandeur, all too often, was specious trash. And now fragrant Anna stood in front of me, vibrating with excitement. I dismissed my thoughts.

'What d'you think?' She performed a modest rotation, in slow motion, on one foot.

'You look beautiful. I would like to put you in a music box. And you smell like a rose.' I fossicked with the bread knife. 'Have a piece of toast. Have a banana.'

'No thanks. I feel a bit sick.' She belched. 'Must be nerves!'

'No one is here yet.' Some gesture seemed to be required of me, but I was not sure what. 'Shall we go out?'

We stopped at the front door, without touching, looking out over the lawn. I remember that I felt liquid, as if something were sliding and slipping inside me, and that this wateriness seemed to be part of the day, too. The grass was shiny with summer dew. The unbroken silence of Sunday morning filled every space like embalming fluid. Somewhere inside the house I could hear a tap running.

Anna frowned and bit her thumbnail. 'I feel terribly guilty to be the only person living here. It looks so uneconomical.' Above the scooped neckline of her dress her tan collarbone did a frenzied dance. She gave a little moan. 'Maybe I'm just not used to people.'

'You'll be fine,' I ventured cruelly. I was suddenly tired of the whole elaborate game of bluff, and of my own emotion. 'Your mother would be proud of you, and *all you're doing to help her.*'

Anna stared at me with an odd deliberateness. 'Don't bet on it that I will,' she said, in a voice lightly, shockingly, poised between irony and disclosure. 'Help, I mean. Don't you know – can't you see – that I sometimes just hate her?'

She plaited her willowy arm confidingly through mine, but did not say any more.

An escutcheon-shaped photo of Mawle (lawn sinister, donkey rampant) emblazoned with the date of our Open Day had appeared in the *Berkshire Herald* and, courtesy of Harry, on selected pub noticeboards in the market towns around Mawle. The first visitors arrived at ten o'clock, a Captain and Mrs Francis Butts from Abingdon. We watched them as they parked their gargantuan saloon – something beige, and vintage, with fins – and advanced unsteadily across the gravel. He was kitted out in pale wrinkled linen, with a preposterous boater stuck on his sweating head. She had what would once have been called a well-supported figure and wore – actually wore, and a scented one, too – a handkerchief lodged in her wattled bosom.

'Welcome, welcome,' I cawed. 'Lovely day, lovely car. Difficult to get the parts these days, eh?'

'You don't say. Francis Butts. Cap'n. This is Poppy.'

Mrs Butts regarded me equivocally. She seemed about to curtsey. Below the noxious hanky her cantilevered body was swathed in polka dots. She turned to her husband and tapped him smartly on the arm.

'Go on, Frank, pay the man. You must be –?'

'A friend of the family. I am currently cataloguing the Mawle art collection. Would you care for a guided tour?'

'Oh, yes, delighted. Frank was quite the painter when he was younger.'

'Not really. Pilot in the war, you know. Italy. Dabbled a bit afterwards.'

'Do have a guide book.' Anna fanned her clutch of pamphlets against her chest. Captain Butts helped himself, shaving a nipple. Filthy sod.

'Charming girl. Daughter of the house?'

'Quite.' I touched Anna briefly on her flushed cheek. 'My godchild.' She smiled colludingly. I had begun to feel mildly excited.

'You are Catholics, of course?' asked Captain Butts. 'Poppy and I wondered – would you ever consider having a parish mass here, in your chapel? We know such a lovely priest.'

A chapel. Mawle had a chapel! How the hell had I failed to find it? Hadn't it occurred to Anna that I should be steered in that direction if I were ever to stand a chance of delivering the Bellini? Foolish, remiss child!

'Naturally. Do come and have a look at it.' I realized that I did not have even the slightest idea of where the chapel might be. I puffed up my voice with reproof. 'Anna, my dear?'

The shameless girl didn't even look guilty. 'Of course.'

She led the Buttses up the oak staircase, while I brought

up the rear in a wake of violets. As we walked my heart began to jump about urgently. The chapel! Where would the Bellini Madonna be, if not in the chapel? Darkened by time and dirt, no doubt, but to the trained eye still perfectly recognizable. The Ropers, in their hapless dim way, had probably been genuflecting in front of it for years.

We went up to the first floor of the east wing and passed through three or four bedrooms. Mrs Butts followed with a proprietorial air, pausing once to finger the stuff of a curtain. Then we came to a room where everything was yellow, and stopped dead at a closet door.

'It's this way.' Anna smiled, as if she were about to present a troop of particularly well-behaved infants with a special birthday surprise, and turned the closet handle.

Behind it was a flight of shallow wooden steps leading from what seemed to be a very large cupboard into a bare, stale room with a low wooden ceiling and a plain stone altar without an altar light. A melting reddish gleam fell across the floor from two stained glass windows – the very windows which I had caught a glimpse of before from the dusty little anteroom containing the trunk. Immediately afterwards my heart plummeted. There weren't any pictures on the walls at all.

'Ho,' said Captain Butts, looking around. 'It's very, hum, effective.'

'No stations, my dear?' asked Mrs Butts. 'Are you having them restored?'

'It's always been like this,' answered Anna simply.

'Consecrated?' This was said with a little snuffle.

'Oh, yes. But we don't use it now.'

'Well, well.' Mrs Butts exhaled decisively. 'We shall have to remedy *that*. I will give Father Tim a bell this very evening.'

'Yes, dear lady,' I whispered in her ear as we descended the stairs, cupping her buttressed butt in my hand. 'And do tell Father Timmy to bring any altar boys he particularly likes.' This shut her up. She did not say a word as I steered her past a large Circumcision – 'Just look at that ducky little prepuce' – although the violet stench around her intensified, like the oil secreted by certain types of insect when faced with the unwelcome attentions of a predator.

The Buttses left soon afterwards. 'I think they were disappointed,' said Anna hopefully as the saloon crawled away. 'What horrible people. My God, what a mistake this whole thing was. If we're lucky they won't be back.'

'Dear girl,' I said, 'I wouldn't lose a moment's sleep over it.'

Only two other couples came: a hoarse-voiced family from London with their three bored brats, attended by a spotted, sulky nanny, up for the weekend with nothing to do; and a randy pair of teen emaciates who giggled hysterically at the sight of every painted tit.

At teatime, having earned precisely £13.75, we shut the gates. Harry still hunkered at the bottom of the drive, holding Rosie by the bridle. All day he had not moved. Anna shooed Vicky out of the kitchen, to which she had been banished for the afternoon, and helped her into the saddle. Then she got up behind the child and waved timidly at me, her silver-sandalled feet swinging. I led them up and down the gravel and around the lake. Anna hummed a tuneless song under her breath all the while. Small clouds began to stray across the sky. When it started to rain a tentative summer rain, we went in.

At dusk I stood at the drawing room window, gazing at a pale smudge on the lawn – what was it? A rat, a mole? No, it lay inert, one of Anna's fairy sandals, orphaned in the mizzle – and realized with a tender shock of surprise that I had been at Mawle a full week.

CHAPTER THIRTEEN

In those seven hazy summer days I had begun to experience a peculiar doubling of my vision. Everything had acquired a glittering twin, a bewitching shadow of itself: the whispering birch by the gate, the hard blue bean of the lake, the bucket in the kitchen sink, for God's sake. I, too, felt double. No: divided. There were two of me: a brutal boor, and a preposterous fledgling, full of feeling. Anna's awkward grace moved me to the core of my rotten heart. I imagined her tending to the Bellini, a frowning handmaid, her polished brown face stooped over the Madonna's older one, the same smooth hair, the same centre parting . . .

'Oh Christ,' says Anna, 'I forgot the bread.'

We have just come back from a trip to the supermarket and my girl is standing at the open refrigerator door, balancing a domed onion in each hand. 'Would you be a love and pop back to the shops for me? Ta.'

Anna pirouettes this way and that in front of the stacked tomatoes and courgettes in the belly of the vegetable morgue. She lifts her arm to stow a cucumber and I see that her velvet armpit is marred by a single mole. I want to sink to my knees among the empty plastic bags on the cold stone floor and clasp her tightly in my arms. Lobbing a sack of frozen peas across the table instead, I smile at her gravely.

'Consider it done, my dear.'

Had I utterly lost my sense of reality, or gained what I'd never had before? Was I twice the man I was previously, or only half? Every day around noon I would hear Anna in the kitchen, and some time later she would call me to the table for lunch, together with Harry and Vicky. We ate nursery food: boiled eggs, sausages, and devilishly grinning discs of synthetic potato called Happy Faces. We ate baked beans, washed down with milk. We ate Cream of Vegetable soup. We ate tuna sandwiches made with tuna that slid, already slathered in mayonnaise, from a tin. We ate, usually, in tense silence, punctuated by resentful whimpers from Vicky and warning grunts from Harry.

'Anna, I don't like this soup. It has bits in it.'

'It can't have. It's not vegetable, it's *Cream* of Vegetable. Ask Dr Lynch.'

'Yes, that's absolutely right. There are no bits in the fruit of the Cream of Vegetable plant.'

We slurp grumpily for a minute or two. Vicky spits out a splinter of carrot. Harry emits a low growl of barely suppressed irritation.

'Oh, for fuck's sake!' he roars.

Anna's head jerks as if she has been switched across the face with a whip.

'Say, Harry, have you seen the latest score?' I ask manfully.

'Nah, T.J. No bloody time.' He stops glaring at Vicky and turns to me. 'How'd them Rangers do, then?'

It seemed that Harry had a television in his shack, and he and I sometimes talked about American football or ice hockey or baseball. Then he would loosen up a little and tip back in his chair, his bronzed trunk at ease, his arm supine like a rough branch along the table, and Anna would relax, and we would all breathe more freely. Anna occasionally fetched us some beers from the refrigerator. Harry had a little trick of prising the bottle tops off with his front teeth, which only Vicky and I failed to applaud. I hated these lunches because he was there; hated him for the long shade of erotically charged misery he cast, and for the etiolated droop of Anna's shoulders. He took away all her light. Why had she taken up with him? Was there really nobody better? Was the gravitational pull of this black hole on my poor star that compelling?

Once lunch was over I followed Anna to the garden, to her evident embarrassment, and kept close to her while she snipped and pruned and deadheaded. I remember telling her about my childhood one afternoon in the garden at Mawle, a memory that is steeped in the sensation of prickling heat and the resurrected throaty smell of foxglove, and having a sagging, awful apprehension that she would not understand – and, as I'd feared (and no doubt counted on) she didn't. What could she have known about the meagre, shabby genteel world that had produced me, with my rapacious hunger for beauty, my starved sense of being always an onlooker at the feast, and my deadly skill with the outward forms of respectability? Anna had been brought up in savagery of a different kind, namely a complete ignorance of any life beyond the walls of her father's Georgian manor. She had the unbudgeable sense of entitlement, the atrocious innocence, of her tribe, and she took my surface polish for the real thing, never dreaming – any more than a lady in a Victorian drawing room would dream, on being presented with a cannibal who submitted to being displayed wearing a smoking jacket and a fob watch – that my appetites were fundamentally alien to hers. On these occasions, scorched by the hot sun, I would wait for the anticipated sting of dismissal. She was not at all intimidated by me now.

'Go on, Dr Lynch. Don't feel that you have to keep me company, you know. I won't find it rude if you have to work. What do you think of our pictures, anyway? It's meant to be quite a decent collection. Do we really have anything good?' There.

'Oh, they're wonderful, all very fine. But if I may say so, *you* look as pretty as a picture in that hat.'

'Pssshht. Really?' She reddened. Even the tritest compliments always caught her off guard.

'Absolutely. If I were only twenty years younger . . .'

'Now don't say that. You're not old, not old at all!' She checked me over, and stopped pruning. She had meant the remark as a courtesy, but seemed genuinely disconcerted by what she saw. 'Well. You really are quite dishy, aren't you?' The scarlet stain on her cheeks intensified, spreading slowly down her neck to join the clay-dark sunburn at the top of her breasts. Her tatty shirt was wide open at the collar. Her shirt – my Lord, her shirt . . .

I said nothing: I was trying to control the violent bifurcation of my perception. Anna resumed her cutting and trimming, unaware that there were now two of her, one a votive figurine smothered in my sighs. 'You must find me very boring. I've never been anywhere, never seen anything. I went to boarding school in Cheltenham but I didn't stay on till the end – too homesick. Daddy let me come back. After that he thought there wasn't much point in my leaving home and getting a job because I'd only have to look after

Mawle one day. And anyway, the school fees were astronomical and I was never any good at lessons.'

Condemned to be the guardian of this heap of shadows! 'Sometimes home's best,' I lied.

'Do you think so? You're so clever. You're Ivy League, one can tell. And you must have travelled the world.' She nodded absently to herself. 'It must be great to be an American. The world is your mussel.'

'Oyster.'

'Sorry?' Anna glanced up pinkly.

I could not help smiling. My oyster, my caviare, my crayfish, my *zuppa di cozze*, my *risotto alle seppie*. My tuna sandwich! My underfed stomach gave a heave. A wild new sensation had invaded my gut. I wanted to gobble her up. I felt completely reckless. 'I'm not really American at all, you know.'

'Gosh, really? What are you, then?'

'I'm Irish. We Irishmen aren't really fond of fish anyway. It's a penitential dish for us.' She accepted this little dig without batting an eye. 'And my education wasn't all that grand either. I went to a very ordinary school, and then to a very ordinary college.'

'Never!' She had put down her shears now and was, I sensed with tumescent pleasure, quietly receptive. 'Where did you grow up?'

'Oh, in a very ordinary town. It was grimy and rainy, and had many churches and many bridges. My school was founded as an apostolic school, to train up young men to the priesthood. By the time I went there, though it still had a seminarians' section attached, it was really just a boarding school, plain and simple.'

'It still sounds rather grand.'

'I assure you, it was not. Many boys with less loving and determined mothers than mine were forced into the seminary. They didn't have a choice.'

Anna looked at me kindly. 'But you weren't forced,' she observed. 'You could choose your future.'

'Yes, I could. And just look at what I've chosen.'

She glanced about humorously, and then down at herself. 'Doesn't look so bad to me. Holidays in the country. Nice house, lovely people.' She lopped the brown shaft of a foxglove and sat back on her dirty soles. There was affectionate laughter in her eyes. 'Go on, get along now. We don't want you falling behind.' The sunlight, hot and sweet, picked out the fine gold hairs on her arms. I felt a strong desire to stroke them. 'You ever going to do anything useful, then?' she asked.

'Well, my dear. I just might.'

I was always astonished at how much Anna's quiet insistence on our respective purposes wounded me. Expelled from paradise in this way, I stalked the corridors of Mawle in pursuit of the Madonna, adding haphazardly to my notes all the while.

Library: Stale-wedding-cake Gothic. Portrait of James Roper and family, no value whatsoever. Standard Grand Canal by Guardi; unexciting Dughet picnic scene.

Stables: No horses or other beasts of any kind in here, unless we count Harry the Stud. No Bellini either.

Outbuildings: Fuck shack with own power supply. Must have satellite link somewhere too.

Cellar: 'Creeps me out,' to quote my tiny pal. Waterfall of booze. Prodigious coal bin. Also some sort of disused storage room (nineteenth-century addition?), nearly cause of second fainting fit. Who or what was *Eloïse*? A ship?

Kitchen: Where my love holds court. Crammed with crap.

Entrance Hall: Heartburn-inducing fondue of minor Dutch Masters. Edam. Leyden. Gouda. Leerdammer. All fine cheeses, but artists unknown.

Dining Room: Second-rate Sheraton; two of the chairs don't match. Alcoves no doubt contained busts or other statuary once. Broken? Clumsy Anna?

Drawing Room: Oak and bay ceiling carvings, very inferior; egg and dart panelling. Meissen with hairline cracks, obviously glued at some stage (*vide* above). Some English crockery. Incidental domestic portraits. Twee gilded floral French porcelain. Hilarious pianola by Steck, a rarity, probably the most valuable item in the room. Vulgar Great Exhibition plaster relief redeemed by rather lifelike goateed Judas.

Rose Room: Mid-period Murillo, excellent example of generic Our Lady of Sorrows (c.1650?) worth perhaps £1½ million? But no cash potential, presumably, since already hanging in full view and so inalienable from estate.

Chinese Suite: Hand-painted wallpaper, superb saturated blues and cantaloupe greens. Silk curtains on bed with asymmetrical avian motif, high thread count in gold. Very stealable inlaid Dutch marquetry table, late eighteenth century.

Primrose Parlour: Yellow, yellow, yellow. Satin and chintz, furbelows, tassels, fringes. Probably once lady's sitting room or bedroom. Thus entry to chapel would have been concealed among her underthings (see below).

Chapel: Pre-Restoration; access ingeniously disguised by large wardrobe, interior deliberately plain. Windows like congealing blood. Might as well be cell or torture chamber. Now unused; Maddalena obviously not the mass-going type.

Tapestry Room: Some good examples of verdure Gobelins. Villa with garden. Leda being rogered by the swan. Washing Day at the mill.

Painted Salon: Some insignificant murals of a biblical nature; cabinets (Italian Empire?) chock-full of Herend and Murano.

Various smaller bedrooms; landings, corridors: Item: one Flight Into Egypt, perhaps by Biscaino. One Capriccio, quite fine. Possibly Panini? Apollo in style of Balducci but most likely by follower. Item: Longhi (?) Rococo parlour piece, not bad. Holy Family which might be by Bertucci (Giovan Battista, not Giacomo). Large Zuccarelli Pastorale; Bernini cartoon the size of my thumb. Canova marbles of the four seasons personified. Latter unfortunately the size of circus midgets.

Bathrooms: Urgently need a good clean.

Billiard Room: Vile Victorian den: green baize table with marble-effect legs, cherrywood cues; loud brass Tiffany lamp; dead butterfly collection on wall; tobacco-coloured hunting prints: *Ready and Waiting. On the Scent. Out Foxed. Home for Tea.*

Smoking Room: Ditto the prints, only shooting scenes. Stinks of old smoke. Mystery as to how this could be so. Anna not an addict of the weed. Have never seen Hardbodied Harry puffing either. Who has been lighting up in here? Sultry, Turkish Delight smell. Cigars?

Dressing room with trunk: The only promising discovery so far. Must reinvestigate as soon as Anna is out of the house for any decent length of time.

Gun Room: Full of guns.

Et cetera. Sometimes I sat in the warm lap of the library, dredging the diary. Although deciphering it was infernally slow work, Roper's account of that far away autumn in Asolo was fast becoming as real to me as my own unreal life at Mawle. I told myself that the answer to my search lay within it, that I was navigating the broadest possible current in my trawl for the Bellini and had to follow it doggedly since I had no other obvious beacons, but the truth was that my initial passion had mutated, and grown lungs and the buds of legs, and was now threatening to leave the shallow waters of my private experience. Oh, to hell with these metaphors. In short, I was developing an interest in Anna and James Roper for their own sakes.

And, most unexpectedly of all, in the child. Vicky sometimes came in without warning and would sit opposite me in the armchair for an hour at a time, watching with sibylline eyes as I turned the pages of the diary. At first I made a great show of flipping through Roper's library books and taking notes whenever she was with me, but later I grew careless and slouched openly. To my own surprise I became used to having her there and found that I missed her impassive presence when she was tagging along behind Harry, or when the house had swallowed her up in one of a series of mysterious disappearances that would send Anna, apologetic and agitated, to my door at supper time to form a search party. Then I reverted to being the scholar at his desk, who raised his austere head from his labours (that inventory!) with infinite patience in order to address the problem. In a few days' time, what would we discover? A ransom note, sent anonymously, lurking in the breakfast post? A heap of small bones, whitening behind the jammed door of a concealed passageway? But no, the child was always found in the same place – under her bed, kicking her cracked heels, staring her unblinking stare.

Vicky seemed to me more than ever like a figure on an old medallion or an engraving in a book: an achieved thing, hardly human, already enjoying the repose of art. I did not notice how completely this had become my vision of her until she accompanied me on my ramble to the village shop one morning.

'Vicky, where are your parents?' I asked her as she jounced along the pavement, swiping at conkers with a stick. She was so graceful that she contrived to make even this mindless choreography look like Swan Lake. I was hypnotized. 'Where's your mother?'

'Dead.' She said this very decisively.

'Oh, my dear!' My eyes swam. 'I shouldn't have pried.'

'It's OK. I can't even remember her.' Another fluid *thwack*, and a conker went flying past my shins. 'Anna only looks after me because I don't have anyone else.'

Ah – now it all came into focus. Little displaced cygnet! 'So Anna's related to you?'

'Second cousin. Twice removed. I don't belong here, you know. I'm from an entirely different branch of the family. The, um, Italian one.' She puffed up her cheeks and blew out the air with an insolent report. '*Much* older.'

Well, that explained the high finish, the priceless lustre of that face. She was something on Maddalena's side, without any Roper admixture. It also explained Anna's unrelenting resentment.

'Hey!' Stopping at a wire fence and pointing proudly to the muck-brown prefab behind it, Vicky suddenly called out, 'There's my school.'

She actually went to school, and in this backwater! I was incensed that no proper provision had been made for this self-possessed, clever girl by her Italian relatives. She should have been at some historic ladies' college like the one Anna had flunked out of; she should, at the very least, have been hand-reared by an antique Oxford Fellow or two put out to grass as private tutors, instead of being dumped in the battery farm now standing in front of us. And this of course was her summer holiday, and my tiny patrician would be back there in September, sharing a desk with a humdrum mortal child and learning how to dissect frogs and to subtract apples from pears. It hardly seemed possible.

'You're not working very hard, are you?' It was an astonishing ultramarine Tuesday afternoon, two days after our Open Day, and Vicky's flawless ivory face was angled at me knowingly. I had a volume, some random, fancily-bound edition from Roper's shelves, ready to hand.

Good Lord – was the child part of the plot to keep me at it, too?

'Oh yes I am. I am doing essential research. Right now I am reading a book called,' I scanned the spine and the contents page quickly, 'called, in fact, *Historic Girls*, which is all about clever little female children who achieved greatness by being very, very good, and very kind to others, just as you should be. Would you like to hear some of it?'

'Sounds bollocky, but all right,' said Vicky, with a grotesquely exaggerated sigh.

'Well then, listen up.' I burrowed through the gilt-edged pages until I came to a familiar story. 'This is the tale of Catarina of Venice, the Girl of the Grand Canal. Afterward known as Queen of Cyprus and Daughter of the Republic. She is about to clap eyes for the first time on James Lusignan, the little boy who will become her husband one day, so pay attention.'

More sighing, accompanied by eyeball-rolling, but she sat up obediently. I began to read in a sonorous voice.

> 'Who is he? Why, do you not know, Catarina mia? 'Tis his Most Puissant Excellency, the mighty Lord of Lusignan, the runaway Heir of Jerusalem, the beggar Prince of Cyprus, with more titles to his name – ho, ho, ho! – than he hath jackets to his back; and with more dodging than ducats, so 'tis said, when the time to pay for his lodging draweth nigh. Holo, Messer Principino! Give you good-day, Lord of Lusignan! Ho, below there is tribute for you.'
>
> And down upon the head of a certain sad young fellow in the piazza, or square, beneath, descended a rattling shower of bonbons, thrown by the hand of the speaker, a brown-faced Venetian lad of sixteen.

But little Catarina Cornaro, just freed from the imprisonment of her convent school at Padua, felt her heart go out in pity towards this homeless young prince, who just now seemed to be the butt for all the riot and teasing of the boys of the Great Republic . . .

'Blech, I'm going to be sick,' said Vicky. 'In a moment there's going to be *kissing*.'

'I doubt it very much. Katie is a virtuous young girl, and her only concern is to be of service to her family. She will kiss only those whom they expressly order her to kiss. Let it be a lesson to you.'

'Smoochy-smoochy, coochy-coochy,' chanted Vicky, propelling herself from her chair with a flick of her finely-sprung calves and falling to the floor in a pantomime of vomiting. 'I'm going to find Anna. You coming?'

'No. Leave me in peace, you wild child. I only like nice children.'

'Well, *you're* not nice. Harry says you're a disgusting old man.'

'And so I am, too. Be off with you now.'

She hesitated. 'Well,' she said, '*I* quite like you. A little bit.' She sidled out of the room, picking her nose. When I was satisfied that she had gone I slipped the diary out of the end pages of *Historic Girls* and carried on untangling Roper's script where I had left off.

On the evening of the 3rd of September Roper had joined Mrs Bronson and her daughter in the drawing room at La Mura, where they corralled him with tables bearing silver dishes filled with peppermint chocolates, dried flowers, and volumes of Italian poetry. Mrs B rested on the sofa with her pugs at her feet, Edith at her elbow, while Roper had stretched himself out at full length in a low chair close to Miss Bronson, his legs thrust straight out and his hands clasped behind his head.

'Edie, my love,' commanded Mrs B by and by, alive to the picturesque potential of the scene, 'you shall play the spinet for us.'

Miss Bronson sat down at the keyboard with a great show of reluctance. After dithering a little over her music she struck up a light-hearted tune, but the tinny tone, half mandolin and half guitar, of the stubby little instrument fell on my ears like the stilted efforts of an organ-grinder; and I could not help thinking that Miss Bronson herself, with her pert tremulous nose and her distended grey eyes fixed soulfully on me, looked distressingly like the monkey.

'Dear Mrs Bronson,' I reminded my hostess, who had to lean forward to catch my words over the din, 'you did promise, didn't you now, that you would introduce me to the family at Ca' Buccari?'

A monkey. The image seemed to detach itself and float into the hot silence like an absurd little hologram. The library was sweltering – I could feel the sweat coursing down my spine. The scuffed white walls were a cipher; even the barred back of the chaise longue seemed suddenly sinister, a cage of chintz.

What was happening to me? I myself was becoming ever more like a monkey at a spinet, a monkey on a barrel organ! Why was I so easily led by these fools? Why couldn't I act decisively, either to seize Anna or to find the Bellini? Yes, and then what? I was certain that Anna depended on me not only to find the painting, but to share my discovery with her. Indeed, I reflected, she *does* know that I want her. She knows and she is counting on it, the little flirt. Her interest in me, her attentiveness – it's all a sham. And what will the poor obtuse girl do with my devotion, once I've laid the Bellini at her feet? She'll take the picture to Mamma and boot me out. Ah, no. This was not going to happen. On, Lynch, on, I urged myself. They didn't know where James Roper had concealed the thing. How could they even be certain that it was really in the house at all? And how, when we came to the moment of revelation, could I ever rely on them to acknowledge the invaluable part I'd have played in unearthing this prize?

Maddalena was up to something; she had, I feared, some plan of her own for the Madonna. John Roper had made the interest earned by Mawle Estates over to his disregarded daughter rather than his wife, which told me all I needed to know, by the by, about his relations with the mutinous Mrs Roper. He'd turned Anna into a surrogate, an uncomplaining helpmeet, and so that she would always remain safe from the temptation to stray the bastard had locked her away here, out of the world, asleep in her own life. Yet though the income from the estate might belong to Anna in name, it was Maddalena's for any practical purposes that really mattered; and while the bitch affected despair at her daughter's lack of sophistication it clearly suited her to keep my darling slumbering soundly in her glass coffin.

Mawle was only scraping by, but Maddalena was living it up in Italy for half the year, no doubt maintained by some Venetian grandee in the time-honoured way reserved for women of her spectacular attributes. Would she really care if the place went down the drain completely? Wasn't the truth, rather, that she'd be only too happy if she could declare Mawle bankrupt and skedaddle to Venice forever with the Bellini in her pocket? If Mamma had her way, unsuspecting Anna could find herself penniless in the blink of an eye, and the painting permanently out of reach. Insidiously, seductively, a new possibility presented itself to me. Surely there was only one proper custodian for the picture – only one person who was fitted, by long dedication, by years of training and, let us be blunt about it, by the quality of his sensibility, to be the arbiter of its future. I would find the Bellini, tell no one, and *keep it for myself.*

I felt along the line of my jaw with my thumb and forefinger. I tugged at the flesh of my neck. I might even have rapped my chest (a ridiculously theatrical gesture, I admit): still firm. If Anna could capture me, then I could waylay her in turn. The Madonna wasn't a listed part of the estate; there was no evidence that it was at Mawle at all; no public proof that it even existed. If I were to decamp with it Maddalena would, in all likelihood, find herself treading thin air should she try to go after me. I felt suddenly alive, and full of fresh possibilities. My fingers rubbed up and down the page, registering its fine grain, the nicks in the paper made by Roper's pen. The interstice between the past and the present seemed as insubstantial as gauze. The truth lay within my grasp.

The telephone rang shrilly in the kitchen, an impertinently mechanical sound in that crypt-like house. No one came to answer it. I closed the diary, tingling along every nerve, and left my sunny patch. I was sliding along the corridor, still clutching my decoy copy of *Historic Girls*, when I heard the back door bang, followed by a scraping and a stamping of boots, and then the low whine of Anna's voice. As I was about to turn around and retreat once more to my chair, something in her tone stopped me. I was too far away to catch the detail of what she was saying, but her sullen listlessness gave her away at once. Slithering the last few yards to the kitchen, I tilted my head against the hinge of the door. Through the crack I could see Anna with her back to me, holding the receiver, her shoulders hunched in the peculiar marionettish way she had. An open bottle of lime juice cordial, lurid staple of an English summer, glittered on the counter beside her. She had on one muddy wellington; the other sprawled across the threshold of the back door like the severed leg of a corpse. Her gardening gloves and hat lay in the middle of the table on an altar of soil.

'*Si, Mamma*,' she wailed. 'I'm not sure. Oh, Christ. Three, maybe four months. No, I haven't told him yet. No, he hasn't asked me, OK? *Non me l' ha chiesto.*' A furious cicada hopped about in the receiver.

'Then tell him your bloody self!' shouted Anna.

I swung into view from behind the kitchen door, brandishing my open book before me.

'Ah, good afternoon, my dear.'

With a squeak Anna dropped the telephone on the floor, where it lay chirruping.

'I was just going to fetch myself a lime cordial. The afternoons are so hot now, you know.' I stared deliberately at the sink.

'Yes hot, of course, let me.' Seizing a tumbler from the draining board she filled it three-quarters of the way with cordial, and with quaking fingers coaxed the tap to spit a dribble of water into the centre of the gloop.

I shut the telephone up by yanking out its cord, and took a little sip of this bilious cocktail. 'Thank you, my dear. You seem somewhat flustered. Was that your mother on the phone?'

'No, oh no!'

I raised my eyebrows and supped my syrup again.

'Well, OK, yes.'

'Nothing the matter, I hope?'

'No, nothing at all. Mummy just called to chat. About this and that – and the other.'

'The other too, eh? Did your dear Mamma enquire after me?'

'Oh, no! That is – oh *shit* – *yes*, she did.' Anna ran her hands over her wretched red face, as if trying to remember an irrelevant detail. 'She asked if you were still comfortable and I said that I believed you were, on the whole. Well, I think – ' she threw out desperately, 'that is – you are, aren't you?'

'Very comfortable, thank you.' I put the glass down on the table and regarded her tenderly, tucking *Historic Girls* under my arm. I would take action, and swiftly. 'My dear Miss Roper, I hope you will forgive me if I am frank. In spite of her generous hospitality I am aware that your mother cannot entertain me here as a guest indefinitely, and does not – I speak quite openly, you realize – perhaps even much *like* me. I depend on you, who have always been the soul of honesty in your dealings with me, to tell me truthfully if I have outstayed my welcome. In short,' I knitted my fingers together as if in prayer, 'would you like me to go?'

Anna looked aghast. 'Oh, Dr Lynch – Tom – please don't say that! How can you think that I want you to go?' She seemed about to cry. 'Maybe Mummy didn't like you much at first, before she met you, but now she wants you to stay too – she particularly wants you to stay!'

'Does she, indeed?' I considered this for a moment. 'And what good does she think it will do us, if I do stay?'

'She thinks it might be useful,' said Anna simply.

'Useful? To her, or to me?'

'Why, useful to *me*,' replied Anna, with an ever deeper blush. 'In a – a practical, day-to-day sort of way.'

'Useful to you, *of course*,' I assented, seizing her sparrow-like elbows in my moist hands. 'Of course, useful to you.' We gazed at each other solemnly. Anna's brown stare seemed afloat on a sea of brine. I felt as if she might dissolve in my grasp at any moment and run to a puddle about my feet, and so I held her tighter. 'But, my nymph,' I continued, 'if I can be useful to you, then so you, too, may be useful to me.'

'Useful to *you*?' Did I imagine it, or did the swell of her emotion subside a notch?

'Yes, dear child. Shall I tell you how?'

'Tell me,' said Anna, dully.

I gripped her elbows again. 'My dear girl – I would like to say, my dear friend – you may not be entirely surprised to learn that I am looking for something. Yes, I am in search of something.' She squirmed a little, but I held her fast. 'I have been in search of it my whole life, and now I mean to find it. I know, oh I absolutely *know* that it is here in this house. And I think you know it too. But I cannot help you unless you trust me. You say that you don't love your mother. You can see perfectly well that your mother doesn't care about you. And we have divined that she doesn't really give a fuck about me. But we can get the better of her if we only work together – *we can find what we are both looking for, together!* You are more familiar with this house than anyone. For God's sake, though she doesn't care about you, I do! I care – I care very much.'

Anna looked at me in open fear. 'I don't understand what you mean.'

'My dear, I think you do. I rather think you do. Will you trust me? Will you help me?' I clasped her arms tighter. My long femur was pressed against her fragile pubic girdle, all the way down to her jittery knee. She took a few steps backwards and I followed her. We did a desperate foxtrot to the fridge, one-two-three, where Anna's hazel hair fanned out flat against a selection of fridge magnets and a shopping list.

'I don't know what you want from me,' she cried. 'I really don't know!'

Her body was shaking, but her eyes were still fixed on mine. Her elbow was grinding away, chafing my paw. What if I had it all wrong? In that moment a maddening doubt about the depth of her immersion in her mother's plans overtook me, and I let her go. Behind her head the sheer albino face of the icebox whined and shivered miserably.

'My dear Anna, only this.' Battling to control myself I gentled her with my hands, and she stopped struggling. 'I mean only this. Your sweetness is the thing I've been looking for all my life.' My breath came in rasps and stutters. 'I'm a foolish man. Forgive me. I won't touch you again.'

A strange thing happened then. Though I had let go of Anna's elbows, she hovered in my grasp. Her small fingers encircled my wrists, but her eyes were quite still.

'You're a stupid blind bastard, all right,' she said, cradling both my hands in hers. She put her palms on my shoulders and kissed me very softly on the lips. Then she slammed out of the room.

The fridge continued to hum its madman's hum. Stunned, I scrutinized the shopping list. Apparently we were short of cream, butter and cheese. What damned use, then, were all those cows?

There was a lump under my arm: the laughable book, now fluttering butterfly wings spotted with my sweat. It took me a moment to recognize what it was. It seemed like a century since I had read from it. I opened it unthinkingly and saw through my tears, for the first time, that there was a faint inscription on the fly leaf. The book hadn't belonged to Roper after all.

'To dear Giulia, on the occasion of her twentieth birthday,' the inscription read. 'Affectionately, cousin Laetitia.'

CHAPTER FOURTEEN

After that, Anna ignored me for two nights. It was not that she avoided me in obvious ways – she was simply never to be found. That evening I deduced that she hadn't come back to the house until I'd firmly knotted the cord of her father's dressing gown and was already scraping away at my teeth over the scarred sink in my garret. With immense relief I heard the companionable rumble of pipes down the passage and concluded (erroneously, as it turned out) that she must be home at last, and running a bath.

On Wednesday the 18th I didn't hear the pipes at all and suspected that Anna had camped for the night, with the child, in Harry's lean-to.

Had I been wrong about her? Did she by some remote chance really have no idea about my purpose at Mawle? Or was the truth that she had given up on me; that she no longer cared about the Bellini, or about what her mother would say if I, and it, slipped through her fingers? Had she decided that I was a dead loss, that I'd never find it? If so, then I began to fear again that she was right, and this gut-wrenching dread was even more painful than my resentment of her former vigilance. And what in the world had she meant by calling me blind? Perhaps there was something that I was failing to see, but if that was so I couldn't, even after hours of sozzled melancholy guesswork, arrive at what it was. I felt charmed by Anna's kiss; inebriated. The pressure of her hands on my shoulders, during our brief moment of contact, had been as light as a cloak. Her mouth had tasted dry and faintly sweet, like a child's.

On each of those Annaless evenings Mawle was unspeakably dreary, a vault of chafing shadows and teasing whispers. I wandered from room to room with my bottle of grappa, peering at the pictures, trying to find some sign – but of what, I hardly knew. I confess that I spent the first night of my isolation rolling around wilfully on the Chinese Bed with my shoes on, and the second kneeling in tears against the counterpane of the bed in the Rose Room, scene of our distant tendresse. I felt weary and sick and sad.

When I thought of the Madonna *del prato* as Dürer had described it I realized, too, in the course of those two days without Anna, that I had pathetically misunderstood Bellini's intention in painting the picture. It was only now, when I myself felt so bereaved, that I could see a meaning behind it far darker than anything I'd intuited before. Had I really thought that Bellini intended the painting as a testament to the Virgin as loving creator, as a triumphant imaginative artist of sorts? What nonsense. Her only son was dead; there was no triumph in that. 'Now that I am old myself,' he had said, 'I can only see her as she was when her son had at last left her, the great work of her life, the work of her imagination, behind her, but with the weary days of her earthly life still to be lived.'

If Bellini had thought of the Madonna as an artist, then it was as one who had been destroyed by the sacrifice demanded of her by her art. That 'hard, hollow' gaze of hers, as Dürer called it – what else did it signify, other than that she was utterly spent; defeated? She'd been the casualty of a ruthless force. Call it God, or Love – it was immaterial. By being obedient to her calling she had lost everything. She was a silenced and lonely woman who knew that the price she'd paid had been too high. Here at last was the human truth, stripped of its religious gilding; that was what Bellini had seen. *Sunt lacrimae rerum et mentem mortalia tangunt.* There are tears at the heart of all mortal things. When thrown in the scales with human suffering, art was not just lightweight, it was irrelevant.

I sank into a malaise. What was the point of looking for the picture at all any more? It had vanished, lost forever in that house, just as Anna was lost to me . . . That Wednesday I lay on the chaise longue in the study and read aimlessly, pulling down from the mitred shelves expensive-smelling volumes about agriculture and fishing that bored me into a doze from which I would wake, sweating, my pulse rattling and my face scalded by the sun that streamed through the window. Sometimes during the course of the never-ending afternoon I imagined that I could hear Vicky's petulant voice in the garden and would start up and run to the back door of the kitchen, or through the musty hall to the front door, only to see the glazed emerald lawn, the beds of sleepy foxgloves, the placid lake, unmoving and untouched, like a landscape in a hushed exhibition into which I had rudely crashed.

Harry was still visible, however. In fact, it seemed to me that on Wednesday he was, if anything, more visible than ever. His smug, ruddy face wobbled on the library windowsill at the most unexpected moments, as if his head had somehow managed to detach itself from the figure manning the mowing car that was parked, ready to devour a three-course repast of grass, rubble and weed, at the edge of the tennis court. Why wasn't he taking the afternoon off to watch endless baseball reruns, as he usually did?

'Hiyar, T.J. Work going OK, then? All them pictures doing what you want them to do?'

'Not really, no.' Where's Anna, you blackguard, you Bluebeard? Where have you buried her? I took a swig of grappa from the bottle on the desk. 'Want some?'

He looked quickly about him. 'Yeah, why not? I never touch the stuff, me. But yeah, why not?'

We passed the bottle swiftly back and forth a few times through the window. I realized that we were standing on a stage. Scene One: a country house, two villains. After a few gulps Harry thrust his fingers into the front pocket of his overalls and produced a bloated paper bag. 'Sausage roll?'

'Since you're offering. Eating in a library! Tsk, tsk. But who's to see, eh?' He did not take me up on this question. I persisted. 'Anna about?'

Still no answer. He was engaged in italicized chewing, and had a pensive look in his eye. Perhaps he was trying to remember his lines. A minute later he spat out a flake of pastry. 'Naw. Not today.' He scrunched up the bag and rolled it about between his horned palms before flicking it over the window sill. It landed on the carpet. 'Skirts, eh,' he grunted. 'Never know where you are with 'em.'

'Never know where they are, you mean,' I prompted.

'Yep. That's so. No idea how the world works. Full of cock-eyed ideas.' He ran his tongue around his teeth. 'You take your life in your bleedin' hands if you get involved.'

Was I really having this conversation, or was the drink

making me hallucinate? In a spirit of scientific enquiry I took another slug of grappa.

'Say, T.J.,' said Harry after swallowing heavily, 'you got a missus?'

'No. I've never been married.'

'Bleedin' right. Don't wanna get caught that way meself.' He leaned over the windowsill conspiratorially. 'Take our Anna, now. Pretty girl. Fit too.' He shook his head dumbly, his great mouth turned down at the corners, like a clown who had just been dealt a box on the ear. To my amazement I sensed that somewhere in the fog of his stupidity there lurked a hard lump of genuine confusion and unhappiness. 'Bloody good shag. But she's got a temper on her. Yar, she's a moody one, all right. Just can't be happy. Always wants more. Whass that all about, hey? I mean, whass she up to now? We're meant to be here on the job and she's off buggering about—'

He stopped and looked up at the eaves in scarlet bewilderment. *On the job*. I was certain that this last soliloquy was not part of the script, oh no.

I asked casually, 'You serious about her, then?'

'Hmmmrff. But I'm just about through here. Can't be doing with this all me life. Place is falling apart.' He shoved his cambered shoulder up against the house wall, as if daring it to collapse on him. 'I got plans of me own. Think mebbe I'll make this my last year here. OK, so I've thought of asking her to come with me, but it's only an idea, mind. Sort of try it out.'

'See how it goes?'

'Yeah, thass right.' He looked at me admiringly, as if I'd provided him with a fantastically elegant formula. 'See how it goes, y' know?'

Harry stuck out his hand for the grappa again. In passing it to him my fingers brushed his very briefly. I winked.

'Oi, mate,' he yelped. 'Sod off!'

My God. I nearly choked on a lump of pork. The arrogant oik. Did he think that I was trying to seduce him?

It had occurred to me in the course of this exchange that perhaps they weren't suddenly indifferent to my movements after all. Perhaps they had merely changed their tactics. The details of the manoeuvre, though, had me stumped. Had Anna really gone off somewhere of her own accord? Or was this new regime of *laissez-faire*, of ol' buddies shooting the breeze and boozing it up, a ploy to see what I could achieve if I thought myself unwatched? Well, to hell with them.

My fury at being manipulated by this pair of amateurs was so immense that I couldn't look for the picture at all after that. I deliberately squandered my chance. If anyone was going to be doing any manipulating around here, it would bloody well be me! As the day passed, though, my rage declined into a depression. I ate biscuits and stale crackers from the stash in the pantry, leaving crumbs on the leather inlay of Roper's desk. I pissed luxuriously in every toilet in the house, including, once, the one next to Anna's bedroom, where I felt my cock grow unaccountably hard. A shrivelled cake of pink soap squatted in the sink, embossed with a single hair. Oh Anna, I thought, is this yours?

I did not dare enter her bedroom itself, but darted my shifty, sullying gaze around the door. It was a very little room, with a rattling window and a sloping roof just like my own. The air seemed hot and spicily fragrant, like the innards of a freshly baked apple pie. A pair of tennis shoes sat in a corner, lapping the frayed carpet with two long tongues;

from the closet handle drooped the blue dress that Anna had worn on our Open Day, now reproachfully empty, its sleeves running to sad creases. The coverlet on the bed was only faintly rumpled. Wherever she was to be found, it was not there.

It was in this mood, torpid and tragic, that I discovered the door in the garden wall later that afternoon, like a door drawn with a child's lumpish crayons on a scrap of paper long since tossed away.

The peculiar thing about my wanderings in that deserted house was that, try as I might, I could never again find the room with the carved Italian tester and the peacock screen, or the chalky little antechamber containing the trunk. They had disintegrated, a chimera. I recalled the square of dirty glass behind its sclerotic green blind, and the narrow view of roses clustered behind it, and beyond that, somewhere in the red brick of the house wall, the redder gleam of stained glass – but although I located the chapel easily enough, and sat sulkily in its hectic glow like an imp in a bottle, I couldn't make my way from there to the room that held the trunk. I simply could not do it. The plan of the building baffled me. The long splintered corridor, which I expected to find around several corners, was never there.

In the savage light of day the house, oddly, looked not just battered but blurred: wallpaper torn, boards buckling, door-frames peeling. The canvases which I had admired before, in the initial excitement of the chase, seemed to have shed their clarity, as if a veil hung between them and me. Was it the light, or the dust, or had I fallen into a semi-swoon? I hoiked myself up the oak staircase through a storm of golden motes.

Bottle in hand, I retraced my steps to the Rose Room, and stood before the curtained bed with its acres of inflamed fabric. The counterpane was still wrinkled from my writhings. Where had I gone from here on that first morning, when Anna was out fornicating with Harry?

There weren't one but two doors leading from the room, one to the east and one to the south; both unexceptional, with deep-set panels and dull brass handles. I opened the southern door carefully, a trill of anticipation threading through my bowels. Here was a dressing room smelling of senile face-powder; a modern built-in wardrobe sheltering an arthritic wire hanger, and an upended white melamine footstool with stiff dead legs. A William Morris paper of morose willows was losing its grip on the wall.

It was all simply too sad. Turning back, I chose the eastern door. Behind it stretched a carpeted passage. I staggered along it, less cautious now, trying every knob along the way. Door after door opened into the dumb folds of dressing rooms, bedrooms – even, once, a sleazy bathroom crammed with tortured pipes, where a bulbous, cowed chamber pot moped in the shadow of a chipped enamel bath – some of which seemed vaguely familiar, as if I had once dreamed them, and others fantastically strange. I expected at any moment to turn a corner into the dark wooden corridor of memory, but was always disappointed.

Nor could I, trying a different angle of attack, identify which of several silted windows set into the side of the house that particular window overlooking the wild garden might be. I thrashed about in the undergrowth for a while and got badly scratched, pulling at branches and fiercely unhooking long fronds of ivy, like a seducer unbuttoning his reluctant mistress. I was on the point of giving up when all at once, after tearing away a tightly gartered convolvulus, I stopped in a heap of withered apples, slap bang in front of the musky bark of an old crab squeezed up against a stone wall. To the right of the rotten trunk was a comical little door, just like the secret door in a fairy tale, arched and low, with a lion's head for a handle. It opened to my touch, as I knew it would, and I laughed triumphantly as I went in.

As I looked about I saw that I stood in a courtyard, in a towering tangle of roses. My previous brief glimpse from the high window hadn't prepared me for instant intoxication. Lashed into the black soil were several species of rose bush and tree: soaring, loose-limbed ramblers bowed under white ruffs that deepened through blush to rhodamine at the edges; raspberry-pink damasks, bushy and sleek-leaved; antique chiffon cultivars with tight pale eyes whose scent must once have caressed the skin of the Medicis; a fibrillar mass trussed in feathery foliage that spread from rhubarb red to buffed pewter and bedded itself down among the gilt wands of gigantic nettles in a perfumed, jewelled haze.

In the very heart of this tissue, swallowed up in a rich pulse of colour, was a cracked stone flag topped by a green-winged lion. The mossy left paw of the lion was curved about a shield, and its flexed stone pinions supported a tarnished sundial. This luminous nest was riddled with thorns that tore my hands as I wrenched at it. Above me the windows of the building stared out onto the distant sky, among them one with a pale green eyelid drawn partly down in a sly wink. Yet I somehow knew that, even if I ran back into the house immediately to find that room, it would once again have disappeared.

The lion's face was blotched like a tippler's with black lichen that spread up through its stone mane and along its wings, bursting into sooty scabs on the plinth of the sundial. I scraped away a few flakes with my nail. Along the edge ran a faint inscription which I cleared, steadily dislodging the dry fungus until I had spelled out a scrolled phrase in the corrupt old French of heraldry: *pour lialte' maintenir.*

'Remain faithful.'

Squatting down against the haunch of the beast, I contemplated the interlacing crescents and serifs of the engraved words, but they meant nothing to me. Faithful to whom? Was it a family motto? Who had planted this elaborate garden, and for what purpose? Someone, once, had cared about it; had selected and grafted and pruned the stock to achieve nuances of richness and depth that, untended and unchecked, now ran to the baroque. The cloying disorder, the unguarded overabundance of it all, was a physical and emotional affront. Was I losing my mind? It made me want to cry out in fear and loneliness. My head felt as foul as a cauldron, and the passionate stench that pressed in on me from all sides compounded my sense of disorientation.

I couldn't bear to stay among those roses a minute longer. When I left, the garden outside looked curiously drained and colourless by contrast, as drained as I myself felt. A long, slow summer dusk was falling, thick with birdsong. The house walls were disappearing in an ascent of cool shadows. I lingered irresolutely on the dim lawn. In that desolate moment, as if brought into being by the pressure of my yearning alone, I swear that a figure seemed to take form out of the twilight, a female shape darting through the distant beeches. My hopes surged. I could not see who or what it was, but I had an impression of urgency and of blown-back hair. The figure seemed to pause on the brink of the ditch behind the tennis court before vanishing into the dark field, and in that moment I fancied that I could feel the current of its movement coming towards me as a frantic torsion of the dissolving grass.

Part Two

CHAPTER FIFTEEN

Sitting here in the dim parlour of Puppi's house with the diary open on my lap, I imagine myself in command of a hall of mirrors: the tired sage, about to exit from the present, holding a speckled glass up to the past. Five centuries slowly reverse themselves. The cold grate in the room bursts into an exuberant blaze. Old Buccari, the queen's courtier, sits at his writing table by the hearth, warming his hands and feet at a late autumn fire. As is his custom at the end of every month, he has been going over the household accounts with the steward of his estate. The rents accumulated, tithes and duties paid, and profits made and lost in the sumptuous textile markets of Venice have all been duly entered in the estate ledgers. Now all that remains is to tally any gifts of goods or monies received against such debts to the estate as are still owing. All these items have to be carefully assessed, weighed or counted before being removed to the storerooms, and a clerk perches at the overseer's side with his inkwell and pen at the ready. Also on the table, within easy reach, are a flask of wine and a cup.

'Received from the Conte Marcello, a silver candelabrum.'

'Silver. Bah. What weight?'

'Two pounds, four ounces.'

The old Count coughs derisively. 'That is not much. What else?'

'From the Contarini in Venice, a grey Barbary mare, fourteen hands high.'

'Just the one? Where is this mare?'

'Already stabled, my lord. She is a goodly mount; I saw her myself this morning.'

Buccari waves his hand. 'Very well, let be. Has Her Grace's secretary, Messer Bembo, repaid any part of my loan to him yet? It was made a good twelvemonth ago, or even more.'

'No, Signore. But the Queen's Grace herself has pledged to stand surety for any debts at court still owing to your household, due to the great love she bears her ladyship your daughter.' He rummages in his leather bags and produces a folio of some kind. 'And as a pledge of his eternal good will, Messer Bembo bids me give your lordship this, with his compliments.'

'Indeed? What is it? Aha, of course. That damned book of his. *Gli Asolani*. Fiammetta is fortunate to have such a patron in Her Grace, even if we must suffer this cobbler of couplets as a result.'

By and by there are only the smaller sums still left to account for. The estate manager unwraps a rectangular parcel that has been swaddled in sacking, and places a wooden board about five or six palms in length on the table.

'And here, my lord, we have a Madonna by Messer Bellini, in settlement of the loan of eighty ducats which you were pleased to make to the Master's workshop six months ago.'

Buccari draws himself up, his features alert with interest for the first time. 'Ah, this I must look at. I have been promised something especially fine by Messer Giovann'. Hold it higher so that I may see it.'

The steward does so. The old Count's eyes travel over the

thin scrubland, the gathering sky, finding at last the eyes of the Madonna. He soon averts his own with a discomfited laugh. At length he sits back, ankles crossed on the black and white flagged floor, frowning up at the rose relief on the ceiling. 'Is it some jest, do you think? Why does the old fool send me this? *Al diavolo ogni cosa!* I asked for a Virgin, fresh and sweet, not a hag.'

'Shall I recall the debt again, my lord?'

'No, no,' sighs Buccari, reaching irritably for his cup of wine. 'The old man has clearly lost his skill. We can expect nothing more from that quarter, it would seem. But what to do with this trash?'

'The board is of good quality, if a trifle rough. Poplar, I'd say.'

'Well, then. Note down: one good poplar board. Value?'

'About a hundred and twenty soldi, my lord.'

'Very good. Put it in the storeroom.'

This scene, or one like it, must have played itself out in the room where I now sit. All the facts support it, but the facts in themselves are nothing. It's the historian's job to dream something real into being. Here all around me five hundred years later are the very tendrilled ceiling roses, now leached of colour, the black and white flags of the *sala*, the unlit grate, the tall shutters bolted fast against the heat . . . One by one the last lights on the hill are extinguished. Night falls, the ancient house sighs, the diary slips imperceptibly from my knee. The scholar's nodding head is still. What a neat conclusion this would be, to cop it in this palazzo full of echoes! What a superbly symmetrical death!

But I sentimentalize. This place isn't Palazzo Puppi, it's

Palazzo Pigsty. My bed is never made. A thin layer of grease coats every surface like a preservative. Whatever the little sod pays her, Artemisia isn't worth it. This afternoon I caught her in the kitchen using one of my pink shirts as a duster, and accosted her sharply.

'If you please, Signore, I am on my way to wash your shirt in this pot.' She cocked her elbow at an enamel tureen that had earlier held my lunch, and still sat on the stove, richly redolent of tomatoes.

'In *this* pot? This is a soup pot.'

'*Si*, Signore, but there is no soup in it now.'

'But why are you using a pot at all? What has happened to the washing machine?'

'By your eminence's gracious leave, the washing machine does not exist.'

'Well, what about the washtub, then? Does *that* exist?'

'Why yes, Signore, it exists, but it was stolen.'

You see what I mean. The elegiac is constantly being scuppered by the absurd.

In the cool part of the day I shamble over to the window overlooking the hill and sit there in a sagging armchair. I am immensely tired, so tired that below me there often seems to be only darkness and a murmuring of waters. The years uncoil and slip away like a greased chain through a hatch, going down, down, with a rattle and a groan. Folly. Pain. Longing. Is this all that I can find to say about them? Even my old obsession with the Bellini has loosened its fangs and scuttled off to squat in a corner. How little is left to me to feel, after all.

Asolo is just like a perverse pop-up book, each row of

thickly layered façades, each sudden shallow angle, revealing a crazy and implausible perspective. I turn my head; I look up or down, and the angles collapse into each other, queasily shifting parallelograms. Above me across the rooftops rises the Queen's Castle, stark and high against the south-western sky, its yellow walls strapped with iron braces. Ferns and grasses and stonecrops grow out of the crevices, smearing the single remaining indistinct fresco: an arabesque curling under the slanting roof of the tower, supported by a painted column. The hands of the clock on the broad western face are permanently stopped at twenty-five minutes past twelve. A little way up hangs a cracked sundial which once marked the hours of the lonely Cornaro. Nothing remains of the queen and her court now, or of the people in Roper's diary: they have vanished, just as I have vanished from Mawle. The book claps shut. The remnants of the morning market are scattered across the cobbles – a bit of plastic netting, an upturned crate, the husk of an onion. The present is no more palpable than the past. It is there and not there, comes and goes. Just like that. How can we ever see it for what it is?

There are moments when the temptation to depart from strict verisimilitude and to force the pattern of my confession – to prune, to add a jolly trellis here and an artfully disposed frond there – is very strong. But I always resist it, remembering the advice Bellini gave to Dürer at the end of his Venetian stay of 1506. You will find it in one of the last letters that Dürer wrote to his friend Willibald Pirkheimer from Venice before his return to Nürnberg, the German original having recently resurfaced as a result of an inventory made of the Pirkheimer estate for the Humanist restrospective at the Alte Pinakothek in München.

I myself did not manage to read the letter until October last year, shortly before I was given the sack, and then only in quotation in an academic article. It was a Stygian Friday afternoon in the college staff room. The stale grey spaces of that fastness, with its olde worlde leaded windows and distressed sofas, were ponderous with dead pipe smoke. A tasselled lamp on the bookshelf by the door tried ineffectually to penetrate the fug, but no one bothered to light another: most of my colleagues had already left for the weekend, departing with cheery goodbyes to overnight in log cabins and root under patchwork quilts and down schooners of brandy in the amber hills. Someone had forgotten a bag of golf clubs that stood in a corner, unmuddied, with the price tag still on. Its expensive brace of glittering steel felt like a snub. I had little to do and nowhere to go, and was contemplating the wisdom of returning home to uncork a bottle of Mrs Platt's finest, when Heidi Klug-Birkenstock sailed in. On the flat of her broad palm she bore a stack of term papers, like a waitress serving *Pfannkuchen*. She saw me, naturally, but pretended to be enjoying a rare solitude, settling her ample rear on a groaning sofa with a turbulent sigh and flipping her marking onto a coffee table. She patted the plait of hair stapled to her head, stifled a yawn. Her plump lips gaped a fraction, like the split cherries on a pie. Then she squared her round shoulders and raised her doughy chin at me.

'Ah, Thomas Joseph! I didn't see you over there. Who are you hiding from?' She laughed fruitily. 'No weekend plans, then? I sent you a letter a few days ago by internal mail. Did you get it?'

'I was about to go home, actually. To do a little reading, a little writing. And yes, I did get your letter.'

'Good, good! Does that mean that we may expect something in print from you soon?'

'Oh, very soon, I hope. Although I cannot, of course, pretend to be as, ah, *fecund* on the research front as you are, dear Heidi.' Her raisin-like eyes grew, if possible, harder and tighter. 'No,' I continued, 'my output must necessarily be more limited. I fear that I have been trained in a different tradition, and – well – just possibly serve a different master. My interest, always, is in truth – in scrupulous truth, and those assertions that may be empirically tested. I venture nothing in print until I am assured that it rests on a bedrock of solid fact. I am not a hack. I am keenly aware that it is my good name that is at stake whenever an article appears from my pen, and I always endeavour to maintain the highest standards of scholarly—'

'Oh, whatever,' snaps Heidi. 'Look, just see to it that you get something out there before you finally retire, OK? I have something here that might give you a jump start.' She digs around in her handbag and pulls out a scruffy scroll of some kind which she tosses to me. 'You've been ruminating Bellini's influence on Dürer for years now, haven't you? So go chew on this.' She cackles unbecomingly, gathers up her stuff, and steers her big butt out into the October dusk.

I am left holding the latest copy of an abstruse arts journal, rolled back to an article about Dürer's sojourn in Venice. There is a reprint of Dürer's dreadlocked self-portrait at thirty-five, those overexposed praying hands, and the *Melancholia*. The text is slight, a mere scaffolding showcasing a 'surprise missive', recently unearthed from the München archive, which the artist wrote to Pirkheimer at the end of October 1506. I begin to read, and the prolapsed sofas, the stink of pipe smoke, and the menacing glint of golf clubs all disappear.

The autumn is drawing to a close; the chill cast of winter steals across the Venetian plain. Christmas is just around the corner, and so too is the inevitable return to Nürnberg: the choking swirl of wood smoke in the Stube; Agnes's worn wooden pattens lying in their pool of dirty snowmelt under the settle; the festive carp, its doleful eye glazed, frying in a pan. Dear God, prays Dürer, spare me my wife's unhappiness. Spare me the darkness and the loneliness.

> Thanks to Bellini's patronage I have completed several commissions for the exiled Queen at Asolo: a portrait of her dwarf – a hunchback with a cruel habit of whipping the palace dogs with his staff, so that the hall seems forever to ring with the angry jangle of his bells – and another of her pet lady-in-waiting, the Contessa Fiammetta, daughter of the Conte Buccari; a long nosed, leather-faced girl in honour of whose marriage Messer Bembo wrote his much praised book of love poetry last year, which I regret to say I have not read. I apologized for my barbarous ignorance of this renowned *Gli Asolani*, which all have hailed as a masterpiece of refined courtly verse. But Bellini merely snorted, saying, 'Be comforted, *Bello*, by the thought that whatever the fashion of wasting God's daylight may be at Court, whether by playing the lute, writing love poetry, or sitting in the sun all day, we are working men and will have no time for it, or for conversation about it either.' He so delighted Her Grace with reports of my industry that I have never

been called on to *dissipate my talents in idle chit-chat*, or *asolare*, as he dubs it.

The Queen was greatly pleased with my work, and clapped her small hands before saying sadly: 'Signore, in your going the hard North will gain a distinction which the poor South must lose.' I replied that I would gladly remain, but that my wife wanted me, and Her Grace seemed equally pleased with this answer, and invited me to walk a little way with her in the palace gardens.

I wish that you could see this absurd little court. We have nothing like it at home. I pity Her Grace, a widow and an exile, obliged to make merry with these Italian fools and smilingly call a kingdom what is in truth a prison. She is surrounded all day by scented fops and philosophers; by a retinue of courtiers who are barely past childhood and are perpetually on heat for each other; by pipers and lutenists and fiddlers, who strut about playing so feelingly that they weep over their own music. The pleasure gardens are very fine in their way: sectioned into sparkling flowerbeds like trays of sweetmeats, shaded by wild fig and nut trees, among which a swarm of gardeners flit all day with rakes and wheelbarrows. The grounds are as fragrant, even in late autumn, as a perfumer's. Yet it tired and irritated me to stroll in them, and after Her Grace had dismissed me I felt vexed.

I confess that this country baffles me. I am constantly astonished that such an abandoned love of the physical and profane should have produced an art that is so spiritual and pure. Bellini scolds me, saying, 'To magnify the essence of a thing is not to kill it, but to reveal it. If you are to become a great painter then you must love this flower *because* it is a flower, this tree because it is a tree. They mean themselves, nothing more. You must paint what you see, not what you wish to see.'

But know, my dear Pirkheimer, that I have silenced all those here who said that I was only good at engraving, and did not know how to work with paints. My Madonna for the German merchants is at last done, and it is such a one as I have never succeeded in painting before. After I made my first sketches, many months ago now, Bellini pressed his own oils into my hands, urging me forward with words that went to my thirsty soul like wine. '*Giovanetto*,' he said, 'if you would only forget your pursuit of symbols, and revel in things themselves, you would easily surpass an old man like me.'

And so my German Madonna is a glowing girl enthroned in a green field, surrounded by those pink putti of which Giambellin is so fond, who are about to give her a jewelled diadem like a starred honeycomb. The Holy Father is in the picture, and so are our Emperor and his colossal nose, and every blessed member of my munificent body of sponsors. I have piled up my merchants in a pyramid of red and gold and blue and crowned every man jack of them with blushing rose garlands, the Pope and the Emperor too. And I have put myself in also, dressed in my new winter coat, ready to depart for Nürnberg. And next to myself, my dear friend, I have put you.

Bellini was not wrong. My *Madonna of the Rose Garlands*, as all here have come to call it, is a success. The Doge himself has come in person to view the panel. I am known throughout Venice; I have money in my pocket at last.

But alas, my dear Pirkheimer, the truth is that although the picture is good, it falls short of my imagining. I admit this only to you. I am plagued by the memory of the work that Bellini showed me in September, and know that mine is only a clever manipulation, not yet the fully realized vision as it might be; not a living woman. On looking in the glass after completing my painting I found a grey hair on my head, which was produced by sheer misery and frustration.

Like Dürer, I admit to having once been easily annoyed by the trivial circumstantial details of which our daily life is so inconveniently full. Bellini taught Dürer to let go of his dependence on contour and line. Bellini taught Dürer naturalism. And yet, I quibbled – do we really have to include carp? Wheelbarrows? Art must imitate life, to be sure, but isn't a little editing, I wondered, permitted to stress its essential outlines? It is only in the last few weeks, as a result of the time I spent at Mawle, that I have begun to wonder whether such ephemera might not be as essential to the overall composition of my narrative as Bellini's miraculous Madonna herself. Isn't it at least possible that everything – not only the deliberate brush stroke, the sure line, the achieved form, but equally, the fly buzzing at the kitchen window, the banging of the garden gate, the smell of fish frying; the most insignificant things, in short – should in fact be part of one concealed pattern? And who am I to impose my own pinched sense of order on this bounty? I have never before or since had such an overwhelming awareness of the world as a machine, an automaton, as I did while I was in that house: one of those fantastic, arch, remorseless engines that you see in old engravings, all cupolas and turrets and blasts of the trumpet. What chance does art finally stand against this fearful cosmic machinery? Art records only the accidents of life, never the process. The world remains intractable.

So let me try as faithfully as possible to reproduce the pattern that was beginning to emerge while I was at Mawle, primitive and raw and rambling as it is. Here, still resting on my lap in Puppi's darkening parlour, is the diary. And here, falling noiselessly into time's waiting furrow, is the moment in which Roper first speaks to the girl who will later become his wife. Did he love her? Was she also his victim, as Anna was mine? It's all a blur. And I see, now, that there is no way out. I must tell you about the oddest and most inconvenient thing I came across next while all alone in Mawle House that Wednesday, as I was reading this entry.

On the 8th of September Roper records that he'd outmanoeuvred Mrs Bronson. On the previous day, after continued skilful pressure from him, she had secured and accepted an invitation on his behalf to the Palazzo Buccari. Their party was joined at the last minute by 'an elderly and rather well-known poet of her acquaintance' – another Englishman like himself, writes Roper – who was in Asolo to finish his latest book.

The little knot of expatriates walked in state to the great wooden doors of Ca' Buccari, which were crowned with a weather-beaten coat of arms bearing a faded phoenix. The three olive-green shutters above the massive balcony overlooking the piazzetta were closed, displaying torch-shaped bosses. Thick iron grilles barred the low square windows of the portico. The place filled Roper with such a sense of foreboding that he almost wished he had not come, but the bolts were already being withdrawn. The doors began to creak, and he crossed a courtyard into a wide bare *sala* that was empty of everything but shattering sunlight. A frowsy little maid led the group through two enormous portals of turquoise and gold with cast gilt bronze handles, into the drawing room. This was a large neglected parlour with a high stuccoed ceiling covered in sheaves of painted roses and sunflowers, and a floor of worn black and white hexagonal flags. The shutters of the far window were half closed, revealing ancient stables and an avenued garden. A crooked-nosed Italian youth leaned against a square writing table, talking earnestly in low whispers with a child who had her back to the visitors. In the middle of the apartment gaped a deep marble fireplace without a fire, in front of which sat a stiff, very upright person with a narrow freckled face surrounded by a cluster of dry brown curls, whom Roper immediately recognized as the lady from the carriage.

'My dear Mrs Bronson,' she exhaled, in an accent that was faintly transatlantic. 'I am so very pleased to see you. Julia, please pay attention.' This was directed at the child, who turned around, revealing herself to be not a child at all, but the young woman with the face like a Lippi who had waved at Roper. She faced the visitors with lowered eyes. Mrs B swept ahead and kissed both ladies on the cheek. The ramrod lady turned to the poet.

'We have so longed, of course,' she continued, smiling frugally, 'to meet the illustrious Mr Robert Browning. No sir, do not deny it. Your immortal poetry has a permanent place in my heart.'

Browning! Robert Browning! I had to read the passage twice before I could take in the sense of it. Browning – colluder in my secret childhood suffering, my shame!

'Ah, my dear madam, you flatter me. Which poem in particular?' asked Mr Browning solemnly, taking her hand.

'Why, all of them. The dear Lord knows, I read a verse of yours every night. I could not fall asleep, otherwise.'

Mr Browning was momentarily nonplussed.

'And this,' the upright lady went on, ignoring the Italian youth and turning to the childlike young woman, 'this is my cousin, the Contessa Julia Buccari.' She gave the name an English, or rather an American, pronunciation. 'Julia, stand up.'

The girl did as she was told and executed a silky curtsey.

'I have raised her,' the stiff lady said, 'as far as possible in the American tradition.'

'I am very pleased to have made your acquaintance,' said the young Contessa gravely, in near-perfect English.

Yes, there was no mistake: it *was* Browning. That name was still, to me, suggestive of an embarrassing foulness, of a personal, private stain; of the impossibility of innocence. Of a misshapen incarnation of tenderness. Of need, that most guileless form of desire. Had I imagined it? I had not. Oh God, oh God, here it was again . . .

'Mrs Bronson whispered to me,' wrote Roper, 'that Mr Browning came to Asolo at her invitation and intends to spend the entire autumn here as her near neighbour, so that he might finish his latest volume of verses. The Poet once loved Asolo as a young man, and this visit represents a communion with the past – a *spiritual reawakening*, no less.'

The black letters on the open page seemed to dart and wriggle; to raise their snouts inquisitively, like tiny snakes. The crooked-nosed boy came in with wine. As Roper drank, the little Contessina slipped out of the room.

'Don't *you* find the heat here excessive, Miss Spragg?' I asked dully. 'I believe that you are used to milder climes.'

'Miss Spragg,' observed Mr Browning, gravely stroking his silver beard, 'is clearly a staunch rose of New England, whom not even the persuasive Italian sun has been able to vanquish.'

Miss Spragg rewarded him with one of her Lenten smiles. Then she turned to me. 'You must have a fine rose garden at Mawle, Mr Roper. Your great English country houses always have roses.'

'No, indeed, Miss Spragg,' I admitted. 'There is no rose garden at Mawle.'

Robert Browning was evidently a slyboots practised in ambiguous flatteries, a socially promiscuous prick. My God, how that poet got about! Here to finish his book, was he? Well, in Asolo, too, the old swaggerer was talking, always talking . . . I vented a torrent of sour air: in my shock I had forgotten to breathe.

The conversation lapsed into desultory chat about hybrids and strains. After a few moments of this Roper excused himself and wandered to the *sala*. The tall room with its stone walls was chilly and still, lit by wax candles that leaned spinelessly on the sideboard. There was no one there but the

Contessina, who was curled up in a blistered chair, chewing her thumbnail. She was reading a book.

'Julia,' called out Miss Spragg tartly, 'what are you doing? Come and converse with the company. Our subject is horticulture.'

The Contessina looked up at me in bewilderment.

'Please do not disturb yourself,' I said roughly, realizing as soon as I'd opened my mouth that it was I who was doing the disturbing. I felt inexplicably angry – with myself? With her? 'You were quite lost in your book.'

'It is only a girls' history book,' she replied, getting quickly to her feet and pushing past me. The bone of her bare elbow grazed me as she did so. I noticed with a tremor that her movements were naturally quick and lithe, like those of a young cat. 'Excuse me, my cousin wants me.'

'A young woman who reads history by choice!' exclaimed Browning when we had rejoined the circle by the cold fireplace and the Contessina had shyly explained her absence. 'Now there's a delightful rarity. Let's have a look at this book. Ah, hum. *Historic Girls*. I don't believe I know it.'

'Julia is very well educated,' said Miss Spragg. 'I taught her myself.'

'Why, then, she must be,' Browning assented.

The girl flushed again with pleasure, her foreign little face looking animated for the first time, and unfairly beautiful.

'Julia speaks English almost like a home-born American,' said Miss Spragg.

'High praise indeed,' returned Browning. 'Now, I pose the

question: if the Contessa Giulia were a rose, what sort of rose would she be? A Musk rose? A slip of Maiden's Blush?'

'A very pink one, I'd say,' suggested Miss Spragg, smiling archly at me.

The following Tuesday Miss Spragg and the little Contessina called on Mrs Bronson, and it was decided, at Miss Spragg's polite but ruthless insistence, that the Contessa Buccari should join the other young people for luncheon at La Mura that Saturday.

When I read the above I was dismayed. What was Browning doing here? How was *this* part of the larger pattern of my search for the Bellini? He'd added a sour footnote to what was, in every other way, an exalted undertaking. Why couldn't I excise the past? I winced as I paced the boards of my attic room, stung to the pith by the mannerless intrusion of this overpraised wordsmith into my life at Mawle.

And what about Roper and the Contessa? In this entry with its random gossip about rose gardens I tried to discern the distant rumbling of wheels, the encroaching shadow. Fate, I thought, should be a terrible engine, unstoppable steel.

But I was kidding myself. I now know that it's all pleasantries, all carp and wheelbarrows and soup pots, and that is how I will have to tell it.

CHAPTER SIXTEEN

As I went downstairs to forage in the pantry on the morning of Thursday the 19th after a second restless solitary night, I found Anna and Vicky sitting at the kitchen table, calmly eating toast. Anna's nut brown hair was looped back in a sensible bun. She wore her stolid look and her gardening clothes: bobbled socks, baggy dungarees, and a plaid shirt with an enormous collar under which her clavicles tumbled like dropped matchsticks. The child was dressed in a decaying silver lace evening gown and satin slippers: a little ghoul about to go to a dance. In front of Anna lay an open newspaper, propped up by a loaf of bread.

'Hi, Dr Lynch,' she said matter-of-factly, as if Tuesday's scene in the kitchen had never happened. 'Did you sleep OK?' The ancient toaster, a chrome beast with a gut of violent red coils and an armoured exoskeleton of black dials, spat out another round of toast with a snarling *krrr-ching*.

I was impressed by Anna's lack of embarrassment at her absence, and looked at her long and curiously.

'Oh, I'm sorry,' she yawned, squinting vacantly at the charred spine of the monstrosity. 'Have some toast?'

Vicky stared at me, winding her black hair around a buttery finger. 'We got sour cherry jam in London. You can have some. Anna said it would be delish, but it's *foul*.'

'Oh, shut up,' said Anna, turning back to the paper. 'I wish you were back at school.'

'I wish I was too.'

'Wish you *were*.'

'That's what I said.'

'Sweet Jesus,' said Anna, sighing powerfully enough to expel a lung while circling something fiercely on the page in front of her with a bitten biro. 'Cherry tomatoes look good but they have to be fucking *forced*. Pardon my French. In bloody little cold frames.'

'Ah, like the toes of Chinese courtesans,' I jabbered. A berserk joy was carousing through my parched heart as I realized that she really had been about her business somewhere, and not secretly spying on me. 'My dear. Were you in *London* just recently?'

'Yes – we got back last night. Didn't you get my note?'

I wondered with a tingle if it was Anna, after all, whom I had seen in the garden at dusk.

'Note? What note was there to get? If there was one to get I would surely have gotten it.'

Anna ignored my levity. 'Well there, of course,' she stabbed at the air between us with an apocalyptic finger, 'on the fridge.'

'The fridge, why yes!' In a thunderclap of happiness I saw that the shopping list now read, 'We need: cream, butter, cheese. Hey Dr Lynch gone to Covent Garden Show, meet Minnie, back Thurs maybe Fri. Cheers Anna.' Ah, Fri! Maybe Fri, indeed! As yet it was only Thurs, prematurely transfigured Thurs, and she had returned a day early and so ended my suffering by a single stroke of pure grace.

'Any good, the show, no?' My voice sounded high and taut.

'Oh, so-so. We checked out the veg.'

'Good for you! Did you find any?'

Now Anna was mirthfully grave, like a woman trying to smooth down her dress in a strong draft. 'Just a few bits here and there.' She laughed out loud. 'The whole show was fruit and veg, you twerp.'

'Delighted to hear it. You can never have too many vegetables, you know.' My obscenely expanding joy threatened to engulf the table, the toaster, every cretinous crumb. 'Tell me their names.' If I could have lured her into the circumference of my arm, her gabbling head on my shoulder, her restless hand in my lap, my transfiguration would have been complete.

'Well, we did see a lot of tomatoes. But Minnie thinks asparagus would be better. And maybe those things that look like old ladies' boobs.'

'Aubergine,' intoned Vicky, wiggling her silvery bottom.

'My dear, are you about to become a market gardener?' The thought of this girl trying to fatten the family purse by tilling the ornamental lawns was laughable, absurdly noble, and almost more than I could bear.

'Yes, why not? I've got to do *something*. Our Open Day was such a disaster. It's not a big thing. I'm just going to make our garden productive. Throughout history the home landscape was expected to produce as well as please.' I studied her from the corner of my eye. She spoke with utter conviction. 'Why should that be so different now?' she continued. 'Most people today seem to think that only greenery – only ornamental greenery – will do.'

'And it won't?'

'Oh, no! We've become lazy, we've got used to buying

everything and growing nothing. Our palates have become—' She gave me a limpid look.

'Bland.'

'Yes! They're bland. *Disgustingly* bland.'

'I see – so we at Mawle are about to start producing our own crops.'

I was gratified that Anna took that 'we' in her stride. 'Well, not really. Not really each and *every* crop. I mean, many people seem to feel that a vegetable garden needs to be nutritionally complete, you know, with everything in it, whether they actually like to eat those vegetables or not.'

'I loathe parsnips,' said Vicky.

'So do I,' I admitted.

'OK, fine, so we won't grow those!' Anna's face shone as if the Holy Ghost were moving in her. 'But why not plant the things people shell out mega bucks for at the supermarket? Like asparagus. All those soggy sticks you get in the veg section. We could grow our own and market them for a knock-down price. If you're going to expend time and energy on your landscape, why not have the landscape reward you for that time and energy in return?'

'Yay!' I carolled. 'The Garden Productive!'

She regarded me warily, suspicious of mockery, but the amused adoration in my face must have won her over. 'Yes, that's just what Minnie called it!' She sat back expansively, her little paps almost heaving. She was magnificent, august.

'Very well, my dear,' I laughed, sliding my slippery hand over hers. 'When do we start digging up the back garden?'

Oh, Anna was a fool all right, but her foolish enthusiasms had a way of irradiating her, of making her fizzle from within, of changing her very substance. Whenever she came into a room I was swept through with a sense of sheer possibility and ridiculous anticipation. I didn't want to watch her, but I simply could not stop myself.

An instance: it is later on the morning of Anna's return, and I am fanning myself at the kitchen table with our dirty washing, of which I have now taken charge. Anna enters from the garden, flushed with sunlight, and her salmon and fawn beauty excites me beyond (for once) words.

'My God!' she whistles. 'It's so bloody hot! Should we install air conditioning, I wonder? Minnie says it's a waste of money. What do you think? Maybe just a small vent in the kitchen?'

'I don't think air conditioning works that way,' sniggers Vicky, who is sprawled under the table in her vest and knickers, reading a comic book.

A ravishing tickling sensation scurries along my ribs. 'Oh, the child knows, indeed she does. Doesn't air conditioning involve miles of tubing, and a reservoir in the cellar full of some dangerous substance such as liquid nitrogen?'

'Perhaps,' Anna says, doubtfully. 'Yes, perhaps you're right. Could it explode and kill us, I wonder? How on earth would we get it up the staircase? Could we pipe it up?'

Her whole body collapses, and with it, my reserve. Oh Anna, only a feeble joke. Forgive me my facetiousness. I only meant to. And she smiles at me, infinitely patient, infinitely forgiving, as if she's always been used to these small cruelties.

At these times she had a painfully introspective look, as if she were battling to turn the grit that I had fired into her quivering centre into something that might yet be valuable, some precious thing that she could offer me in time. How desperately she wanted to prove herself! A few hours after the above exchange I caught her in the library, balancing one of the lugubrious volumes of Murray's dictionary in the crook of her reed-like arm, furtively looking up, it transpired, some word that I had used earlier that afternoon which she hadn't understood.

'Conducting some research for your degree, my dear?'

'Well, not really.' She fumbled with the whispering pages of the *OED*. 'I'm just, um, checking something, you know.'

'Don't let me disturb you.' I sat down at Roper's desk (for by now I no longer worked at the makeshift table which Anna had set up for me at the window, but had taken up residence in the centre of the room) and shuffled my papers about a bit. Stained with sunlight, they crackled under my fingers like tea leaves. 'Item: one Flight Into Egypt, perhaps by Biscaino,' I read. 'One Capriccio, quite fine. Possibly Panini?' How dry, how ridiculous the words were. I stared at them so fervidly that they dwindled into random fissures, cracks in the texture of the paper itself. It was no good. My imagination had been breached, and was now wholly ruled by the fused image of a colossal, winsome Anna-Madonna.

A blast of impatience tore through me: I longed, more than ever, to possess the Bellini. Fragments of the letter in which Dürer had first mentioned the painting of that other, more worn woman came back to me with a sere and chastening pain. I had read it so many times that I could recite it word for word.

Again I smelled the stagnant Venetian evening, so unlike the crisp pine-and-smoke scented nights of Nürnberg, rippling behind the bubbled glass of Dürer's window. I could see a canal-borne insect insert a fine proboscis into

Dürer's cheek as he wrote, punctuating it with a comma of blood.

On that distant autumn afternoon of 1506, Dürer had been so mesmerized by the otherworldly verisimilitude of the picture, its extraordinary skill, that he had for a while failed to spot what was most obvious about it.

> I gazed and gazed, and then I saw it. 'You have made the Madonna a tired old woman,' I said. 'Yes,' said Bellini, 'and her lap is empty.'
>
> It was so – the plainest detail of all had entirely escaped me.
>
> I simply could not see how it was done. The irises of that suffering face seemed when viewed from a certain angle to protrude from the canvas, but the centres were flat, even vacant.
>
> 'What dark art have you used here?' I asked him. 'What witchcraft, to make her so sad and so uncannily alive? You have studied some secret lore. Tell me, for I am ready to be sworn to it.'
>
> 'Why none,' replied Bellini with a chuckle, 'I have used only oils. We must find the unearthly in the earthly; there is no other way. Next time, *Bello*, why not simply try to paint what is *in front of your nose*?' And at that he laughed loudly.

A finch flew past the window, its wings on fire. I too wanted to laugh. In spite of the painting's cruel intimation of the mortality of things the whole business of living seemed, in that instant, monumentally simple and light. We must find the unearthly in the earthly. No other way. No other way . . . I glanced up at Anna. How young she still was! Surely she deserved happiness; surely her unassuming life should never be smudged by bitterness or disappointment? Her glittering hair was spread over her shoulders like a veil. Her timid breasts rose, felicitously scooped, from the blue bodice of her dungarees. Her eyes flickered like stars. As I watched her she seemed to gain in power, in presence, to absorb and magnify my emotion until it threatened to transcend us both in its intensity. My Anna! I was overcome by such a fervent, breathless sense of veneration that I felt I would surely swoon at any moment. The room was full of sun and the hot emerald smell of recently cut summer grass. Still Anna turned the rice paper pages of the dictionary. To my surprise I saw that she was scowling, almost on the point of tears.

'Shit, shit,' she mewled. 'It's just not in here.'

'Highly unlikely, my dear,' I wheezed. 'The correct spelling of most things can be found in there, as long as you already know how to spell them. An irony, that, I've always thought. Anyway, may I be of some help?'

Anna winced. 'Maybe. But promise not to laugh.'

I arranged my face into its most earnest lines. 'I wouldn't dream of it. Let's have a look, then.' The book on her slender loins lay open at *fasces*, a bundle of rods with a projecting axe blade, emblem of authority; *fascia*, a long flat surface of wood or stone, a covering, a façade; and *fascinate*, for which I could effortlessly have expanded and rewritten and illustrated the definition.

'You see? It's just not there. What a *cheat*.'

'What is the word? Might you give me a teensy clue?'

'Oh, you know, that word you used this morning. That

word. You said you were sorry for being so fas – so fas – Oh Christ! You're laughing! You promised not to laugh!'

'Dear girl, dear girl! If I ever hurt you again, deliberately or un-deliberately, if such a word exists, then beat me.' I took her dirty hot hand in my big mitt, and brought it down on my own head. 'Here, beat me hard, like this!'

After Anna had pummelled me once or twice as directed she began to smile, and to smear her face thoroughly with snot and smooth down her hair, and the treacherous weight of the dictionary slid from her lap and was quite forgotten.

But I do not want you to think that Anna knew nothing, that she was ignorant: far from it. It was simply that I could not find, or did not know, the words for what she knew. In the three weeks I lived at Mawle I must have sat with her for hours in the garden, watching her work. She could train a crooked vine and espalier a twisted shoot, and fondle blown heads out of the tightest bud, yakking all the while about the stinginess of the electrical store she had frequented for the past three years in Didcot, some five miles away, which refused to do a free repair job on the vacuum cleaner they'd sold her (a psychedelic machine, covered in neon plastic piping, which sat lifelessly in the kitchen like a clone of the Pompidou Centre); the surprising pain of having her ears pierced six weeks previously – here she twiddled the tiny gold studs in her rosy lobes with mucky fingers – and the teenage slag in the village newsagent's, who pretended that the last copy of the Sunday paper had been sold even though Anna could see with her own peepers that there was still a whole stash behind the counter.

'She had her eye on Harry for a long time, of course, but he wasn't having any of her. Stupid cow.'

'I should hope not. My dear, is he true to you?'

'Oh well, you know. Are they ever?'

I thought about this for a while. 'Do your ears still hurt?'

'Yes, off and on. Harry says they're dead cute now.'

I know, yes, I know. And yet – those flowering foxgloves, like exploding rods of giant popcorn; the dolphin-budded delphiniums; the snouted orange snapdragons; the shy, thirsty peonies, which she raised as if by magic out of the dumb earth – no, don't tell me that she wasn't wise, wise beyond my simple understanding! Whenever I think of Anna, it is of a bent figure, its slender back stitched with perspiration long before it was stitched with pain under my hands on that last night, and the murmur of her voice, irrelevant but entirely hypnotic, in a green shade.

Why had she never left Mawle? Was this isolated life of gardening and village gossip really enough for her? It pained me that she seemed resigned to act day in and day out as nursemaid to a child who wasn't even an immediate relation of hers. Oh, I blamed Maddalena for manipulating her – but I also blamed Anna's father, John Roper, with his casual masculine contempt for his daughter, for having stunted her in the first place. No bloody good to him, was she? Evidently he'd thought she wasn't, and this was the result. At some stage in her girlhood she'd been deformed by a carelessly unkind hand, pounded into ductility, stripped of a sense of expectation. Perhaps Papa had never actually laid a finger on her in anger, but there were, as I knew, other equally effective ways of bruising a soul.

Anna was barely educated, of course: the degree was a joke; that essay on the feminist cinema of the 1940s, which she was supposed to be writing to meet a deadline that had long since expired, never forthcoming. She would sit in the kitchen for hours at a time, making laborious notes in her bubbled handwriting from the same tatty textbook, trying to breathe life into this cadaver. When I tried to engage her in conversation about her labours, though, she was reluctant, or perhaps just genuinely not interested. Who could blame her? 'The focus of this corpse [no: course] is on both the screenings and readings of women in films, covering a wide range of positions . . .'

I was learning, by now, to keep a straight face. On her file paper, my very modern Madonna had copied out, very neatly, a catechism of filmography. 'Q: Is anything ever *necessary* in a film? A: No, we should ask: what is this *doing* in the film. Q: How much attention should we give to any one element of a film? A: There may be, and often is, some irritating aspect or element of a film, and we may still decide to give the film rather than the distraction a reading.'

'What about those films that consist of little more than a series of distractions and annoyances?' I asked. I never did learn to shut up! 'How do we read those, eh? No, no – don't try to give me an answer' – for she had already begun to search, reverently, head bowed down, for the solution somewhere on the page.

At last I couldn't stand it any more. She was so dense: it should have been easy for me to get her to do what I wanted! Removing the file paper from her hands, I looked at her squarely.

'Anna,' I said, 'this must stop. I meant what I said in the kitchen the other day. I need your help; I need you on my side.'

'Tom, I am on your side!' she laughed. 'But how could I

possibly help you any more than I already am? Of course I'm happy to muck in with your research if you need an assistant, but I really don't know much about art at all. Plants are my thing.' She chewed her pen. 'Maybe I could number all the pictures for you? Would *that* help? There should be some sticky labels somewhere. No. Shit. I think we used them for jam. Shall I run over to the shops? Could you lend me a few quid?'

Christ. It was hopeless. At the end of each day, feeling variously full of pity, enchanted or vaguely exasperated, I would leave her and go up to my room. At times Anna's passiveness could seem annoyingly like strength. In herself she was completely inexpressive; why, then, couldn't I bend her more easily to my will? It was like picking up mercury with my bare hands, and the strangest thing of all was that her fluidity made me feel toothless and tame.

How fastidious and dull everything was in my hutch: the narrow bed, my thin valise (for I no longer hid my notes, but left them, loosely concealed, on the desk in the library – who could see them but Anna?), my brush and comb parallel and inert on the edge of the sink. The cake of brown soap never seemed to get any smaller, or to release any smell particular to itself. My second jacket hung on the peg behind the door, limply. In those hours, when I was alone with myself, only the mattress on the bed, concealing Roper's diary in its maw, seemed to contain any real life. And then, like an unsatisfied lover who'd been teased and titillated beyond endurance, I would be overcome by impotent yearning for the Bellini.

CHAPTER SEVENTEEN

Our asparagus, the Mawle asparagus, came as a hank of sprawling, skinny roots with a centre full of alveolar buds, shrink-wrapped and all the way from Spain. I looked up 'asparagus' in Roper's funereal dictionary and found that it was an herbaceous perennial boasting a root system with a megalomaniac drive to expand. The immature edible shoots sprout from the lung-like crown buried in the soil. Oddly enough it is the male plants that are supposed to live longer and yield higher than the females; this is because the female plants spend energy on forming flowers and setting seeds and other fripperies of that sort, taking away from the metabolic reserves directed to the roots. The male plants, on the other hand, are tenacious and produce rippling rows of spears.

To increase the vigour of the crop it is best to transplant a one-year-old cutting that has been seeded elsewhere. With good weed control and fertility, an asparagus bed established in this way can yield generations of productive harvest. Or, as Anna put it with the new, messianic look in her eye, 'A weekend's worth of effort spent planting an asparagus bed will produce pounds of delicious shoots for twenty years or more. But,' she chanted from *Get Your Greens*, a shiny coffee table book, prodigal of illustration and scant of print, that had winged its way to her through the ether from a virtual bookshop and was now our authority on these matters, 'do not start from older root stock. This has been proven to delay production.'

She was standing at the mouth of the shallow trench that Harry was digging at her behest in the field behind Mawle. It was the 20th of August, Friday morning. Harry's sun-darkened ribs were irrigated with rivulets of sweat.

'You can start from old stock or from tiddlers,' he grunted. 'It won't make a blind bit of difference. This is the wrong time for planting. And this is the wrong soil. Nothing will grow.'

He was right; even I could see that. One of the most disturbing things about this whole venture was that, in her determination to generate the cash that Mawle so obviously needed, Anna's instincts as a gardener seemed to have deserted her.

'Look, just dig, OK? The book says that it shouldn't actually be *cold*, and it's not cold, is it?'

'BLOODY right it's not.' Vicky sat with her legs crossed by the side of the strip of turned earth, wiping her beaded nose. The sun above us was brazen and hard. Beyond the long, limp grass of the field, across the shrivelled ditch, the walls of Mawle were rawly rouged; the old collapsed tennis court crudely daubed with nodding jasmine. The air seemed at once bright and swollen, like an overfilled balloon, and there was a menacing drone of insect traffic underfoot.

'Watch yourn mouth, girl,' Harry said, without pausing in his toil.

'Oh shut up, Harry,' snapped Anna. 'She's just a child. Why must you always be so mean to her?'

Harry goes on digging. And then this happens. Anna stretches her arm across the pit to rumple his damp hair, but his hand flies up spontaneously from the spade to ward off her touch. Anna stops dead, her face stiffened into a welt of astonishment and terror. The spade stabs at the soil, flies up, stabs down. Harry's sweating back is rounded to its long shaft like a gravedigger's. The child promptly lies down in the dirt and makes an angel in the scattered soil, expecting, wanting, a scolding. But no one says a word. We are as tensed as a group of mourners in a churchyard. At long last Anna folds her hands and bows her petrified head.

That time seems crazy to me now. And indeed, how difficult it is to trace the true pattern of things. It is difficult enough to do it with the benefit of hindsight, while sitting here in Puppi's parlour; it was almost impossible to do it in the lived moment, at Mawle. All my usual tools are, were, inadequate for the job. Now, of course, knowing what I know about the shadowy, fumbled events leading up to James Roper's hasty marriage, and about Anna's own paternity, I can see the crass ironies that eluded me at the time. *Transplanted seedlings.* Oh, ha, ha. What a rude, crude pattern. What a graceless motif. Is time really such a clumsy artisan that it must aim for the most obvious, most unmitigated effects? Apparently so.

That Friday afternoon Anna asked me an apparently trivial question to which I should have paid much more attention than I did. She was 'tidying', as she called it, picking up various items of clothing that Vicky had sloughed off, like so many shed chrysales, around the library.

'Dr Lynch. When you're done here – will you go home?'

'Well now, I can't stay at Mawle forever, can I?'

'I suppose not. Of course not.' She gnawed her finger ends. 'Will you go back to America or – or Ireland, I mean?'

Anna was loitering, I remember, near the desk. My, it was good to have her back, doing ordinary Annaish things! She leaned her hip against the wood; she was holding a red cardigan and one diminutive shoe. She gave the cardigan a yank and folded it in half, and then into quarters along the arms.

'No, never to Ireland. Never again. And come to think of it, I can't really go back to Vermont either; for reasons, dear child,' I checked her sharp inhalation with the raised heel of my hand, 'that I don't wish to go into just now.' It was all, in fact, too frighteningly true. I sidestepped the temptation to pursue the realization any further. 'Hmmm. Let me see. Could I remain here, in England? It's possible.' I grinned wolfishly, tapped a tooth with my nail: all the better to eat you with. 'At least the galleries are free. There would have to be a very good incentive, though, to make it really worth my while.' I had begun these maunderings carelessly, for the pleasure of hearing my idle ideas circle and rub up against her. I did not expect a reply.

'Oh,' gasped Anna. 'I didn't think – I never thought! That you would ever even *consider* staying—' I looked up, surprised. Her voice, husky and low, had broken on the last word. 'Oh, I don't know what to do,' she suddenly stormed. 'I just don't know! Do you believe that people can change, Dr Lynch? Really change, in themselves? Not just for a little while, the way you can put a new coat of paint on something that's a different colour altogether – but, well, for always?' Anna's eyes were dark; she seemed on the brink of tears. A whoop and a few bars of song, shouted off key, came from the garden, blurred by the *pitter patter* of the sprinkler. Another whoop, and the swooshing slap of water: lured by the heat of the day, Vicky had earlier flown away from her armchair, into the blue sky.

My stomach constricted. 'Dear girl, are you all right?'

Anna stared at me so wildly, in such pure feral panic, that I dropped my pen.

'No, I'm not – I'm not—'

'It's your mother, isn't it? Has she telephoned again? Is she wondering what's taking me so long? Oh, my dear, how I wish that you and I would stop pretending!' I creaked to my feet. 'I wish that you would tell me the truth—'

'No, it's not Mummy. For once. That's the truth.'

I surveyed her ashy face, the tremor of her shoulders. Her eyes were turned towards the open window by a mere fraction, but it was enough. 'It's Harry, isn't it?'

She grimaced her assent. Her arms were clasped around her middle, as if she had a cramp. She looked very young, very tired, and very alone.

'Well, if you want my opinion, he's not a good bet, Anna. Not reliable' – as if I knew about such things! On the other hand, I thought with a sudden involuntary prickle of shame, perhaps I knew more than most. 'If you're waiting for him to pop the question, my girl, you'll be waiting a long time. Is that what all this tension is about?'

She flapped her hands a little, in distress. 'Oh shit. You're right,' she said. 'I know you're right.' Then she leaned towards me across the table, her face seething. She opened her mouth. She was about to speak.

'Anna, I need a towel! This water is FUCKING freezing!' All at once the child was bouncing up and down at the window sill, whirring her arms. Anna shifted her weight away from me with a simulated smile. The shudder of her lips, though, was real. There was an indentation on her hip where the desk corner had stabbed it.

'OK, just wait there. I'm coming,' she said in a flat, quenched voice. And she went. It's nothing after all, I thought, sitting down again, it's nothing. Just women's troubles. I will ask her again later.

With difficulty I put the thought of Anna aside and trained my attention on the diary again. The picture – where was the picture? I stood behind a high wall separating me from the Bellini, and at any moment I might, with a little effort, turn that long-awaited corner and arrive at a revelation. Roper's link with Giulia Buccari was the only thread I had to guide me through this maze. Forget Anna! The painting; *that* was what mattered! I didn't care for the monetary value of the Madonna. I wanted to make good my famished life in another way – to own this one solid and true thing; to finger and fold my hands over it and savour it with the licence that came only with private possession. I couldn't care less now if the world never saw the picture; all I wanted was to feed off it in secret, without the risk of ever being disturbed; and in trying to satisfy this exquisite craving I was determined not to allow myself to be deflected by irrelevant emotion. Having decided this, I turned back to the diary with a refreshed appetite. I remembered that Roper had inveigled Mrs Bronson into inviting the Contessa to La Mura. Other than at the entry for the 1st of September there were no further pictures of male genitalia (or female genitalia, as it happens), but the mix of literary gravitas and lubriciousness in Roper's account of this lunch party on the 14th of September left me so hot and bothered that I had to engage in some solitary prophylactic activity on my cot before dinner, followed up with a cold flannel pressed to my groin.

Thanks to a caprice of Browning's – who had, to my disgust, again joined them, armed with a shiny new Panama hat – Mrs Bronson's guests had taken up their positions under the sunny windows of her loggia, within view of the smouldering Rocca on its distant mountain top. The Contessina arrived punctually at noon, panting slightly in the heat and escorted by the scowling young man from Casa Buccari. This time Roper had the opportunity to take a better look at him. Apart from his twisted nose he was fine-boned, and rather short. A slice of blue-black hair fell across his moody brown forehead, but Roper was most struck by his clever, wounded, liverish eyes: with those hooded beads and that tormented nose, he resembled a sulky cuckoo. Although the Italian was rather grandly introduced by the girl as her tutor, he appeared to be some species of poor relation or general factotum, for she dismissed his solicitous attentions with an impatient '*Va', Giuseppe!*' almost as soon as he had shut up her parasol – which he continued, however, to present to her with an urgent little shake.

Nevertheless they sat in the sun, unshaded. Mrs Bronson, as ever, was energetically manufacturing woollen goods which it was a torture to imagine next to the skin while Thisbe or Trolley lay blinking in the penumbra of a newspaper stand. Her daughter jabbed listlessly at her tapestry, a showy design of a peacock fanning its feathers beneath an apple tree, and occasionally rubbed at the drops of perspiration that rolled from her chin down to her bosom. Mrs B pressed Browning to read aloud from the manuscript of the book which he was then preparing for publication, but he refused, adding that as he planned to dedicate its contents to her, they would be hers to command once it had gone to press; but that on that particular afternoon he had an old man's fancy to sit in the sun and do nothing. His words seemed to make the treacle-coloured walls of La Mura fall away, revealing the sweating group inside like the figures in a doll's house.

I, too, settled down for an afternoon's happy voyeurism. I had a clandestine feeling that I was about to discover something toothsome.

'Oh, it is too hot,' moaned Miss Bronson. 'It is too hot to live!'

'Come, my dear young lady,' Browning admonished her. 'Four centuries ago, almost to the month, Catarina Cornaro took possession of this town. And here we are today, at the court of Kate the Queen. Does that not make a pretty pattern? Is that not a detail to be savoured?' He made Mrs B a chivalrous little bow. She smiled and paused encouragingly in her knitting.

'Yes, but I do not like to sit in the sun all day doing nothing,' Miss Bronson grimaced. 'It is a waste of time.'

'*Edie*,' said her mother in a warning voice, lifting her needle.

'Then you do not know how to *asolare*, my dear,' insisted Browning. 'Wasting time is an important part of living, rather like being in love.' He smiled at Mrs B.

'I would rather be in love than bored,' retorted Edith. 'Wouldn't you, Giulia?'

'Perhaps,' purred the little Contessina.

Everyone laughed. Miss Bronson, however, was nimble. If Mr Browning wouldn't read for them, then Mr Roper would recite a poem from memory. She was sure that he had a great collection of love poems by heart.

Gullible Roper admitted that he did know one, by a contemporary of Shakespeare's.

'Shakespeare, yes,' nodded Browning, biting into a piece of cheese. 'Shakespeare is very good. Do begin.' Roper murmured that this poem was by a Bartholomew Griffin. However – he cleared his throat.

'My Lady's hair is threads of beaten gold;
Her front the purest crystal eye hath seen;
Her eyes the brightest stars the heavens hold;
Her cheeks, red roses, such as seld have been;
Her pretty lips of red vermilion dye;
Her hand of ivory the purest white;
Her blush Aurora, or the morning sky.
Her breast displays two silver fountains bright—'

Roper had not recited eight lines when Browning banged the luncheon table so hard that the tisana rocked on its silver salver.

'No, no, no!' he bayed. 'Why, sir, you said we were to have Shakespeare! How easily this versifying fool strips the woman he loves of all her true features and turns her into an allegory! Who can't in a moment convert his lady love into Aurora, or a rosebush, or a silver fountain? Or a thousand other metaphorical flim-flams? No, do not give me this pale *love poetry*. It reeks of bloodless deceit.'

Grandiloquent gobshite. I felt about to pop with pique on Roper's behalf.

'But surely the highest purpose of poetry,' the poor

stooge was saying, 'is to show us the essence of Beauty! Of Love! How can one do that by describing an ordinary woman?'

'Ah, my dear boy, I see!' frowned Browning with the greatest seriousness. 'You mean the Beautiful itself, clear and unmixed – not infected with human flesh and colour and a lot of other mortal nonsense. You would like your love poetry to depict pure soul. Have I guessed it? Am I right?'

'Yes, exactly so!'

The old know-all twinkled with laughter. 'Pish! That is what my late wife believed, you know. Her poetry was as clean and pure as church marble. But I'll take sense, too. If I am to love, then let me love entire and whole – with my body too – not just with my *soul*!'

'Little pitchers, Robert, little pitchers,' tutted Mrs B. 'We are not in the smoking room now.'

'Peace, Kate! My dear boy,' grumbled Browning, 'when you fall in love, then love a girl for her human self – no lower word will serve.'

Well, they could not all be of his opinion, said Mrs B sweetly. *She* found Mr Griffin's poetry rather fine. Browning sniped that she never could keep to the point. Who was this Mr Griffin she referred to? They began to quarrel, and the afternoon ended badly.

It occurred to me that Browning talked a great deal about passion, but that he was lecturing the others on something of which he was himself incapable. His marriage had been founded on, had been animated and sustained by poetry, for chrissakes. The widow Bronson was on heat for him, and the old fraud tickled her while affecting not to notice. This book-writing was a charade. She had invited him to Asolo to propose to her, but he could not bring himself to do it. With a hoot, I composed my own love poem:

> There once was a poet named Browning
> Who wooed a fat widow, though mourning.
> When she begged, 'Try my cunt'
> He replied, 'No, I can't!
> For I dread the sensation of drowning.'

All right. Perhaps I have been excessively self-effacing. I must admit that there is, after all, a certain pleasing symmetry, a coherence, to these passages detailing the lost history of that autumn of 1889. In arranging them thus I feel as if I have embarked on a secret adventure of order.

Why was Roper really making the Grand Tour? Did he himself know what his true purpose was? To buy pictures, of course, but this was surely merely the public reason, the pretext, in the shadow of which a hundred rarer and more delicate intentions promised to spring to life. Oh, the women around him knew, and were magnificently shrewd in their instinct to supply his need. In their covert glances and complicit smothered silences I began to glimpse the shape of a much more elaborate design; a half anxious, half triumphant acknowledgement of the truth that Roper had come to Italy – a little apprehensively, perhaps, and with enough bluster and bonhomie to conceal the full realization even from himself – not only to collect pictures, but to pick up a wife.

There was sex in the air.

CHAPTER EIGHTEEN

In those last days of August it suddenly turned even hotter. Sun gases converged in the garden's dip, on the flat stretch of the fields. In the midday light the shadows of the chestnut tree threw slats over the spumy grass: an elusively cool filigree on a carpet of heat. The strip of skin between my hairline and collar rang with pain. Harry worked on in the asparagus bed, a distant figure, charcoal against the white-hot sky, lunging and bobbing in a diabolical clockwork motion that made me obscurely uneasy.

Since our abortive conversation in the library I had become aware, at first dimly and then quite irresistibly, of a change in Anna's bearing. At times that Saturday I caught her gazing at me, as though she were trying unsuccessfully to decipher a message in a foreign tongue. Sometimes she would elbow me, as if by accident, while we were doing the washing-up. Once, I am almost certain, her dungareed knee poked my corduroys under the dinner table. She even took to hovering outside the library door, entering, after a few minutes' apparently aimless pacing, carrying an armful of tattered brown envelopes, or a noisome ledger, which she would deposit in front of me before starting a little light dusting.

'What's this, dear child? A gift?'

'Well, I've been thinking about what you said. About me

and you – about us helping each other. And I sort of thought that if, you know, you were, um, looking for – looking at – the family pictures, you might want these. Records and receipts and stuff. Just a thought,' she offered breezily.

Could she see how lost I was, and was she trying to give me a nudge? Or had she really had a change of heart? Was she at last parting company with her mother and throwing in her lot with me? 'And how very thoughtful you are. I will peruse these documents with the utmost care.'

I was rewarded, every time, with a slow suffusion of pink in her tan cheek and tossed head: a tea rose, nodding its budding beauty on the stalk.

What I liked best about these exchanges, however, apart from my privileged glimpses of Anna's shyly ripening loveliness, was that in them Harry was never mentioned.

'Should I offer to assist him, my dear?' I asked her when we met on Sunday morning at the kitchen sink. Behind the window, as if in a hellish peepshow, Harry was performing his dervish dance. Although Anna's hands were green I had noticed that in between her visits to me she mostly kept a cautious distance from the pit, circling it hungrily, like a bee at the calyx of a heavily perfumed but possibly carnivorous flower.

'No, he's just pissed off. He's trying to prove a point,' she said meaningfully.

'I don't quite follow.' A distended summer fly butted its relentless head against the glass pane before settling on the tap, where it rubbed its forelegs together wisely.

'Oh, you know. It was just me and him before. And now there's you.'

'There is? I am?'

'Why yes,' she said promptly, avoiding my gaze. 'Of course.'

I sometimes find it difficult, you understand, when remembering or reconstructing these interludes, to focus on the true business of scholarship – on the real task in hand, I mean. There should be a single idea informing the work, and it should emerge from the marble entire, a long-submerged figure slowly disclosed by the stately recession of the tide of thought. Instead of this an insane fist seems to strike out, wielding a novelty-shop hatchet, and the whole edifice flies to pieces: a splinter here, a sliver there. I scurry about with my pot of glue, trying to stick them back together, trying to avoid the leering cracks.

I am no longer always even sure whose story I am supposed to be telling. Oh, mine, naturally, but for the first time in my life I wonder what it's worth. A lost painting, a beautiful young woman, a besotted failure, a botched quest – like a *scagliola* marble, its impurities give it a specious appearance of solidity and depth. While I was at Mawle my whole day was wound up and down and over Anna. I felt her stir everywhere. Were there moments, when we were apart, when I was glad to be free of her gaze? Were there moments, even, when I deliberately put her out of my mind – and then, later, quite unintentionally, really and truly forgot her?

Terrible, treacherous, prophetic thoughts. I was weeping great fat salt tears at James Roper's desk that afternoon when Anna came in.

'Dr Lynch!' she clucked, flinging down her offering of dirty paper and putting her stringy arms around me. 'Tom, oh Tom! Whatever is the matter? Whatever are you doing?'

Reclining against the hollows of Anna's body I realized

that she had scarcely ever called me by my first name. I could feel her bony fingers in my hair, and pressed my wet face more firmly into her scented belly.

'Why are you so tender to me, Anna?' I mumbled. 'Why do you overlook my faults?'

'Shut up, idiot,' she commanded, very gently. 'Just stop talking for five minutes, won't you? What faults? Before you came we were totally alone. No one has ever paid the slightest attention to Vicky before.' She stroked my head. 'You've made all the difference to her. And to me. Is it possible that you can't see it?'

We held onto each other in the shimmering dusk. The crevices of her flesh were ripe with lilies. I remember the dampness of her skin, and a crease near her navel in the shape of a star. Yes, what *was* I doing?

The papers that Anna had deposited on my desk were of little interest. The Biscaino turned out to be a fake, acquired, according to a gangrenous bill of sale which bore Roper's signature, from a copyist in Florence. The tearful Madonna in the Rose Room was, however, a real Murillo: its authenticity was attested by a wad of crackling parchment studded with black and red wax seals, embossed with ducal crowns and coats of arms and other fancy stuff. I tossed this to one side. The crumbling ledgers were full of pernickety accounts detailing the acquisition of inlaid boxes, tortoiseshell fans, goblets of Venetian glass, salt cellars, reams of fine paper, ivory brooches, and countless further examples of such junk. Nothing on this list seemed remotely familiar from my weeks at Mawle. These objects were, no doubt, scattered all about the house, but I was as unmoved by them as is an actor by the props on a stage where only his emotion has weight and meaning. Only once, on glancing up from the diary at the library shelves, did I spot something that appeared in Roper's ledgers: a pistachio-green bronze of Neptune, now doing duty as a book-end, which resembled a wad of wet toilet paper. I was surprised to discover that it had cost him several thousand lire.

But then, just when I'd given up hope of establishing anything concrete at all, Anna produced the Bible.

I'd been getting increasingly irritated with this pile of twaddle, and was perhaps a trifle snappish with her on Sunday evening as she hovered over me. Her hand flittered here and there; in the next minute she was – blissful torment – palpating my arm.

'Forget it, my dear,' I said curtly. 'It's all rubbish. Don't you have any other records? Family ones, for instance?'

'Give me a chance, Tom!' Anna cried – annoyed? Yes, definitely annoyed, and quite abruptly and not a little rudely letting go of my bicep. 'Can't think of anything off the top of my head, but Daddy did show me an old Bible once, with my name in it. I haven't been very good at keeping it up to date, though. It's upstairs in the Painted Salon. Shall I root it out?'

Oh, root away, my Anna, root away! It was my turn to hover around her now, her lapdog, a truffle dog, as she ascended the Great Staircase to the second floor. We were headed for a long dark room in the west wing which I'd previously inventoried and quickly dismissed. It was gallery-shaped, with a detail of narrow semicircular arches running along the walls. The arches enclosed a glum biblical frieze: Adam salivating in a grey glade; Bathsheba at her bath;

the lusty elders ogling Susannah by the painted flames of painted torches. Anna opened the curtains to let in the evening light. Four Italian cabinets stood in the corners of the room, each crammed full of china and glass, with rows of heavy drawers beneath. I eased myself into a damp wing-back chair and settled down to wait as Anna began to crawl about in the lower reaches of the cabinet nearest to me. The chalky torches seemed to dance while she scratched and prodded, her arse in the air.

'Found it!'

Crouched and swivelling on the pads of her feet, Anna held up a leathery slab, a welt of paper bound in the hide of a long-perished Georgian calf, stamped all over with gold. My eager hands reached towards it.

'Oh no, no, no! Ah, ah, ah!'

Anna patted her cheek with a finger – her nail, I noticed, was stickily painted in bubblegum pink. I leaned forward and kissed her face.

'Signorina.' I drew an arabesque in the air with my fingers.

'Signore.' I was touched, always, that her Italian accent was about as convincing as mine.

She handed over the Bible. In taking it I tried to kiss her again when she wasn't expecting me to, and just managed to graze her earlobe with my mouth. She laughed in surprise, put her bitten pink fingers to her lips. My gut was still somersaulting as I waved her away.

'Don't rush now,' she said shyly. 'Take your time. I'll just go on downstairs and do a few things around the house that need doing.'

'Oh, Anna.' I gave her a smile that was weighted with a tender unspoken reproach. 'Don't you realize how difficult it is for *me* to get anything done at all when I know that I could be enjoying a quiet evening with you instead?'

Her face turned as red as a cooking apple as she hung on the doorknob, grinning like a loon. The door closed behind her with a breathless thud.

The Bible was sumptuous, soapy to the touch; an expensive musky King James edition with a London imprint. The inside cover and facing page were blood-red, bordered with gold fleurs-de-lis. Then came a thick spotty interleaving page, like a geometrical pancake, that must once have been white. Behind this there was a skin of tissue paper obscuring a further page, covered in something curling and curved. An incisor of pain lodged itself in my chest. I lifted this membrane in a state of fearful excitement.

Under the tissue lay an apple tree that sprawled from margin to margin, its teeming branches heavily inked with the multiplications of several generations of Ropers. The trunk of the tree sheltered the original Liverpudlian and his wife and was overspread by a sprouting canopy of successive and collateral James Ropers. There were three Georgian Jameses, one stillborn; a Regency James who died in infancy; a James who must have marvelled at the advent of the steam locomotive, and another who might have been the fossil collector. And then, finally, on a higher branch, in the ornate handwriting of the diary, I found James Edward Roper, b. 2nd of February 1866, m. Giulia Anna Maria Buccari (b. 15th of August 1869, d. 4th of April 1890), daughter of Giovanni Pietro Maria Buccari and Julia Anne Buccari, née van der Veen. There was no wedding date, but here at last was evidence outside Sanderson of the marriage – an open-handed invitation to believe that the Bellini might indeed have come into James Roper's possession thanks to that meeting in 1889.

These final details were recorded in the looped script I had come to know so well, as was the birth of Giulia's son, Edward Peter James, on the 1st of April 1890 – evidently a premature child; the previous September she'd still been unmarried. Had the wedding taken place in October? Another hand, cramped and precise, using a thick blue pen like a schoolboy's, had filled in the day and year of James Roper's death, the 22nd of March 1940, and the exact date of Edward's marriage to a Rosalie Marks of Kew: 1st of June 1940. A bit of a daddy's boy who couldn't bring himself to take that step while James Roper still lived; or had he wanted to come into his inheritance first? Whatever the reason, the union was successful at the most basic level: the same pen had noted the birth of John Peter Edward on the 7th of May 1945. Edward Roper's death date had been added to it in pencil: 23rd of December 1953. This must have been a particular blow, coming so close to Christmas; even more so as his son John, Anna's father, was only eight at the time. On the 4th of January 1969 this John (the keeper of the book had changed again, and was now writing in a fickle brown ink that reminded me, like a stealthy twinge, of something I had seen or read not long ago – but what?) had married Maddalena Teresa Marcello. Anna Maria Julia Roper was born on the 20th of July 1969.

My God. I touched the month, the year. 1969! My fresh-faced, childish love was nowhere near as young as I'd thought. She was – what? Thirty-four? No, thirty-five! She'd had her birthday last month. And the dates didn't add up at all. Her parents were married in January, and she was born seven months later. This abbreviated pregnancy was as odd, in its own way, as that other premature birth in 1890. Had Papa and Mamma Roper jumped the gun?

Anna's father – the unformed note in red biro had undoubtedly been made by her – had died seventeen years ago on the 13th of August 1987, as Maddalena had divulged. That much, then, was true. After Anna's there were no further names, just naked branches and empty foliage.

The sombre old walls of the room seemed to stare at me, their arches expectantly raised. I studied Adam's bare frescoed legs. Something in the family history didn't fit, something in the design wasn't flush . . . Why was there no record of when James Roper and his Contessa were married? The details stuck out brokenly. All the other marriages were carefully recorded, down to the day. Why not this one? I felt a strange, creeping sense of unease, and a sudden overpowering desire to confront Anna with the full blast of my frustration.

The day was drawing to a close. The cabinet in the far corner by the window had vanished, gobbled up by the dusk. The chair had left a cold patch on the seat of my trousers that made walking feel mildly obscene. I fumbled uncomfortably in the gloom for the door and stepped out onto the landing. How dark it suddenly was! All around me the felted shadows seemed to muffle sound, so that my descending steps fell silently on the staircase. I clutched the banister tightly, guided by a faint light coming from below, where someone must have turned on the lamps. When I reached the ground floor, however, it was dark too: the light came from the library. In the distance I heard a squeaking sound, as of a heavy chair being pushed or pulled along a floor. Something fell in that remotely lit space with a slithering, cascading sound like water. Then there was silence.

I approached the library door slowly, my legs shaking: the chill seemed to have crept all the way down my calves. On the threshold I drew back. There was something or someone in the room already, bending over the desk. It was, unmistakably, a human shape, silhouetted blackly against the orange aura of the lamp. The looming curves of its body belled from floor to ceiling. It was making a strange transverse movement over the surface of the desk with attenuated arms, as if bestowing a ritual blessing. A dazzling lake of white was spread around its feet.

I felt at once, with a bulge of terror, that I had strayed over the invisible line separating the present from the past. Sensing my presence, the apparition lifted its shadowed head and turned towards me in a swift, angry movement. Its widened eyes were black and wild. It was a woman, and she held a wand of some sort in her left hand. With a low cry she raised this sceptre towards me.

'Oh!' the wraith cried in a voice that was terrible, yet familiar.

With hirpling nerves I pounced on the overhead light switch.

'Anna! What in God's name are you up to?'

'Jesus Christ, Dr Lynch! Don't go creeping up on people like that!' Anna flopped down heavily in my chair, which was, I noticed, pulled back some way from the desk so as to allow free access to it. Her thighs were trembling. She gave the feather duster in her hand an agitated shake. 'It's filthy in here. Why didn't you *tell* me? I could so easily have given it a good clean for you before now.'

The bright light showed that the tabletop was indeed covered in a week's worth of dust, swirled here and there with what appeared to be the clawmarks of a large bird. I whimpered in weary relief.

'You've – you've been dusting my things.'

'Yup, and not before time. Just get a sniff of this.' The diary was lying at her elbow. She picked it up and gave it a careless wallop. An ashy curl scrolled from its pages into the lamplight. My heart nearly stopped.

Anna tossed the diary back onto the desk. 'It's a miracle you haven't been eaten alive by dust mites, you know.'

'Oh, your discerning dust mite isn't interested in tired old flesh like mine. Here,' I chided, joining her on the carpet on my hands and knees, 'let me do that. You've tipped nearly all my papers on the floor, you silly girl.'

It was true: they were pooled on the floor.

'Heavens, Anna, you really are a goose, aren't you? You couldn't have made a bigger mess if you'd tried.' I sneezed crossly.

'Look, aren't you even a little grateful to me for protecting you from an asthma attack or worse?' she pouted, giving me a flirtatious dig in the ribs with her duster. 'Just a tiny little bit?'

'Stop that! Yes, of course I am. It's just that I had the most awful premonition as I was coming down the stairs, and then, when I saw you, I stupidly assumed – I thought you were a – well, that is – you startled me.'

'*I* startled *you*? I thought you'd be up there for hours and that I'd be able to give you a nice surprise. You've been so tense these past few days.' She crossed her lissome arms thoughtfully. 'I'll just have to finish this tomorrow now. Did you get any joy from that Bible, anyway?'

'No,' I lied. 'Not a smidgen. Oh, I grant that it's very comprehensive, but it didn't give me any new, ah, information that would help with your family pictures, unfortunately.'

Anna laid an anxious hand on my wrist. A wrinkle was spreading across her forehead. 'But – but the lines of descent and all that. The dates. *They* must be interesting, mustn't they? Don't they speak to you at all?'

'My dear child, it's pictures that tell us about people, not vice versa.'

'Really? I would've thought it was exactly the other way around.' I could feel the hectic pressure of her fingers through my sleeve. 'Oh well – you're the expert,' she sighed, rubbing her brow. 'It's late. I'd better get supper on.' She took a deep breath and patted my hand regretfully.

Then she said a strange thing, just as she was about to go out of the room.

'Tell me, Dr Lynch. Do you like picnics?'

My guts baulked at the possibilities. 'Nothing adventurous tonight, please, Anna. Just a simple wholesome sandwich will do.'

'OK, José,' she smiled tightly, and left with the most unsettling swagger of her hips.

CHAPTER NINETEEN

I sensed with a fastidious shrinking of the stomach that Anna and I were now converging on each other. She may have started off as an agent of entrapment, and I as a nobly-intentioned predator (all right, all right, a common or garden thief) but this pattern was slowly inverting itself. At some as yet unplotted point, I knew, we would meet. I could see that she was finding it harder and harder to remain indifferent to me, and I – well, I was finding it harder and harder to go on circling around her.

By now it was already Monday the 23rd of August. I'd been in the house for a fortnight, and I had nothing to show for it. So. Roper *had* married Giulia Buccari – this had been the means by which he'd got his hands on the Madonna. But how had the deal been clinched? And where, and *why*, had he hidden the Bellini? The landscape of his journal overlay another that was always implicitly there though occluded by time: remote, ideal, complete; distinct from the lush ugliness and rebarbative vulgarities of these nineteenth-century people and their world. It was Giambellin's landscape, the landscape of the Venetian Renaissance.

I began to feel impatient again to peel back this hyperreal, overbright Victorian film and re-enter that other more subtle country; to have a view, once more, of its enamelled blue skies, swelling behind spindly *campanili* and squat towers capped with rusty tiled roofs; its carefully combed fields stretching their luxuriant golden arms towards the margins of slender rivers; its stony paths walked by diminutive jerkined men and wimpled women. On Monday morning I decided not to waste any more time. I would no longer allow myself to get sidetracked by futile aesthetic and biographical speculations. I would summon up one final effort and whip through the showy Victoriana of the diary.

I was beginning to think that Anna's newly roused interest in my efforts was acting as a lucky charm. How odd it was that she'd mentioned picnics, and here – well, here one was. On the 20th of September Roper expressed a wish, after a light midday repast of salami and oranges, to drive out into the countryside to see Canova's marbles at Possagno.

'My dear Mr Roper,' protested Mrs B, 'this is folly – it will soon be hot. Let us wait until three o'clock. Those statues will still be there after tea-time, you know,' she added comfortably.

'Must we then persist in these pitiful Anglo-Saxon habits even *here*?' returned I, exasperated. 'Is Canova to wait on a confounded cup of tea?'

But it appeared that the coachman, Vittorio, could not, through tacit agreement sanctified by long custom, be imposed on so soon after the noon meal, and that the barometer, in spite of the unencumbered sky, clearly indicated a looming Venetian *tempesta*.

'Ha!' I exclaimed, 'I hadn't expected such a lack of spirit from *you*, Mrs Bronson. It is not Italian – no, it is not in the Italian temper of things at all.'

This did the trick. Mrs Bronson dispatched a servant to Casa Buccari to beg the Contessa for the loan of her coachman. After a half hour in which they sat in baited silence broken only by the occasional intestinal rumble, the dogsbody returned with a note. Mrs B read it and flashed Roper a proud Yankee look. They could do better than Vittorio – Miss Spragg was sending them her own carriage along with Giuseppe, the surly young tutor, to drive it, and the ladies from Ca' Buccari would be joining the party too. Sound the bugles!

They were soon on the road to Possagno, which was bordered on each side by thick hedges and fields in which stood great wains of autumn hay. As they rattled along, Roper enthusiastically observed everything observable for subsequent notation – the brooks between hedges and high road, the apple orchards, and stretch upon stretch of tall chestnut trees. Then he fell silent. 'This landscape is most strange,' he remarked after a while, when the carriage had passed another hedgerow. 'It does not seem Italian at all – it could almost be English. Yes, it has a decidedly English character. That hay cart, now – pure Constable.' He lapsed into a disgruntled contemplation of the scene.

Fortunately the hedges gave way, near Monfumo, to borders of alders and shivering aspens, the yellow fields to the gentle slopes of vineyards, and the offensive hay wains to broad wooden *carri* piled high with white or purple grapes. Roper was satisfied. Touching his hat to a bemused rustic, who lifted his own in the manner of the country, he sighed that it was very Italian. It was Italianissimo. They would not go on to Possagno – they would stop there, among these simple people, and sit by that pleasant river he could see flowing not far off. The order to halt drew unexpected protests from the usually taciturn Giuseppe, who wagged his head angrily at the rows of vines. But Miss Spragg – I chuckled at this; the old stick knew what she was about – shut him up. He was made to drive the carriage under a high awning which was only half taken up by a collapsed *carro*, and after Roper had insisted that he pay the astonished owner handsomely for this privilege, they made their way down on foot to a muddy dribble of water. By now the afternoon sun had burned away the morning's vapours and the bright valley, hard and gemlike, glinted all around. They carried with them four bottles of lemonade in a netted bag, which Giuseppe lowered into the glittering rivulet and secured to the washy bank by a few baleful jabs with a branch.

'*Per piacere, Signori,*' he cautioned irritably, wiping his hands on his knees, 'do not sit so close to the water. The air is not so good here – *non è salubre,* it is full of creatures.' To the Contessina he added, more gently, '*Per favore, Giulia, non metterti qui. Siediti più in su.*' The girl, who had lingered close to him, dutifully went to sit under an aspen, followed in single file by the other ladies.

'A charming scene,' I applauded. 'You might all serve as models in a procession to Bacchus.'

Miss Bronson gave me a grin that split her plump chops from ear to ear. 'Pray, Mr Roper, come sit with us and be our Silenus,' she cajoled.

'I do congratulate you on your daughter, Mrs Bronson,' said Miss Spragg in a dry whisper when we were all seated. The Contessa had laid her head on her cousin's knee. 'She is already so very much the young woman. My Julia is frightfully innocent, scarcely more than a child.' She paused portentously, leaving us to surmise how young the unconscious Giulia might be. Dozing now in the shadow of the aspens, I must admit, she did not look very old; no more than fifteen or sixteen, a smooth marble effigy of a girl.

'Has Miss Bronson been "out" for long?' pressed Miss Spragg.

'No,' said Mrs B, coolly plaining and purling, 'but she has her fair share of admirers.'

'In this country women marry early, of course,' continued Miss Spragg. 'But I cannot condone it. The undeveloped female system cannot cope with that particular strain.'

The squat heat of the afternoon, bearing down on us from under a gathering ruffle of brown cloud, gave weight to her words.

I felt a rolling in the air. The pregnant moment, swelling dangerously, seemed about to suffocate the present. Then Miss Spragg drew her pistols and fired from the hip. 'What do you think of my Julia, Mr Roper?' she unexpectedly asked.

'She too is charming, charming,' Roper replied; stupefied by the sunshine.

The Contessina shivered a little and whimpered in her sleep. A bubble of spit appeared at the corner of her lip.

After that everything happened with alarming speed – I had to peer hard and close to catch the meaning of it. Miss Spragg leaned over the girl, patting her glossy face.

'You have slept enough, Julia,' she wittered, 'Julia, wake up. This heavy sleep cannot be good. Wake up and fan yourself.' Her anxious eyes fleetingly met Mrs Bronson's unyielding gaze.

'*Fra breve*,' the girl mumbled, turning her blank cheek into her cousin's skirts.

'A little lemonade, Giuseppe!' Miss Spragg called down nervously to the water's edge.

'No, no, let me,' I cried. In my haste I slipped and slithered to the riverbank. In a minute or two I'd hoisted the bottle out of the stream. 'Here, hold up the young lady's head. There you are.'

The Contessina coughed.

'You have been talking about me, Laetitia, I know it,' she said, sitting up with an accusing look. 'And now I have the head-egg.' She put her thin hands to her flushed face.

All the while Giuseppe had been silently watching this scene from the bank with his keen scavenger's gaze. Now, to my irritation, he jumped up abruptly, shouting that theirs had been a foolish journey. '*Che stolta!*' the boy spat at Miss Spragg. '*Te l'avevo detto! Vuoi uccidere lei e poi me? Alzati, Giulia, ti aiuto io!*'

I felt a spasm of apprehension and excitement. The heat of the day seemed to press down on me with fiery screws; it was hard to get a grip on anything. Giuseppe had said something grossly out of key. 'You idiot,' he'd called out. 'I warned you! Do you want to kill her, and me, too?' It made no sense . . . But what came next was as unexpected, and as eccentric.

'I am surprised that you allow your servants to speak to you in this way, my dear,' gasped Mrs Bronson.

'He is not a servant, he is my cousin,' gurgled the Contessina, and vomited inconsequently onto the ground.

Here the picture threatens to disintegrate into garish smears and outré effects. Ignoring Mrs Bronson's scandalized bleats, Giuseppe lifted the Contessina to his chest and, clasping her tightly under the armpits and knees, strode up the slope with her, while the rest of the party scampered after them in confused retreat. As they reached the crest of the hill and limped towards the carriage hail began to fall: lumps of hail, grains as big as Klondike nuggets. Giuseppe settled the girl among the red velvet cushions and hung about her anxiously, fussing over her skirts. Then he reassumed his position on the driver's seat, where he sat in a sullen fury with his coat over his head, like a melancholic trying to ignore the music at a concert. *Ka-whupp. Ka-whupp* – the next moment the picnickers were assaulted by a different kind of thumping. Three peasant boys, ignoring the shower, had climbed onto the high wheels of the rotten *carro* next door, and leaning across, banged the carriage roof and jiggled grapes at them. Giuseppe began to shoo them off impatiently, but Roper, too, was by now in a stinking mood. Things were going obscurely wrong. 'Yes, yes, let us have them,' he bellowed, gathering the bruised fruit in his hands and bending over the Contessina, whose face was lustrous with sweat. 'Please,' he begged, 'please eat a grape to make *me* happy.'

The girl raised herself on an obedient elbow, bit with sharp teeth into the grape he'd thrust at her, and hey presto! She was soon asking for another, and then another, and so they all began to call to the boys to *ancora un po' d'uva, per favore*, and when the urchins brought them not just bunches of the cool fruit, but hailstones the size of walnuts to marvel at, the prisoners in the carriage handed this fool's gold around feverishly. In the midst of the chaos Roper pressed one of the nuggets into the Contessa's palm, and she wrapped her childish fingers around his and shrieked a laugh. The hail was lighter now and her laughter bounced off the carriage walls in a frenzied echo of its scatter.

After half an hour the storm had blown over, and the old carriage set off for Asolo with an attenuated groan. Giuseppe drove slowly, as if he resented every inch. The road was white and slippery, the hail piled high in corners and ditches.

'Is your cousin often ill?' I asked Miss Spragg quietly while the others were exclaiming over the eldritch landscape.

'My Julia is perfectly hale,' replied Miss Spragg. Her smile was like the scratch of a needle. 'But I do wish,' she continued in a low voice, 'oh, Mr Roper, how I wish that she did not have to be exposed constantly to this extreme climate.'

'A more temperate zone would be infinitely preferable.'

'Infinitely – yes.'

'I wonder,' I asked, 'that you have not thought of returning to America?'

'What, to settle Julia in a brownstone smelling of varnish?' Miss Spragg's pinched face was florid with contempt. 'She has her *dot*, and a handsome one too. And she has her title, you know. This is her proper setting, this or another place like it. I promised her mother that I would *never*,' she squeezed the word out through bolted teeth, 'let her daughter marry beneath her. In America they would not understand Julia's true worth.'

She smiled wisely at me, her mouth clamped tight.

'She is very lovely,' I agreed. 'But her worth, my dear lady, does not lie in her title – it lies in her beauty – in her freshness! Someone should paint her.' I thumped the floor of the carriage with my cane. 'Someone should fix her forever, before it is too late.'

The Contessina turned from the carriage window with a blush. Miss Spragg seized the girl's hand. 'You have hit on an excellent idea, sir,' she breathed. 'As Julia's tutor, Giuseppe will do it. He has a talent for representation – all the Italians do, you know. It's in their blood.'

'Is it really, ma'am?' asked I, astonished. 'The ability to paint?'

'The ability to represent things in the most handsome light possible,' murmured Miss Spragg. 'We depend on him for it.'

A spark had flashed out of the darkness as I was reading this and its white traces now hung before me like the afterimage of a flare. It was all so distant, and yet at the same time the blazing sun, the golden fields, the compliant, frail girl seemed instantly known to me, indefinably near. There was a terrifying moment of overlap between past and present, a gemination of relationships. In the sunlight of that vineyard, in the diaphanous shape of an implied desire, in a dozen apparently random phrases and associations, I had recognized the fragments of my experience shaken up and jarringly recombined, but still clearly distinguishable. Oh, what was it? In Roper's hungry possessiveness towards Giulia Buccari I caught a brute echo of my affronted feelings of custodianship whenever Anna's attention was diverted from me. As I gazed into the foxed glass of the diary I felt like someone confronting a double exposure of his own face, and my heart rang with anguish and a newly urgent, explosive sense of lust.

'Come on, Fred. I've been upstairs for a GODDAMN hour with my face on and you're not even dressed yet!'

It was Vicky, festooned in silver lace, with a cloche hat rammed on her head. Her eyes were stencilled with black kohl, *à la* Maddalena Roper. The ghostly mirror shattered, scattering my thoughts to the four corners of the afternoon. The flare with its inverted afterimage vanished in a squiggle of smoke. I remembered with a sense of curious contentment that I had promised to entertain the child before lunch, while Anna finished dusting the library.

I meant to search for the Bellini, you see; I really did. But I was increasingly susceptible to an involuntary, almost sensual reluctance to do so; a readiness, in spite of my best intentions, to let myself be ambushed by the life, past and present, of that house. And Anna was right: quite apart from my intrusive feelings for her there was the question of Vicky. Insensibly, without my noticing, the little girl had insinuated her tentacles about my heart. Our moments together were an endless source of distraction. That silver dress she now wore almost daily came from a plasterboard cupboard in a little room on the third floor – our floor – that Anna called 'the Sewing Room'. Slicks of blue paint and the faint corolla of a daisy above the skirting suggested that it was once a child's playroom, or a nursery. Underneath the window vanished hands, by the steady application of a now vanished toy, had managed to work a set of parallel grooves into the spidering linoleum that spread, dull as old ivory, from wall to wall. I remember that the window sash was lopsided and gave onto a view of the steps behind the kitchen, and that a smell of boiled rice always hung about the place, regardless of what was cooking below. There was no furniture at all, apart from the cupboard and a treadle Singer machine with a black-latticed frame that sat behind the door, and was never used for sewing.

The cupboard was stuffed full of someone's old clothes, or rather several people's, most of them female or very young – a child's pair of navy velvet knickerbockers, a crêpe-de-chine wedding dress of war-time vintage, and, tossed in a heap at the back, a hideous black and yellow check gown of an even older cut that had begun to decompose at the seams. In the afternoons, while Anna fretted by the widening asparagus bed, Vicky squirmed in and out of the stinking cloth like a silverfish.

'This is for you. It's a bit dirty but it's very swanky.' She held up a paralysed tweed gentleman's motoring jacket, circa 1910.

'Vroom, vroom. Where's the motor car? Has the man brought it round yet, Daphne?' She was Daphne and I Frederick, her long-suffering husband, enlisted hour after hour in pedalling the unthreaded Singer, or submitting to act as the mannequin for her sartorial experiments.

'Noo-o.' Her eyes arched upwards, a paroxysm of despair in which I again recognized a tracery of La Roper. Vicky seemed to be in the grip of a repellent ventriloquism. 'I've had to let him go. We can't afford him any more! I think I'm going to have to sell some of these clothes. Oh, my lovely clothes!' She supported herself against the Singer, a middle-aged woman overcome by the plebeian mercenariness of life. 'Really, this house is killing me. First this *wretched* painting which we just can't find, even though we know we're sitting on a fucking mine of gold, and now the antics of this interfering American *fool* . . .'

The old house creaks, protests, settles again on its gravel

foundations. I am aghast, as transfixed as an unwilling client at a séance. I stare at my middle-aged wife. 'Yes, my dear Daphne – the interfering American fool. As to him – now what?'

The moment of revelation floats into view: a soap bubble, a fugitive thing of glints and curves; floats, bobs into my line of vision, and vanishes. Vicky stares at me blankly, as if I were speaking a foreign language, and stops quoting.

'Oh, I dunno. Here, do you want to try this on? I found it today.' She scrambles in the froth of fabric at our feet, her thin shoulder blades rotating furiously, and pulls out a lace tea gown with a limp crocheted rose tacked to its shrivelled shoulder.

'My dear, I'd like to, but I don't think I can – I've suddenly got such a headache, you see.'

'Poor old Fred. Then we must sit you down. Come on.' She sweeps back the tide of clothing on the floor with her dirty foot and I sink against it awkwardly, a mass of popping bones. 'Close your eyes.'

I do so, and I am filled with a sensation of pure pain, a grubby green pain that rinses down from my wicked brain to my left arm, where it forks into a trident hand of darting agony. As I kneel, groaning, in the foamy silks and tweeds, Vicky takes my palm. She sits beside me, the fine feelers of her being curled around my corruption. I believe I can see her heart through my closed lids, the berry-like heart of a seahorse, a glassfish; a doll's purse of crimson threads, cradling its miniature throbs. I open an eye. She is perfectly poised, her spine taut, gazing at me wetly. Memory raises its head above the waters, sinks down again. Where have I seen that look?

'Are you all right now?'

'Yes, my dear. It must be the heat.'

She fans me with her little fins. 'There, there. We'll soon have you better.'

Delicately she dips and sways towards me. I take her in: the shell-like curve of her dark hair, her inward look, the look of an intent marine creature painstakingly hatching its pearl, and then it comes to me. I realize what has been perfectly obvious all along. Of course – of course! Second cousin? My aunt! That was merely the childish fantasy of a little girl who wished herself elsewhere. How could I have failed to see it before? It didn't need a family tree to tell me this. She is just like Anna, if a less defeated, undimmed Anna. She is Anna's child.

CHAPTER TWENTY

Since his quarrel with Anna, Harry had taken to scraping all day at the cavity in the yellow field and no longer came to join us at the kitchen table. That Monday afternoon as we ate our lunch his radio bleeped and blopped at us across the thickening air. At my behest Anna had shopped for and cooked proper food: wedges of venous sirloin, fat with blood; pompom-sized peas, and a bag of ruched organic cabbage. I'd hoped to put some iron into her. But she ate steadily, unseeingly, saying little; a patient beyond the help of medication. She was in pain again, and I could do nothing about it.

I began to study her – to tamp my fingers, as I thought, in her hollows, over her quivering face; but she was already hardening, a piece of scrimshaw to my touch, rutted and unyielding. Bloody hell. Not only was she thirty-five, she wasn't an inexperienced girleen at all. I guessed that she'd fallen pregnant with the child when she was twenty-six, twenty-seven. Was Harry here then, pruning the blowsy flowerbeds and tilling the land, a juvenile combine harvester, a toothed harrowing machine, yanking her lank ponytail and pinning her down in the furrows? Come on, bend over this bale of straw, this clod of earth, let me squeeze your juicy bum . . .

Or – a worse thought, this – was she the hunter, the rustling serpent, the splay-legged clay woman; her tender umbilicus already rippling out across the creamy silt, the gaping fields? I couldn't stand not knowing. She had already stacked our dirty lunch plates in the sink and had started to drag bags of manure out of the back of Harry's van when I approached her.

'Anna, Vicky's yours, isn't she?'

'Yes of course she's mine, worse luck.' She held a bag of fertilizer in a clinch and gawped, huffing, at me over the top. 'I told you that ages ago.'

'Well, technically, my dear, you know, you didn't.'

'Didn't I? Well, whose did you think she was? Come on, give me a hand with this compost. I want to give the foxglove bed a good turning over before summer ends.' Sliding the bag to the ground, she dusted off her palms. She smelled faintly, insinuatingly, of shit. 'You're a funny one sometimes, d'you know that?'

I manhandled the manure as directed, but the ground was still tilting madly under my feet. How could I have got it all so wrong? Though I'd meant to, I simply couldn't ask her who the father was, or if she'd even wanted this child. The question suddenly struck me as grossly intrusive; my rigid embarrassment a measure of the infinite distance that lay between us. She was as unguarded, as open, as ever, but she had never seemed so difficult to read. I longed for her, but I couldn't find a point of entry. Anna! When I think of you now I only see a mask, a lozenge of polished stone, the almond lure of your lips; later I plumbed your deadened depths, but we were never, never, no, no matter what I tell myself – never, by any feat of the imagination, except in the meanest physical sense – really lovers.

*

After lunch I withdrew to the library, full of woe, and read Roper's journal again. Once I had begun to listen for it I caught it often: the thin whine of desire, like the tinny shiver of a cymbal, running counter to the diary's surface ebullience. The Contessa was clearly unwell in some way, she was weak, but Roper preferred her to the more obviously promising Miss Bronson. Was it Giulia's pliableness, her lack of definition, that drew him? She didn't give him hope, but she offered no resistance. She was like clay or wax, soft to the hands. Perhaps her very malleability was a kind of strength, her formlessness a source of possibility. She drew him, just as Anna drew me, and he thought that the propulsion was all his. And I could see that she drew her cousin, Giuseppe, too, though her girlishness and easy susceptibility seemed to irritate him as much as they charmed him. The day after the picnic these tensions threatened to come to a head when Roper returned to the Palazzo Buccari to ask after the Contessina's health. The door under the ghostly phoenix was opened by the little servant girl, who rocked teasingly in its crack.

'*Mi dispiace, ma la Signora Spragg* is resting, *sta dormendo*.' The *serva* folded her plump hands under her speckled cheek in a helpful dumb show of exhaustion.

'Ah, that does not matter. It is the Contessa Buccari I have come to see.'

'Signore, she is at her painting lesson.' The girl smiled at him naughtily. 'I will show you where.'

She led Roper across the courtyard and out by a side gate to the corner of the *barchessa*, where an avenue of ilex trees dwindled shaggily into the distance, bordered by thick shadow like a mourning card. At the bottom of a dark garden edged with statues stood Giuseppe, throwing paint at a board inclined against an easel. The Contessa held herself bolt upright before him in the rigidly self-conscious pose of a bad model. The two were watched by an elderly woman in black bombazine with three colossal chins, to whom Roper was introduced, although he couldn't later remember her name.

The purpling sky was so dismal, the light falling through the gnarled old trees so thin, the mood of the huddled group so sombre, that it might have been a scene in a morgue. The Contessina ducked her glossy head when she saw Roper and giggled nervously. The fat old woman opened her jaws and brayed at Giuseppe, *Beppe, lasciaci*, after which she became mute again.

Stopping him from leaving, Roper stepped up to the easel.

'No – if you please – do not go.' I turned to the Contessina. 'I am sorry; I have interrupted your sacred hour. You are studying – you are learning the principles of composition, of paint, of portraits – you are learning.' I'm afraid that I was not at all sure what she was learning.

'Yes,' said the cousin, 'we are attempting to learn. But *is* she learning, I ask you? *Giulia, che vergogna!* She has no concentration, no application. I have tried to teach her how to hold her brush, how to thin and mix the colours, *ma Giulia non ce la fa*, she will not listen, she idles and runs back to her *novelli*, her silly stories about princesses in love, and other women's rubbish.' He bit his lips angrily. 'She has no sense of what can and *cannot be*.'

In spite of myself I rather liked him. 'You are a sensible sort of fellow, you know, Giuseppe.'

'Signore,' he shook his oily head. 'It is my duty and my desire to serve reason in all things.'

'And what's this picture, then? May I see it?'

'It would be an honour which I have already anticipated most keenly. For it was you, Signore, who commissioned it. I have called it *The Maiden*.'

'Well, don't let's anticipate it. It's the work of a mere moment, old fellow.'

I shouldered him aside.

He had begun a sterile, faux Classical little portrait, executed in a cream tint, of the Contessina. The insipid vanilla face planted on its vanilla neck was as undistinguished and bald, under its sculpturally massed braids, as a darning egg. The dead eyes of the figure were duller than soap, the dead mouth under its apple cheeks rucked into a simpering pout. Two nerveless hands lay crossed over a quiver of arrows that reclined on its breast. I admit that I almost uttered a cry of disgust.

'It is very skilful,' I offered. 'It is a soulful work. Yes, most soulful and – and symbolic of all that is pure and beautiful in womanhood itself.'

Giuseppe bowed briefly. '*È vero*. I believe that art should stand for something ideal and absolute if it is to touch the nobler emotions. It should have no dealings with irrational, superstitious nonsense.' As if to illustrate this remark, he faced the portrait contemptuously towards the easel. On the back of the old board was a rather good if dirty landscape that seemed vaguely religious. I was half minded to offer him something for it, and would have – but the fellow was becoming a bore.

The Contessina had come back to life and wandered over

to us. 'I like that old picture,' she said pettishly. 'You shouldn't have taken it without asking me, even if it was only lying in the store room. It is not your house, it is mine.' Pulling a face, she peeped around at the other side of the board. 'And what's more, you have made me look like a frog, Beppe,' she scolded, and erupted in peals of laughter.

The young man shut up his box of paints. 'We have painted enough for one day,' he said sternly. Turning to me, he offered me his supple hand. 'Signore, it is a rare pleasure, in this house, to speak to someone of learning and understanding. If you will pardon me, I am expected elsewhere.' So saying, he trotted briskly up the avenue and disappeared behind the wall of the palazzo.

'Pah,' called the Contessina as he went. 'He has only gone to flirt with that Ludovica Contanto. That girl is not so pretty as she thinks. And she smells of hops.' When her cousin had vanished without a backward glance, though, she looked both despondent and perplexed in turns. Our triple-chinned chaperone had not stirred and still sat without speaking. 'Ah, do not mind her,' said the Contessina. 'She is only my aunt. She is deaf and cannot hear us, no matter what we say.' She forced a smile again, and seemed to flick out her tongue at me.

In spite of this promising beginning, however, they said little to each other. They lingered side by side for a while on a stone bench, and Roper studied the moss on its claw feet.

My protégé asked if the Contessina were quite recovered, and she shrugged. They agreed that it was very hot that day, but not as hot as it had been two days ago, and that English temperatures were far cooler, the climate positively rainy, in fact – or rather, Roper made these sage observations, and the girl did not dispute them. He told her that it rained so much at home that the roof of Mawle sometimes leaked. To his delight, this strange young woman appeared to take an enthusiastic interest in his roof. '*Ohimè*, to get your feet so wet! Is your home very big and cold?' she asked. 'And does it have – the stone animals – those animals of Mrs Radcliffe?' It took them some time to arrive at the fact that she was referring to gargoyles, and for Roper to explain that Mawle was not a gloomy ruin but really quite modern, with a pretty lake and good books and wallpaper and whatnot. The Contessina found the wallpaper very amusing. Why would he cover up his frescoes? Did his father approve of this? Roper explained that the plaster at Mawle was unadorned in this way, and that he was his late father's heir, and his own master for some two years past, and therefore free to do precisely as he liked.

'Here we order things differently,' the girl remarked flatly.

They sat for a while in silence. The statues seemed to grow whiter and more ghostly. At last Roper risked a flaccid remark on the beauty of the grim garden. '*Si, è una vista incantevole*,' murmured the Contessina sadly. He did not know what else to say to her. Their duenna had nodded off, a most ineffectual Cerberus, and only her three chins shook forbiddingly. Roper thought of making an elaborate gesture: of taking the Contessina's hand and putting it to his lips, of whispering urgent words of comfort and consolation in her ear; 'For,' he writes, 'she had certainly given me enough encouragement.' But in spite of the tomb-like silence and isolation of the darkening garden he did not dare, and he took his leave soon afterwards.

Oh, the sensation of power! I was approaching the Bellini with thundering strides, loping high above the small fry around me with their pathetic plans of capture. I would boot Maddalena into a corner. Didn't those few apparently barren words between James Roper and Giulia Buccari contain an appeal, the promise of an imminent transaction? In a heart-beat I would arrive at Roper's account of his marriage, the details of his wife's property, and the picture itself – and from there it would be but a skip and a jump to its hiding place. I held the book up to my ear, as if I could eavesdrop on tiny voices continuing the conversation. My nerves warbled. Steady, Lynch, steady! I gave my pockets an exploratory pat and was cheered to discover a precious shred of dried mushroom (*Psilocybe cubensis*), a quaalude or two, and an analgesic powder of some sort.

In the kitchen I poured myself a celebratory shot of grappa and drank it in a single swallow. After stuffing the dry ingredients in my mouth and giving them a good chomp I prepared another shot as a chaser, into which I tipped the powder. But I lacked a suitable implement with which to whisk up my potion. Where had Anna hidden the teaspoons today? The kitchen had no system; its utensils were allowed to roam freely. I opened a few likely cupboards and found plenty of other things, including a herd of nomadic pastry cutters camped around a bag of flour, but there wasn't a spoon in sight. There was a watchful ladle, though, poking its head out of a pottery jug on top of the refrigerator. It would do. Come here, my lovely. I could just about reach it without the aid of a chair by balancing on the rims of my brogues.

As I did so the jug executed a suicidal double roll and hopped into my hands, spilling its intestines all over the floor. Scraps of newsprint fell around me with an enervated flitter. I crouched to shunt them together with my palm, and had brought the buggers into some sort of order when I realized that the cutting now squeezed between my thumb and forefinger was all about Ludovico Puppi. And so were the five or six after that. I held a chattering trove of newspaper articles of different lengths, printed in Italian. The oldest went back seven years; the most recent was only four months old. I offer a rough translation of their jabber.

'Professor Ludovico Puppi was the principal speaker at the well-attended conference funded by the *Istituto dei Arti Plastiche* on epithalamial Northern Renaissance bas-reliefs, entitled "Beauty and Duty: The Artful Business of Renaissance Marriage."' 'Ludovico Puppi, acclaimed scholar, author and critic, who was yesterday awarded the *Palle d'Oro* medal for his contribution to art criticism, spoke warmly of his pleasure at being able to wield this formidable tool in the service of the public . . .' 'Professor Puppi himself proposed the toast at the annual dinner of Padua's Department of Medieval and Modern Art History by recalling his own happy years as a carefree student at the University in the 1960s . . .' And so on and so on, climaxing in this piece of po-faced tripe from the books section of a pompous Milan quarterly: 'Pietro Bembo's discourse on courtly love in his *Gli Asolani*, argues Ludovico Puppi, fits beautifully into the Renaissance paradigm of the country villa and its garden as a space dedicated to *otium*, or the retreat from reality.'

And here, oh horrors, was a dedication, forced into the margin in eensy-weensy letters: '*Alla mia Annetta. Che ragazza in gamba sei stata ad aver trovato questi Da Vinci. Grazie mille carissima. Bacioni da Ludo.*'

'To my little Anna. What a clever girl you are to find those Da Vincis. A thousand thanks, my dearest one. Kisses from Ludo.'

Da Vincis! His little Anna! I nearly fell to the floor. What in the name of all that was unholy were these Da Vincis she'd been sending Puppi's way? Did the Ropers own a previously undiscovered Leonardo cartoon? Pages from a notebook? A whole folio? Was the homunculus planning to publish this material? I was on the verge of having another angina attack, when a vision reared before me of a still steaming Ludovico, freshly showered, offering me a cigar.

I calmed myself. Why, wasn't Da Vinci the name of the brand he smoked? Puppi had boasted that it hailed from Nicaragua. Presumably it wasn't easy to get hold of in this sleepy village. Anna wasn't in the habit of transatlantic travel; why on earth was she taking the trouble to shop mail order for special cigs for this puffing poppet?

And, oh my, the articles: those smug, self-congratulatory locutions! Paradigm! Courtly love! The priapic poseur, the concupiscent creep! How I despised Bembo's skimmed-milk version of desire, the whole absurd pretence that the human body didn't exist. To my chagrin, I found myself agreeing with Browning. It was as he'd said: when it came to love I'd take sense any day, too.

Had Anna collected these clippings? Had Puppi *sent* the whole lot to her? How long had they been corresponding with each other and sending each other nauseating love gifts? Well, the detail didn't matter. I'd been braced against one rival, but the sudden re-emergence of the dwarf was a bitter blow. I was ambushed by heartache, revulsion and a piercing, premature mood of nostalgia, as if a sad shadow, a presage of future disaster, had passed between us and caused me to lose Anna before I'd even possessed her.

Above all, the cuttings were heinously indicative of intimacy, not to mention scholarly activity; evidence that Puppi had been to Mawle. He'd been here, at the house, searching for the Madonna. He had spent days or even weeks grubbing around for the painting, he'd tried to worm his way into Anna's simple heart with his clever talk, and afterwards – yes, that was it – he'd bombarded the poor child with boasts about his scholarship. And she'd stuffed the lot in a jar – she probably didn't understand a word of it all. Had she helped him? She couldn't have! Wasn't my presence at Mawle proof of that? Did she like him? Was she really taken in by this plausible gnome? No, no: he was too short. He was bald. He was *Italian*. It was all too risibly, unimaginably revolting.

Everything was subtly altered. I stood at the kitchen window in a slew of sunlight. My mouth was dry from the pills and the booze. Suddenly I could feel something unlooked for, something simple but terrifying in its novelty, raising its bashful head inside me. What I felt for Anna wasn't just infatuation; it was something ordinary but sublime.

Hers was the voice I listened for when I descended the stairs in the morning; her knock-kneed, shy waddle in the corridor outside the library or in the kitchen was a constant, reassuring reminder that life hadn't stalled, but persisted in its usual passage from breakfast to lunch to supper to bath, and would continue to do so the next day, and the next. Her familiar, dropsical smile was balm to my trilling nerves, and seemed to contain my only promise of security. It was not in the least what I'd ever thought love would be like: it was perversely unspectacular, and disconcertingly rooted in the most unprepossessing details of our life together. Anna's bra slung across the back of a kitchen chair to dry, the concertina'd tissues she was forever shedding from her sleeve (this green-fingered girl suffered from hayfever!), a lump of chewing gum she'd saved on a saucer next to the sink – none of these perishable things disgusted me as it should, and once would, have, but instead triggered an indulgent, lascivious tenderness, a sense of fleshly companionableness, that seemed to sum up my whole relation to her now.

I wanted Anna simply to be.

Above Mawle the sky strained like a parachute with its seams full of wind, dilating over the twisting garden, whose green hollows seemed to recede into infinity like a succession of doors opening into the past. At once I saw her step out onto the lawn and stop in a square of brightness, her hair lifted by the breeze. Anna? Giulia? The fabric of reality was so stretched that I no longer knew. She could have been a girl out of any century. Why, it might even have been the Cornaro herself, pacing her garden in search of something to distract her from the knowledge of what she had lost. Her fist gripped her skirts as she urgently mouthed an appeal to someone concealed beyond my field of vision. I was unable to tear my eyes away from her, this woman caught in amber and held aloof, in her ungraspable, inflammatory loveliness, from the present hour. A bolt of shame tore through me: the cuttings seemed to singe my fingers.

As I stood there, swaying woozily on the brink of insight, the telephone rang. Its note of shrill alarm seemed to spew from my own jealousy and compunction, and it felt entirely natural for me to pick up the receiver.

'*Ciao* Anna? Why have you not been calling me with any news? I am sickening with worry! *Sto andando fuori di testa!*'

I knew that sultry, slightly hysterical voice: it was Maddalena Roper.

'Signora Roper? This is Thomas Lynch. Anna is gardening, and I am just enjoying a small *riposo* before returning to work. May *I* help you instead?'

There was a sudden alarmed silence, a crackling that was more than static, that was the essence of indignant tension distilled. I could imagine Maddalena running her nail along the silvered surface of her hoisted breasts; her confused rage and humiliation as, caught out, she weighed up the advantages and possible disadvantages of replying.

'Signora Roper?' I repeated. 'Won't you speak to me? Let me help you. Things could be so much easier for us all if you did.'

Still there was silence. I could not even hear her breath. The walls of the kitchen pressed closer, in stunned fascination at what might happen next. A second later my ears rang with the long flatline beep of a broken connection.

CHAPTER TWENTY-ONE

That evening Anna sat with me in the library. It had become her habit to have a glass of milk, a boiled egg, or some other wholesome titbit to hand. Her appetite was enormous. Since her return from London she had mostly given up her t-shirts and leggings in favour of buttercup or cherry or plum incarnations of the yoked dress she had worn on our Open Day, all cut to the same pattern. I remember, yes I remember, that there was one sprigged with strawberries on a white ground, uneven scarlet stitching snagging the hem, in which she looked like a pattern-book pixie. The Singer in the Sewing Room must have been put to use at some point after all during her lonely days here, before I came.

The evening of the 23rd was the last such Monday evening I was to spend at Mawle, although I didn't know it. The calf-bound books on the shelves were streaked with mulberry shadows. Anna was eating one of those small summer tangerines that smell of fever, of sleepy skin, and seemed more than usually soporific and mute. Her wiry arms were pale; a tendon jumped in her thin wrist as she unwound the pocked rind. A fine summer dew of citrus hung about the room, pricking my nose. Although she'd hardly spoken all evening, I sensed that she was waiting for me to say or do something. Had her mother rung her back? Did she know that I'd tried to force Maddalena's hand that afternoon? I had toyed since supper with the few feeble notes I'd been pretending to make, shuffling my papers and wiping my pen, and now I rose. Anna glanced up at me expectantly.

What did she want from me? All at once I was aware that I was being sent a clear sexual signal, and for the first time in my life in such a situation I was viscerally afraid. 'My dear,' I said nervously, 'I am very tired, and really must sleep. Will you excuse me?'

She flashed me a look of pure hatred. Then she did something that scared the bejesus out of me. Thrusting the last segments of the fruit into her mouth, the crazy girl bit down hard on her lip, so that juice and blood ran mingled down her chin and dripped onto the rind in her hand. On her way to the door she stopped in front of me and wordlessly tipped the peel into my lap.

I sat for a long while without moving, contemplating the meaning of this action. What did she want me to understand by it? 'Here, you phoney, this is all you deserve'? Or: 'Look, this is all that's left of me'? Or even, 'I bleed, and you have done nothing about it'? I knew that I'd failed her in some way, that I had somehow missed my moment, but beyond this I fumbled in darkness. To my annoyance I was also distracted by the memory of a bright fleck of blood, like the flake of a rare shell, on the yoke of her dress. This fleck seemed to grow, to expand in my mind's eye, until it became a pulsating clue, part of a gigantic puzzle, the origin and purpose of which were indecipherable.

I must have fallen asleep. When I opened my eyes it was black night, the sky behind the window thick with stars, its last twinges of cerulean expunged. The room was eerily white, every table and chair transparent, irradiated by fierce moonlight. I felt like a condemned man suddenly woken in his cell by the eye of the warder's torch, and crept up to my room, heavy with unspecifiable guilt and regret. A blade of light from Anna's door pinioned me at the top of the stairs. Through the blazing crack I saw her averted head. Her dressing gown was half unbuttoned; she was trying to pull the elastic band from her hair. A small porcelain lamp burned on the dressing table. Had she been reading? A magazine lay open on the bed. I was transfixed by her sharp elbows, moving vaguely in their loose sleeves. The August wind, more heat than air, blew through the branches of the elms outside and lifted the curtain, exposing a moon as thick as a cheese. She got up to close the window and I left.

It was midnight when I opened Roper's diary again, but I made scarcely any progress. Though the whine or hum, the vibrating chord, of desire was more clearly audible than ever, the handwriting was so poor that I groped in darkness. Following the account of his visit to the Palazzo Buccari there was a longish passage in which his usually energetic script became stooped and dyspeptic, and was veiled on one page by an inky nebula, as if he'd shaken his pen in a frenzy.

Some time shortly after his afternoon at Ca' Buccari, it seems, in late September or thereabouts, something happened that brought about a peculiar alteration in Roper's relationship with the Contessa. The very next entry after his record of this visit had no date, but 'Friday or Saturday?' seared across the top like lightning. Beneath it he had simply penned the single sentence, 'In a day or two we go to Treviso, & I will [approach? assay? attempt?] her again there.'

Then came the furious thicket of writing with the ink

spatters, which must have been the record of the Trevisan trip. It was almost illegible, spiked with ambiguities and ampersands. I skipped over this and stepped into a clearing: a clipped entry for Tuesday, the 1st of October, where Roper had apparently recovered his composure and his orthography.

> *Intermissa, Venus.* I will make it all right with the girl. In spite of all that has passed between us she did not speak a word to me or even look my way all evening.

'In spite of all that has passed between us'? What in God's name *had* happened at Treviso?

On the landing, Anna's door closed with a bang. I rammed the diary under my pillow and snapped off my light. But there were no sly footfalls on the dusty linoleum outside; no skirmishes with my doorknob – I'd locked my door that night for the first time since coming to Mawle – not even (I had to get out of bed and lie with my ear pressed to the slit under the door to make absolutely certain of this) any plaintive sobs coming from that direction. I was both terrified and repelled. Trying to seduce me for her own purposes that evening, Anna had reminded me of Maddalena in ways that I didn't want to think about too closely. I shrank from her, but I pitied her too. I pitied her more than ever. Her lamp was still on. I waited there until two o'clock, willing it to go out, so that I would not have to feel the weight of her wakeful presence across the corridor.

This, I admit, is where my attempt at writing Roper's story threatens to disintegrate. I could easily accommodate his desire. The thing that eluded me was what he had done about it. I lay in the dark, tracing shapes in its changing texture, surrendered to sensual turmoil. In the midst of this flux and reflux I had a peculiarly powerful apprehension of the Bellini. The picture was there somewhere in that black interior, of one fabric with it, still exerting its unbearable pressure on my imagination . . . For an excruciating moment I thought that I could discern its spectral outline towering over me, a rectangle not five feet from the end of my bed. I edged twitching towards it across the blackness, only to strike solid glass. The window pane, a deeper thickness in the thickness of shifting shadows, stared out into nothingness. I drew back the catch and let in a sliver of night. Small rustlings and pipings came from the invisible garden. The crushed air smelled of sap. Here James Roper had walked, had sat, on his return from Italy. Here, after his marriage, for reasons which were still mysterious to me, he'd concealed the Madonna *del prato* in such a way that no one would ever find it. Why, oh why? I was beginning to think that I knew. In a corner of my mind a possible motive had announced itself slyly, like a manifestation of my own wishes. Roper had collected a mass of pictures and bibelots of varying quality, but the Bellini occupied another plane of beauty in his collection entirely. It was the one thing he owned which he couldn't bring himself to share with anyone else. Perhaps he'd tried at first to imagine where such a picture could go, and simply drawn a blank. Soon after this he must have realized that he couldn't bring himself to display the painting at all, that he would never be able to tolerate other eyes assessing its strangeness, making free with its mystery. He'd hidden it in such a way that his hand alone could draw aside the curtain screening it from the world.

And he'd taken his secret to the grave. Was that it? If I could only see! If I could only look right into the heart of that briefly resurrected life, and really *see*—

I began my study of that final, most frustrating section of the diary the very next day. Anna spent Tuesday morning in the kitchen, earnestly studying gardening supply catalogues and occasionally writing down an order. Since leaving me alone in the library with my lap full of orange peel the previous evening her bearing towards me had become fearful and prim, as if I were a drooling rottweiler, or a notoriously lecherous old uncle whom she was obliged to entertain while remaining perfectly aware of the risk she was running. She worked at the beech table as usual, her ankles crossed under her chair (she was wearing knee socks!), her toffee-coloured hair plumped into a plait (or does my spiteful memory invent these details?). In any case, I clearly recall her handwriting, which was large, childish and round, and in which she had just shaped the words 'Green Fuse Fertilizer' on a notepad. Above this she had written 'peat pellets, peat pots, seeds, Sunshine A-Frame Garden House'. There was a forked crimson weal on her bottom lip.

'I'll be going out in a minute to the garden centre to do a little shopping with Harry,' she announced brightly when she saw me lurking in the shadows of the fridge.

'Everything all right, then? Garden coming along well?'

'Couldn't be better, thanks.'

'Good-oh.'

And off I crawled to the library, the disgusting old cur, the randy uncle, to while away the day with weeping and reading. In a quarter of an hour I heard Harry's van starting, the shuddering spray of gravel, the creaking sweep of the gate. I was all alone.

Let me begin the delicate job of restoration, then, painful as it may be. Roper's next diary entry for October after that mysterious Trevisan visit – the account of which is, as I've already indicated, virtually illegible – concerns an enigmatic incident that occurred five or six days later, at Asolo's grape festival. On Sunday the 6th he woke to the peal of bells: many-tongued, insistent, coming as it seemed from every corner of the town. At about ten he at last staggered into the sloping main street of the town. It was dense with bodies, all straining upwards towards the Piazza Maggiore, and the morning sun beat down on the wide-brimmed straw hats and black skirts of the townspeople. A brown sheen of heat lay over the shutters and balconies of the brightly-painted house fronts, over the baking tiles of the roofs, over the thick dark junipers and cypresses thronging the ascent to the Rocca. The town seemed squeezed dry of air; pressing, urgent.

Roper followed the surge into the square and was delivered in front of the cathedral, which the locals call Santa Maria di Breda: a spanking new flat brick façade, three-doored, with twinkling pediments. An old priest waited under the portico, dressed in a frayed surplice and stole, with an aspergillum in his hand. Before him dawdled a motley array of children, carrying grapes in straw panniers fixed around their necks with ribbon, and a row of girls in embroidered blouses, leading a clutch of donkeys. The donkeys' ears were garlanded with red and white paper roses, their backs draped with wildly-stitched blankets of orange and yellow. Two girls approached the main door, carrying a plaster Virgin on a trestle, and lowered it, wobbling, to the ground. The lonely sound of a tambourine sank through the heavy air. The old priest shook holy water vigorously over the statue, the girls and the donkeys, and a loud cheer went up from the crowd.

Some way in front of him Roper spied a linen shirt with a fine blue stripe; grizzled hair, a Panama hat. When he touched the yoke of the shirt, Browning turned around and greeted him boisterously.

'My dear boy,' said Browning, 'isn't this fine? Isn't this the thing?'

'I feel rather hot,' I replied. 'Is there any chance of going in?'

'Why, yes,' Browning smiled. 'I believe that Miss Spragg is securing us a guide.'

Miss Spragg stood by the sputtering fountain mounted by its winged lion in the middle of the square, her hand pressed to her temple, arguing with a sharp-faced fellow in a gay violet waistcoat. On seeing me talking to our poet, the popinjay came right over, wrinkling his nose.

'Signore. This gentleman,' nodding at Browning, 'bids me show you our famous Duomo. But I cannot do it for the money suggested by,' he flicked his fingers contemptuously at Miss Spragg, who had followed hot on his heels, 'this lady.' Then he stood back, stuck out his hip and folded his arms. Drawing heavy breaths in the heat, Miss Spragg returned defiantly that she could not see how it should be right to be *drained dry* when visiting God's House.

Browning let out a guffaw.

'Mr Browning, you are no help,' she flashed back in a pugnacious whisper.

Roper, however, had noticed the two younger ladies drooping near the cathedral door in the full glare of the sun, trying to pat the donkeys. He had not met the Contessina again since their afternoon in Treviso. She was dressed all in white, with a white hat and white gloves, and carried a parasol, and he flinched at seeing that her face was white, too: she looked like a ghost at the festival. At this he immediately agreed to an extortionate price with the young man in the waistcoat, and they went in without further delay.

The stone interior of the cathedral was cobwebby and malodorous. Roper took the Contessa's white parasol. He writes, puzzlingly, that her drawn eyes widened in anger.

'Please to look around, also at pavement,' said our guide. We glanced at our feet. A spider scuttled across my boot and disappeared into a crack in the travertine.

'The Duomo is very ancient, built on a *primitivo* Roman place, found during digging jobs. Most famous event here was welcome of the Cornaro. She was a *patrizia* been born to Venice, married by proxy the great king to Cyprus, Giacomo Lusignano.' The fop paused dramatically. 'But the lady very sad, her husband die, her son die in tender age.'

'Alas,' said Miss Spragg.

'*Si*,' said our guide waspishly. 'The Queen was told, give Cyprus to Venice and return in native land. So she come back to the Repubblica Veneta a widow to live at Asolo. When she arrive there were many *festeggiamenti*. She come with her jolly dwarf, her ladies and *gentiluomini*, her secretary the well-read very clever Monsignor Pietro

Bembo.' He hopped about a little in a festive way. 'In the Dome the Cornaro listen to the *Te Deum* and under the loggia to a speech of pronounced welcome. She was given the honour of being *dominates*, the Mrs of Asolo. Yes! She gave many *ducati* and was a great patron. She donate to the Dome the baptismal bathtub of Grazioli.' He pointed with a swagger at a roly-poly marble font carved with ribbons and a sword. 'But ah, in 1509 the flag of the imperial ones waves on the civic tower once more. Queen Cornaro scarper to Venice. She dies there alone.'

The Contessina leaned against a pew. Browning approached her quietly.

'Are you tired, Contessa? This place is too close. And I fear our guide is not very good.'

'Oh no, Mr Browning. I wish we could continue this *asolando* forever.'

'You are a clever girl. You have given me the title of my book.' He turned to me. 'Mr Roper, your arm is needed.'

She and I went out alone into the sunshine.

What could have happened at Treviso to make Roper lose the Contessa's favour? Had he, as I suspected, pressed his suit too hard; had he risked a familiarity too far? But why, if he did, should proof of his ardour have offended her so? The entry following, for the 10th of October, is equally bewildering. On the face of it this passage, too, has as its central motif the tradition of wine-making on which the area then depended – though, as I will shortly reveal, some of its ostensibly most innocent details are shrouded in a peculiar haze. So much in it is mysterious that I have wondered if it is some sort of elaborate private code. I have even hesitated as to whether I should include such a possibly compromised piece of evidence in this otherwise meticulous dossier. OK, I was drinking heavily, I admit, and it was difficult to tell fact from fancy; at times, indeed, I felt that it was I who no longer existed, and only that long-ago autumn in Asolo and its strange chimes with the present that rang true. But I put it in so as to be absolutely impartial, absolutely exact.

Roper appears to have found it impossible to keep his thoughts from returning to that earlier Trevisan excursion. After a week they kept reverting to it, and what he calls 'the memory of the dancing water, and the heat, and the willows', and even of the Contessina's unsmiling white face and her stern hand on his arm a few days later outside the cathedral in Asolo, had become, he says, a surprising, furtive, incomprehensible joy, made all the sharper by the blank of absence – for after that he didn't see her again until the following Thursday morning. He felt his insides twist when Mrs Bronson suggested a visit to Bassano del Grappa. He hoped that the Contessa would come; he lived in fear that she would not. But she did, and his breath quickened when he saw Miss Spragg leading Giulia up the worn steps of La Mura.

'You are in good spirits, Mr Roper,' observed Miss Spragg with a sideways simper at her charge. 'I think that Asolo must agree with you.'

'It does, ma'am. It agrees with me more than I can say. *È una vista incantevole*.'

'You have learned a new phrase, sir,' said Miss Spragg.

'Yes,' I reddened, 'I have. It's a beautiful view.'

To my chagrin the Contessa merely looked down at the scratched flags of the *sala*, chewing the inside of her lip as though she tasted something bitter there.

They struck out for Bassano later that morning in Mrs Bronson's carriage, driven by Vittorio. Browning, obnoxiously helpful as ever, went with them, making up a sixth member of the party. Roper had great difficulty in preventing his knees from rubbing up against the Contessa's skirts in the crush. They were seated directly opposite each other, and he kept his eyes, when he did not look out of the window, fixed resolutely on the toe of her boot, as she did hers on his. Behind them rolled the plain with its moving shadows, bordered by the lacy outline of the Euganean Hills; ahead to the west lay the remote mountains, capped with snow. The carriage entered Bassano as it trundled alongside the spangled Brenta, which flowed between buttressed and corbelled houses and was spanned by Palladio's grand old wooden bridge at its broadest point.

The travellers stood for a while on the broad timbers of this structure, watching the ducks float past, and the gulls swooping overhead past Monte Grappa. Then they walked along until they came to an inn with a peaked wooden roof at the eastern entrance of the bridge. Roper caught the fiery blur of geraniums growing in balconied terracotta pots, carved wooden tables and chairs, girls with plaited hair milling about in white aprons. A metallic breeze blew from the river. The place did not look or feel Italian at all, but he was so tamped with volcanic emotion that he could not care. Browning commandeered one of the carved tables and called for the speciality of the town.

The word sent me ricocheting between past and present. Which was which? Their grappa came in a squat bottle, drawn straight from the cask, with thistle-shaped glasses and a dish of dried cod. Every detail of this scene seemed golden, as solid as sense; it was I who was fraying at the edges.

The clear spirit had the very palest sheen of sun-bleached straw, and I could taste its coldness in Roper's mouth, the latent germ of fire that flickered over the tongue and cauterized his throat. *Alla salute!* The years seemed to scumble and bleed together as I read. I drank greedily from my own bottle; the effect was identical.

Miss Bronson also drank, coughed wildly, and held out her glass to be refilled. 'Mamma never allows me to have this divine beverage when we are at home,' she laughed roguishly.

'Yes, and now you may see why, madam,' said Mrs B, who was nevertheless amused rather than reproving. 'Is it to your taste, Mr Roper?'

Roper belched that it had a most tonic effect – he, too, would try just a little more. The Contessina observed that her Papa had been very fond of grappa. Her upside down head swam reflected in the bulb of Roper's glass, cushioned by blue sky and restless cloud. He had never heard her mention her father before. 'Then you, too, must have another drop,' he urged, flourishing the bottle.

'He did not live long,' added the Contessa simply, taking a sip of the sugary brandy. I – did I really write *I?* I mean, of course, Roper – felt obscurely wrong-footed, and so refilled her glass again.

How diffuse I felt, as if I were being spread thinly across time . . .

'Oh, I can't be doing with this cod,' Miss Bronson broke out, pushing the dish away. 'I have such a craving now for some nice cold asparagus that I could simply die!'

'Yes, the white asparagus at Bassano is especially delicate,' agreed her mother. 'But this is October, you know,' she added. 'You shall have to wait until May to satisfy your appetite, miss.'

Miss Bronson made a sour face. 'I won't wait!' She turned to Browning, her mouth twitching wilfully. 'Dear Mr Browning, please find me some. No one could refuse you, or your genius. You could conjure asparagus out of a coal-scuttle!'

'Even Robert cannot turn autumn into spring,' murmured Mrs B with a wry smile.

'Well now, Kate,' returned Browning, strangely nettled, 'we shall see. This is a dilemma to which the application of the *creative imagination* would not go amiss.'

The page fermented under my hands as they roamed Bassano's quiet alleys in the heat in search of Miss Bronson's asparagus. Roper's perceptions have the feverish heightened cast of a dream: he seems to have drifted, that afternoon, through shifting layers of excitement and apprehension. After a while the party dispersed and he lost sight of the others. The trefoiled windows of the houses gave way to painted fronts: a variegated deck of cards that fanned out as far as the eye could see. Roper wandered under a portico and came across a busy market at the foot of a sheer white church, where stall after stall reared steeply up at him, disgorging onions, leather, silk, figs and majolica wares. A slalom brought him to the Contessina. She stood under a striped canvas awning, gazing mournfully at a shelf of china dolls, her childish arms huddled around her waist. The legs of the dolls stuck out from under their skirts, their useless dwarf feet shod in leather pumps. He noticed with despair that Giulia drew back a little when she saw him.

'Oh, Mr Roper, aren't they pretty?' she smiled wanly, and in that moment I thought they were the most remarkable things in God's creation, and bought her three, one with a head of tousled walnut, one with wiry black hair pasted into a widow's peak, and one with a lacquered hazel plait. They all had identical snub noses, and after I'd persuaded Giulia to put her hand in mine the dolls sat in the crook of her free arm, turning their noses up at me.

They found Browning at last, not in the market, but haggling with a crone in a dirty little shop down an alleyway where bottles of preserves filled the curtained shelves: transparent chillies, bruised discs of purple aubergine, flared artichoke hearts, all swilling in oil, beneath which the poet leaned across the grainy counter, gossiping companionably with the old woman.

'My dear boy,' Browning blared as I entered, with the Contessina still clinging to my wrist. 'See what treasure I've found! All the fruits of the seasons, look! If we don't get our autumn asparagus here, my name is not Robert Browning.'

The crone grunted that if it was asparagus we wanted she had a jar or two, shuffled off into the back of the shop, and returned with three golden bottles in which hung suspended some stumpy white stalks with tufted heads.

'Indeed,' breathed Browning, entranced. 'And how do we eat this?'

'You take the asparagus, you shake it gently. You roast it in its oil, you pepper it, you salt it. You slice mozzarella very fine, and roll the stalks in the cheese, and roast them again until they bubble and pop, and douse them in grappa, and throw *parmigiano* on top while they are still hot, as much as you can, and a tongue of butter. *Eccolà!*' She winked lewdly at the Contessina. 'Your husband will not be able to resist it, Signora. It aids the deep sleep, but first,' she fluttered her lips, 'it pricks the fires.'

I realized in an engulfing rush of blood that she was referring to me. The Contessa looked down in consternation.

'Clearly a speciality of the region,' boomed Browning, indecorously amused. 'My dear boy, we must try it. I will buy all three jars of this pale asparagus, and we shall have it as suggested for supper tonight. Come, *Signora Roper*, do I have your consent?'

The Contessina nodded her head agitatedly, shook it and nodded it, and they left carrying their bottles of asparagus wrapped in soiled paper tied with twine, like triumphant midwives after a successful delivery.

Reluctantly I watched them go. The room hardened into its familiar lines; I was left with the quaking of my gut. As I dragged my eyes away from the page the grudging minutes began their forward impetus again.

Aside from the discomfiting questions this entry again raised about Roper's mysteriously altered relations with the Contessa, it arrested my attention because it contained that rather adventurous recipe for roast asparagus. I took some time and care over preparing this dish for Anna's supper, once she and Harry had stopped ransacking the local nurseries.

They returned with their spoils in a state of high excitement, and I listened all that Tuesday afternoon to the bubble and splutter of their voices percolating in the pit. The glowing garden chirped and whistled beyond the windows of Mawle, spasmodically disturbed by the clanging of Harry's hammer on the metal struts of the ascending glasshouse. Anna's eager voice wove in and out of this rhythm in syncopated encouragement and praise, and once or twice Vicky swore cheerfully from the fringes of that green world. How distant it seemed, how self-enclosed, like a toy scene sealed in a plastic dome. Were they reconciled, had they buried the hatchet; had they, in cutesy common parlance, 'made up'? I guessed so. By nine o'clock the shiny white skeleton of a greenhouse glinted next to the asparagus bed. Anna stole in through the back door at twilight with her soiled gum boots in her hand, like a guilty girl tiptoeing home after her curfew. She took in the crystal, the eggshell-thin Sèvres, the stone cold asparagus spears in their cheesy hods; the shavings of parmesan settled, like a giant's dandruff, in twin ramekins.

'Oh, Dr Lynch, you haven't been cooking, have you?'

I tightened the pinny nastily around my waist. 'I have.'

'Where's Vicky?'

'Bathed and in bed. I explained to her that you were *very* busy. She asked me to give you a special kiss goodnight.'

How her neglectful maternal heart must have been stabbed by this! She even came up to me and dutifully presented her cheek. I felt like a schoolmaster administering a beating. Her face was soft, and smelled of sweat.

'I feel terrible,' she moaned. 'I've so ignored you.'

'You've been working far too hard. You must eat. You are wasting away.' (This was obviously untrue. While her arms remained gaunt she had, in the last fortnight, become noticeably bloated around the stomach and buttocks, a pincushion dolly.)

'You're right. I must keep my strength up.' She sniffed hungrily at the asparagus.

'Would you like me to warm it up for you?' I snapped.

'No, don't bother.' Anna slid back her chair and fell to. I watched in admiration as her strong young jaws shredded the woody shafts and scissored the stringy mozzarella. 'Oh, this is fantastic,' she gasped between mouthfuls. 'This is just what I needed. Aren't you having any?'

'No, my dear. This is all for you.' I steered my plate towards her. My appetite had disappeared, together with my anger. If she could only have managed to eat every last scrap, not just my supper but the plate itself, the kitchen table, the kitchen, the house, and me in it, I would have been entirely happy, entirely fulfilled. In that half hour, I admit, I examined the possibility of a new life for us both, in which I cooked her food and washed her child and saw her chastely to bed in a lawn nightgown every night, and sometimes wiped the mud from her boots when she crawled in from the shack in the field.

I plied Anna with a pre-war Chablis which I had found in the cellar, and which was no doubt priceless. She drank down two glasses, kissed me clumsily on the mouth, and went to her room. The next morning she slept late. I fretted and fussed over a breakfast tray, but didn't have the courage to carry it up to her. In retrospect I am glad, because as it turned out she needed every ounce of her strength for what was about to happen.

CHAPTER TWENTY-TWO

Unlike Anna I did not sleep well that Tuesday night, the night of the asparagus, perhaps because I hadn't eaten any of this soporific vegetable. In fact I had great trouble sleeping at all, for it was now, as if they had simply been waiting for an inopportune moment to come calling, that my old friends and enemies began to appear to me. No sooner was I alone in my room after supper than the visits began. As I was about to don my pyjamas I was alarmed to find Father Gabriel, the old Jesuit who had sent me into Paine's arms, standing dolorously at my bedside, eyebrows fizzing with disappointment. I stopped to fight him off with extended fingers, dazzled by the envelope of acid light surrounding the old bastard, only to find myself gripping the switch of the bedside lamp, propelled into full wakefulness as if by an electric shock.

Later I was interrupted as I strained biliously on the lavatory by the spectre of Mrs Platt, reeking of fermented fruit. I was even called on at dawn by my first lover himself, manifesting as a pair of thin, roughly-trousered legs and pimply buttocks that painfully resolved themselves, as the slow day broke, into the worn curtains and fly-blown glass of my little window. With these visits came a low-voltage trembling that shook my whole body, as if the poles of my being had been rammed into an enormous socket. The quake crawled slowly through my flesh, a fiery caterpillar furred with pain.

The funny thing was that these attacks began within hours of my last tipple. They were accompanied by a savage coldness that seemed to crystallize in my marrow and sprout out of my very bones, making my scalp itch and my arms and legs twitch wildly, until I put the bottle of grappa to my mouth again – and then the blessed sensation of warmth and ease was like the kiss of the sun, so that I drank more. I drank all night, stopping only to pick up the diary. Certain words still have the round flavour and bountiful scent of the spirit – 'October', for instance, or 'Contessa'.

Oh, I knew what this was called; I knew the term for it, this drenched quaking, this nervous paralysis. I had to admit to myself that I was entering the physical stage of alcohol poisoning, the deadly downwards hurtle of delirium tremens. But I didn't give a damn.

I had become too obsessed by that cursed diary. The slow unpicking of its pages was a compulsion which I rationed as carefully as a miser rations the pawing of his hoard. Some of the entries which I'd so laboriously deciphered I read over and over that night, until I came to know them by heart. Their shard-like reflections of another place and another time were superimposed on my memory of the daily comings and goings at Mawle, merging with them in a palimpsest in which it was difficult to distinguish past from present. I could see James Roper's face with absolute clarity – I could see the blond hairs that sprouted on his lip; and the thin bones of Giulia's arms . . . Squatting inside my maze, dazed in my isolation, I continued to disentangle the skein of the past. Yes, something had happened at Treviso. I couldn't help feeling that this was the puzzle at the heart of Roper's story, and that if I could only follow it to its source

I would be able to feel the thread of the mystery jerking in my clutch.

But what did I find when I went back to that snarled section of the diary and pored over it with a tumbler full of magnifying water to hand? Only more metaphors, more poetry, more phantoms.

Treviso, then. Let me see if I can disentangle fancy from fact. Fact: it seems that Mrs Bronson, Browning, Edith, the Contessa and Roper visited the little town, famed for its position on the River Sile, its Venetian-style canals and bridges, in the last week or so of September. The date, as I mentioned earlier, is indistinct, but their excursion must have taken place some time between Roper's scrawled entry in late September, and the sudden improvement in his mood on the 1st of October, when he so bafflingly wrote that he would 'make it all right'. I will backtrack to that earlier passage, which I have so far avoided because it was the very devil to decipher. Here Roper tried, as far as I could see, to describe the topography of the town as it struck him on arrival. But is the account that follows fact or fancy, or that hyperreal blend of both which, I now suspect, is the best that we can hope for from experience?

Treviso was hot. It was all water, Roper writes, and appeared, at first, uncannily like a [shrunken?] Venice: an infinite regress of miniature canals, minute marble-clad bridges, and abbreviated arches with gap-toothed balustrades, as if a drowning dwarf had grinned a final, despairing grin before sinking under the waves. Façades of roasted red and orange jutted among the scalding shadows. The brows of the houses were tattooed with strange frescoes of angels and mythological beasts. In the Calmaggiore he saw a thickly matted faun and a cherub nestling side by side, with their limbs entwined, as if the creatures were [indecipherable. Possibly 'frolicking'?]. The heat, which had reared up at midday like a hungry flame, made walking uncomfortable. The flagging group stood for some time in the Piazza dei Signori, a close little square like a sitting room, wondering where to turn next, and unable, in spite of the domestic proportions of the piazza, which powerfully suggested the proximity of sofas and armchairs, to find any place to rest.

'I smell fish,' said Miss Bronson.

'My dear child,' began her mother, mopping her face peevishly with a handkerchief, 'pray do not, *please* do not, embark on one of your whims.'

'No, no, Mrs Bronson,' said Roper, 'I believe that we passed a signpost for a fish market not long since. That is,' he added, 'if a *pescheria* means a fish market, as I think it does.'

'Good Lord,' exclaimed Browning, 'are we to go traipsing after fish in this weather? Very well, very well,' he conceded when Miss Bronson began whiningly to protest, 'fish it will be. Fish it is. Jonah,' he waved at Roper, 'lead on.'

By pressing down an alley, and then crossing a stone bridge, they came to a striking [stinking?] island in the middle of the main canal of the town, packed with wooden trestles that brimmed with fish. The crinkly innards of fish streamed festively into buckets; the blunt heads of fish lay like shed arrow-heads in the sawdusty cobbles; the butterflied bodies of fish gaped on rosettes of rose-red blood. Boxes of coffined crabs jostled against tubs full of octopus, oysters and mussels, pans crammed with shrimp, and platters of tinselly sardines. Siren-like voices called from every corner, and all around, like a hammer, clanged the ferrous tang of the sea. As Roper gazed at the accusing lips of a halibut he was taken aback to feel the Contessina's hand gripping his arm. Feeling more than a little unsteady himself, he asked her if she were unwell.

'I am – I am. It is the smell – the blood. Can we go somewhere else?' Her little tongue darted around & about between her teeth. 'My cousin told me that I was to entrust myself entirely to you.'

Her cousin? Which cousin? Miss Spragg, or Giuseppe? A mantle of perspiration lapped Giulia's thin wrist, and Roper saw from the tug of her bodice that she was breathing rapidly and shallowly.

'Oh please,' she repeated urgently, 'let us go from here.'

I looked about, but could not see Mrs Bronson or the others. I wasn't certain, even then, where Giulia & I went, or what exactly was required of me. I remember that I led her past a water mill dully scooping its water with square wooden paddles, down [tangled?] streets full of people, across a succession of bridges. There was a dark smear of blood on her skirt. I was aware of the glint of marble, of balconies & wrought iron lanterns, & once, on a house corner, of a grinning stone face with an enormous nose. The sun stood high in the sky, a dish full of shallow fire. After several minutes we crossed a broader bridge & came to a quiet bend in the river. My heart was beating hard: I could feel its frantic pulse in my neck, my temples, in the hollow of my nauseated stomach. The heat was terrible. Giulia's hand was still on my arm.

Finally a band of trembling water stretched before us in the distance, thickly hemmed along its banks by willows. Here there was no one. By now my [passion?] had risen to match hers, & I guided her firmly onwards by the elbow. Had I interpreted her docility correctly? I hoped; I scarcely dared to hope—

A short way along the river the canal & the drooping boughs of the bank met above our heads in an endlessly repeating arabesque, as if the willows had flung their heads down to the water to drink or to despair. The light was green & low. At this spot I persuaded Giulia, although she appeared suitably reluctant, to proceed a little way with me into the coolness of the trees & to [recline?] against the mossy slope of the bank. Her skirts caught once or twice on the reeds & nettles that grew along the path, & she made a little show of resisting when I stooped to free them – I remember that my hand caressed her ankle – & of wanting to go back. Once there, however, she saw the futility of any further protest & sat down with a tremulous thud – indeed, I flatter myself, she [embraced?] the inevitability of the encounter to which she had invited me.

When they made their way back a little later to rejoin the rest of the party, however, the Contessina was utterly silent. Her cheek was colourless; her gloved hand, on the cuff of which there was a muddy stain, lay rigidly in the hinge of Roper's elbow. Although he tried to divert her with conversation she showed him only her stunned [profile?], like a sleepwalker. She would not let him [comfort? confront?] her for the rest of the afternoon. The papery faces of the houses they passed seemed to blush a stinging scarlet in the afternoon sun. As they walked Roper could make out, through low windows, the interiors of unfamiliar rooms: a clock on a wall, striking the hour, a birdcage, some pictures. 'I have never,' he admits, 'felt so sad.'

I couldn't decipher any more: the handwriting was abysmal. I tried to find hidden coherences between this entry and the others, but its morphology defeated me. The echoes came and went: sunlight, the heat of a fading summer, the tang of asparagus, the smell of salt and blood; the snap and bite of random appetites, randomly expressed. Something had happened at Treviso, all right. When I'd at last combed through Roper's confession I couldn't but see the main fact. That moment on the riverbank threw an unnervingly slant light on his later encounter with the Contessa at the cathedral in Asolo.

Awkwardly and ignobly short of the ideal as the truth was, it was clear that Roper had done more than risk an over-familiarity under the willows. He'd had sex with Giulia.

Oh, he'd had her, that's for sure. But why did Roper describe the girl's eyes, on meeting his at Santa Maria later that week, as widening in anger? As I cast about for an answer I seemed to catch the sharp edge of a darker shape glinting under the sunlit surface of the diary; glinting and turning slowly, like the back of a monstrous, still submerged creature that would soon begin to rise from the depths to shatter the calm surface of my suppositions.

Was the Contessa's surrender to him at Treviso calculated, as Roper implies, or was it rape? I sat up for hours, trying to arrive at an answer, but I always failed.

You will have to judge the case. All I am able to see is that it is very likely that everything I have put down here is going to have to be rewritten.

CHAPTER TWENTY-THREE

Anna, newly emerged on Wednesday morning from her long sleep, stooped as reverently as a priestess at her shrine over the junk she had bought for the greenhouse: plastic irrigation troughs and pot-bellied thermometers; outlandish funnels and chalice-shaped cups for dissolving magical cubes; stinking powders promising instant fertilization. My heart was momentarily eased, quite cured. How couldn't it be? She was near, and spread out all around me was the glorious world: the racing blue summer sky, the sparkling air, a stray Cabbage White flitting across the shingled roof of Mawle.

And then, around mid-morning, as I was about to go into the kitchen, I saw them. Harry had his right arm around Anna's waist, buckling its tender hollow backwards, over the edge of the wooden table. His body was naked to the waist, burned scarlet by the sun: a red king, claiming his queen. Her hand gripped his neck, either to pull him towards her or push him away. Her t-shirt had ridden up to reveal a fold of brown flesh. Even at that distance I imagined that I could inhale Anna's bruised lily smell. The tips of her bare feet were lifted off the floor, each toe a rigid little tongue.

As I looked on the two stopped, frozen, even though they had not noticed me. A sense of desolation seemed to have come over them; their very muscles appeared to slacken. Giving Harry an impatient tap on the chest, Anna freed herself and went to slouch by the sink, her spine limp. At that moment they both had the air of prisoners, of captives: large animals left in their cage to mate or not, at will.

Was she vacillating disastrously, even then, between him and me? If I had quit the field, packed up my bag and gone home, or even just shut my gob, would all have been well? Perhaps – oh, a more than speculative yes to that! Sheer inertia might still have kept Harry by her side, or the disabling pressure of that nugget of desire which I'd glimpsed in him before. One could see Anna in ten years' time, a blubbery Mrs Mop with a sullen teenage kid and several more homunculi that had popped from her midriff in the meanwhile, fixing the oaf his lunch, watering the tomato plants, treadling her Singer on winter evenings in that shabby little room . . .

But the fact is that I really don't know. I still don't know! I'm inclined to believe now that my failure to understand Anna was, quite literally, a matter of perspective: it was not that I didn't bother to look, but that I was standing too close to her to discern the larger picture of which she was a part. And I was harried by shadows. I was inhabiting a ghost story. I was helplessly snagged in the diary's spectral web, surrounded by the chatter of wraiths whose voices were by now so loud that they threatened to drown out the voices of the living. That morning I waited in Roper's study in a state of convulsive expectation, intensely alert but at the same time not properly awake, and after spending an hour or so in this condition I came to myself with a start and realized that there was a bloody taste in my mouth, that I had a cramp in my foot and that I still held the notebook in my quaking hands.

Roper was falling in love. I treasure it, that first glimpse of an emotion that was, on the face of it, so improbable, and at the same time so predictable. He had forced himself on Giulia, or she had yielded to him; at any rate, he had fucked her, and out of nothing the alchemy of sex had produced this most homely of flowers, this modest little bloom.

At the time I found it laughable and rather touching; absurdly touching, too, were Roper's shy attempts at keeping the blossom alive, as if it were a rare species the world had never seen before. He sat, tongue-tied, with the Contessa in the parlour of Ca' Buccari while the jowled and snoring aunt acted as duenna. He describes himself, on another day, as voluptuously humbled when the girl indicated with a wary nod that he, and not Giuseppe – who always lingered, it seems, on the fringes – should fetch her fan. Roper, who noticed that Giulia remained skittishly aloof from Giuseppe's ostentatious bustling, supposed that Italians could not help talking in such dramatically imploring tones even about glasses of water or the necessity of opening the window. He bought Giulia a box of watercolours, which she accepted politely and laid to one side. Although he hoped to surprise her painting with them one afternoon, he never did.

By doing violence to her he had done violence to himself. He was slowly being taken apart and reconstituted. What had happened at Treviso might have involved the act of love, but it wasn't yet love: *that* was a stealthy, preposterous, and yet unavoidable thing. And of course he dreamed about her at night: sometimes just as she was, a brown-eyed child in a bad dress, in need of his tenderness and protection; at other times as the pressure of a body in the darkness, and once, intoxicatingly, as a lapping fire.

A sense of strain had descended on Mrs Bronson's party: everyone seemed to be waiting for a crisis that would break the deadlock of the autumn. On a Thursday evening towards the end of October, Roper remembers, Mrs B had rounded up her scalps in the parlour at La Mura. It was growing cold, and the curtains were partly drawn against the blossoming dusk. The side tables had been pulled forwards to allow the light from their fringed lamps to fall in a broad muddy wash on the Turkey carpet, in the middle of which snored a huddle of dogs. Edith had almost completed her tapestry. Browning, who had been in an awkward, louring temper during dinner, sat by the wood stove, loudly cracking and shelling walnuts. The whole scene had an air of muffled menace, of smothered hopes; in stray phrases I could detect the sour whiff of rut on the turn. The Contessina was restless, and lingered wistfully by Miss Bronson's chair.

'I have never seen anything so beautiful,' sighed the girl. 'It is like a real bird, but better.'

I could picture it: an apple tree with plump russet apples into which I might sink my teeth, and in front of this a great strapping male peacock with its immense blue and green train spread out in a descending stellar curve, on which the iridescent centre of each feather glowed like a burnished eye . . .

Miss Bronson dipped her head modestly, but looked secretly triumphant. 'Oh, I like to keep my hand in. Though I am not an *artist* like our dear Mr Browning, of course.'

'What's that, eh, Edie?' Browning gloomed, looking up from his exertions over the nutcracker. 'Have you finished that beast at last?'

Miss Bronson said nothing.

Roper had tried to engage the Contessina in conversation all afternoon, but with scant success: she answered in monosyllables, and refused to meet his gaze.

'Oh, Mamma, Mr Roper, look at the sun.' It was Miss Bronson, from her chair under the tall windows, who had spoken again. Her face was turned from her embroidery towards the distant hilltop.

They all looked up in amazement. In setting, the sun that now flamed beyond the curtains resembled a phosphorescent disc – vibrating, shooting out cords of purple and scarlet in all directions. Every tree, stone and leaf was coloured red by its rays.

'Oh, it is like a rose,' said the Contessina, with parted lips. 'Or perhaps the souls of the dead, like a thousand petals, flying up to heaven.'

Browning regarded Giulia with keen interest. 'You have the imagination of a poet, my dear,' he said. 'You know things as a poet knows them.'

The girl was abashed. 'Oh, no, I do not know very much.'

'But you love what you see. And knowledge without love is lifeless. Eh, Mr Roper? Isn't that so?'

I did not know what to say to this. What had he guessed?

They lapsed into troubled silence again. To fill it Mrs B began, in her hovering drawl, to recount a dream she'd had the previous night about a pedlar who had come to the door with his cheap sweets and a tray of charms.

'I hope you sent him away, Mamma,' Miss Bronson interrupted her crisply, returning to her needlework.

'Well, no, not exactly,' Mrs B admitted guiltily. 'I was not tempted by the candy, and I could feel no excitement at the prospect of a new gown.' She smoothed down the folds of her plain housedress with its heavy satin mantle. Above her head, an old tapestry shivered lightly in the heat that rose from the tiled stove. 'But the charms, though, were quite another thing! I had never seen such rare and delightful trinkets. There was a little dog, just like Tubby here,' she nudged an unseen form beneath her skirts, which grunted, 'and a sun and a moon; the smallest, most perfectly fashioned silver rosebud; a miniature wedding ring, a baby's hand, and, prettiest of all, a tiny book, perfect in every detail right down to the lettering on its spine.'

Browning had stopped shelling nuts some moments earlier, and was now listening attentively. 'What was the title of the book?' he asked.

'Do you know, I can't for the life of me recall,' Mrs B replied. 'I sometimes fancy that I can glimpse it again if I turn my head very quickly, just so.' The blue ribbons of her cap jerked to the left and right. 'It is one word, and I think it starts with an *A*. But no. No – it is entirely gone, I'm afraid.'

Browning fell silent again, but did not pick up the nutcracker.

'And which charm did you choose to have as your own, Signora Bronson?' asked the Contessina.

'Well,' said Mrs B kindly, 'for a very long time I simply couldn't choose! My fingers brushed over the silver until it was quite smudged, and the old pedlar became really quite impatient.'

'But you must have had a preference, you know,' said her daughter.

A smile hovered around Mrs B's mouth. 'And so I did – I had two preferences! I liked the solid little book very much, but I also yearned for the ring, which was so plain, and yet perfect. My fingers strayed first to the one, then to the other . . . The pedlar rattled his tray. The ring, or the book? The book, or the ring? Which to choose?'

'Oh, which did you?' asked the Contessina.

'Alas, my dear, I hadn't the chance! For I was so long in deciding that the old man snapped his case shut, and passed from under my gate, leaving me empty-handed.' Mrs B placed her hands, palm up, in her lap, as if to demonstrate.

'Yes, but which *would* it have been? Why won't you tell?' the Contessina persisted, with an artlessness that made Roper smile.

Mrs B pondered. 'Well, my dear, I really don't know which. I truly hadn't made up my mind. Maybe the old pedlar knew this.' She nodded thoughtfully. 'Yes, I do believe that he recognized my indecisiveness. It's an old failing of mine.'

And then something happened that gave the final sprain to this halting evening. Miss Bronson asked audaciously what Roper had dreamed the night before. 'Oh, if we are to speak of dreams we must enquire of Mr Browning,' Roper parried. 'I am sure there is more poetry in his briefest afternoon nap than in all our midnights put together.'

'Indeed not, Mr Roper,' snarled Browning, his broad face startlingly suffused with spite. 'I have no dreams worth remembering – no beautiful or clever dreams.' He gazed at the walnut in his palm. 'The particularity of the world – is agony. When I came here first, as a young man, every stone, every tree, every face,' touching a finger to his cheek, which seemed wet in the light of the slowly setting sun, 'seemed ringed with fire just as they do tonight; ablaze with – I can hardly say with what – with a certain *truth* – with the truth of their own nature.' He stopped and stared unseeing at the tapestry peacock under Miss Bronson's fingers. Mrs B put out her hand, as if to dissuade him from speaking further, but he waved her away.

'Ah, Kate, each thing was full of such terror and beauty – such beauty clothed in terror – like the Bush, burning but unconsumed! And now?' He slid heavily to a footstool near the stove. 'The Bush is bare. I write and nothing comes. Mine is a mimic creation at best – the travailing mountain yields a silly mouse.'

'Nonsense, Robert; only reflect!' countered Mrs B. 'Your new book is finished. Your reputation is secure. The contribution you have made to poetry, to our language itself, cannot fade.'

'Language! What piss! A book is just a book. A flower is just a flower. I am so weary of words.'

Here Mrs Bronson got up, and Roper realized that he had never before seen her perform this simple action with such uncharacteristic abruptness. She crossed the floor to where Browning sat and laid her palm briefly on his white head before leaving the room. Taking the Contessa by the hand, her daughter followed her with a distressed glance at Roper. Roper stood up, sat down, and promptly propped himself up again, like a straw man at a fair. Then he gabbled his good-nights to the poet, who still squatted on the footstool in dejection.

Why, how blindingly obvious it was. It was Browning who was in love, and banal Mrs Bronson who had eluded *him*.

There is something else that happened on that final Wednesday at Mawle which I should record.

I sat in that bleak library all morning like a castaway. There was an iron, thwarted taste on my tongue. *Spare me, Venus!* Anna never appeared, needless to say. Vicky materialized briefly at the door of the library, resplendent and miserable in her silver sheath, saw my equally miserable face, and vanished again. Around midday I began to despair. The sun stood remorselessly high above the frayed curtains, tearing the blue heavens with its invincible blade. Thirsty and comfortless, I turned again to the clump of ledgers and scattered papers that Anna had put on my table, intending to scrape them into a heap and fling them into a drawer. How full of dust and trash, how full of random *things* they were.

My thumb flicked under a loose page, as brittle and brown as a sycamore leaf, which helicoptered to the carpet at my feet. I bent down, throbbing with sorrow in every joint, to pick it up. It was a large sheet that must once have been folded into sharp quarters, because it was lined vertically and crossways with deep creases. In the centre, aligned on the bar of the horizontal crease, was a rapid sketch – just four swift lines – of something approximately rectangular, and radiating out from this point, at regular angles, spread pie-like slices filled with perfectly rendered concentric circles. The whole configuration was boxed in by a thick black border. This wasn't part of a conventional ledger or an account book, and I wondered for a moment if it was a copy of something, some design or pattern in marble or paint, that Roper had seen and coveted in a church or gallery in the course of his travels. Then I saw, on closer inspection, that the spiralling circles were not circles at all, but minute, furled fragments of script. *Rosa centifolia pomponia. Rosa damascena bifera. Rosa gallica officinalis. Rosa gallica versicolor.*

All at once I understood. Each curled knot was a name – the proper, botanical name – of a rose, and each segment of pie represented a bed planted with row on row on row of roses: tight buds, knotted heads, great dissolute loose-petalled cabbages of roses. It was a plan for a rose garden; for the secret overgrown garden I had found behind the concealed stone wall, beyond the low door with the lion's-head handle.

Roper had planted it – it was his garden.

I was suddenly overwhelmed by an irrational desire to visit it again, to put the disturbing power of its degenerate profusion to the test. Not a whisper, not a moan, came from the direction of the kitchen. Refolding the sketch, I stole to the back door. The kitchen was indeed quite empty. I couldn't see Anna and Harry outside; had they repaired to his shack? Or were they upstairs, bouncing about in her apple-scented bed? I cast these thoughts from my mind and strolled nonchalantly past the flowerbeds, sometimes stooping to finger a bloom. Did I see a curtain twitch from somewhere high up? No: it was my imagination . . . The beech trees stood to attention punctually, like the hands of a clock. No ghosts troubled the margins of the day.

When I was certain that no one was watching, I approached the ragged shrubbery to the east of Mawle and slid into its rough darkness. It was damp, as before, and thorny, but this time I expected to get badly scratched, and I asserted my will more roughly. Even the contrary convolvulus seemed compliant. I hacked and tore. And there it was: the door, planted in a sea of shrivelled apples, the jaws of its knocker stretched wide in a noiseless roar. It opened to my touch without a murmur. Hundred-petalled heads surrounded me, a clump of frilled old bloomers hung out to air. The mossy lion crouched motionless, its green legend undisturbed and as withholding as previously: *pour lialte' maintenir.* It was all as I'd remembered it, only if possible more undone, more melancholy, and I was rinsed with a debilitating feeling of foreboding.

'No, indeed. There is no rose garden at Mawle.' And yet there was. What did it mean?

Vicky turned up in the kitchen some time after one o'clock, clamouring for food. She wasn't wearing the costume from the old clothes cupboard she'd had on that morning, but something just as bizarre: flared grey nylon slacks topped off with a white aertex shirt, and a vile pair of black rubber clogs.

'My school uniform,' she said proudly. 'D'you like it? What have we got to eat?. Where's Anna?'

'Ghastly,' I replied. 'Cheese on toast, gone. Why are you wearing that ridiculous getup?'

'Term starts next week.' She rested her chin glumly on her grubby fists. 'We were given tons of homework and I haven't done any of it. I'm trying to get in the mood.' She gazed up at me pleadingly.

'I suppose I could lend a hand. Lunch first.' Inside, I was beginning to ooze melancholy. School! So soon! I swallowed the lump in my throat. Professor Lynch as foster father! 'I just hope you haven't been given any of that incomprehensible trigonometry to do.'

'Dr Lynch, I'm only *nine*.' She rolled her eyes in that exasperating, endearing way of hers.

It didn't happen then, but later that afternoon, once we had eaten the toasted cheese, suffered indigestion, and agonized over the geography of the British Isles. With a burp, Vicky ran off to play. Anna hadn't returned for lunch. The sun was entering its ripest phase: a squat Buddha of gold, dazzling and indifferent on a cloth of blue. I still sat at the kitchen table, tracing the concentric patterns of the plan with my forefinger. Birds twittered callously in the trees.

I noticed the voices first as a counterpoint to the birdsong, erratic and shrill. There was a high shriek, issuing in a frenzied volley, and a low-pitched *stut-stut-stutter* in answer: heavy machinery, ponderous and deadly. This went on for several minutes, and seemed to grow louder before stopping abruptly. I heard a woman bellow briefly in pain. Then there was silence. I got up and went to the back door. There was no one in the garden, and the asparagus bed was deserted, a black slash in the green. The frail bones of the glasshouse teetered in the sunlight.

Slipping along the back wall of the house, I could smell a familiar smell of coconut and passionflower: a faint whiff of the sickly tropical suntan lotion with which Anna liked to baste herself lay curdling on the air. But she was not there. Although the greenery all around was still, the depths of the garden seemed to tremble, as if a storm had just blown through it. Harry leaned against the stable wall, alone, his great carcase braced against his arms, forehead on the brick. As always he was half naked, and this time I saw that his flies were undone. The detail made me strangely angry. His head swung heavily below his lumpy shoulders. He looked at once timid and unnaturally exposed, like an animalcule seen through a microscope, or a man observed by an angel. Going up to him, I greeted him blithely. He shook his head groggily, but did not reply. It was then that I brought down my burning sword.

'Be off with you,' I whispered in his ear. 'Go on, sod off. You've not only screwed her this time, you've hit her, haven't you, you bastard? You've crossed the line. So you can piss off now. You're no good for her – for her or her child.'

His chin jerked up as his unfocused pupils struggled to fix me. He laughed. 'Child? What the hell do you know?' His left eye was already puce and thickening. Clearly Anna, too, was capable of packing a punch. A trickle of blood ran down from the scrub of his eyebrow, along his nose.

'I know this: if you show your face here again, I'll call the police and lay a charge against you. Get going, now. I'll give you an hour. You've not much to take.'

He stared at me incredulously. 'You twat. They've set you up. But you can't see it, can you?'

'What the fuck do you mean by that?'

'You're a sitting duck, mate. Them pictures will be the end of you. Oooh Anna, oooh, Anna.' He swung his arms about like an effete baboon, mimicking my voice. 'Allow *me*. Let *me*. How absolutely *divine* it all is. I've already had a good wank over the walls. Now let me just put my dick—'

I went for him. In spite of his dazed state his reaction was swift. Blocking my hand with his palm, he slid me under his armpit and bent my elbow back until the joint squealed.

He spoke in a leisurely way. 'You're so far up your own hole your brain has turned to shit.'

'You stupid turd,' I gasped. 'You clearly don't know the

meaning of real affection, let alone loyalty. Anna was a fool ever to have put her faith in you.'

'Yeah. That's the long an' the short of it.' He laughed and released me with a contemptuous waltzing swivel of the wrist. 'Catch me raising one of her bastards.'

Then he shrugged his shoulders, still laughing. I watched him for a long time as he went, a small figure staggering off across the smoking field, groping his way through the air.

CHAPTER TWENTY-FOUR

I have now given you almost all the facts at my disposal. There they lie on my square writing table, a heap of chaff. A breath could blow them out of the crumbling windows, into the street, across the violet plain. Two girls are chattering and laughing at the drinking fountain a little way down. In the shrinking sky the evening star begins to flash its distress: dot, dot, dot, dash, dash, dash, dot, dot, dot. Artemisia steps into the parlour for a moment to ask me if I require anything further before she goes home for the night. She looks ill-used, like a greying monument over which children have rudely clambered all day.

'No, indeed, Signora Artemisia, I am not in need of anything. You have been most kind.' Then something occurs to me. 'But wait – I have a question to ask you. I hope that you will not think me impertinent.'

Her head tilts almost imperceptibly, and I continue, 'Signora, you have a son – you are married. You *are* married, I take it, Signora Artemisia?'

'Signore, you insult me deliberately.' She shakes out her apron in anger.

'No, no,' I hastily correct myself, 'I mean, is your husband still living?'

She is appeased: a guarded nod. '*Si*, Signore. He lives.'

'Do you love him? Are you happy together?'

Artemisia regards me with undisguised sympathy, as though I were an imbecile. 'What has marriage to do with love, Signore? We are used to each other.'

'I see. I ask your pardon. And I thank you.'

She smiles stonily and flicks her sleeve over my lamp and papers in a rare gesture of goodwill. '*Allora, buona notte, Signore.* Do not stay up too late writing.' Her worn slippers paddle along the corridor, and she is gone.

The evening light is withdrawing from the hills. Their golden undulations lie along the horizon in broken arcs, giving way below to striped soil, sediment and grass: tracking lines into faraway valleys that are bluing now in the dusk. Brick farm buildings and thatched *casoni* sparkle on the scree. A minute figure appears on a hillside road, slowly rounds its curve, crosses a stile, and is swallowed up by a shorn field. A homely smell of cooking hangs in the air.

I am always astonished to think that these prosaic details are the very facts on which even the great Giambellin had to base his vision. In his grasp they are no longer merely facts, though, but yield something serene and whole, a view of a world in which man and nature are one, and a little greater than either. Where does the first begin and the other end? Rock and flesh share the same substance. Calmness and repose breathe from every crevice, every pore. The landscape does not just exist; it knows and feels: it shares our nature, soothes our anxiety, reassures us that all might yet be well. Held as we are in this gentle clasp, our chains barely chafe. It is utterly simple, and utterly ordinary. I cannot for the life of me see how it is done.

I realize at last how pointless it is to write about art. One might as well try to jot down the biochemical formula for love. Neither conveys what it is like to see, to yearn. It is impossible to bring about a chemical reaction with mere words. When this account is finished, then perhaps I shall simply look, and try to see what is there. But what good will looking do, I wonder? This is a world, I now believe, of shifting surfaces, behind which the human heart staggers about like a blind thing, knocking itself senseless.

Most art historians would agree that it is proper practice to leave the materials they have consulted in the archives. However, I've always felt that these sources should remain in the hands of those who value them most, and I've kept the plan of Roper's rose garden with me. I study it often. In the symbology of my rotten psyche it has assumed the significance of one of those infamous inkblots in the Rorschach test. Is it a butterfly, a pair of breasts, an animal-skin rug? How could I have known then?

By this time I was convinced that Roper's relationship with Giulia Buccari would prove to be not just a matter of biology or impulse or simple acquisition but a test of his mettle – a test, in short, of what he was. He wanted her and he got her. He'd led an obviously inexperienced young woman away from her chaperone and seduced her. He had written that he would 'make it all right', and what else did he mean by this other than that he was going to propose marriage to her? All that was clear. Another question had begun to irk me, though, one that ate into my thoughts of the Bellini with its irresistible symmetry: Roper may have hidden the painting on his return to Mawle, but what did he do with the Contessina once he finally had her in his possession? What was their life together like? Was he – impertinent question – happy? Was *she*? We tried to solve this puzzle later, Anna and I, on that terrible Friday, once everything between us had collapsed and I was left to scrabble about in the ruin of my feeling for her, fighting the impulse to flee – but wait: this is premature; this does not belong here, it must bide its time.

For here's the thing. When it came to it, you see, on the subject of his married life Roper's diary was entirely blank.

I was now possessed by the crowd of phantoms that dogged my every step in that melancholy house: it was impossible to turn my head away; impossible to shut the book and call a halt. Was I watching them, or they me? They seemed to press their faces up against the glass of the journal, mouths agape, in attitudes of sorrow and warning . . . But I was an idiot with an absurd, sodden itch, incapable of understanding. I should have taken the hint and scarpered. It would have cost me the Madonna, but would that have mattered? I'd failed to find it so far; would it have made a difference if I'd left Mawle without finding it at all? At least it would have spared me the humiliating moment of fulfilment that lay in wait at the end.

For I did see it, you know. Before everything went smash, I held the Bellini – undeservedly, inadvertently, through no doing of my own – in my soiled hands. It all happened by accident, in the usual manner of catastrophe.

On Sunday, the 27th of October 1889 Roper went to dinner at the Palazzo Buccari. 'Also there,' he writes, 'were my own Giulia, as I may now call her, Mrs Bronson, Giuseppe and the triple-chinned woman from the garden.' The old aunt ate watchfully, with her dewlaps lowered over her plate, and sat for the rest of the evening on a sofa near the window, a wax doll of freakish proportions. Glittering golden light fell from the glass sconces and chandeliers illuminating the echoing stone chamber. The *serva* brought in shallow bowls brimming with a watery mess of noodles and beans, wistfully fragrant of celery, and then a dish of rice garnished with lobster tails, and after that a platter of small greasy fowl.

'My dear,' said Mrs Bronson, dabbing her mouth appreciatively with her napkin, '*Polenta ed osei* – this is a rare treat! These little birds are a great delicacy here, you know,' she murmured to me.

'Yes, we roast them over a low flame,' said Miss Spragg. She smiled twiggily at Browning, who was filleting a tiny shank. Stirring the Lilliputian remains on his plate enquiringly with his knife tip, he leaned towards Mrs B.

'What sort of poultry did you say this was, Kate?'

'Why, none at all, dear Robert – this is thrush meat.'

'What?' The poet pushed his plate away, aghast. 'Have we dined on the flesh of songbirds?'

Mrs B attempted an embarrassed apology. 'Mr Browning,' she explained, 'has a superstition about these creatures – he shudders to see even their feathers adorning a lady's bonnet.'

'Superstition!' flinched Browning. 'It is no superstition, dear Kate, to abhor the murder of these most musical and harmless beings simply to satisfy our vanity – our grossest appetites!' His anger mounting, he half shouted, 'Would you kill *everything* that sings?'

Oh, the pitiful inanity of frustrated desire! Roper had better luck. After dinner he followed the Contessa onto the terrace.

She was dressed particularly badly in a low-cut lobster-red gown, its wilting basque shrouded in a trailing shawl. A large brooch clutched at her breast. She looked graceless, disarmed, and he notes that he naturally did everything in his power to put her at her ease.

'Isn't this a perfect evening?' I asked her.

'Oh yes, heavenly,' she agreed.

'And isn't this garden a slice of perfection, too?'

'Yes, it is like Paradise,' she assented. She loosened her shawl a little, so that it slipped from her shoulders and slithered to the ground. A tear hurried down her slender neck. From somewhere came a distant tinkling, like a cowbell on the hill, or a teaspoon in a cup.

Giulia put up her face to be kissed. Her stained lips tasted oily and sweet. As my mouth touched hers I felt the tip of her absurd brooch grinding into my breastbone, and the bell went on making its *tinkle tinkle*, as if someone were endlessly stirring their tea. Afterwards she looked just as wan and uncertain as before. She had demanded nothing of me. It touched me deeply. I was torn between the impulse to laugh at her and to put my arms around her.

'When we are married and living at Mawle you shall have a garden, a rose garden, much finer than this,' I whispered.

'You are too kind,' she said, as if I had just passed her something, a sandwich or her shawl, which still lay at her feet.

'What a funny girl you are. Doesn't that cheer you up?'

'Yes, thank you,' she hiccupped. 'Will you go in and ask cousin Laetitia for her permission now?'

'Shouldn't we stay here a little while first, by ourselves?' I pleaded.

'No,' said my wife-to-be decisively. 'It is the proper thing to do.'

She gathered up her shawl and wrapped it awkwardly across her chest. We returned to the *sala*, where Mrs Bronson, hampered by Browning, was putting on her cloak, and I set off to find Miss Spragg so that I could negotiate the terms of my engagement.

I sat up in bed through the long hours of Wednesday night, reading and rereading this. I drank. Perhaps I dozed. My brain felt brittle, a thing of glass, and came up with the most peculiar effects: an explosion of fire, a charred bird, a kaleidoscopic gush of song . . .

I was in hell. My elbow felt sprained, my heart more bruised than ever. Harry's parting words chased each other about my head in a constant raucous echo. 'You twat. They've set you up. Them pictures will be the end of you . . . You can't see it, can you?' It was nonsense, of course, pure vitriolic nonsense. He was humiliated at being driven from the field; he was aiming his clumsy missiles at random. But what did he intend me to understand by it?

I'd fed Vicky tepid sardines and tinned spaghetti as the sun was setting, washed her face and tucked her up in her cot. Anna came back to the house from her hidey hole at ten, still incandescent with anger after her fisticuffs with Harry, and swept upstairs to her room without a word. She was wearing her checked shirt. Where had she been all afternoon and evening? Not in Harry's shack – at four o'clock, still enraged after my altercation with him, I'd searched the place and found it stripped. Even the mattress was gone. His van, too, had disappeared. Did Anna know that he'd left?

Fuelled by grappa, drifting in and out of darkly-coloured dreams, I sweated till dawn at my ghastly retort, heating, calcining, subliming, distilling, but could not work out what Anna was doing or feeling.

Next morning Anna arrived at breakfast with her loose hair carefully curled and glossed, spiralling over her lumberjack collar, throwing off its lights like an *ignis fatuus*. A spice of autumn hung in the air: a crispness, a dryness, indefinably sharp and brittle. The greenhouse, bathed in dew, glistered damply in the mist.

'Good morning, my dear.' I kissed her on her left cheek. It was uncharacteristically taupe and slippery. So that was what she was up to yesterday afternoon – she'd been shopping for cosmetics! Two tiny pustules nestled in the stained corner of her mouth. The pores of her skin were open, glazed.

'What is this *stuff* you have on?'

Anna clapped her hand to the side of her face, a patient with toothache, emitting the sufferer's low moan. The line of her jaw bulged; under its thick layer of make-up it was a pulpy bluish red.

'Tom, Harry's left. We had a fight. I don't know where he's gone.' She began to cry. Her tears were all the more painful for being noiseless.

'Did that bastard hurt you badly?'

A dreadful keening: No, no. And I believe, after all, that the physical blow he had dealt her was the least of it.

In that moment of clarity I became aware, as if by the

cumulative force of an immense inner pressure, that something momentous had happened to me; had been happening to me, in fact, ever since my arrival at Mawle. I had been harried and assaulted by painful and awkward memories; I'd been pursued by apparently random echoes from another time; a flickering dreamscape over which I had no conscious control. Even Browning, that disillusioned emissary from the realm of words, had had his role to play in my dismemberment. And this process had brought me, by smarting intervals, to the brink of a terrible confrontation. I stood at the edge of myself, looking into the cloven heart, not of Thomas Joseph Lynch, connoisseur and aesthete, but of a repulsive stranger. Yes, what a buffoon I was! Not even a harmless buffoon: I was a selfish, badly ageing man who was prepared to ingest that gentle girl, to gobble up her most tender hopes as grist to my own ambition. Worse, I was ready to do it with protestations of sincerity, and to call it concern. To call it love.

I lurched upstairs to my room and dashed cold water at my eyes. On raising my head, I caught sight of the face that was reflected back at me in the tarnished mirror above the sink. A crooked shadow fell across its flesh, slicing the handsome contours from hairline to chin. The features were smooth and sharp, like marble or ice, and as polished. The forehead soared haughtily, as if inflated by a long and steady self-regard. The corners of the eyes sloped downwards in deep folds; the pupil of each eye gleamed black, the eyeball mushroom-white, blind in its ruffle of skin. The coarse red beard beneath the hard mouth was tufted like a goat's. The expression was eager and alert but too extreme for ordinary sympathy; too fierce, too intent. What was most compelling about the face was indistinguishable from what was inhuman; even, perhaps, from what was grotesque. And as I stood there, full of revulsion at the barrenness of this landscape, two other faces swam up at me, each choking me with such a sense of fear and pity that I've been unable to forget them since.

There is something I have not yet confessed. I was not being entirely truthful when I wrote, earlier, that I did not see Paine again after I'd left school. On that single return visit I made to Limerick years ago to bury my father I stopped at the Castle Hotel for a whiskey and a piss. As I was making my way to the lavatory I bumped into a drip-dry-suited drunkard cradling an empty pint glass who was weaving and swaying down the corridor towards me, evidently on his way back to the bar. The door he had just quitted was signposted 'Limerick Youth Workers' Conference'. We paired up in the middle of the passage and danced one of those inelegant jigs where both dancers hop to the left, and then bolt for the right, and then make an undignified attempt at the left again. My semblable stared at me reproachfully. He was, of course, quite pickled, but even so, his next words surprised me.

'Lynch? Is it Thomas Joseph, now? Is it really yer man?' His fat throat pulsed ominously.

I scrutinized my opposite number's beer-swollen face. There was the static downiness of the hair, and a certain pitted and scarred quality about the jaw, but I could not be sure.

'Is it you,' the drunk persisted, 'you bastard divil of a mammy's pet?' He made a hopeful, hopeless grasp at my arm. Astonishingly, his eyes were glazed with menacing tears. 'Why did you throw me over? Oh why? Will you come with me now, Thomas Joseph?' he moaned, 'Will you?'

'Sorry, bud,' I replied in my best American drawl, jabbing him playfully once or twice in the gut. 'I'm not your pal. But is this the way to the john?'

'Two doors down to the left,' he muttered after a moment, and then baptized the wall with a splash of vomit. I went into the lobby and alerted the flinty-eyed young woman defending the desk there to the sudden discomposure of one of her guests. I had no wish to know this gross incarnation of Paine again, if that is indeed who he was.

The second face that remains with me does so not because it is familiar but because it is maddeningly opaque. It's the face of a young woman who sits under flaring lamplight while contriving to remain in shadow; whose expression is so bare, so simple, that hers might already be a long-faded face in an old canvas. When I question it I get no answer. It has the impenetrable look of a doll or an idol, something that appears to have no direct agency, but whose blind power, whether artful or artless is, I sense, immense.

On the 30th of October 1889 Roper wrote in his diary that he planned to spend the winter and spring in Asolo with his wife, returning to Mawle the following June or July to escape the summer heat. His intention was that Giulia should have coolness, and a breeze, to forestall her bewildering faints and spells of sickness. 'How to describe the touching completeness with which she has given herself over to me? She has a charming way, now that I am her *fidanzato*, of leaning on my arm, and whispering almost fearfully, "Don't you think, once we are married, that you may not love me as you do now? Perhaps we should marry quickly." When I ask the comical, innocent thing what could have put such an absurd idea into her head, she replies that it is the way of the world, and her expression is so miserable that I must laugh and kiss the tip of her nose.' He adds, 'Giulia shall have her roses: I have sketched an outline for her garden, and have promised to have a proper plan of it drawn up once we are home again as proof of my love. When I tell her this she seems happy and stilled.'

That evening Miss Spragg, having triumphantly fulfilled her promise to see her ward suitably matched, threw an engagement party at Ca' Buccari. All her slight acquaintance among the Venetian nobility was there, including the Contessa Marcello and the Princess Paul Metternich. The Princess had the narrowest hands Roper had ever seen on a woman, and the most tragic smile. Her hair was dressed with a nodding black ostrich feather that cast a mysterious shade over her hollow face, while the clasp of her gloved fingers on his pulse was so cold that he imagined for a moment that a frost had descended on him. She regarded him very queerly, and rather insolently, before seizing Mrs Bronson by the elbow and drawing her off into a corner. The Contessa Marcello, however, was a pure-bred, blonde-haired Venetian – hers, he makes a point of mentioning, was one of the last of the old aristocratic Venetian families never to have married foreigners – and he was glad to see her greeting the Contessina with what seemed like real kindness. On the glassy table in the dining room rows of sweet biscuits or *golosessi* rippled around a beached pear cake, shored up by bottles of iced Prosecco. The room was brightly lit. After a while Roper's head began to drum: in the relentless effulgence every physical thing before him cast a double shadow.

'Tell me,' rasped the Princess, 'what brings you to the Veneto, Mr Roper? Are you in search of experience? Or merely of culture?' Her vowels were Italian husks, heavily infiltrated by Germanic footsoldiers.

She smiled her crepuscular smile, and he burbled that he came to see the sights. The Serenissima. The eternal city, and so forth.

'Did you? And is Venice eternal? Do you find us immortal?' Her smile revealed teeth that were steeply bevelled.

'It has an undeniable grandeur. St Mark's, now, I've never seen the like. I wish that I could pack it up to take home with me.'

'Really?' said the Contessa Marcello mildly. Her dress was shabby, but she wore it so well that it was nearly impossible to tell. 'And what would you do with San Marco back in Berkshire? Where would you put it?'

Her composed, frugal elegance shamed me. I felt as if I'd failed to understand anything at all about this place. 'Yes. I do see what you mean. Hardly the thing for one's mantelpiece, is it?'

The Princess looked at me approvingly. 'Ah, you are being ironic – an English characteristic. One hears so much about it.'

'I expect that you collect endless pictures, Mr Roper, like all the *inglese*,' interjected the Contessa Marcello.

Turning to the Princess, I tried another tack. 'Your Venetian canals are rather grand, too.'

'Feugh,' said the Princess, looking me up and down. 'The canals. They stink.' She dismissed the topic with a toss of her chilly hand.

At the end of the evening Giuseppe approached Roper and presented him quaveringly with a rectangular paper parcel, which turned out to hold his revolting portrait of Giulia, clamped by a tawdry frame. Giuseppe's eyes were full of tears – how unpredictably sentimental these Italians were!

'Here is my cousin,' he said solemnly. 'I give her to you.'

'Thanks, old fellow.' I was rather at a loss. I guessed that he was anxious about his place in the house, and wished to reassure him. 'As my wife's tutor, you know, you will always be welcome here – for lessons and that sort of thing. And of course we shan't be staying long, and we're going to need a – what's the word? A *guardiano*, a caretaker for the palazzo.'

'Ah, Signore.' Giuseppe cringed alarmingly. 'I will be glad to serve you and the Contessa in any way possible.'

At Giuseppe's approach, however, the Contessa had left Roper's side to sit by Miss Spragg. Roper ventured loudly that she looked pale. Mightn't it be wiser to retire to her room? He was encouraged by the fact that she got up immediately and took her leave without protest: here at last was a sign of true attachment; an indisputable mark of her regard for him. As she did so Browning clasped Roper's hand, though his voice was remote.

'My dear boy,' he said heavily, 'your happy news has made my visit to Asolo complete. I see that you will make an excellent husband.'

But unbegrudging Miss Bronson, generous in defeat, intercepted Giulia before she left the room. Exclaiming that she, too, wanted to give her a present, she pressed a roll of cloth into the Contessa's hands. In her exhaustion and embarrassment Giulia fumbled with the thing, and it unscrolled in her grasp, revealing the peacock tapestry on which Edith Bronson had laboured so long.

'Oh, Miss Bronson! Is it really mine?' cried Giulia.

Miss Bronson smiled. 'Yes, my dear. I don't think it can belong to anyone else.'

My Giulia, across a hushed century, I greet you! For one brief autumn you rubbed shoulders with prolix Robert Browning, but posterity has not seen fit to record that fact. It doesn't bother with those who sit quietly and wait, who simply appear to suffer and observe. It only remembers the doers, the talkers – the self-proclaimed creators, of beauty or of pain. And this raises a question that haunts me: how will I be remembered, if at all?

CHAPTER TWENTY-FIVE

That final Thursday dragged on. August was nearly over and lay wheezing along the tops of the trees in shreds of sepia cloud. Having made herself up to look like a clapped-out child whore, Anna dawdled expectantly at the window, a hooker on the lookout for her favourite customer. Her eyes were puffy. Had that checked shirt been Harry's? Had she fallen asleep, weeping, in her clothes on Wednesday night after storming upstairs? I tried to distract her by enlisting her help in completing my sham inventory of the pictures at Mawle. My notes lay in the library, crisped by the sun, scrolling at the edges. I hadn't touched them for days.

Although she was reluctant, Anna followed me obediently up and down the stairs as I squinnied and assessed and jotted, sometimes stopping to look out onto the dry lawn below, or to gaze dully at her reflection in a dull mirror. Her inertia irritated me inexpressibly. I felt like twisting her arm, or slapping her. And by now, in any case, I had inventoried the whole house; only the attic was left. More for something to say that would snap Anna out of her self-pitying mood than out of any genuine interest, I finally pulled up sharp in front of a poorly executed Diana in one of the third-floor attic bedrooms.

'And what is this?'

'Oh, her.' A sluggish, gluey stare. 'That's *Bisnonna*.'

'Is that an Italian name?'

'Sort of. She – well, she was my great-grandmother. This room was Dad's when he was little.'

My heart began to pump madly. 'Did your *bisnonna* – your great-grandmother – live here, at Mawle?'

'No – she never came to this house. She died when she was very young, Daddy said, in Italy. In Asolo.' Anna looked at me tensely, suddenly oddly alert. 'That's where my great-grandfather met her.'

The girl in the portrait had a trite oval face, burdened with a solid shelf of sable hair. Her hands lay lifelessly across a quiver barbed with pointy gold arrows. The board on which the picture was painted was no bigger than a largish photo album, and was surrounded by a cheap gesso frame.

Why, yes. It had all been duly recorded in the Bible: Giulia Buccari, born 15th of August 1869 – and the precipitous death date: 4th of April 1890.

'Really? How did she die?' I tried to contain my rising excitement. 'Was it – was it of a fever?'

'No, nothing like that. Jesus, if you just think about what women had to go through in those days.'

'Anna, what on earth do you mean?'

'She died giving birth to my Grandpa Teddy. Can you picture it – no painkillers, no proper doctor, just knives and hot water.' She laid a cradling hand on her own belly. 'She must've developed a massive infection immediately after.'

'Dear God, Anna . . .'

'Daddy said that Grandfather never knew her at all,' she went on. 'He came back here, to Mawle, when he was just a month old. He was a premature baby, you know, a weakling, and it affected him his whole life. He died when

Daddy was a little boy. Dad always said that I was the spitting image of him.'

'Your *bisnonna* wasn't all that strong to begin with, was she?' I mused dreamily. The face in the picture was as flavourless as a milk pudding. 'Those fainting spells. And then her parents hadn't lived long . . . But the picture really doesn't do her justice. It makes her look like anyone and no one, and she must have been, above all, *herself* – she must have been unusually beautiful!'

After I had spoken these words I nearly bit off my tongue. In a moment Anna would turn on me, demanding an explanation. How did I know about Miss van der Veen's death of typhoid, Buccari's rapid decline, the orphaned girl's mysterious faints, her beauty? I saw it all: the teapot-stained copy of Sanderson hauled from my holdall; the diary brandished above her head; myself, kneeling on the tattered carpet, weeping, begging her forgiveness for not having been open with her from the start.

But no, there wasn't anything of the kind.

'Yes, apparently she was beautiful,' said Anna cautiously, her eyes still fixed on me. 'Or not beautiful, but incredibly seductive.' She smiled sadly.

I groped for a compliment. 'Then you must resemble her, too.'

Anna crowed with pleasure. 'Oh, go on. That expensive slap must be worth it after all.'

She was in a light, playful mood for the rest of the morning, pinching my arm, carrying my pencils, sportively directing me towards great canvases blotched with colour, but my concentration was shattered. I could grasp nothing clearly.

Just before we turned away, you see, at the bottom of the portrait of Giulia Buccari, coiled beneath her left breast, I had spotted a vermilion scrawl, a crimson worm: the painter's signature – Giuseppe Puppi.

But the diary had no answers; nothing more to tell me.

I opened it again when Anna had gone off to touch up her mask and restarch her hair in her bedroom. There was only one entry left.

Friday, the 1st of November. Mr Browning left yesterday for Venice. Mrs B and I accompanied him to the *diretto* at Castelfranco. Once we had said our goodbyes, and as he was about to step into the railway carriage, Browning looked back at the Venetian plain, flushed with early morning sunlight. Turning to Mrs B, he asked, 'I was right to fall in love with this place fifty years ago, Kate, was I not?'

'Yes, dear Robert,' she replied, grasping his hand in her own, 'you were right.'

'We outlive some places that charmed us in our youth, but the loveliness of this was no disappointment – am I not right? Isn't it more beautiful even now than it was then?'

'Indeed it is, my dearest friend.'

'Ah but I – haven't I changed? I was a young man when last I was here, and now I sometimes feel that I am close to death. To think that I should have been here again! Oh, my dear, what precisely is the connection between then and now? What is fact? And what fancy?'

'Hush, Robert. You are not about to die. I shall not allow it.' The two smiled at each other. Then Browning leaned over and kissed Mrs B on the palm.

'I should hope not, old lady. I do believe that I am good for another ten years yet.'

And so saying, he got onto the train. That was the last we saw of him.

Robert Browning had vanished as inconveniently as he had arrived.

The diary ended there.

I was in freefall. No marriage, no Bellini, no final, heart-stopping disclosure of the Madonna's hiding place. I gave a low groan of baffled agony; I may even, stupidly, have shaken the book as if something more might tumble out. Nothing. This last entry was followed by twenty or thirty blank pages. Some were ringed with mould; many were furred and stippled with dirt; others were mysteriously smeared; but not one of them contained a single word more.

Puppi! The name of that midget, that manikin, that cunning poppet! That name! How for the love of God could there be a Puppi in 1889 too? I raged that afternoon, all evening, and through the long night. I wanted to stamp my feet and crash through the floor, into the belly of the house, the core of the earth, a flaming meteor. Instead, I paddled palms with Anna and circled, hungrily sniffing, around her family tree. I wanted, I demanded, a solution.

When was her great-grandfather married? She didn't know, exactly. What happened to her great-grandmother's possessions after great-grandpa upped sticks and came back to Berkshire? Those painted brown eyes were blank. And what about the palazzo in Asolo? Was it shut up, or sold, or razed to the ground? Or simply stripped, and handed over to the care of someone waiting in the wings, a poor relation, say, who would be grateful to have it? Your guess is as good as mine – and I could hazard a guess, oh yes.

Later that day, when I was alone in the library again, I turned back to the Bible and reconsidered its thickly-inked genealogy. A reek of fruitful respectability steamed from the page. Edward Roper had been born on the 1st of April 1890, and I saw, with a pang, what I should have noticed before: that Giulia had survived his arrival by just three days. Why had Roper written nothing in his diary about his marriage to her, nothing whatsoever about their brief life together? He'd proposed at the end of October. I did some rapid sums. However swiftly and quietly it was done, they couldn't possibly have arranged the wedding to fall before the first or second week of November 1889, and that in itself would have shown a most unseemly haste. This premature child, Anna's sickly Grandpa Teddy, had lived to sixty-three – hardly an indication of great frailty! Was the boy Roper's? Or was he really someone else's?

The room, the house, seemed to fill with an ominous silence, a tickless, hourless, yeasty blank that thickened and spilled into every corner. Josiah Lamb's picture of James Roper and his son glittered like a puddle of oil above the mantelpiece. There was the false pastoral: the waggish garden wall, the door with its brass knocker. The twisty-nosed child was thin and dark, just as he had been when I'd first looked at the painting over two weeks ago, but I was no longer sure if you could really call him delicate. He had a concentrated presence, rather, as he sat within the arm of the old cousin without touching her pied sleeve – the intense, spiky quality of a too-closely-hothoused plant. Laetitia Spragg's shrewd grey eyes were fixed on Roper's face. It was a well-fed face, a resolute face, with the tight set of selfishness, or possibly only disappointment, about the mouth. To my dismay I couldn't tell which.

That afternoon I tried to imagine them – Roper and his son – as they began their long leaving of Asolo. Anna had said – hadn't she? – that her great-grandfather had returned to England with the child when the boy was only a month old. In his journal he'd written that he intended to remain until July, but now, after this birth, he could not go quickly enough. I thought that I could see the little provincial station in the shadow of the hill, where a train waited silently for the signal.

This is a wet spring, the spring of May 1890, and it has rained since dawn, but the showers have stopped for an hour or two and the sky is a watery orange. A young man and a middle-aged woman stand on the platform. They are wearing deep mourning. All around them there is confusion: the guard patrols languidly, his damp tunic collar unbuttoned; lunch baskets, bandboxes and parcels are stacked and topple and are restacked; random terriers assiduously sniff the muddy drains. But the man and the woman themselves remain remote from the bustle. They are alone. Except for two or three light bags, their luggage – the pictures and bibelots acquired by the young gentleman during his Italian tour, and all the portable contents of the Palazzo Buccari, the house he has lived in so briefly, and is now hastily leaving – has already been taken to Venice, where it is lying strapped and stowed in packing cases in the hold of the *Eloïse*, a cargo vessel bound for Portsmouth. Somewhere among them is an inconspicuous box containing the Bellini Madonna, unrecognized and uncherished.

The woman carries a newborn infant – a loose-jointed, plump brat, not the frail babe of family legend – in a shawl, stiffly but quite capably, as if she has done this sort of thing before. The young man helps her into their first-class compartment, a narrow box with green baize seats and a black blind like the pall on a coffin. There they sit, doll-like, without moving.

Fitfully the passengers climb on board, doors are slammed, the whistle blows. The carriage pulls away as the train begins to clack along. Thin drifts of smoke from the cinnamon-roofed houses on the hill disperse in the spring sunshine. A face is pressed against the dusty carriage window; a hand waves blindly, and is gone.

Is that how it was?

I was still fretfully picturing this scene, tweaking and embellishing the details, when there was a faint knock on the door. Anna bobbed on the library threshold in a tide of lamplight. 'Do you mind if I sit with you for a bit?' she mumbled. 'I've just put Vicky to bed.'

I shut the Bible. It was about nine o'clock, and the shadows lay long on the wall outside the library window. I hadn't noticed how late it had become. 'Of course not. Stay as long as you like.' Stay forever! 'How are you feeling now?'

'Oh, you know.' She rowed in the air with her fingers. 'Up and down.' Then, 'I'm worried about Vicky, Tom. She's taken to hiding under her bed again.'

'She senses your unhappiness, Anna.'

Anna climbed into the armchair and crouched there like

a shipwrecked sailor on a raft. 'Look, I know that I'm not a very good mother to her. You don't have to tell me. The truth is, I didn't think that doing it alone would be this hard. But your being here has helped; it's made it all bearable. You've sort of been – an example to me.' After delivering this absurd speech the poor girl blushed, and I was taken aback to find myself both pained and reluctantly moved.

'I'll look after her tomorrow morning while you get some rest, take her out of herself a little,' I offered.

'You've been so good to us.'

'Oh, nonsense.'

'You have. You have, Tom.'

We didn't say anything for a while. Then Anna ventured cautiously, 'I hope that family stuff was useful to you.' She bit her thumb, yawned. 'I feel bad about not putting Vicky's name in the Bible yet. Maybe I'll get around to it tomorrow.'

'Absolutely. Right you are.' It was totally beyond me to tell her how disappointed I felt. I'd discovered no trace of what I had come to find, and what I had unearthed instead depressed me profoundly.

Anna sat in her chair without moving or attempting to smile. Her eyes were shut; I could see her chest rise and fall as if in sleep. The gathering darkness of the night behind the window pane seemed about to wash her away. The dusk spread out towards the edges of the room like tar, seeping against the little island of photographs that I had glanced at so rapidly when I first took possession of the library. I hadn't looked at them again since then, but now I could put names, dates, even, to the faces. If the thin boy in the knickerbockers was the groom in the wedding picture, and if this was indeed Edward Roper, then the girl with the lipstick and heels and the bride must both be Rosalie Marks, Anna's grandmother.

I marvelled again at James Roper's blondness and Edward Roper's incongruous darkness. Let's assume that Edward Roper had really been not James Roper's child, but someone else's. There was only one likely candidate. Although I didn't want to entertain the idea, I was forced to admit that it was possible that Giulia's cousin, Giuseppe Puppi, was the father. Giulia had at times shown a casual hauteur towards him thanks to the difference in their stations, but everything in Roper's account confirmed my impression of her as an affectionate girl who was self-defeatingly incapable of resisting her impulses. And what about Giuseppe? He lectured his cousin and he disparaged her, but he was reluctant to let her go: he was a sentimental rationalist; not such a rare combination, after all. Perhaps he loved her. Yes, I could imagine him as the father of Giulia's child. In that case Edward Roper's colouring came not just from his mother, but from the dark-faced Giuseppe himself, which would explain the indecent discrepancy between Roper's looks and his son's.

The Polaroid of the beehived girl and the young man in flares was also fairly easy to place. That beehive was now a chignon, but Maddalena Roper's hair was still a formidable blonde. Curiously, there was a very strong resemblance between Anna and her grandfather, Edward Roper, although Anna did not look much like her own father. John Roper's face, like that of his mother, Rosalie Marks, was thin; his pale eyes were lashless, his hair sandy and fine – bleached further, in the photograph, by Italian sunlight. Anna's palette was a lustrous pecan while both her parents were fair, but this was evidently a throwback to the genes transmitted – if they had so been – by Giulia Buccari and Giuseppe Puppi.

Puppi – there it was again: that galling name! What was the connection?

Anna was staring at me with wide open eyes. 'Are you looking at those old photos?'

'Yes,' I quacked, startled. 'They're lovely.'

She got up and came over to join me at the desk. Kneeling beside the chair she linked her arm through mine, resting her forehead against my shoulder. 'I love that photo of Mummy and Daddy. They were out on a day trip to a town near Padova' – she pronounced it in the Italian way – 'at Christmastime. I think it was the day Daddy proposed, and that's why Mummy kept the picture. They look so happy, don't you agree?'

'Oh, ecstatic.' In fact the boy looked dazed, as if he'd just been hit over the head with a mallet – although this might have been the effect of the sharp winter sun in his eyes – and the girl hugely pleased with herself.

'Why were they in Padua? Did they meet in Italy, then?'

'Yup. They were both students at the university. Daddy was just finishing his year abroad when they got together. It was a whirlwind romance. Mummy had another boyfriend at the time, but she always said that Daddy was just so groovy that she couldn't resist him – he was already in his twenties, with his own house. He simply swept her off her feet! Her family was rather grand, but they just loved Daddy and they were all for it.'

I didn't take her up on this, because something else had by now dawned on me. That blonde hair! 'Your mother is one of the Venetian Marcellos, isn't she? Aren't they an old family? They must be wealthy in their own right. My dear

Anna, couldn't your Italian relatives assist you with the upkeep of Mawle?'

''Fraid not. They may have a title but they've never had much money. Still, Mamma's parents never looked down on Daddy just because he wasn't Lord somebody or other. They took him for who he was.'

I bet they did. And their daughter took Mawle.

The pieces cohered with uncanny precision, and with such harrowing speed that I felt as if I were being skewered by a rain of arrows. Though Anna still chattered on, I no longer heard her. Somewhere in the back of my mind a dangling fragment was on the point of meeting its target. Swiftly, I made my computations. It was very likely that Giuseppe had married at some point, once he had taken over the Casa Buccari, and had a son of his own – *another* son, I should say. In the normal span of things this boy might have been born somewhere around the beginning of the new century, and if this child, in turn, had had another male child anywhere between twenty to forty years later, that would place the latest Puppi roughly in my generation. The shard drew blood as it fell into place, and I tried not to wince. Hello there, Ludovico! I could see how you must have come to know about the Bellini Madonna. Didn't Sanderson say that the Madonna *del prato* that Roper brought to Mawle, and which had once belonged to the Buccari and hung in their palazzo, did so 'according to a long tradition repeated in the bride's family'? The Madonna was, by anyone's reckoning, as much a family picture of Puppi's as James Roper's.

The stream of prattle under my ear trickled on unchecked. Anna was gurgling about her childhood singing lessons or sewing lessons with Granny, I no longer recall which. I was relieved to note that her spirits had lifted for the moment, and wholly charmed by the fragrant heat of her caramel head on my arm, but I couldn't absorb any more. The pressure in my chest was by now enormous. I noticed that the moon had risen over the lawn: a lemon yellow harvest moon that shed an oppressive light.

I picked up the fuzzed snap of the stodgy infant. 'Wait my dear. You haven't told me – who is the baby?'

Anna blinked at the slurry of pinks and greens. 'Oh, the baby! That's me.'

You? Rose-and-brown skinned, heavy eyed, hypnotically lovely you? This squinting cabbage was *you?*

Did she see my surprise and my delight, the ache I harboured for her, written on my face? Perhaps she did, because she kissed me on the mouth. Then she kissed me on both eyes. She was smiling so guilelessly that my heart broke. The sensation was a revelation. It was a mixture of agony and relief, and of memory, too – the remembered smells and emotions of my boyhood: of warm hair and sleepy roses and urgent clinging and famished, undiluted need, fused by a flash of silvery pain. I kissed her back. From somewhere, whether inside or outside me I couldn't tell, a violent wind appeared to be blowing. I felt weightless, shattered. The mass of our two bodies pressed together seemed indissoluble.

In that long moment, as I held Anna clasped against me, I was convinced that I had done her a profound wrong by ever suspecting her of trying to steer me into finding the thing she desired, and that she knew nothing about the Bellini Madonna after all.

CHAPTER TWENTY-SIX

And now, at last, I could see it. The picture of James Roper that hung in the library was the portrait of a haunted man. His face was not hard or stubborn, but rigid with dread. I looked at it again many times, and it seemed to me on each occasion more and more like the image of someone tormented and distracted by the oblique static of memory, by an apprehension that lay just outside his grasp.

Roper's passion had been founded on a passing fancy and gratified in a moment of random opportunity. Did he marry Giulia just to 'make it all right', as he had written – to correct the wrong he thought he'd done her that day at Treviso? If so, his bitterness at the conclusion would have been unspeakable. Only a fool could have believed that the boy who was born the following 1st of April was a child of a mere six months' gestation. Perhaps it occurred to Roper that the world might have been forgiven for thinking him fool enough for that, since he was already fool enough to have swallowed an even bigger illusion: the idea that he was her first lover. How clever that bony pander, Miss Spragg, had been! If Roper had married the Contessina to make restitution, then the irony that there was, when it came to it, no restitution to be made must have winded him. He'd paid another man's dues. Whose? The answer, in miniature, would have stared him daily in the face. This realization on its own, let alone its living, breathing proof, running about the house in blue knickerbockers, would have been enough to make any husband look haunted.

But there was something else, I reflected, that fed that look: a far greater and more appalling uncertainty as to the degree of *her* knowledge. Had Roper truly loved his wife after all? It was possible. Of all insidious emotions love, as I'd discovered, is the most likely to be founded on the impalpable – on the improbable, on a whim. But did she really care for him in return? Or was she a willing part of the scheme to ensnare him from the beginning? Were her impulsiveness, her innocence, her playfulness, all assumed? In his most unhappy moments he must often have wondered if he'd ever seen her clearly, this spontaneous girl who had just perhaps been a monster of subtlety. Laetitia Spragg had been determined that the Contessina should marry well. Had Giulia, already carrying another man's child, found herself trapped in an impossible situation, and, helped by Miss Spragg, scrabbled out of the only gap in the wire that offered itself?

Roper had thought of all his actions as unprompted and free. How earnestly he must have tried to persuade himself, in the days leading up to his marriage, that his unobserved half hour with Giulia Buccari under the willows on the riverbank was, if not planned by her, then at least mutually desired. Six months later, I imagined, he found himself ready to give almost anything for the simple guarantee that he'd forced her. But she was dead, and, even if he'd had the courage to ask her, unable to reply.

All Friday morning an overactive neighbour stoked and stacked an early bonfire, releasing a filthy plume of nodding smoke into the still air.

'Why don't you go out for a little while?' I suggested. Anna hadn't stirred since coming down to breakfast except to gulp down yoghurt and cheddar from the fridge like an unsated anaconda, and to tell the truth, I was becoming a little tired of her apathy. 'There's still some sunshine at the bottom of the garden.' (A thin sun, like cat's piss or barley water.)

'What for?'

I threw my hands up in exasperation: suit yourself. As I was about to leave the kitchen I turned to take a last look at Anna. She was standing at the sink, still chewing, bearing her weight on her elbow. Her crooked profile was turned towards the window that overlooked the fields. The late morning sun caressed her corkscrewing brown hair, which, in spite of its stiffness, was still very lovely; her rounded cheeks, her dimpled chin. The chequerboard of her shirt ran drunkenly over her full breasts and gently sloping belly. It came to me, with the muted click of a door closing, that she was pregnant.

She was pregnant.

My heart gave a blurt of pain. I was overcome by horror and helpless remorse. Rapidly, frantically, I began to redraft my image of her. Had she really been in love with Harry – that yokel, that oaf? Or had she been wilfully reckless, tossing him the precious gift of herself in the way that spoilt royal children in fairy tales, knowing the danger perfectly well, play with jewels on the brink of a bewitched pond where an ogre squats in wait? Anna's naïvety and helplessness, her passivity, suddenly seemed poisonous, a diseased pearl held in the loathsome jaws of a toad. Other thoughts gnawed at me too. Maddalena Roper's explosive anger that day in the kitchen before lunch a fortnight ago, when she'd called Anna a slut; the furious phone call between Anna and her mother which I'd overheard later – had these eruptions ever been about me at all? I suddenly doubted it, and the doubt was strangely, searingly humbling.

We opened a bottle of the Pol Roger at lunch that afternoon ('To Mawle!' 'To you!' 'To art!') and drank it greedily with our baked beans. Something had needled me all morning, and in that unsober hour it rose to my lips as a question, nudged by the bubbles of the champagne.

'My dear Anna, you can't always have lived only here, at Mawle.'

Anna started to say something, lost her way, and took another swallow. I sat staring at the pale wine in my glass. An opalescent swag of grease curled idly across its surface.

'Yes I have,' she said at last. 'My whole life.'

'What, really *all* of it?'

'Yup. I was born upstairs, you know. The Rose Room was Granny's once, then Mummy's. It wasn't always on show the way it is now.'

'And the Sewing Room used to be your nursery.'

She made a cack-handed attempt at clapping. 'Yes! How did you know?'

I did not reply to this. An insane plan was hatching in my brain. 'Anna, have you never thought of leaving?'

Anna looked narrowly at the kitchen furniture, as if she were totting up the number of chairs. 'Why, no. I've never wanted to. Why should I? First Daddy needed me here. Mamma got so bored at home that she wasn't much help to him. And it's so grey in England. She preferred being in Venice. And then, after Dad's death, there didn't seem to be any point. I've often thought it would be easiest if I just lived out my days at Mawle – you know, fixed up the house. Got married.' Her mouth whitened with pain. 'Fuck it. So much for that idea!' She took a ferocious gulp of the Pol Roger. 'Anyway, where would I go? And who with?'

'Well, what about Italy, perhaps?'

I imagined us three – really four – fleeing to a simple, cut-price villa, and battening there on breast milk, olives and basil. Vicky prattled in the local dialect, and Anna's embalmed curls were streaked crocus by the sun. I made a modest but honest living ushering Americans around the neighbourhood churches, resting in our kitchen in the evenings, where I dandled Harry's bastard on my knee . . .

It was the dream of a poltroon. The cage door, I saw, had stood wide open all along. The princess in the tower was quite free; the prison walls were made of sand. Whatever the forces that shaped her may have been, nothing now kept Anna at Mawle except her own capacity for self-sabotage.

After lunch Anna went back to her room and did not come down again. At three o'clock I knocked timidly at her door. Vicky had followed me upstairs. There was no reply, and I entered, full of fear.

Anna lay on the bed. Her back was turned towards me.

'He isn't coming back; I know he isn't,' she sobbed. 'I don't understand. He *promised* that we would see how things went. Oh Jesus. I ruined it all, didn't I? I told him about the baby and he wanted me to get rid of it. He said—'

It hurt even to breathe. 'What, Anna, what?'

'He said I was a shit mother now, so what made me think I could do it right this time? I just lost it.' She began to cry again. 'I had to go and ruin it all by losing my temper.'

'I'm sure it's not that; I'm sure it's not your fault. Don't make yourself miserable, Anna, please!'

'Why not? How do you know it's not my fault? If it's not, then he's left because Mummy's got rid of him.' My face must have been paralysed by guilt and horror, because she let out a scream of pure agony. 'Oh Christ, she has, hasn't she?'

'Anna, no—'

'She has – she has! She's just kicked him out without even giving me a chance to say goodbye. Oh Jesus. Oh Jesus, Jesus!'

If I'd taken this opportunity to confess that I'd run Harry off myself, everything might still have been different. I truly believe that I wanted to, but I couldn't find the words: they had been sucked away into a subterranean cave of shame. 'My dear child,' I said weakly, 'you are still very young. I'm sure that you will fall in love with a good man one day,' I added inanely, 'marry, and make a happy home.'

Anna turned around to face me. Her heavy nipples were dark against the checks of her shirt, her soupy cheeks mottled white and scarlet. I watched speechlessly as she sat up and began to run her nails over her face. All the while a claw of ivy tapped dully against the window pane. In my chest the familiar wheels of acid began their slow rotation.

'Love,' she said, her voice like a dead woman's. 'Love. I'm going to be forty soon. You are the only person who's ever been truly kind to me.' She stretched out her arms childishly, repeating, 'My head hurts, my head.'

Sinking to her side in terror I touched my mouth to the salty ends of her hair, her swollen chin. Her eyes closed as I rested my forehead against hers. We sat so for a minute during which my blood shook.

The next moment she was standing beside me, smoothing back with a blue-veined hand the hair my lips had kissed.

'Well,' she said, looking around the room with quiet purpose, 'well.' And then, noticing her daughter, who still lingered half in and half out of the doorway, for the first time, 'Go away, Ludovica. Just go away.'

'What did you just say? *What did you call her?*'

But a dreadful quietness had fallen over Anna as soon as she had spoken these words and the door was shut. The child's footsteps clattered down the corridor. That listening, suffering look which I knew and feared had entered Anna's face. Around her badly-curled hair a nimbus of reddish light wavered and blazed. My heart clenched in on itself and murmured, dreading what she would say next; but she said nothing, nothing at all as she walked towards me, still listening and suffering, with a blind gaze of surrender which I had often imagined but never before seen in her eyes.

What happened then? What could possibly happen between a lumbering man of fifty and a twig-limbed girl, the one overwhelmed by an anguish of clumsy feeling and the sudden, preposterous satisfaction of all his half-admitted hopes, the other desperate? She was very brave. Only once that afternoon she gave a cry of pain, and then I felt the dryness and misery of my body as I never had before.

As the bold summer sun was climbing across the roof at six o'clock, Anna surfaced from her sleep. Vicky hadn't reappeared since her mother had chased her away and taken me to bed. Had she bolted to her room; was she hurt; was she crying? It was past her supper time. Was she hungry? What did she make of it all? It felt as if the monstrous transgression

I'd just perpetrated had doused her completely; as if I'd extinguished whatever spark of goodness I'd managed to strike, in spite of myself, from my presence at Mawle. Choked with shame, I put my arms about Anna and, holding her tightly, took my heart in my hands.

'Anna, my love. I have a confession to make. I must tell you what it is I really want.'

She thrust her little bottom resignedly against my crotch.

'No, not that again. It's this. I didn't come here to catalogue your pictures. I came because I was looking for something very special – a painting – a very old and precious painting. It's a Madonna, by an old Italian boy – someone called Bellini.' She did not immediately respond. I picked out the constellation of freckles on her back with my pinkie. 'Long dead,' I added hopelessly.

She yawned. 'I know. Ludo warned us.'

My mind reeled. With a sickening quirk of the stomach I realized that I had been right all along. All these weeks Maddalena had roped this innocent into watching me. However, she had failed, completely failed to reckon with the fleshly weakness, the moral flaw in her little chatelaine; or, dare I say it, with the unexpected robustness of her Abelard. Playing with Anna's uncoiling hair, I puckered my muzzle close to her dainty ear and dissembled.

'*Cara*. Am I supposed to know this Ludo?'

Anna turned halfway around. 'Why, of course you know him. Ludovico Puppi. He's my mother's friend. He told us months ago that you would be coming here.' At once she looked rumpled and forlorn. 'Actually, he said you were queer.'

I let this pass. 'Ludovico! He *told* you?'

Then, while I was staring, stunned, at the curve of her

cold shoulder, the child's name came back to me like a thunderbolt. Oh, I have you, I thought, I have you now. I seized my young mistress's arm and spoke gravely.

'Anna, my poor darling. You must tell me everything. Was, *is* Ludovico Puppi your lover? *Is he Vicky's father?*'

But the exasperating girl gave a snicker of derision. 'My lover? My mother's lover, you mean. Vicky's father was a lad I knew here in the village, years ago, Richard Smith. I wanted a family of my own, but I got it all wrong with him. He didn't stick around.'

Dick, why naturally! Precocious *confrère* of Tom and Harry. But, good God – could it really be that my cinquecento Infanta, my enchanted cygnet, my most rare and imperial Vicky, was a *Smith*?

'After I had Vicky he just left.' Anna's face was dark with misery. 'Ludo is *my* father, you idiot, my *real* father. Oh shit!' She let out a groan and flopped back on the pillow. 'Mummy will never forgive me for telling you.'

'I simply don't understand!'

Anna sighed heavily. 'Mamma had a thing with Ludo years back, when they were still students in Padova. But then she met Daddy and afterwards she found out she was pregnant. She was *so* embarrassed.'

I must have looked sceptical, because Anna uttered a protesting squawk.

'It wasn't her fault! She was only nineteen. She really thought I was Daddy's – she didn't realize the truth till they were back here, and it was too late.' Her cheeks trembled. 'I suppose Ludo was quite a playboy when he was younger. I don't get to see him that much, anyway. He's never around unless Mummy is.'

Ah, those newspaper cuttings in the jug on the fridge! The diligently sourced cigars; an ingratiating offering that was, come to think of it, utterly typical of her. Immediately I regretted my misplaced, barbiturate-tinged jealousy. Poor child, poor lonely child!

'And where exactly is your mother now?' The room was gyrating. I had a sudden awful vision of Maddalena Roper skulking behind the curtains.

'Oh, you know. Waiting in Switzerland with Ludo for you to do your stuff.' Anna's eyes shifted alarmingly from lambent jet to flat craftiness. 'She's not really skiing at all.'

'My stuff?'

'To find the painting, Tom. Ludo said that you were our best bet; he knew it as soon as you started writing to Mummy. He told her you were a total bore on the subject.'

'A *bore*?'

'Yup, he said you'd been stalking him so mercilessly that you must have some idea of where the picture was. He said we just had to let you in, to keep an eye on you; that you'd take us straight to it.' She faltered. For a vertiginous moment everything seemed to hang in the air, as if over an abyss. Then Anna took a tentative step forward on her tightrope. 'OK, Mamma was a little annoyed with you at first for meddling; can you blame her? She was terrified that you were going to discover the Bellini and go and shout about it and ruin our chance to sell. But then, we'd been looking for the thing on our own for simply years, and we'd never got anywhere at all. Ludo talked her round. You know, the picture sort of belongs to him, too.'

'I'm relieved that the estimable Professor Puppi has such a good opinion of me.'

'Oh, he doesn't, you know,' whispered Anna. 'Just the opposite – that's why he has such confidence in you. He said that you're the type who'd be open to anything.'

'*Most* complimentary.'

'Oh, that's a good thing – that you take it that way, I mean,' said Anna with sham lightness. 'They were going to pin you down in Asolo and make you an offer you couldn't refuse. They want you to act as a middleman for them.' Her fatless index finger stirred the bowl of my inner arm, as if she were intent on making soup. 'There's a ton of dosh in it for you, you know. As long as you play ball.'

'"An offer I couldn't refuse"?' Dosh? *Play ball?*

'Yes. Don't you get it? Dad made it an absolute condition of his will that nothing could be sold from Mawle once he was gone. He put the whole house in trust. He knew that there was something remarkable in the collection somewhere, but he'd never managed to discover it. Mummy and Ludo couldn't either – they were going out of their minds! But then you got in touch, and Ludo said you knew your Bellinis. They were going to ask you to flog off the painting for them once you'd – once we'd – found out where it was.'

I was breathless with suppressed fury. 'So I'm to be your mother's fence. And this pleasant little stint in the country has just been an opportunity for me to do the groundwork, free of charge?'

Anna grinned a sickly, quailing grin. 'If you want to put it that way – yes.'

'I see. Oh, I do see. Well, since I'm to sell the picture for her without implicating her, I hope your mother has had the foresight to put together a watertight chain of title for the thing. Problems of provenance can cause a real stink in the

Old Master market. Any respectable auctioneer, if that's what she has in mind, will take the greatest care to avoid handling works of doubtful title. They'd be strictly liable, my dear, if they were to sell on behalf of anyone but the true owner.'

'Don't worry, Mummy has it all worked out. The chain thing will be what it always has been, except that the person selling through you would be Ludo, not Mamma – from his address in Asolo.' Anna sighed ruefully. 'He was always going to be the seller, you know, except of course we didn't have the bloody picture.'

'Quite. A slight hitch there, eh? But I can think of another. How, my darling, was your mother going to make sure that I didn't run off with the Bellini myself, when or rather *if*, I did ah – *locate* it?'

She gave a small, triumphantly coquettish simper. 'Well, it was up to me to make sure that you didn't. And you won't now, will you?' Lacing her arms around my neck the little slut brushed my shoulder with a kiss, still watchful. I cast inside myself for an answer, but could glimpse only the fretful roil and swell of darkness there, agitated by an extreme fatigue.

'Oh, Tom, forgive me. I didn't mean for things to happen quite like this. I hated having to keep you here under false pretences. And I'm sorry about the tisanas. You know, there was a point not so long ago when I nearly gave it all up. I was sick of it! I mean, there had to be – there *has* to be – some other way of making money, some way that doesn't involve lying and ripping people off.'

'Was that why you went to London to learn about asparagus?'

'Yes. But the truth is that I've fallen for you. I really have.

I love you.' She repeated the sentence, slotting her head firmly into my collarbone, as if bald reiteration would transform it into truth. 'I love you. Please don't abandon us.'

I took Anna's clammy fingers in mine and planted crocodile kisses on them one by one. 'I won't ever let on to Ludovico that you told me. Or to your mother,' I said.

Anna looked up at me for a long while, regarding me uncertainly with her child's eyes. Then she smiled a slow, languorous, radiant smile that cut me to the bone.

'Oh God. It's silly for us to go on pretending, isn't it? And you must admit that you haven't made a very good job of it at all so far, have you?'

'No, I haven't,' I allowed.

'Look, we can start again. You're onto several good leads. We can do this together, just as you said!'

'Christ, Anna! "Good leads"? What on earth do you mean?'

'I mean, all this stuff about that German painter and that poet bloke and – and – the nature of art is very interesting, but it's not the real story, is it? Don't you want to find out where the picture actually *is?*' She regarded me shyly. 'I'm sorry to put it like that. But I have wondered.'

I was unable to take in any of the detail of what she had just uttered. A snowdrift had just slid from a distant peak and settled about my vitals. It couldn't be – and yet it was. 'Anna. Have you been reading my notes? *Have you been reading James Roper's diary?*'

'Well, you always left them lying around for anyone to see. I mean, what did you expect?'

'Expect? There was only you to see them! And I expected you to do what you appeared to be doing! What you were supposed to be doing – the tidying! The dusting!'

'Well, I did tidy! And sometimes, while I tidied, I read your notes, OK? This house belongs to *me*, not you. Oh look,' she cajoled, 'for goodness' sake. After the way Mummy's behaved, I don't owe her anything any more. Come on.'

As she jumped out of the bed she looked so much like a tousled page jumping down from the banqueting table that I was close to tears again and wanted to warn her, to call out Stop, stop, stop! Stop, oh stop, my love. Too late. The next minute she was a grown woman again, squeezing her mushrooming thighs wormed with stretch marks, her curving belly, into a pair of discarded black leggings. Hopping about on one foot, she prodded me with a naked toe.

'Come on. Get up.'

I couldn't speak. By inches, my quivering smile was already turning into a grimace. 'Where are we going?'

Leaning over me, Anna exhaled a puff of sweetish-sour breath uncomfortably close to my lips.

'Downstairs. We're going to have another look at the diary.'

CHAPTER TWENTY-SEVEN

'You're wrong, you know, about my great-grandfather. He wasn't unhappy with *Bisnonna*.'

'Unhappy? I never wrote that!'

Anna was sitting cross-legged on the floor of the library with James Roper's diary resting on her knee, her head inclined against the desk. My notes, naked and shivering, were spread out in front of her, and from time to time she singled out their most incriminating features with the tip of a pencil. 'Oh yes you did. "In his most unhappy moments he must often have wondered if he'd ever seen her clearly, this spontaneous girl who had just perhaps been a monster of subtlety."' She leaned back, clutching her elbows, and looked at me accusingly.

'Oh, please!' This was preposterous. Was I really arguing the finer points of biographical exegesis with this ignoramus? 'What right do you have to comment on any of this, sweetheart?'

Anna shrugged. 'About as much right as you have, I'd say.'

I didn't know anything about Anna Roper. Not the first thing.

I was filled with a sudden sense of hilarity, and with a stirring, unexpected appreciation of the novelty of the moment. It was novel and funny and at the same time oddly and comfortingly intimate, as if we were a pair newlyweds having our first marital argument, across the breakfast table of our honeymoon hotel, about the day's itinerary.

'Do you have any other insights? Come on, spit them out.'

She shot me a defiant look. 'OK. I think my great-grandfather loved my great-grandmother. Love doesn't have to be perfect to be real, you know.'

'Real?'

'Yes, real! Everything's always abstract with you, isn't it? Why must you make things so needlessly complicated?'

Oh, my little child-wife!

'Quite the expert on love today, aren't you? Explain this, then. Why didn't he write a word about their married life together? He wrote about everything else leading up to it!'

Anna looked at me with frank compassion. 'Because – because he *was* happy! He had her safe. Once he was married he stopped keeping that stupid diary and got on with living.'

I was impressed, in spite of myself, and went so far as to lift the diary from her knee and flick through it for a few moments. 'Hmm, that might be just about plausible. But you've forgotten one thing.' I held up the mutilated notebook. 'If your great-grandpa loved his bride so much, then why did he try to tear up his account of their courtship?'

'For a clever person you can be very stupid, you know.' Anna jumped up and snatched back the book from me. 'He tried to tear it up, OK,' she fingered the rough edge of the cover, 'but not while she lived, I'll bet.'

'What do you mean, you insufferable girl?'

'Why, it's perfectly clear! He hung on to the thing while she was alive. It only became meaningless to him when she was dead.'

I was flummoxed. 'But why try to tear it up? Why, if – as *you* say – he loved her?'

'Because it was Giulia he loved – not the sentimental story he'd made up about her. He'd got her all wrong, hadn't he? He thought she was just a stupid ignorant girl, and she wasn't at all; she'd given him a run for his money!'

'The pregnancy, yes,' I mumbled. 'I confess that I didn't notice the signs.'

''Course you didn't. She must have been only a few months along when they went on that picnic. Jesus, poor clever Giulia. She and that Spragg did a fine job convincing my great-grandpa that marrying her was his idea.'

I turned away for a moment to hide the emotion that sluiced through me, all at once, like a salt tide. The smooth jade lawn of Mawle rolled away beyond the window sash, muddied by the first hesitant bars of a liver-coloured sunset. At the edge of the tennis court, as if over an uncrossable ocean, I caught a glimpse of Vicky dispiritedly dragging a doll. The child seemed tiny, yet never more painfully vivid, absorbed in her private suffering near the edge of the frame.

'No, it won't stand up. There's no proof for any of this.'

'Of course there is.' Anna's voice came from just behind me: she must have crept over to the window to join me. I felt her hand alight on my shoulder. She spoke very quietly, so that I had to lower my head to hear her. 'He planted the rose garden, didn't he?' she murmured. 'He kept his promise. Why else would he have done that, unless he'd loved her?'

The thought continued to unspool itself in the silence, gathering in unsettling clarity and precision.

'You know about the rose garden,' I brought out at last.

'I found it when I was still little,' said Anna sadly. 'I used to go there when I wanted to hide away. Mummy and Daddy could never find me – they thought every time that I'd vanished into thin air.' She wrung out a smile. 'I had no idea who'd planted it, but it made me feel better just to sit among those roses.'

'Haven't you ever considered trying to rescue the garden – to restore it to what it must once have been?'

'Never.' Anna looked at me in astonishment. 'It doesn't need rescuing! It's the one perfect corner of Mawle. I've never wanted to touch it. And now I know why it's there, I never will.'

What a let-down it all was. Roper's awkward and irregular courtship was, for all I knew, the prelude to a perfectly contented, if brief, bourgeois marriage. And Anna wasn't only less of a fool than I'd thought her, but not even a Roper at all. I gave myself up to this reflection in a luxury of acidly bathetic amusement. She was no more a Roper than her grandfather had been. I considered the implications for her if my theory were correct. Supposing, as I'd calculated, that after getting Giulia Buccari pregnant Giuseppe Puppi had married and had a son and grandson of his own, and if Ludovico was that grandson and Anna's true father, then Maddalena had conceived Anna, not by her husband, but by her husband's first cousin. No wonder Anna was the spitting image of John Roper's dear old dad. Giuseppe Puppi was Anna's great-grandfather twice over, so to speak. Either way, and this was the crowning irony, there hadn't been Ropers at Mawle for half a century.

I was still facing Lamb's portrait of James Roper and his son. How could I have missed the similarities between Anna's face, Ludovico Puppi's and Edward Roper's? It was, after all, exactly the same face. They all shared that wide canvas-like forehead, the dark colouring, the tragic, veiled eyes, the nose that listed slightly. Hadn't those been Giuseppe Puppi's features, too? Ah, pity James Roper, bewildered respectable Roper! There he sat in his garden with his family about him, guessing or not guessing; who could tell? And even if he had guessed – and let's say he had – did he really look haunted, or was his strangely inward air merely a symptom of a staggeringly complacent self-regard? No one knew the truth. He had his house and his knick-knacks. He could, and would, go on living like this for another forty-four years. He was either a very great fool indeed, or a smugly imperturbable cuckold. My tentative liking for him had evaporated and all that was left was a residue of irritation. I had come full circle. How I despised him – how I despised them all!

Fake, fake. It was all a tasteless sham and a fake. The infinitely precious, infinitely fragile reality I had inhabited for the duration of the summer had, in the space of a few hours, begun to wheeze and deflate. I could feel it shrivelling and collapsing around me. My heart thrashed as if it were about to explode.

Turning from the picture to face Anna, I put out my hands to her. She took them uncertainly. There it was again, that lily smell of hers, a little soured by sweat, but no less intoxicating for that. I breathed it in long and gratefully: a final, unanticipated benediction. The split on her lip had sealed over. Her butterscotch skin was still dewy from her afternoon's sleep. How long had I been at Mawle? Two and a half weeks? Nearly three? I let go of her fingers and cupped her face in my hands.

'Goodbye, my dear.'

'What do you mean, *goodbye*?'

'I'm going at last. I should never have come here. I should never have disturbed you all. I'm so sorry.' The silence of the house was as darkly blue and as fathomless as it had always been. 'I can't bear any more.'

Oh, the unavoidable melodrama of parting.

In answer she put her hands over mine and gripped them so hard that I was afraid the bone of her jaw would crack. 'You can't go. You *can't*.'

'Ah, but I can. And I am. Just like this. Bye, bye.'

Anna moved her head a hair's breadth from side to side: No. Her eyes were fixed on mine. I felt her body tremble, unless the shaking came from inside me. I braced myself for tears, for pleading and threats, but I had made up my mind, and the realization was like the return of blood to a limb that has fallen asleep.

What happened then was a surprise. Without a word, still holding my hands fast, Anna led me to the door of the library and out into the corridor. I remember that we stumbled against a chair in the hall and that I caught her beneath her breasts, without letting go of her hands. We went up the staircase like that, a crabbed creature making its way painfully towards the top. The absurd journey seemed to take an hour, two hours, although it could not have lasted for more than a few minutes. I was afraid that at any moment we would slip and fall. All this time we never spoke. When we reached the third floor and stood outside Anna's bedroom, though, I broke her grip.

'Forgive me, my dear, but I can't go in there with you again.' It was true. My desire for her had completely vanished.

'In here? Oh, no.' Bizarrely, she laughed again. 'Don't stop now. Come with me.' She beckoned to me lightly. The late evening sunshine falling from a skylight above her head poured a steady stream of diamonds into her hair. As if in a dream I leaned forward to touch them, but she warded me off. 'Not yet. First, come.'

She led me along the passage where we had slept apart for weeks, separated only by a few feet. We passed my door and the door to Vicky's room. Finally we went into the tiny back bedroom where we had found the portrait of Giulia Buccari. It was still there, hanging in deep shadow on the wall above the iron bed. The coverlet was one of those old-fashioned quilts stitched from hexagons of cast-off fabric – somebody's old dress, a pair of worn-out curtains; perhaps parts of it had been supplied by the costume cupboard in the Sewing Room. The faded greens and ivories bristled like the scales on a snake. Anna led me to the edge of the bed. I felt like weeping. Did she have a fancy, a whim, that I should make love to her here, where her father had slept as a boy?

'No, Anna, no,' I repeated angrily. 'I've told you that I can't.'

'Hush.' She knelt on the bed and reached for the portrait. I swear that I had no idea, even then, of what her gesture meant. She struggled a little at first to get the picture off its hook, which was rusty and bent. Her milky brown arms were so tensed at their labour that I thought she would not succeed. After a minute or two of gentle jolting, however, she lifted the frame away from the wall with a triumphant cry, and stepped back, holding it up.

'Look.' Anna regarded the image of Giulia Buccari reprovingly, as an exasperated mother might look at a troublesome infant. 'Isn't it kitsch? Who would ever have thought it?'

Yes, it was kitsch, but I now saw that it was subtly disturbing too. The round eyes and conventionally smirking lips appeared not just dull, but stupid and unconsciously mendacious. And it *was* froglike, just as the Contessina had said: the curve of the cheek, the childish swelling of the chin. From these harmless elements Giuseppe Puppi had managed to create a portrait of femininity that somehow suggested that the sitter's sex was both a limitation and a meanness. The crudely gilded gesso frame surrounding the picture only added to the effect of cheap irony.

'It's pathetic,' I agreed. 'But why are you returning to this again? It's no use, Anna. There's nothing here that interests me now.'

'Can't you see?' Anna gazed at me. I felt again, as I so often had before, that there was a supplication in her eyes that I was failing either to interpret correctly or to answer. 'You really can't, can you? All right. Sit here by me and I'll do my best to show you.'

She turned the picture around so that it lay face down on her lap. The back was covered over with stained brown paper, like parcel paper, that had begun to wrinkle at the corners where it was stretched. The edges of the frame were roughly secured, over and over again, with thick strips of yellow tape, and a length of twisted wire swung, slackly threaded, through two flaky eyelet screws fixed into either side of the gesso.

'It was when I read that bit about the painting lesson,' said Anna, with her eyes still on mine. 'It was then – then, I think, that I knew. Not at first, not immediately. Maybe only later, when they were at that depressing engagement party . . . It took me a while to *see* it, you know? And I'm not altogether sure that I do see, even now. I've been afraid to look, in case none of this turns out to be true.'

No, I did not know what she was talking about. I didn't know at all.

Inserting her finger under the topmost skin of tape, Anna began very slowly to work the left corner of the frame free. The tape was so old that its adhesive had long since crystallized, and it tore off easily. Still Anna did not hurry. She peeled off the dry strips one by one and laid them carefully on the coverlet, until the frame was loose at last. Then she applied a light pressure to the rectangle with her thumbs. It stuck for a second or two before shifting gracefully sideways, like a skater. As it did so, the brown paper backing that still clung to it came away with a sigh. Behind the paper lay a wooden board, like a child's slate, and I realized all at once, with a painful fibrillation of the heart, that someone had painted a picture on this side of the wood too.

And there it was. The setting sun bronzing the window fell plainly on an oil portrait of great age and delicacy; fell on a bowed head covered in a black robe and white cowl, a broad frieze of ochre hills, and a roseate sky scarred with pearly cloud, just like the sky outside the window pane.

I looked down at the Bellini Madonna.

Anna turned to me with a soft moan. 'Would you like to hold it?'

'*Would* I? May I?'

She put the thing into my outstretched arms. I clasped it anxiously. The passing minutes seemed to fold and contract, one into the other. Somehow, I don't know quite how, I found myself kneeling on the floor. Anna knelt by my side. For a while I simply could not speak. After a little I felt her expectant eyes on me, and knew that I had to say something.

'I never believed that I would live to see this. No, I never believed it.' My own voice seemed to reach me from infinitely far away, distorted and remote, as if it had travelled stellar distances.

Anna looked at me questioningly. 'Is it really all that?'

'My dear child! All that – and more.'

Oh, and it was. I have never held anything so utterly itself. The picture seemed to pulse in my hands, to stir with ready life, as pure and complete, underneath its veneer of surface dirt, as on the day it was made. I did a quick assessment of its condition. It was wonderfully far from being a difficult work to restore: its unassuming history had seen to that. It had never been sold or violently snatched or passed on as a trophy; it had never lain in a leaking barn, or a skip; it had never been rammed by a burglar's foot. It had existed, so far, entirely in the shadows, always quietly there but essentially unseen. After being stored undisturbed and unprized in Ca' Buccari for centuries it had come, in its veiled state, to Mawle, and had been forgotten. There were no signs of flaking or whitening or foxing; no warping or cracking of the panel. Apart from a little atmospheric pollution it was perfect in every detail: perfectly transparent, perfectly beautiful, and bewilderingly mysterious. Very gently, I rubbed away the smoky accretion covering it from one corner. In spite of their great age, the colours in which the picture was painted gleamed under their film of grime like dew, or newly spilt blood. I drank in the red-roofed hilltop town, the broken winch above the well; the worn Madonna, her dispossessed hands resting on her knees. Her eyes numbed me. Their naked, direct gaze was calm, but not merely that. All their emotion was spent. They seemed to launch a deadly shaft, skewering me with what was in one minute an accusation, and in another, an appeal.

The Madonna's faintly lined face, too, had a film like sweat, the porous resilience of real flesh. And yet – I stroked her cheek with my fingertip to feel the paint – if you looked closely, you could see that the ageing skin was made up of feathery brushstrokes, each caress adding a layer, like a breath, to the one beneath. And this contrivance was somehow more precious than simple perfection would have been. Everything permanent is rooted in impermanence, I thought, and the knowledge made me sob out loud. And Giuseppe Puppi had decided to deface this jewel, this masterpiece, with his own stillborn version of a human face! I recalled his high-handed attempts at teaching the giggling Contessina about art. How easily that sentimental ideologue would have dismissed Bellini's Madonna! And how disappointed he must have been in Giulia Buccari too. He had chosen to paint his ghastly travesty of a virgin on the back of this picture, rather than any other, because he had feared the humanity of both.

'Don't cry, please don't cry!'

I came to myself to find Anna clutching my arm. 'We can go anywhere with our share of the money, you know.'

'What, and lose this? How could you bear it?'

'But we don't have to lose the picture, do we? No one even knows it's at Mawle. We can stay here. We don't have to go through with the plan if you don't want to. If you stick by me, I feel I can do anything, just anything! I'll simply tell them you couldn't find it, even though you did your best.'

She looked at the painting and twined her tendril arms firmly about my waist. 'Would you like to have the Madonna?' she asked in a timid whisper. 'It could be yours, you know, if you wanted it.'

'Oh Anna, how can it ever belong to me?'

'We could get married,' she urged quietly. 'I could marry you. And then everything I have would be yours too, the picture included. It would be just as much yours as mine! We've been happy enough together, Tom, haven't we?'

I howled.

'Why are you angry with me?'

'I'm not angry.'

'Then what have I done?'

'Everything, Anna, everything.'

My words fell between us like lead, with a dismal mortal clang. The spell was broken, Anna's faery aura snuffed out. What had she done, my pixie, my prisoner of the Castle Perilous? She had given up her power, her extraordinary mystery, and become a plain, pregnant frump in widow's clothing. I could hardly bear to look at her.

Instead I put my hand on her narrow ribcage, feeling her heart beating faintly somewhere above my thumb. Her face was dangerously close to mine, rising up out of the fog of my rage and disappointment like the figurehead of a ship. When I sought her mouth her forehead collided with my chin, but she turned her head deftly to guide me. The space between our bodies seemed arid and unnavigable, my skin like sand, furling and swaying under its own weight. The sudden ghastly touch of Anna's fingers on my stomach appalled me. Her hair had come out of its rubber band. There was one glittering strand, I remember, that flickered from her temple like a bolt of silk, or lightning. Her scalp, patchily visible at the roots, was dirty. Her ear, surprisingly alive and warm, lay just under my nose.

'I do love you, you know,' she mumbled.

'What?' I asked, although I had heard her perfectly clearly. 'What?'

I slid my finger under the waistband of her leggings. Her tailbone was covered in fine down. Her flesh was warm and sticky, all the way down to the cleft of her arse. I probed the little purse of her anus with the edge of my nail and felt it contract.

'Love you,' she repeated.

'Do you? Are you sure?'

'Yes, of course.' She put her hand over mine, forcing my finger in deeper. I saw her wince. 'You don't have to be nice, Tom. I belong to you now.'

She had never looked so much like a waif. Her bruised eyes were half closed, as though in rapt supplication; her bony arms, held out above her swollen waist, were extended as if to embrace whatever form of immolation I might choose to inflict on her. A salt smell of desperation came off her like the fetor of a disease.

And so I bedded Anna for a second time, right there in that little room, and submitted several times that night, and again the following morning, with a drained sick feeling, to her piteous requests that I should hurt her – and hurt her.

In spite of my aching heart, cram-full of confused love for her, in spite of her pregnant belly, I hurt her.

*

On Saturday the three of us ate a strained, fatty breakfast of bacon and fried eggs; the child staring at me, the mother keeping her eyes on her plate. At midday, having seen a subdued Anna off to bed alone to rest and Ludovica (for so I must now call her), dumbly sullen, to play in the Sewing Room, I got into my car and left for the airport. I took only the holdall which I had brought with me to Mawle. In it, wrapped inside my rancid pink pyjamas, I had stuffed Roper's diary. When the car was three-quarters of the way up the gravel drive I made the mistake of looking back. Alerted by the noise of the engine, Anna had run out onto the front-door steps. As I swung past the gate I had a blurred impression of her tossed brown hair and strangely white face, in which the mouth was a soundless O. She was wearing a nightie with blue ribbons at the throat, blown upwards against her chin by the autumn breeze. Their flutterings were the last thing I saw at Mawle.

CHAPTER TWENTY-EIGHT

By early evening I was in Asolo. Awash with aeroplane gin and remorse, I stumbled out under the Porta Loreggia on the corner of La Mura, where my taxi had deposited me. The scalloped *fontanella* on the corner babbled away to itself. Ahead of me snaked the cobbled twists of the silent Via Roberto Browning, its rows of snaggle-toothed arches bared in a long malicious smile. High above, a shutter banged twice in the autumn wind. In my hurry to leave Mawle I had forgotten the map which Puppi had enclosed with his protestations, in absentia, of hospitality, but by this stage I did not need it.

'My housekeeper Artemisia,' he had written, 'will be honoured to welcome you, but like many of our good northern-bred women she is a little tight-fisted. You will find, in the bottom drawer of the chest in your room, a spare key to the pantry.'

Excellent Ludovico! When you invited me here for what I now realize was to have been a business proposition, you didn't know that I would arrive with mortification, not triumph, in my heart. I stumbled past the street named after that damned English poet in a blaze of alcoholic grief. I recognized your house at once by its heavy arch of stone and the phoenix on its faded escutcheon, a short way up the Via Marconi from La Mura. The sight of a red geranium growing in its dirty pot by the massive wooden doors made me stagger for a moment. A polished brass nameplate read, ornately, *Prof. L. Puppi.* There was also an iron knocker, shedding rust, with which I rapped twice at the door. The taps seemed to become lost in the fabric of the wood itself, passing from there into the heavy stillness of the waiting day and on into a weightless zone in which I imagined I could hear the distant susurration of the atmosphere's thick gases, an inhumanly mournful sound like the sighing of atoms, which somehow reached my guilty ears with perfect clarity.

Why do I feel, now, as if the whole of the natural world accuses me? Since coming here I have had this sensation many times and have stopped to listen – to listen – trying to find in it a recognizable word, but without success. Is it a freak effect of the town's high altitude, built as it is on the hazy blue gradient that rises up towards the distant Alps? I don't think so. I must turn from fancy; I must try to look the truth in the face. And yet I wish that I could step once more, just for a moment, into the unspoiled pages of that recessed world that I have lost – whether Bellini's or Roper's hardly matters, as long as I could reinhabit the sealed landscape of my former imaginings.

I waited for a few minutes, inhaling with a bilious hunger the salty aromas of the local dinner hour as they began to unfold, one by one, a hundred savoury roses from the half-open windows of the unpeopled street. At last a shuffle and a grinding of locks and bolts made me perk up and prepare to put my foot in the door if necessary. It swung aside to reveal a stout, long-faced troll with a fine set of barred white teeth, who eyed me critically, legs akimbo, and prepared to withdraw again.

'Not so fast, Signora,' I insisted, flourishing my letter under her nose. '*Permesso!* I am here as a guest of Signor Puppi and although I have arrived a little *in anticipo* – ahead of time – I am sure the good Professore *si arrabbierebbe se sapesse che mi avete mandato via*. Would take it personally, in fact, if I were sent away.'

Artemisia was a woman of sense. Having made a show of studying the letter she nodded grudgingly, wiping her nails on her apron and crossing herself before releasing the chain. And so I was admitted to the Palazzo Buccari.

I know that you will already have spotted the irony in all of this. James Roper had never even known that he had the Bellini.

And I betrayed Anna in the end. She had played the game skilfully, much more skilfully than I had given her credit for, but she hadn't reckoned with my defective heart. She thought that in my world, as in hers, sex, the utter and excruciating surrender of herself to my grubby little cock, would be some sort of guarantee. She had no inkling of what I really was. She mistook me for her great-grandfather. She took me for a gentleman. Anna may have been a puppet, a schemer, even, but she was above all appallingly naïve. She'd trusted me. She'd hesitated, but then she'd made up her mind. And in the way of such tired old stories, I'd seduced her and then abandoned her. The ludicrous pattern of it all appals me. Roper and Lynch! With her very name she gave me the noose I needed, and I duly hanged her. In the great cosmic lexicon our two names surely appear side by side, still in their stranglehold, as a warning and a joke.

I know that I will never go back to Mawle. I have realized

in the last day or two that I really am very ill. There is a telltale purple colour spreading across the bed of my nails and over my tongue. I am dying, and I have had the bad taste once more to choose Anna's father's house in which to hide. But where else could I go? The world, which once seemed so wide and free and full of difference, has shrunk to the size of a comically bitter grain. Vermont is an impossibility. Ireland is a distant nightmare from which I have long since awoken. I no longer belong anywhere.

So here we go again. I get up in the mornings and put on one of Puppi's dressing gowns. I position myself at the table in the parlour, under the plaster roses, arrange my sheet of paper, and open the diary. Artemisia brings me coffee. I take up my pen, and get ready to write. But I do not write. There is nothing left to say. Words have deserted me. Who would ever have believed it possible?

I write only one word on the blank page, over and over again: Anna.

You offered me everything, including yourself, and in return I used you in the way I knew best. My little accomplice! In certain moods I interpret your proposal as a challenge, a fine, final throwing down of the gauntlet. Bankrupt and helpless, you still had this one weapon up your sleeve: you could give me the thing I'd most wanted, the one yearned for and unattainable thing, but your asking price was that I should stay. And why not – after all, why not? Would it be such a burden?

But I was unable to receive what you were prepared to give. In that engulfing moment when we stood together before the Madonna you made me feel the full extent of my emotional failure, and my overriding feeling for you, against all my expectations, was hatred.

What was it you'd said? 'Everything's always abstract with you, isn't it?' How I resented you for speaking that fact! Giving you pain was easy because it was exactly what I most wanted to do. Not to shield you, or caress you, but to make you suffer. How could the sum of my longing have turned out to be – this? Am I really not capable of more; am I doomed never to pass the test?

That is the most agonizing possibility of all. There are moments when it seems that running away from you was a final and necessary act of renunciation, one on which I mustn't go back. Perhaps it would be truer to say that I've spared you.

Do you think of me with loathing? I wouldn't blame you if you did. You might be consoled though, or perhaps amused – as if it were ever in your nature to be amused at someone else's hurt! – to know that my sexual instinct is quite dead. Immediately after you had handed yourself over to me I felt I couldn't summon up a shred of real desire for you ever again, but could only take you as if you were a thing of no importance. That sensation persists. It is not just you, my dear – nobody, literally no other body, moves me any more. The brown-skinned girls and boys of the town, loitering by the drinking fountain, or congregating in the piazza underneath the obdurately spread wings of the stone lion, are as irrelevant as shadows or smudges on glass. I am done with mystery. I am done with sex. I am done with words! And I am most definitely done with art.

But here's the funny thing. At the centre of my resentment, even as I knelt all that last long night with your flinching torso under my hands, lay a hot bud of agony that pulsed, pitifully and insistently, like a second, dwarf heart, and that has continued to make its plaintive wishes felt. It beats and beats. It cries out to me to speak, to return, to clasp you, you of all people, for pity's sake, in my arms. How, it says, could you ever have imagined that a pattern in paint, an *idea*, could make up for the loss of a living woman? The girl was right. You were happy with her. Go back to her, go – she is your daily life now, such as it is; she and her child. Go back and *be* happy.

I fear, though, that it is too late. The trembling that has wrung me in the last month is worse, and my marrow seems to ooze ice. I can smell my own sour stink, a mixture of ethanol and despairing sweat, wherever I go. There is a permanent, smouldering fire around my liver. This morning I spat up a bright mouthful of blood. Yes, I do believe I'm for the chop.

Oh well. *Tempus edax rerum!* You know how it is.

Artemisia knows too, of course; she must have seen it as soon as she opened the door to me, a stooped, shaking emaciate, reeking of booze. I hope I will not give her too much trouble. Her wary concern for me has at last overpowered her natural sloth: yesterday, her unexpected guest having by now been installed in the palazzo a week, I overheard her at last reporting his presence to someone on the house telephone. In her opinion the English gentleman was not at all well. He did not like her cooking. He walked with an unsteady gait, often in the midday sun. He wrote much, late into the night, and slept little. He had an unaccountable aversion to her listening to the radio. He even objected to her performing the most basic functions of daily life, such as the washing. No, he had said nothing to her about pictures, although he asked about many other strange things. In her opinion he might not be quite right in the – but no, *poverino! Dio ci scampi e liberi!* – God forbid!

I heard all this as if from far away, as a feverish patient, lying in his sickbed, listens to dreamlike voices billowing in the corner of the room. Artemisia had tipped Puppi off to the fact that I was here. It wouldn't take him long to alert Maddalena and for the two to descend on Mawle. I didn't fear for myself; I cared only about you, Anna. What would you say when they questioned you? Would you tell them that we'd found the painting after all; would you give yourself over to the enemy yet again? Or would you, in a rare moment of grace, find the strength simply to turn the Madonna to the wall?

Somewhere in this muffled hour Puppi and Maddalena are no doubt already regrouping, but I am beyond the reach of all plots. There's been only one more thing that I have wanted to clear up, and I did that today without any real difficulty. I put it off for a long time, wondering whether I should make the effort. After all, what can it possibly matter now? Once I had made up my mind to do it, however, I hobbled into the kitchen with a rare sense of determination. Artemisia was rearranging the dirt on the floor, and was, as always, amenable to being interrupted.

'Signora, I have been wondering,' I began. 'Your family has always lived in this town; am I correct?'

'*Si*, Professore. My mother worked for the Professore's father before me.'

'And has the Puppi family always lived here at the palazzo?'

She sighed indulgently, as if to indicate that she was getting used to my silly questions and, though she did not welcome them, would try out of Christian charity to tolerate them.

'No, Signore. The Professore's great-grandmother, before she marry Signor Puppi, she was a Buccari. She return here as a widow to her brother's house with her child when he was still a boy.'

Ah, the fat woman with the jowls. And her son, of course, was Giuseppe. 'The boy – that was the Professore's grandfather?'

'*Si*, Signore. He was Giuseppe Tomasi Puppi.'

'But the Professore is called Ludovico, no? Is that a family name?'

'*Va bene!*' Artemisia is by now completely convinced of my imbecility, and she is scrupulously tender with me as a result. 'The Professore's grandfather, Giuseppe Puppi, he marry a local girl of good family, Signorina Ludovica Contanto, the daughter of old Contanto the brewer, and bring her to live here. And when their grandchild the Professore was born he was named for her.'

I bow my head in deference to this genealogy. It was as I'd thought: Giuseppe had comforted himself with the brewer's daughter. Her beery blood had gone into the making of my rival's little barrel-like body.

'You say that the Professore's great-grandmother – Signora Puppi – that this lady came to the palazzo after she was widowed, to live with her brother. Presumably he owned the house then?'

'*È esatto*. Her brother was master. The Buccari live here a very long time. But Giovanni Buccari had only a daughter, and she die young – *buon' anima* – and her husband was an Englishman who went back to his own country.' She says this in an incredulous, sepulchral voice, as if such perversity were scarcely to be believed. 'So the Professore's grandfather take the house. And the Puppi are here now.'

Artemisia smiles at me clemently and knocks the dirt out of her broom, unaware that she has merely confirmed what I have already guessed. It is all quite clear, and I am suffused with good feeling towards her for so innocently slotting the last missing piece of the puzzle into place.

Otherwise, however, I am unmoved. I am ready to go. One of these fine mornings, my Anna (and they are very fine, backed by broadening ribbons of cloudless sky, real tanning weather!), Artemisia will notice that I have failed to report for my task of annoying her, and will shuffle along the passageway into my room to find me lying in bed as still as a baby. All in all, you know, I will not be sorry. I will be glad to get off this carousel.

I never think of the Bellini now. My long obsession with it is finished, and the funny thing is that I can't really bring myself to care. Could it be that my brush with real emotion has finally killed off my aesthetic sense? There's a certain drollness in that speculation. I might so easily have taken the painting, lifted it from the tangled sheets with their pitiful human smudge of shit and blood while you were still asleep that last morning, and run away with it. The thought never even crossed my mind.

You see, my thoughts are all elsewhere. I hate to admit it but your proposal of marriage, so ridiculous, so extravagant, touches me more than I can say. It torments me, in fact. What did you mean by it? Did you really expect me to accept? Did you think me so eager, so possessed by the Bellini; so desperate – as desperate as you yourself were to break the deadlock of your life at Mawle – that I would agree to this insane bargain? Or was it another of your self-destructive moves? I don't think so. I believe – I know – that it was a real offer, a last wild gamble. I don't deceive myself for a moment that you loved me. Oh, you were fond of me, true enough, but you really thought you had no other options left: I'd seen to that.

But you do, you know. Why not escape? Why not do the one thing that it has never occurred to you to do? Take your daughter and go. Leave Mawle and the detritus of four hundred years. Walk away from that coffin; go and plant your garden somewhere else. Forget about the Bellini. And for God's sake forget about me.

I must make a final confession. As I drove away from Mawle I saw your face quite clearly in the rear-view mirror, illuminated like a face in a painting. My last view of you was not blurred at all, as I have pretended, but perfectly distinct. Your lips were stretched in a rigid cry, like the lips of a corpse to which death had come too suddenly; but your uncomprehending eyes were still living. Your hands twitched pitifully at your breast. I knew that I had given you a mortal wound, that I had shovelled the first spadeful of dirt into your still breathing mouth, but I didn't stay to see the job properly done.

Who were you really? I thought I knew you, but I did not. The three weeks I spent with you, or my countless visions of you, were some of the strangest and the happiest, as well as the most anguished, I have known. But I could not have lived with you in the way that you wanted me to, you now dearest to me of all women; the one person whom of all, I do believe, I most want to protect from myself. If I have learned nothing else from all of this, it is that our intentions are not painted in lasting pigments, and that no instance of human suffering is unique.

Ours is an old story, surely, my Anna, or rather an old image; an illumination in a still bright psalter: a green garden, a flowering rose bush, an older man leading the young woman he adores, but must not possess, on a donkey.

But I lay all these sterile speculations aside. I am finally done with theories. I still dream, but my dreams are of a garden at sunset, and need no interpretation. Let me put aside the curtain shielding you for the last time, Anna. How my hands tremble! Surely, this time, it is not from drink, for I have drunk nothing for the last night and day. I am immensely tired.

In my dreams I am always with you, walking across the grass at Mawle. Isn't that strange? Your face is not as I saw it last, the face of a woman about to be buried alive, but naked and serene. I kiss your lowered eyelids, the hot parting of your silky brown head. Vicky runs backwards and forwards through the brilliant flower beds, her silver skirts torn, her tawny legs dusty with pollen. Your belly is ripening, straining the cornflower blue cloth of your summer dress. The heat of the day is fading. Soon it will be autumn, and then winter again. At dusk the foxgloves close their sleepy throats; a thrush calls from the hedge: the savage, enduring world is all around. The old house looms over us, an ark of stone. The calm blankness of your face extends to the air, the sky, the very light itself, until it becomes the aspect of everything. Nothing stirs. The garden is silent. I take your hand. I put my lips to the lips of the Madonna.

NOTE

Robert Browning's final collection of poetry, *Asolando*, was published in London in December 1889. On the afternoon of the 12th of December, as Browning lay ill in Venice with a bronchial infection, he received a telegram from his publishers to tell him that the edition was doing well. He died at ten o'clock that night, of heart failure.

My Last Duchess

FERRARA

That's my last Duchess painted on the wall,
Looking as if she were alive. I call
That piece a wonder, now: Frà Pandolf's hands
Worked busily a day, and there she stands.
Will 't please you sit and look at her? I said
'Frà Pandolf' by design, for never read
Strangers like you that pictured countenance,
The depth and passion of its earnest glance,
But to myself they turned (since none puts by
The curtain I have drawn for you, but I)
And seemed as they would ask me, if they durst,
How such a glance came there; so, not the first
Are you to turn and ask thus. Sir, 't was not
Her husband's presence only, called that spot
Of joy into the Duchess' cheek: perhaps
Frà Pandolf chanced to say, 'Her mantle laps
Over my lady's wrist too much,' or 'Paint
Must never hope to reproduce the faint
Half-flush that dies along her throat': such stuff
Was courtesy, she thought, and cause enough
For calling up that spot of joy. She had
A heart – how shall I say? – too soon made glad,
Too easily impressed; she liked whate'er
She looked on, and her looks went everywhere.
Sir, 't was all one! My favour at her breast,
The dropping of the daylight in the West,
The bough of cherries some officious fool

Broke in the orchard for her, the white mule
She rode with round the terrace – all and each
Would draw from her alike the approving speech,
Or blush, at least. She thanked men, – good! But thanked
Somehow – I know not how – as if she ranked
My gift of a nine-hundred-years-old name
With anybody's gift. Who'd stoop to blame
This sort of trifling? Even had you skill
In speech – (which I have not) – to make your will
Quite clear to such an one, and say, 'Just this
Or that in you disgusts me; here you miss,
Or there exceed the mark' – and if she let
Herself be lessoned so, nor plainly set
Her wits to yours, forsooth, and made excuse,
– E'en then would be some stooping; and I choose
Never to stoop. Oh sir, she smiled, no doubt,
Whene'er I passed her; but who passed without
Much the same smile? This grew; I gave commands;
Then all smiles stopped together. There she stands
As if alive. Will 't please you rise? We'll meet
The company below, then. I repeat,
The Count your master's known munificence
Is ample warrant that no just pretence
Of mine for dowry will be disallowed;
Though his fair daughter's self, as I avowed
At starting, is my object. Nay, we'll go
Together down, sir. Notice Neptune, though,
Taming a sea-horse, thought a rarity,
Which Claus of Innsbruck cast in bronze for me!

Robert Browning, *Dramatic Lyrics*

ACKNOWLEDGEMENTS

I would like to acknowledge the following sources for the novel:

Albrecht Dürer's *Records of Journeys to Venice and the Low Countries*, edited by Roger Fry (Boston: Merrymount Press, 1913); Fry's *Giovanni Bellini* (1899; reprinted New York: Ursus, 1995); *Historic Girls* by Elbridge Streeter Brooks (New York: G.P. Putnam's Sons, 1885), where you will find the story of 'Catarina of Venice, the Girl of the Grand Canal'; Mrs Lawrence Turnbull's *The Golden Book of Venice* (New York: Century Co., 1900), which contains the song sung by Puppi in the shower, and, of course, Pietro Bembo's *Gli Asolani* (1505), the book about love which neither Roper nor Dürer has read. The sonnet that Roper recites is one of Bartholomew Griffin's sonnets in *Fidessa* (1596). The poem that Lynch studies at school is William Hayley's *The Triumphs of Temper* (1781), and Lynch's unflattering thoughts about it are based on comments made by George Saintsbury. Lynch's ideas about art and the ephemeral in Chapter Fifteen also owe a debt to T.S. Eliot's *The Metaphysical Poets* (1921).

Katharine de Kay Bronson's 'Browning in Asolo' and 'Browning in Venice', and 'Robert Browning' by Daniel Sargent Curtis. All three memoirs may be found in the appendices to *More Than Friend: The Letters of Robert Browning to Katharine de Kay Bronson*, edited by Michael Meredith

(Texas and Kansas: Armstrong Browning Library of Baylor University and Wedgestone Press, 1985).

Henry James's fictional account of Browning in 'The Private Life' (from the volume *The Private Life*, London: Osgood, McIlvaine, 1893); as well as James's 'Recollections of Katharine de Kay Bronson' in *The Cornhill Magazine*, vol. 12, 1902, and *William Wetmore Story and his Friends* (London: Blackwood, 1903).

Richard S. Kennedy's *Robert Browning's Asolando: The Indian Summer of a Poet* (Columbia and London: University of Missouri Press, 1993); A.S. Byatt's 'Precipice-encurled' in *Sugar and Other Stories* (London: Penguin, 1988) and 'Robert Browning: Fact, Fiction, Lies, Incarnation and Art' in *Passions of the Mind* (London: Vintage, 1993) were also early inspirations. My main quarry for Browning, however, was Betty Miller's by now classic biography, *Robert Browning: A Portrait* (London: John Murray, 1952).

Apologies are due to the innocent posters of articles and term papers about art on the worldwide web, which I have shamelessly spoofed and plundered.

My thanks go to Maria Teresa Caprotti for her patient and generous help in correcting my Italian, to Mike Macnair and David Robertson of St Hugh's College, Oxford, for clarifying an important point of British inheritance law, and to James Bruce-Gardyne at Christie's for his expertise in assigning an estimated value to two of the (entirely imaginary) paintings in this book.

I'm immensely grateful to Bill Hamilton and all at A.M. Heath for their unfailing good humour and for making this job such a pleasure, and to my English and American editors, Jon Riley and Courtney Hodell, and Mary Mount at Viking, who also read the manuscript at an early stage, for countless improvements.

Casa La Mura in Asolo is today in the possession of Mrs Bronson's great-granddaughter, Maria Todorow, and is available for rent during the warmer months. Mawle House and the Palazzo Buccari, as described here, at least, do not exist.